Praise for *Across Time and Starlight*

"An engrossing fantasy romance featuring a vast world and plenty of time-traveling adventure. But it's the romance that shines."

—INDEPENDENT BOOK REVIEW

"A wonderful read! Fantasy fanatics will rejoice in this magical tale that transports the readers to a different world with amazing world-building detail . . . An immersive love story with a hint of magic, adventure, and fantasy. Lovers of J. R. R. Tolkien's beloved Lord of the Rings books will very much enjoy this story, as well as Neil Gaiman's audience for *Sandman* and fans of The Witcher series by Andrzej Sapkowski."

—C. R. C., best-selling author of *The Persistence of Fate*

"This is an absorbing and engaging read . . . visual and visceral, this hero/heroine quest will appeal to readers who love the fantasy genre."

—DORIAN HAARHOFF, author of *The Writer's Voice*

Across Time and Starlight

Alessandro Candotti

River Grove
Books

Published by River Grove Books
Austin, TX
www.rivergrovebooks.com

Distributed by River Grove Books

Design and composition by Greenleaf Book Group
Cover design by Greenleaf Book Group

Publisher's Cataloging-in-Publication data is available.

Print ISBN: 978-1-63299-843-9

eBook ISBN: 978-1-63299-844-6

First Edition

To my parents, who showed me the way.
To my wife, who keeps me on the path.

✦ 1 ✦

SAYA

New Time

THERE WAS ONLY ONE THING I remembered about the boy I loved. He didn't believe I existed. Perhaps that was only natural, since we met in a dream. Mine or his, or the World Trees' who dreamed our lives into existence, that I never truly figured out. Now all I had left of him was his voice, just a whisper of breath under the bright stars of my imagination.

"What if I told you you're not real?
That I just made you up
so I don't feel so lonely all the time?"

he asked, and I replied,

"I would like that.

It would mean something inside you poured itself into making me.
Just so I could love you.
So, in a way, I'm a love letter to you.
From your deepest self.
Wouldn't you want to be something so beautiful?"

And for a long time, I believed in that.

The expanse held my body on a cushion of weightlessness. I floated beneath a vault of stars, blazed through wisps of cloud backlit by the moon. Below, the ocean sighed and cascaded into ripples of light. My chest strummed with something immense and full of longing, unafraid.

I rolled and cut through the night sky, my hair streaming out behind me. Wind streaked over the wings he had dreamed for me. On my back they beat and rose, effortless—the wings that set me free to love him, even if I knew I'd never see him again. With their power they thrilled me, the air brimming with possibility.

Now I was free.

Higher and higher, they took me away from this world, from everything. Then came the mechanical thudding, the sleek machines slicing through the cloud banks. They never tired, hunting me across this expanse. My lungs burned as I dived and danced away from their searchlights. They broke me, league by league, until my only escape was a desperate surge toward the moon.

But soon the air grew too thin to breathe, and I wavered before a summit of stars. My wings faltered, barely keeping me afloat. The moon was like a portal to a dream, too far to touch. Everything became soaked in a hideous and wondrous slowness. The lights of the universe burned as the machines circled below me. And gasping, I plummeted toward the hungry sea.

Their nets caught me, abrasive, tearing into skin and feather. I tangled myself, thrashing like an animal. Men with black holes for eyes pulled me from that web, clubs at the ready. Then there was darkness.

I didn't know how much time had passed when I awoke to another night's stars. I had been bound with leather straps, spread-eagled on a table, my wings pinned with nails. Blood pooled around my wrists. I tasted copper in my teeth, my knuckles tight as a brace squeezed on my forehead. Saws glinted, their teeth sharp. Bitterness coated my tongue from a surgeon's morphine. The branches of a gigantic twisted tree crawled over the sky, blotting out the last of the twinkling lights.

I tried to remember him. I could not.

I screwed my eyes shut and saw a kaleidoscope of dancing red, green, and black. Soon, I couldn't feel my wings anymore. Soon, I didn't believe they could ever have existed.

✦

"Approach, my child," came the priestess's voice. "Sit at her feet."

As I knelt in front of a temple pew, the ancient woman guided the urchin toward me. His eyes were downcast, cheeks smudged with dirt, milky-blond hair standing on end like a wick of pale flame. As the orphan neared, I lifted myself to sit back on the wooden bench, brushing off the memories of that night sky, letting my old self float further and further away.

This was to be my third conversation with a child, and my chest was wild and tender, stung by the hope in the little ones' eyes. But it was not them I was here for.

I studied how the Mother guided the orphan forward, one hand on the small of his back and the other on his shirtsleeve. He lurched into the pew, his soft fingers groping the seats. The priestess watched him. A bronze circlet gleamed in her close-cropped hair that had turned entirely white, a shock against her dusky skin.

Above us, inky roots crawled across the stories of the Beginnings on the temple's dome, choking this place of worship. They gleamed an unearthly blue and I was prickled by a sense they were somehow aware of us.

This night and every night before it, they had taken our dreams back to the citadel, to the Black Tree that feasted on the nightly imagination of our people. But the Tree and its Regent hungered for more than just our inner worlds, as I understood only too well.

In the pew opposite, the First Mother pressed her mouth together in muted hope this orphan would be a good fit, and I sensed she had seen too many little hearts broken. The lines on her face told me she was pragmatic, used to making hard decisions. Her only vanity was the purple polish at the base of each nail.

"Are you a faerie?" the little boy asked, gumming his teeth. As I smiled at him, he gaped, his fingers dropping out of his mouth.

Like the priestess, I too had a copper band on my forehead. I had added a string of yellow flowers to my flowing golden hair and was sitting cross-legged in the white lace dress I had chosen for the moment, dangling one bare foot.

The orphan's eyes and mine locked. His were fox brown and alive with trust. Everything in me wanted to take care of this tiny person, and there was something so natural about it. I found myself wondering if this was the same feeling my father had when he plucked me as a babe from the river. I took a deep breath, aiming for an artful lightness.

"Perhaps I seem so, but I am a creature just like you." I slid off the bench and crouched before him, offering my hand.

"Will you be my mother?" he asked.

My breath caught in my chest, as if I'd inhaled a cloud of warm, heady smoke. If I could not have a mother of my own, shouldn't I know how it feels to become one? I deserved this at least. I tucked my golden locks behind my ear. Hesitantly, the boy reached for my hand, his pudgy fingers tugging on mine.

"What is your name?" I asked.

"Salerio," he replied in a small voice. He looked at me as if I had descended from the moon to rescue him.

"Salerio, tell her about your drawings," instructed the Mother from behind.

"My black monster!" he blurted, digging into his pants behind his back. The First Mother watched me as he removed a crumpled manuscript. On its back he'd scrawled and colored his beasts, variations of the same sinister amber eyes and muscled humps.

"Salerio has talent and should imagine while he can," I replied, offering a shy glance at the First Mother.

Her eyes signaled agreement. I had passed one of her tests. We both knew it would not be long before all of his fanciful dreams would be taken from him.

"Salerio, can you sing?" I asked.

He fidgeted with his drawing, folding the page into a grimy square and stuffing it back into his pants.

"Let me sing you a song of the white dragon of Aiyan, the Eternally Blooming." I gathered myself to make use of that fragile feeling in my chest. The first verse told of a snow dragon who flew through time searching for his own tail.

Dragon, dragon, come and go
As your heart lost in the flow
Find your tail and time will show . . .

There was a charged silence. Wide-eyed boys and girls appeared from the doorways of the temple on the left and right of the altar. I opened my arms to my audience. Salerio dived in and the others snuck forward, curious heads bobbing in a huddle around us in the pews as others crowded to my knees.

"Where did you learn this verse?" The Mother's words were sharp, a warning. She stood and peeled the more enthusiastic children off me, grabbing their shirts like the scruffs of their necks. I didn't think they'd ever heard someone sing before.

"Mother, may we speak privately?"

She nodded, brushing off the last little hands that tugged at my dress, and indicated we should pass into the aisle. She guided me toward the altar, and there for a second I saw within it the wasted body of a child, entombed in the black roots, sacrificial eyes only showing the whites. But the altar was simply a statue, tangled in the dark latticework of the Black Tree. I turned away from the Mother so she wouldn't see the horror that crawled over my face.

"Bye, Salerio," I sang over my shoulder, keeping my composure. The orphan's eyes swelled, and I was spiked with guilt. I forced a smile, wiped my eyes, and waved to the others. I couldn't tell them I wouldn't be back, that I would never be a mother to any of them.

"You've done such a wonderful job," I gushed at the First Mother. She nodded again, curtly taking us past the altar to a circular door. The wrinkles on her forehead and the corners of her eyes crinkled as she pushed it open and we entered into her makeshift study. Shuffling, she gestured with hands clasped as if in prayer that I should join her.

Inside were two chairs, no decorations, just an oval mirror and a carpet with a pattern of concentric circles hanging on the wall. Here too the roots had grown across the roof to obscure whatever murals had once been there. Their rustling seemed to register us entering.

There was a table between the chairs and a fireplace full of sullen embers. I crossed my legs and perched on the edge of my seat while the Mother coaxed a glow from the ashes. A sweet smoke wrinkled my nose as she sprinkled blossoms into a tea-pot. I stared at my nails and listened to the timid crackle of the embers, the hush of her unhurried breath. These were the only sounds in the room.

"The ballad borders on . . . treachery," she finally said. The scent of chamomile mixed with the woodsmoke while I fidgeted.

"Yes," I demurred, toying with a braid of my hair.

The Mother said nothing for a while. When the tea bubbled, she served it in clay cups. "I don't need to tell you what would happen if you were discovered lifting your voice to dreams long lost."

I held the heating clay with both hands, blowing shyly as she took her seat on the other side of the table, scratching the small rash on the inside step of her foot.

"Mother, do you know this song?" I preempted, cloaking my face with a curtain of golden hair. My soprano bloomed in the room.

One day, lovely, we'll be free
Oh lovely, we'll be free, oh lovely

As I sang, shock had registered, but quickly she regained control. Her mouth and posture softened as she leaned back, her arms draped over the wicker chair. A small sigh filled her breast. There was a warm core beneath the iron.

"It has been many moons since I last enjoyed this," the priestess mused once I had finished. Her purple nails shifted into a steeple position as she considered me. Her eyes flicked to the copper ringlet around my temples. Mine involuntarily jumped to hers too.

"Mother, I am one of the few who keep the faith of the Beginnings alive. I have heard there is a Traveler from another time who can return our stolen dreams . . ."

"Who told you this?" she demanded. "You foolish girl, you should not be mixed up in this!"

I shrank away, pulling my legs up onto my chair. This seemed to mollify her. I waited as she regarded me in charged silence.

"I'm not asking for the same emancipation," I began.

"Do not bring this abomination upon our heads!" Had I imagined it or did the roots above us quiver as if she'd mentioned them by name?

I placed my arms around my knees, burrowing my face in them and making a small hurt noise. Then I waited. For a moment, I thought it was too much. Then I sensed her approach and felt her hand resting on the crown of my head.

"There now, child. The old ways are gone." Experienced fingers found my chin; rough calluses brushed against my skin. When she raised my face, my eyes were as bright and trusting as Salerio's.

"Mother, I wish to see the *sai maran*, the sanctuary of Beginnings where we once prayed for the rebirth of the world. There are so few of us left, and I fear . . . I cannot bear children . . ."

Slowly, the resolve softened in her face. "Come, my child, don't fret, don't fret." She grasped my wrist with the same firmness she had shown the orphans and took me to the back of the room. "Does your husband not approve?"

"He doesn't."

"Mine didn't either." She offered me a wry smile and squeezed my hand.

She reached out and dragged the carpet of concentric rings from the wall, revealing the stone beneath. We both coughed, dust tickling our noses.

"Help me, child." The Mother carefully positioned her fingers in a set of tiny grooves in the stone. "Now pull!"

The groan of a hidden mechanism filled the room, cogs and wheels croaking to life. Then the stone slab rumbled aside. My eyes adjusted to the hues of lilac and emerald emanating from the cavern within. I could make out prismatic crystals, spires of gleaming gemstones with a speckled honeycomb of living spaces carved from the rock. There were sleeping bunks, pools of water, groves of sacred plants, shrines that depicted the rings of time, ghostly in the ethereal light of the crystals.

"These holy places were built to house the First Mothers when we entered the Life Praise," the Mother said as she entered into the expanse. "A week of prayer to the roots of the world, to the World Trees we call the Fates, who dream our lives into being, imagining time as we know it. These plants and waters are their descendants, and they give the Mothers all the sustenance we need."

She gestured to the pools, where strange flowers arched upward. They resembled lilies but for a kaleidoscopic pollen that twinkled from tightly bound cones. "The *sai maran* can also be understood as an *arkh*. The Mothers locked themselves inside these caverns, sustained by the plants with no way to return until they had completed their—" She turned around and cried out at the sight of me, her palm reaching to her mouth.

I had not followed her in. I was holding on to the stone slab, but it was no longer with the dainty hands of the maiden I had been just moments before. My hands were now old and compact with purple fingernails—identical to hers, as the rest of me was. She stared back at a mirror image of herself.

I had recreated her image, transforming my shape despite the agony it caused me within. Now I was wearing her body like a second skin, down to the smallest detail.

My name was Saya, and I was the girl whose dreams came true. But since that night I found myself spread-eagled on a table, all I ever dreamed of was becoming someone else. A dream that brought me here to locate the time Traveler or find myself caged once more by servants of the Black Tree.

"May the Beginnings guide your Life Praise," I whispered, pushing the stone slab of the sanctuary shut. The Mother did not move as the shadow of the rock door crossed her face, but only cried out again, a frightened gasp. The mechanism groaned, then gave a final click as the door locked, leaving the wall precisely as we had found it. I rehung the carpet, then dusted off my calloused palms, shivering as reverberations of the transformation continued to knit pain through every inch of me.

Gritting my teeth, I ran my hands through my hair, short and wiry, surprised at how gummy my knees were from exertion. I felt sick. I touched my round new body and put my ear to the carpet, barely able to hear her pleas: "Why are you doing this?" I turned and leaned my back against the wall. Soon there was only silence. A tear fell onto my immaculate priestess's habit, pooling and absorbing into the brown wool.

"Because I too am a prisoner, Mother . . ." I whispered. When the men who'd taken my wings saw me shape-shift for the first time, they'd understood my potential. They'd opened the door to my cage. But the moment I'd stepped out, I'd exchanged my old self for a new one, swapping one prison for another.

Gingerly I started testing out my limbs. My new body hurt, arthritis in the left knee. But that pain was nothing compared to the fractures within me. It felt as if every particle inside was splintering, as if the fabric of me was being ripped apart and put back together again. This was the changeling. It had started after my wings were taken from me, during my long imprisonment at the hands of the Tree and its Regent.

I shuffled to inspect my lined face in the mirror. It had the same roundness, severe lips, and benevolent wrinkles as the First Mother. For a second it flickered, and I saw fragments of the girl I had once been, her hair streaming rainbows, her eyes flashing through colors, her lips blossoming and thinning into so many shapes. With a grunt, I wrenched it back to the Mother. I was the changeling now. That Saya was gone. I wasn't even sure I remembered her.

I leaned heavily against the table to inspect my ankle: the rash I'd spotted the old priestess scratching, a tiny but necessary detail. Satisfied, the nausea lifting, I placed my fingers into a steeple and looked back at the Mother in the mirror.

"I will come back for you," I told my reflection. "I promise."

I inspected the bare room. That she hadn't lost her religious fervor was suspicious enough. The Black Tree had all but eradicated her faith. As our inner visions and dreams were taken from us, so too was our belief in a higher plane. Sensations that were once sacred had lost their meaning—love and fear, reason and religion, holiness and hate, joy and music, the invisible breath of life—all were fading into memory.

Those who refused to offer them as tribute were hunted by the *kai talan*, inquisitors charged with extracting dreams by any means necessary. And the Tree had only grown bigger with each succeeding year.

The Mother had retained other contraband, faded books and sheets of music, making it clear she had not been contributing for years, decades even, evading inspections. For most who lived in the ruins beneath the Tree, these items would no longer be of interest. But my suspicions ran deeper.

The Mother had known what I meant when I spoke of the Traveler prophecy. She knew of the possibility of returning lost dreams. While it was circumstantial evidence, the unease would not leave me.

I paused and glanced upward at the gleaming roots above me that choked the religious paintings on the ceiling. The prophecy spoke to the very heart of why our dreams could never come back. Why those who sought to do so threatened the lives of us all.

The Black Tree and its Regent weren't just our rulers. They were the only things that kept our people from extinction.

◆

It was barely three months ago when I had found myself huddling in a cave's mouth in the mountains. Lime and sandstone stalagmites guarded the opening like teeth; a wet mineral smell clogged my throat. Rain fell past me many hundreds of feet, all the way down to the ground no one had touched in generations.

Gently, I reached down to the abandoned bird nests at my feet, plucking a white feather. Cupping it in my hands, I let the wind take it out into the storm. Caught in the swirls, it floated and pirouetted as if dancing, as miraculously as the Floating City we lived on ourselves. Then, as if the fragile dreams that powered it had disappeared, it vanished from our sight.

Behind me was my captor and handler, Favian. A *kai talan* inquisitor and the son of a legendary spymaster, he was dressed, as always, in black, with a white tree on his chest and a blue stripe in his short blond hair. An efficient, elegant figure, he did not have a speck of dirt on him.

For a moment, as we looked out at an earth blurred by the rain and clouds, so far below us, I wondered what it would feel like to leap onto those clouds and glide free across the sky of that unknown world below. And then stop flying once and for all.

"Do you ever wonder what's down there in the Flat Lands?" I asked.

Favian didn't answer. We just looked at the rain together. I couldn't tell if, like me, he was nostalgic, longing for a place he had never seen. I never knew what Favian was thinking. It was one of the things I hated about him. We listened to the falling water, and for once, he let the moment be. Maybe we were both reflecting on the strangeness of it all and the roles in which we now found ourselves. But then again, I didn't think he ever questioned his.

"The distilled dreams of those who have Risen are harnessed through the roots of the Tree." He quoted the law of the Regent in his crisp luxurious croon. "It is the fuel that keeps us and our glorious home afloat. To maintain it, all citizens are required to offer their dreams to the Tree. . ." He paused significantly and let the tension build. *To avoid a catastrophic fall to our deaths* were words he didn't need to say.

I shivered, droplets trickling from the teeth of the stalactites around us. I couldn't look at him, sensing his cold black eyes boring into my skull.

"Show me our enemies, Saya." His voice slithered over my body.

I gritted my teeth and slipped off my frock, revealing my bare breasts and undergarments. My nipples were hard in the cold. I'd made it through this test before but here, so far from my cage in the citadel, I felt different, more exposed. Flecks of rain prickled my skin, blown in by the swirling winds.

"Change," he commanded. Crushing a whimper, I screwed my eyes shut, searching for the rippling pain of the changeling. It took so much of me to remain subdued. *Breathe.* I couldn't slide the awareness of his eyes off me.

I imagined myself standing down on the Flat Lands, at the edge of the crater where the gargantuan mass of the Floating City had ripped from the earth. Gazing up at the impossible miracle of our home in the clouds.

I envisioned myself as a knight of the Marauda Empire, a member of the legions who had invaded us. One who knelt among the graves of my fallen comrades who had tumbled from the cliffs as they tore up into the sky on Our Day Of Rising. I grasped for their fury, their sorrow, their conviction, but still the shape of the enemy would not come.

"Change," he ordered again. That cold voice belied his true nature, so velvety it hid all signs of the rage within him. I was shaking more violently now, each particle of me ripping and returning together. All I could hear was the water cascading, a distant, endless drumming.

Favian's hand slid up my neck, his breath warm on my skin, his scent whispering of saffron and leather. He began to squeeze and I groaned hoarsely, pulling on the agony of the changeling, the tiniest pieces of me shredding and reknitting themselves.

"Change," he hissed.

I am a willing servant of the Empire. My muscles spasmed and crinkled, the rippling within me reconfiguring itself. *I vow to slaughter the people of the Floating City.* My back widened, my chest heaving, my jaw reconstructing itself as Favian let go.

The heretics will travel the forbidden way, across time and starlight. My skin sliced open into the traditional scars of Maurada knife fighting. *This will crack open the fabric of time itself, pulling apart our world as we know it.* The yellow cloak of the Empire draped down my back, as I swelled into my powerful new body. *Not one of them can surivive.*

I gasped for air, my lips ill fitting and severe. Favian strode around me, examining every inch. I was a Marauda in all but soul, tendons hardened by war and devotion, clean shaven and hunched, with an angular face and hooded eyes. He stopped and pushed his foot squarely into my back. I collapsed like a newborn infant.

"Change," he repeated mercilessly. My vision was blurry, my broad soldier's shoulders shaking, the wind licking at my close-cropped hair.

I heard him unfurl the whip he'd used to train me. Faster, I had to do it faster. "Saya." His voice held a warning. "My gorgeous Saya." I closed my eyes again, hammering my chest with a fist thick as a gauntlet.

"Change. You know who they are."

I imagined myself in the deepest alleyways of the old city, among the crumbling ruins of the Temples of Beginnings. Swarms of ragged fanatics following me like rats in a stream of the faithful, the ever-present shadow of the Black Tree looming over our passage.

I am one of the Last Men, those who resist the monstrous Tree and its Regent.

I saw myself whispering in hallways charged with prophecy, the blessings of the First Mothers pulsing in my heart. *I believe the time Traveler will return our stolen dreams.* The whip cracked against a stalagmite next to me, pinging my cheeks with powdery sandstone.

My body suctioned inward, becoming more starved, haggard. I groaned and cried out, my voice vibrating into a higher pitch. *The Black Tree is a dark World Tree, a harbinger of the end of times.* My hair sprouted, my beard lengthening, the cloak on my back slithering into rags. *It devours not just our dreams but our very souls.*

We must save the people of the Floating Lands by any means necessary. My eyes became wider and rimmed in red, hollow and manic. *Even if it means working with those who would exterminate us, our ancestral enemies, the Marauda.* I turned on my knees, flashing a look of rage at Favian. He had crossed his arms with a smirk, like I was a pet learning how to walk.

I collapsed onto my elbows, exhausted by the pain. Favian strolled up to me with his whip and gently rolled me over, examining my new face. He tugged his hand through my chest-length beard, testing its integrity. "Good girl." Was that a touch of pride?

Shuddering in the dim cave light, my form reversed back from the withered rebel into Ciana, to the dainty and elegant girl who was to be my next mission's camouflage. She came easier than the others, a relief from the burden of our enemies' minds.

He sat me up, gently placing my frock over me and then retreated, tucking the whip into his belt. I lay still for a few seconds to gather myself, shivering before the gaping maw in the cliff face.

The rain fell, down down down. At last I stood like a fawn, my knees rubbery and awkward, dragging the frock over my shoulders.

"Excellent, my darling." Favian perched cross-legged on a

mushroom limestone, keenly observing for any flickers of my old self. For the briefest of seconds, did a hint of self-loathing ghost over his face?

No, I was so scrambled from the changeling, I wasn't seeing things clearly. My captor composed himself as I leaned on a cold column of rock. Finally I was stable.

"Saya," Favian leaned forward. "This time Traveler prophecy has been designated a *satar* threat." He waited while I absorbed this.

"*Satar* means. . . existential?" I ran my fingers through my long blonde locks, my scalp tingling.

He blinked his delicate eyelashes.

It wouldn't be dangerous unless it had some truth to it. Favian fixed me with piercing black eyes, swirling and mesmerizing. I had always hated how confused his eyes could make me, the way they baited and invited, penetrated or thrilled. He regarded me now with that inky analysis.

"Does an existential threat excite you?" he asked, snakebite in his eyes.

"Does it excite you?" I retorted. He enjoyed that, bestowing on me a lavish smile, and I couldn't help being impressed by how numerous and small his teeth were.

"How are you finding Ciana?" he asked, somehow gentle now.

The delicate farmer's daughter from the Outer Rim liked to dance through the streets, put flowers in her hair, and care for the elderly. Some of these poor souls even believed she was their grandchild, having sacrificed any dreams of their own to the Tree. She was innocent in all the ways I could never be—an ideal subject to infiltrate the First Mother's heart—and I'd spent the last week studying her like a sculptor. Favian paused before me, weighing a bag of silver in his hand before tossing it to me.

"For your needs." His eyes flicked to the abandoned bird nests as I snatched the tinkling coins from the air.

Then he took an envelope from his inside breast pocket. I wished he would not open it. Projects of his were so secretive they could only mean dancing along a razor's edge. Even other *kai talan* would not know of our mission, putting me at risk from both the Last Men and my own supposed allies.

The cave's stalactites hung down around us like some ancient, fossilized monster, the hush of the rain loud in my ears.

"From what we can make out, the prophecy around the Traveler first surfaced in the old Temple of Beginnings in the ruins of the old village." If there was one thing I knew for sure about him, it was that his ambition was limitless. "As you know, we have had suspicions—"

"Please, not me," I begged.

He stood up and approached, without taking his inky black eyes off me. "Saya, darling, it will be better than last time." He reached out to touch my hand, making me flinch away.

"You sent those old women to join the Forgotten without trial!" The pouch of silver coins dug into my palm.

His whole demeanor hardened, his many tiny teeth frozen. He had changed since being promoted to hunting people. He was a boy no longer. "The First Mothers panicked. We only wanted to understand—"

"Don't lie to me, Favian."

He folded the report succinctly, his fingers precise and controlled. The sheets of rain were falling forever behind him, blotting out the sky.

"I hate it when you lie to me." I could not cut from my memory the hunted look on the old priestesses' wrinkled faces as members of the *kai talan* held them down in their habits and anointed them on their brows with a single drop of the extract of the Tree's poisonous blue flowers. Their pupils filled first with horror, then with darkness, and finally, worst of all, with gratefulness as spidery black tears welled and streaked down their cheeks as the burden of their dreams was taken from them.

At that moment they joined the Forgotten—those who had been drained of their dreams so completely that they were only empty husks. For what were our lives, our purpose, but the dreams of the World Trees?

"Saya, do you not recall the Regent's words? That you will become whole again?"

I loosened my clutch on the pouch. The clinking of the coins cascaded through me.

Both of us waited. The moment could cut either way.

Once there had been a ragged girl on her way to the capital, huddling under the only blanket I'd ever owned: a patchwork quilt smelling faintly of horse manure and home. My mother, abandoning me on a desolate cliffside, had vanished into the night. I woke to the crunch of footsteps and cried out for her, hopeful and ready to forgive.

Instead, a centipede of fingers tore my quilt off me, and manacles bit into my tender young wrists. In my confusion and panic, the secrets in my back flared—my wings burst forth, ethereal and glowing in the platinum moonlight. The soldiers staggered back in wonder as my wings beat and thundered with my panicked heart. The soles of my feet rose from the ground, and whirlpools of wind clutched at the soldiers' disheveled hair.

Then an ugly jolt, for from my manacled wrists there was a chain, a gnarled steel worm crawling with soldiers that twisted and wrestled me back to the cold ground. And there was Favian, dropping a pouch of silver into my mother's open palm. The coins tinkled into her hand as he smiled with his tiny white teeth.

"The Regent pays handsomely for miracles." I hissed the same words he had spoken then and pitched the pouch of silver at his chest. He grunted as it thudded and burst open, showers of dancing light exploding onto the cave ground. The rain poured past the cave opening, all the way down to the Flat Lands.

I froze as my handler stepped forward, whipping a slap up to my cheek. He faltered at the last second, and his hand merely brushed against my jaw, tender, almost afraid. A droplet trickled from the blue stripe in his hair, pooling and then dripping over his eyebrow. I did not move, staring him down. He swallowed the accusation, and for a split second, I saw the lonely boy he hid inside.

At that, I turned and fled back into the tunnels of the Skala Mines, into the warren of the Forgotten.

"Saya!" His voice had echoed after me.

I winced at the recollection, wishing it, along with many other memories of Favian, could be taken from me like the dreams of so many others. We'd known each other for a long time, and none of it had been easy between us. He'd been the first to imprison me and the first to release me after my failed escape into the stars. I'd been his "bird in a cage," and he'd ministered to me when I was most broken. Once, on a mission hunting the Last Men, he'd pressed me up against a wall, and I was afraid of what he might do. Afraid of what I might have wanted him to do.

✦ ✦ ✦

I shivered away my memories of that cave and its portal of falling rain. It was far warmer here in the First Mother's office, a humble temple room of stone. I found more faded books, religious artwork, and other contraband under the false bottom of one of her desk drawers. Since the resurgence of the resistance, the Regent had cracked down on any evidence of a deep inner life. Nothing I found directly confirmed she was one of the Last Men; anyone could hoard these precious artifacts. I decided to widen my search to the temple more broadly.

Closing the door behind me, I reentered the dome. The beam of sunlight was coming down at a slightly different angle. No orphans in sight. I inspected the root system feeding on the altar. I could see twinkles of blue in the dark tangle. Somehow the dreams of the ancients embedded in the walls of the temple itself were feeding the Tree, maintaining enough of a threshold not to alert the inquisitors without the Mother having to sacrifice any dreams of her own.

"Fascinating," I murmured to myself. Could this have been where the Last Men began? These orphans, free from giving to the Tree, able to dream of a different life? Perhaps the temples were shielding their inhabitants from the taxes, incubating new rebels with each generation.

I walked around the dome's circumference and opened a circular doorway leading into the kitchen, where a fire blazed under several pots. Two volunteers peeling yams for the evening soup waved at me, one younger, one elder, but both with the same chestnut braids. I acknowledged them and headed through the steam.

"We are following the recipe, Mother!" they assured me.

I nodded, mimicking the Mother's curtness.

On the other side of the kitchen, I stepped through a doorway into a courtyard. Around it were simple living quarters built into the cliff face, an elongated stone house with a thatched roof for the children on the right, the Mother's personal quarters to the left, and across the way, a small natural waterfall enclosed by a waist-high wall, which acted as a washroom.

Faded clothing hung from a washing line. A gingerbread cat yawned from the steps of the Mother's hut and then meowed at me. With the exception of the run-down root system running from the temple and between the stone buildings, the setting was primitive, and I crushed a whisper of nostalgia for a home long ago lost to me. These memories were so deeply buried they only surfaced in dreams. I should let the Black Tree take them and be done with it.

The bubbling excitement of noisy kids running stopped me in my tracks.

"Mother! Mother!" From around the corner came Salerio with a younger girl in tow. They were both dirty from head to toe and grinning with a mad glint in their eyes. Salerio slowed in front of me, a frown furrowing his brow. "Mother?" His voice wavered, and with it his pale wick of hair. The girl echoed her brother. She had placed a big dirty flower in her hair, the roots behind her ear.

"Yes, my children," I said, striving for the Mother's confidence. "Why are you running?"

"We saw the time Traveler!" He jumped excitedly.

My heart skipped a beat.

✦ 2 ✦

ANDREAS

Old Time

I'D BEEN WANDERING FOR DAYS with your poem in my pocket when, in the early dawn, I came to what looked like the last village on earth. Alongside it a river streamed, shimmering with rainbows, reeds brushing the sky. Minerals from the hot spring water had colored the mud red and brown.

If time really did move in a circle, as the First Mothers taught, then by the Fates, this was as good a place as any. If our stories were ever to loop and find each other again, then it would be here.

Upstream a peasant was fishing from a lashed bamboo boat, dipping a pole into the misty crystal waters. Beyond him, dilapidated huts lined the shore, fuzzy in the cream-and-rose morning. A footprint suctioned into the mud before me was like a signpost for the first of our kind. The air was scalded with the scent of rusting iron.

I'd drifted into this wasteland following a long, beaten road of aimless turns, through a windblown, dizzying landscape of mesas and delicate colors, skeletal ribs and mammoth skulls my only companions. The winds had swept reminders of the ever-spreading sands of the Great Thirst all the way here into the Uncharted Lands.

White dust from the reeds coated my cloak as I crunched past the papyrus and thorn trees. I took from my backpack a small box, a flint, and tinder and placed them in a dry spot among the reeds. In the box was a floating lantern—a rice paper shell with an opening at the bottom. I took your poem and laced it with strips of reed to create a bamboo frame. I struck the flint, blowing the tinder until sparks caught and a single lonely flame licked. Then I took out a candle and kindled the wick.

The fisherman spooned his oar into the steamy water, drifting toward me.

"What ye doing, young stranger?" His face was one for the ages, a chaos of kinky hair and rank sweat. Gray skin crinkled around a neglected beard, his limbs small as a child's, wiry and emaciated.

"Saying goodbye." I placed the candle inside the lantern, careful to keep it away from your poem.

"Where is she?" he asked. I eyed him from under my brow. He put his palms up as if to calm a beast. Smarter than he looked. Above his raised hands, the full moon hovered in the breaking day, the same pale color as the infinite sands. Its circle was as distant as the night you'd walked down in its light.

"In a dream," I replied. Fallen in love with a girl in my dreams. How did that make any sense? Yet it was true. I stepped into the mud footprint and waded into the stream. The water, first pleasantly warm between my toes, became hot as a bath at my waist.

I'd forgotten so much of our lives together, your face, even your name. You, my lovely Traveler, girl from another time, who'd wandered so innocently into my life—were you ever real or just a figment of my deepest fantasy? I had only glimmers of you left, just a memory of that everlasting shore in the Dreaming, our feet together in the turquoise waves, the ocean a twinkling mirror of a star-studded universe above us. This was where the present and the future were born, where our waking world was imagined.

I saw flashes of me pushing you up on the swing, your feet lifting up above the waves, the wings on your back gleaming like brushstrokes against the sky of stars. The foam flowed in front of you, the great tree reaching above us in pink and gold.

"Promise me we'll find each other again."

Your whisper rippled in my chest, your urgency like an echo of a past life.

If you're not real, I thought, *it doesn't matter. If I just made you up, then you're a part of me that I can say goodbye to. So it's right that you become my last love letter. To you, or to myself.*

I let the floating lantern go downstream, its light pulsing gently in the mist. Together, the fisherman and I watched the poem disappear into the reflection of the moon.

A presence stalked through the dappled shadows of the thorn trees behind me.

✦

On the anniversary of the day I said goodbye to you, the amber eyes of the creature, bleak and pitiless, were waiting for me to fall. It paced just behind the sparse tree line in the ravine below, many leagues south of the Uncharted Lands in the tangled forests near the Village of the Second Sun.

The beast's long pink-red tongue lashed through the air, hardly visible in the darkness under the trees. I stared down, sweating on the wall of granite a hundred feet above, my fingers braced in a lightning-shaped crack of stone.

I adjusted my grip, the muscles of my back burning as I scowled over my shoulder. The creature faded into shadow and dust, only the outlines of its eyes remaining, like afterburn in the fabric of the world.

"Hey, murder poodle!" I shouted. "Come back!"

The summer light cut through the gloom of the tree line in patches, but I could not pick out the creature's shape among the shaded brush.

I thought you'd saved me, my Traveler girl, from this hump-backed monster in the Dreaming. But as you had tiptoed down from the full moon and into my heart, so it had hunted me since I first found myself awake without you, my dreams manifesting around me like phantoms. It had stalked me all the way into the Uncharted Lands and back—yet now this creature too was fading, just like my memories of you.

"You potbellied hairball!" I gritted my teeth, trying to hide the desperation in my voice, peering down the sheer cliff face. "Where are you?"

I had begun climbing these giant cliff faces barefoot, without rope, every week since I'd returned. The more frightening the ascent, the more likely the beast would show its face. Seeing it again helped prove you were real, that you weren't gone forever. I'd seen nothing for a fortnight, but now, as I clung on this dizzying precipice of stone, the creature had returned.

"Fiend!" I shouted again, hating the high note in my voice. Maybe if I could still see the creature, I could see you again.

It wasn't only my memories of our Dreaming together that were fading. For all of us from our village, recalling anything of that strange reality that had leaked from the Rift was like grasping clouds of mist floating down a hillside.

I swung my foot out, the clawed fingers of one arm lodged into the cliff, desperately seeking a trace of the beast below. But only shadows lingered and swayed in the north wind as pebbles tumbled into the rooftops of green.

Maybe I should just let go, I thought suddenly, my gaze following the winds over the sea of forest pine, all the way to the gray-purple mountains in the distance and the Uncharted Lands beyond. *Of everything*. Beneath me, the cliff face cut downward, a dizzying, stomach-churning wall of sheer rock to the forest floor. Then the beast's eyes flickered once more between the trunks, leering amber. I grinned, baring my teeth at it, half in victory, half in relief.

"Haaaah! Haaaah!" I roared down at it.

Plastering myself to the granite that towered hundreds of feet around me, I pincered the fingers of my right hand onto a nodule for leverage. Then I braced my left leg into a crescent-shaped crack and swung. My right leg lunged out, hamstring burning, toes slipping off a hold thin as a pencil.

"By the hairless ball sacks of the Fates!" I flung my leg out again, and this time my toes caught. I grimaced, sweating and panting as I dug my toenails in, my heart thundering in my chest. Panic yapping in my ear like a rabid dog. The sun burning my bare back, droplets running down my spine. No room for fear or regret. Free, treading lightly on the world, doing it right.

I shifted my weight onto the toehold, my big nail ripping painfully as I strained for a tiny ledge. My hand gripped and held. *Yes,*

you ugly bastard, I can feel your disappointment down there. It fuels me.
I bared my teeth at the summit, goose pimples on my neck.

I was at the crest of the climb now, but there was no hold or crack or even nodule on the sheer slab above me. And it was barely a few feet to the top. Of course I should have scouted before coming up here without a harness, pick, ropes, or even gloves. Only me and the chalk on my fingers and toes. I had figured I would rise to the moment, whatever moment that would be. Into the sky or into the ground.

A jump then. Through the gusting wind, above a sea of trees and into the merciless expanse. I leaped up, my hands gripping, pulling, my legs swinging into the nothingness. My right hand hooked and slipped, left arm twisting with the momentum as my body swung out and I almost fell.

"Andreas!" a panicked voice called up from the ravine.

I didn't have time, the muscles of my left shoulder ripping. I swung my right hand around and clawed again, my life depending on the power in my fingertips. Both hands now, pulling, and up!

"*Zabibti Mai!*" echoed an angry shout. *Brain the size of a raisin,* in the old tongue. I crawled over the edge and flopped onto my back, my lungs burning, pulse racing like a rabbit. I wanted to laugh.

"I'm coming up!" Heron, my oldest friend. He'd have to take the long way; I had time. I took a few deep breaths and checked my toe. It was grisly. I rolled over and glanced down. No more yellow eyes. Bastard.

Wouldn't it just be better to live a normal life, without glimpses of beasts or girls who tiptoe down from the moon? Maybe it would be better to forget your dreams forever?

I rolled back the other way and rose to my feet, wincing. Thick clouds of mist settled over the chasms, bringing a muffled hush.

Then sunlight broke over the Passage of Ravines, the day basking between the clouds, light beaming over jagged emerald forests.

On the horizon, the purple ice-capped spine of the Sentinel Mountains encircled the Village of the Second Sun and the ravines in which it was hidden like a half ring of spikes. Tunneled inside them were the mountain people of Skala, and on the other side of those peaks crashed seas of ice and storm, cutting our lands off from the Marauda Empire. I shifted my gaze north, following the desert wind of the Great Thirst and beyond into the Uncharted Lands I'd returned from barely a year ago.

"Haaaah!" I shouted again, hoping for an echo, a response, something. None came.

I turned back to the dense forests behind me, the maze of sheer valleys that cloaked the Village of the Second Sun.

I'd been living out here in the deep forest among the ravines, hunting and crafting my cabin, ever since my wanderings in the Uncharted Lands. Too many unnecessary fights before that, too many mornings waking up in prison cells, greeted by the consequences of my black temper.

The Dreaming had begun when the beggar Melasquez had found what might have been a black World Tree and, using its power, torn open a Rift into another plane. For two years this strange world had seeped through the Rift. Its terrors and wonders had driven away the Marauda invaders and by the time the Rift finally closed, the armies of the Empire had scattered back across the seas.

The Elders forbade the Rift from ever being reopened, even though it was my only way back to you, my Traveler. Yet by then, Melasquez—never the most stable even before his miraculous feat—had sunk into a grotesque madness. So I didn't care about his ramblings about being the savior or the Elders' ruling.

For trespassing, brawling, skulking around the Rift, and conspiring with anyone who would listen about how to bring back the Dreaming, I spent nights in prison nursing my bruised ribs. Now here I was in the ravines, an outcast taunting the mountains.

I hunkered down, listening for Heron to come up through the tree line. I wondered what had brought him here so early and in such a panic. Not that I resented his position as Elder-to-be, but he had better things to do than babysit me. Since he was so brilliant at everything. I heard the whinny of horses, sweet and full of passion.

Heron trotted out of the tree line on a chestnut stallion, leading a gray. "When you slip and fall, can I have that hunchbacked cabin you built?" he shouted. He was annoyingly handsome even when he was upset.

Balanced and elegant, not lean and abrasive like me, he was made for being looked at. Full lips, square jaw, jaunty gait. His glacial-blue eyes, usually accompanied by a swashbuckling smirk, shocked and warmed at a glance. Today they sparkled with the luminous intensity that signaled knowing or suffering or both. It was pointless chasing girls with him; he stole the whole room. And of course, married the next Eldress, Leah. I would do anything for the two of them.

I shuffled over to meet him as he dismounted, his tan leather boots of finer quality than I could ever afford. He landed with panache, his pale blue robe embroidered with starlings. As I neared, he faked a right-hand punch, our ritual greeting. As teenagers, we'd fancied one day we'd fight over Leah's hand and trained for the *sai maga*, the wedding challenge. Traditionally, suitors would vie for love through hand-to-hand combat, but he'd won her heart easily and I'd never contested it. Still, the game continued. I dodged and feigned a takedown, enjoying the pain in my injured toe.

"Watch out, Golden Boy." I grinned. I was bigger than him, bigger than most, and he knew it.

"It's your girl, isn't it?" he said, falling into a fighting stance, skipping from foot to foot, his robe billowing around his fancy boots. "Your Traveler girl?" The way he emphasized the word tickled my irritation. His hair gleamed bronze in the sun as he measured the distance between us with a pawing fist.

"What girl?" I shook out my arms from the climb, baiting him with my chin out. The ravine grass was spiky underfoot, but there was room to maneuver among the stones and old roots on this outcrop.

"Get your head right," he said, an edge to his voice. He faked a one-two and then kicked me lightly in the thigh. "You proposed to Rosana a week ago." My thigh ached with his reminder. He was right, as always. "The *potato* farmer's daughter." He laughed, the mockery in his voice worse than the blow.

"My head is right," I said, pressing forward anyway and forcing him back as he switched stances. "Free-climbing in the ravines, I can't make a single mistake."

He shot a look at me. He knew I'd been climbing without rope. I was looking for an opening.

"I still don't get why you asked her." He juked twice, cautious, bobbing on his toes.

I'd caught him before. I didn't answer, just kept pressing forward, driving him back toward the horses. I'd glimpsed the beast at the engagement too, in the tree line beyond the shallows of the lake where Rosana and I'd stood hand in hand. It had seemed to relish that union.

"I overheard the scouts talking to Elder Pan," Heron said, skipping backward, light on his feet, not daring to glance behind him.

"I'm not allowed to say but . . ." He threw his left as he spoke, and I ducked under, clasping both his legs, lifting him up over my shoulder.

"Andreas!" he gasped. I spun and marched him toward a pile of brush. "The Marauda have returned." I froze as he elbowed me in the small of my bare back. A cloud masked the sun overhead. Suddenly, I understood the ice behind his eyes.

The Marauda Empire. Their soldiers had once occupied our village in their black steel armor, screaming at us to live in this time and this time alone. They hunted our people for traveling the forbidden way—between times—a heresy we hadn't even committed yet. Invaders from beyond the ocean, always needing a mythology to justify their endless expansion. Three years ago they'd come to exterminate us, but the Dreaming had saved us. Now they'd returned to finish the job.

"Melasquez won't open the Rift into the Dreaming again," Heron sputtered. "He says he speaks with the Fates, that they will save us."

My chest squeezed tight like a fist. Melasquez the beggar, once the most pathetic man in the village, had transformed into a twenty-foot-tall giant during the Dreaming. Now he was loved by the Elders, heralded as the savior of the village, even as he had become gripped by a madness in the aftermath that none could explain.

"Probably not the best time to mention it," he said in futility as I dumped him into the tough mountain grass.

I grunted and stepped back.

Heron put his hands up and assessed me with keen blue eyes. "Don't be stupid, *Zabibti Mai*." His smile widened as my mood darkened. "The Marauda were right, the Dreaming *is* a heresy." His voice hardened.

Was my hunger to reopen the Rift and bring back the Dreaming so transparent? Hadn't I paid enough for it? I glared past him into the spiky sea of birch and pine that now seemed to surround me.

"*Zabibti*." A pine cone plopped off my chest. I inclined my head in warning. Heron flinched, the quirk on his lips turning playful as he scrambled to his feet, brushing twigs off his robe. "Forget about your Traveler girl. Think of Rosana and the future you've planned together. Planting potatoes."

I hesitated.

He put his arm on my shoulder in a brotherly fashion, almost manipulative. "Do you want a real girl or a dream girl?"

Strands of my sweaty hair blotted him out as I was forced to examine my feet. "The Marauda—" I began, reaching down for a cone near his boot.

"We will negotiate." Heron cut me off, his voice sharper. "Reopening the Rift is a fool's solution. They know that as well as we do."

He spoke the truth. In the aftermath of the Dreaming, not only had we forgotten what had happened in those two strange years; it seemed we were forgetting something deep within ourselves as well. An awful passivity had descended on the village.

I straightened and searched the ice in his eyes. Pity crushed my anger. Did Heron really believe Melasquez that the Fates would save us? Or was he convinced like the rest of the village that there was no escaping destiny, that it was pointless to fight the inevitable?

"Did you come here to stop me from reopening the Rift?" I crushed the pine cone, savoring the pain of the spines in my grip. Heron did not back down, his nails digging into my shoulder. I should stop now, before I hurt myself again. Had I not already said goodbye to her?

"I came here to warn you," he said.

I growled down at him, half a head taller as we stood nearly chest to chest, my limbs reverberating from the climb. Up close, Heron looked slender, though he was not a slim man.

"We were forced to tie the giant to that tree for a reason," he added, his voice barbed.

Then Heron sighed. The sound curdled the black rage in my chest into guilt. Heron cared for me—his wild, broken friend, trying to get himself killed in these jagged ravines.

"Are you sure you want to reopen the Rift? Did you not see the price of it, the madness that grips Melasquez, that grips you both?" Heron snarled as he spoke the final word.

"He is a parasite!" I cursed darkly. The protest was louder than I intended. I picked up a rock and flung it off the edge.

"Hating Melasquez won't bring her back, my friend, even if your Traveler girl was . . ." Heron trailed off. *Real.* He meant to say real. I glanced back at him, and I could see he didn't like what he saw in my eyes. He put his hands on his hips, close to the knife in his belt.

How many times had he dissuaded me in a drunken rage from tossing aside Melasquez's *mayaa*, the women who served and protected him? Counseled me to accept Rosana, my now fiancée, joining them, despite my most ferocious arguments? How many times had he picked me up from the jails for brawling with the Guard, demanding our "savior" be freed to reopen the Rift to the Dreaming? He knew well what I was capable of.

"We should trust in the Fates," he said. His voice was oddly distant as he rubbed his diamond-shaped jawline. Golden Boy, devout as ever. My dearest friend was as lost as everyone else.

I hobbled past him toward the horses.

"Where are you going?"

"To find Rosana. The Fates only know what madness he will visit upon his faithful."

Heron came running after me. He grabbed on to my calf as I mounted the gray filly, his hand on the hilt of his blade.

"Tell the *mayaa* who shield him I want to talk," I growled down at him.

"Andreas!" he hissed, digging his fingers in again.

"Are we nothing but the playthings of the Fates?" I said, looking down at him, my tone brutal.

He let me go.

I dragged viciously at the reins of the filly, Zahara, clicking my tongue. We trotted the way Heron had come, along a path of loose pebbles that wound around the chasm and down into the stream, picking up the pace as we clipped onto the dusty road. I kicked her into a gallop as the road widened. South, home to the Village of the Second Sun.

I dearly hoped the Elder-to-be could negotiate an audience for me with the *mayaa*. It would be no easy task, given my less-than-stellar reputation.

Promise me we'll find each other again. My Traveler's whisper rippled in my chest. Was this really happening? It was as if something in me had made the decision. A self beyond myself. An invisible string tugging from within.

✦ 3 ✦

SAYA

New Time

"YOU SAW THE TRAVELER?" I blurted out to Salerio. The afternoon sun in the courtyard beyond the temple seemed to deepen, bathing the little boy's cheeks in a reddish hue.

His words and the wonder in his voice spirited me away to a similar place, a scarlet-tinted light just like this. My first mission, barely a year ago. And that same phrase, spoken by an older boy with cinnamon-colored skin and handsome gray eyes he would grow into.

Eyes that suggested a wide imagination once, maybe too much of it. The boy's name was Seven, and he might have battled with girls in a sandpit and dazzled strangers with his spirit had he been gifted with a boyhood. But Seven had been born into the crumbling streets of Old Town alongside the group of thieves he ran with. The neglect of these alleyways had soaked into his young heart, darker than the muck that shadowed his cheeks.

Seven had spoken these same words to a hooded figure circled by scrawny pickpockets. I shuffled awkwardly among them in the shape of an urchin, a little boy of their own named Three. It was right before the Dreaming Curfew, the hour when citizens were commanded to enter their homes, the taxation of the dreams to begin shortly.

A crimson sun cast purple shadows, and dust danced around our feet. In the dimming light, the gang gathered here in the crumbling remains of the market to hear stories: the only things that kept these kids going, that supplied them with their most forbidden treasure—dreams.

"Aye, laddie," the hooded figure replied. "I 'ave indeed seen the Traveler." His hair was cropped close to his head, and his chin was sleek as a monk's under his hood. I noticed in the murky light how his wrists were thick and his palms calloused.

A drop of sweat ran down my spine under my shirt of rags.

"The Traveler cometh, setting us free to dream once again!" The hooded man tapped Seven's forehead with a crooked finger. His lip was split open, an old wound or a birth defect, I couldn't tell. Was this preacher one of the Last Men I was seeking—those who spread rumors of the Traveler prophecy to the lowest among us in the Floating Lands, fomenting rebellion?

"I don't dream no more." Seven flinched away, flicking those gray eyes at me, righteous and vulnerable. *Me neither*, I wanted to reply. *I stopped dreaming a long time ago. You should stop too, for the boy you look at with that naked love is not here.*

I dropped my eyes to my feet, bare, brown, and cherubic, their cracked nails the size of a twelve-year-old's. Hiding in the disguise of the urchin Three, I too was a scuffed and dirty little street hustler, doing my best to forget. The real boy called Three had disappeared a week ago, according to the brief I'd received from Favian's gloved fingers.

"Once, I dreamed I could fly, but I can't remember." Seven's sullen voice brought me back. At the sound of his words, down my back the needles of the changeling began reknitting themselves like phantom limbs, a thousand thousand of them stitching along the brutal scars that flared across my shoulder blades. This was my first time trying to control a transformation beyond the walls of my cage, and the effort was pulling me apart. No! There would not be another chance to prove myself valuable to Favian. Only a prison awaited me if I failed; he'd left no doubt about that.

Mercifully, the gang's attention was fixed on the preacher. My palms were clammy, my temples pounding as I willed the needles back inside, shoving down my true self. I would not be exposed! The other kids huddled in closer as the dark triangle of the hood floated in my direction, then turned back to Seven. The man's voice was husky, the pitch building into ecstatic revelation.

"Dreams . . . they be the essence of us. They be the voice of the Fates! Given to us by the World Trees, our creators." The preacher paused for effect, pursing his split lips, then raised both fists above his head. "The Traveler will return them to us!"

There was a whoosh of expectation, my gasp coming half a second too late. Again, the tower of the hood flicked to me.

I saw Seven frowning, biting his lip, his gray eyes clouded with concern. When we'd met earlier, he'd asked where I had been, tossing his arms over my shoulders as we sauntered to the old market. I lied and said I'd had to go underground for a while after a botched job. I didn't give him details, and he didn't believe me. He seemed scared to press further. Three had clearly been involved in something dangerous before his disappearance.

"You shouldn't say this. The *kai talan*—" said another young thief, her ribs poking through her rags as she fiddled with her headband.

The hooded man cut her off with a crooked finger pointed upward. "Behold ye, the first sign."

As one, we looked up to the rising blood moon, eerie in a red sky. The moon had always reminded me of a portal to another world, of the boy who had taken my heart in a dream. Suddenly I missed him with the last shimmering inch of me.

"Spread the word, laddies."

I realized the figure was once again staring at me from the darkness under his hood, and I grew uncomfortable.

"Thy dreams shall be returned. Even those you have lost." There was something strange about his word choice, discordant, too deliberate.

"Shhh!" The cry came from our spotter, two parallel alleyways down. "The Guard!"

Just then we heard the horn of the patrol approaching rapidly. The urchins scattered like rats across the pavement, scurrying into the shadows. The preacher swept his cloak and shouldered himself into a rounded doorway, an old iron grate screeching. Having made sure Seven had bolted with the others, I stuck to the walls and followed after my quarry, desperate to not lose my one chance to escape my cage.

Goodbye, Seven. I hope you find another boy to love.

I slipped carefully past the half-opened gate, into a room crusted in dust and stacked with abandoned furniture. Footsteps creaked overhead as I crept around a chair and slipped into a dim corridor, hesitating for a second before a rickety ladder. Taking a gulp, I crawled up and peeked into an attic gleaming with spider silk, a few floorboards remaining.

The fading sunlight beamed in through a man-sized hole in the ceiling. A rocking chair beneath it swayed. I stepped toward it and climbed onto the seat, crouching to find my balance. The joints of it creaked, my legs shaking. I stared up at the crack of sky, a whisper of cloud an eternity away yet so close I could almost remember what it felt like. I jumped toward it, my arms shuddering as I pulled myself up, rough stone cutting into my palms, and rolled onto my feet.

There! A cloaked figure was running across the rooftops. Ducking low, I followed across the wooden slats that crisscrossed the deserted neighborhoods, gripped by a mounting fear the Black Tree was somehow watching. Its gargantuan branches arched above us into the sky like some kind of god, while its dark roots wove their way through the rooftops and into every home.

There were thousands beneath me who would soon be asleep, dreaming away their souls to the Tree that oversaw them. It would soon bathe their eyelids in a soft bluish light, draining their fears and hopes.

The preacher had not yet glanced behind him, but my paranoia that the Tree was watching was becoming unbearable. Without warning, he disappeared, vanishing down into an alley. My chest burning, I traced his way over the beams, taking two steps for every one of his. I skidded to a stop at the edge of a crumbling storehouse. Below was a dead-end alley. I flicked my gaze up at the Tree, its branches reaching out into the sky like a deity's fingers, blotting out the first stars. Then down into the alley, maroon with shadow, from which rose the sickly-sweet scent of rot from the open sewers and heaped trash. I crinkled my nose.

Had he jumped all the way down? In the dim light I spotted a frayed rope that had disturbed the dust, and traced it to where it was wrapped around a broken chimney. Wincing at the thought, I gripped and tugged. I imagined Favian's unreadable eyes as he briefed me on my task, his smile black with ambition as he slicked his blond hair back over his head.

"Locate the Last Men, my little bird." He'd turned and ambled away from me. With a series of rapid clicks, I heard the door to my cage unlock. "And once you do, return to me and sing." He glanced back over his uniformed shoulder as the gate swung shut. In the cruel corners of his smile, I saw that the door would never unlock again if I failed him.

Shaking off the memory, I backed to the edge of the roof, looping the rope around my wrist. I pulled as hard as I could, testing the weight. The rope quivered like a live creature between my fingers but held. I gulped, leaning back. Fates protect me!

I bent my knees, my bare toes gripping the stone as I shuffled over the edge. One step. Two steps. The twine creaked and twisted, spinning me with it. I gave a muffled squawk as my shoulder crunched into the wall, rope tearing through my hands, slamming me hard into the stones below. My hip took the impact, and I had to slap my hand over my mouth to keep myself from crying out.

"You look just like the other street rat who tattles on us." The preacher's hoarse voice came from my right, blocking the exit to the alley. I huddled on the pebbled street, my heart thundering in my chest. Did he know the boy Three? My hip was numb.

"Where is he?" I managed in my high young voice, forcing myself up, my eyes darting around for an escape. The hooded man emerged from behind a trash pile with a curved knife in his hand.

He spun it round and round hypnotically. I'd never seen such a blade, wicked and runed. I imagined it slitting my neck, blood pouring out, my body discarded and listless in the trash. A nameless boy on a nameless street.

"The street rat speaks like a believer." He stood, his cloak billowing toward me. The last of the red light caught his eyes like pinpoints. "But like you, he be but a snitch." His voice had changed completely, colder, with none of the strange intonations of earlier. I heard the horns of the Guard, distantly, too far. A sneer spread across the preacher's lip, splitting open like an old wound, a yellow canine poking through. There was nowhere to go, the rope hanging useless next to me.

To my boy from my dream. Goodbye. I'm sorry I forgot almost all of you.

The blade spun in an infinite pattern, taking me ever deeper as the changeling began within. I forced myself to stand, and as I did, I grew and widened, the bones of my face flattening and my hair receding. My lips sneered open, teeth yellow and chipped. A wart with two perfectly placed hairs stung on my cheek. My chest ballooned, my limbs thickening, pulsing. I staggered as if drunk, the agony of the transformation making my eyes swim. My crude new body felt massive, disorienting. But there was no time—I had to find a way.

"In the name of the Traveler," I wailed in the preacher's cruel and unfamiliar baritone back at him, shaking like the child I had been a moment before. "Your dreams have returned!"

The hooded preacher stopped dead, his pinpoint eyes popping from his head, his sneer turned into a snarl of fright. He raised his knife like an accusation and stepped forward.

"It is as we are taught! Traveling the forbidden way has broken the world. Heresy! This be heresy!" He spat at his feet, his eyes popping and blinking. The horns of the Guard sounded again, closer.

I blinked, swaying slightly in front of him. This was surely not the reaction of a true believer, of the Last Men who waited for the Traveler's prophesied return. They should be praising this moment, at least confused by the dreamlike image of themselves staring back at them. I needed to delay, to play for time until the . . .

"Be silent!" a second voice croaked from the open sewer. A small dark cloak rose from the stench, weapon raised. I'd never seen a device like it before. A small crossbow, pistol-gripped and double-winged, it had two bolts that could be fired in quick succession.

"Heresy!" the preacher hissed again, backing away into the trash, pointing his knife at me. "Kill it!"

My new body was strumming with pain; I was barely able to respond. All my mind could hear was *kill*. I shook my head at the crossbow with its twin wings, pulling myself upward into a dignified bearing.

The answer came with sudden clarity. If time traveling was heresy, both these men were Marauda.

The preacher continued to gesticulate, his compatriot's weapon snaking toward me and back to him again. The Guard's horns grew louder, closer. It would only be moments now.

"Do you not know that it is I, brother?" the preacher whined at the dark cloak. The whites of his eyes showed as the crossbow bolts shifted toward me, his teeth locked in a death grin. There was no way out, no way I could prove I was the true preacher. I held my chin out and pointed at my double, who was cowering against the wall.

"The shape-shifter fears for its life," I forced myself to sneer, my split lip tugging as I spoke. "But we Marauda do not fear death, for we live in the eternal present." I held my fist up to the cloaked figure. "You will never know which of us is the real one, brother. The only way to be sure, to protect our mission, is to kill us both." I met the gaze of the crossbow and brought my fist to my chest.

I closed my eyes. *Heretic, heretic, kill the heretic.* I heard the crossbow twang twice as my chest constricted. There was an awful gurgle. I dared a glance. The preacher lay slumped in the trash, dark liquid vomiting from bolts in his throat and belly. Beside him lay the hooked blade, with its bewitching runes that had almost finished me.

"Brother!" The cloaked figure at the sewer entrance beckoned me. I sprinted toward him, bending to scoop up the knife as the cacophony of horns rounded the corner. I dived after him into the sewer, felt his arms catching and dragging me in. Tumbling into stinking muck, I spun to see my savior slide the grate closed over our heads and swing home a heavy bolt. Boots thumped overhead. His arm slid under mine as he helped me to my feet, driving me against the wall.

"A true knight of Marauda gives himself for the Empire!" he hissed as he thrust his elbow into my throat. Then he backed away, and I caught a glimpse of his shaved cheeks, a hatchet face with a narrow chin and hostile eyes. "Never lose your blade!" Then he was moving. I chased after him, through a maze of running sewers, rodents scuttling over our boots. My new body was powerful, but I felt my knees would buckle at any moment from relief. As my fingers dug around the hilt, all I could think of was how the knife's keen edge had almost sawn into my jugular.

Down low, the Marauda kept a heady pace in the circular tunnels, the only light streaking from the occasional grates above. I wanted to retch as the filth lodged in the back of my throat. I nearly dropped the knife and glanced at my hand. I was shaking, but not just on the outside. My grasp shimmered between the calloused knuckles of the preacher and my own girlish fingers, slim and vulnerable. My hold on the changeling was fracturing, and as my hands transformed, they began to emit an unearthly rainbow light. I hid them behind my back, praying to the Fates my leader would not turn.

Low voices and firelight flickered ahead. We emerged into an opening beneath a grate, through which light slanted dimly from above. Two clean-shaven men brandished torches, framed by the dark holes of the tunnels. There was silence at our arrival, but for trickling water and the hiss of smoke.

"Knights of Marauda," the man whom I'd arrived with said softly, his voice burning with anger. "There are shape-shifters among us!" He tossed the crossbow at the man to the right, who snatched it out of the air.

"You speak of faeries?" The reply came from the man to my left, a powerful warrior with close-set eyes, wrapped in a crimson cloak too small for him. Between the two, I heard a whimper from within the tunnel.

"I speak of the Dreaming." The Marauda who'd saved me swore low and viciously. "The heresy that corrupts our first occupation of the Village of the Second Sun." He spoke in the present tense, as did all of his people. The preacher whom I imitated must have been highly trained for his words to have come out with confidence in the streets of Old Town. Unsure if my tongue would betray me, I stayed silent, edging my way around the group.

"We are wiping every last one from this living earth," agreed the third, whiplash lean with a dancer's grace to his movements. He flipped the crossbow, catching it deftly by the grip. I brushed against the tunnel walls, continuing to move around them as they spoke.

"The Last Men fester the city with rumors. They believe their dreams will be returned to them," the big one grumbled, shifting uncomfortably. "Perhaps it is true?"

Now that the two men's backs were to me, I glanced as casually as I could behind us into the tunnel where the whimpering had come from. Tied to a chair was a small boy, identical to the one I'd imitated a few minutes earlier. Except Three was gagged with blood caking his forehead, his brown skinny limbs bound. This little urchin who had nothing but the love of another had made a mistake snitching on these men. Had he been spying for Favian before me? Was I just his replacement in the spymaster's web?

"We must return to the Flat Lands," insisted the Marauda I had arrived with. Their leader perhaps, by the authority in his tone.

Behind them, I slipped into the darkened sewer. I'd studied this boy who was bound before me. His eyes were frightened, but I knew also his street swagger, his laughing smile that could light up your heart right before he took off with your purse. Could I leave him? What would they do with him if they returned to the Flat Lands?

"Should we send word to the Last Men?"

"No. Their time is coming."

I held my finger to my split lip, slipping the curved blade from my cloak. Three's eyes rolled in panic, his legs, bound at the ankle, kicking uselessly. "Seven says he misses you," I whispered, snaking my hand around his foot. With my other, I cut him free. "Find the one who loves you." At my words I felt my disguise splintering, something inside me breaking with it. Three's mouth gaped as I collapsed in the muck, shimmering in light. The urchin turned and ran, scampering into the darkness of the tunnels, his shadows dancing along the walls.

"Heresy finds us!"

I twisted around, my form shaking and unearthly, nearly see-through.

"It is from the Dreaming!" The men stared at me, mouths agape, as Three's footsteps faded into the maze beyond. My essence was trying to find another shape, anything other than the girl I had been. But instead I was disappearing into nothing, my glowing hair flaring out like a ghost. I opened my mouth to speak, but from my throat came only a vibration, strumming like a song.

"This is the shape-shifter?" The lithe one strung two bolts into the crossbow with practiced speed. I thought of tossing the knife at him, but it had slipped straight through my fingers as if they barely existed.

"Nay, this is a faerie." The big one circled around me, narrowing his pig eyes. "The old ones speak of her kind." He gestured with his chin as the lean one collected my blade, then shrugged and handed it over to his bigger friend, who crouched in front of me, scratching his chin. "Legend says . . ."

"If you carve out a faerie's living heart, you can live forever," finished the lean one for him, leaning down to inspect my chest. The flaring colors of my unstable light reflected in his hungry eyes, dancing over his face in blues, golds, reds, and yellows.

Suddenly he grunted in surprise. Black tendrils erupted from under his shirt, crawling up his neck, over his chin, and behind his eyes, black liquid filling up their whites. Rivers of black tears leaked down his cheeks, and his expression changed into one of relief. Then he plummeted face down into the sewer water, the hilt of a blade lodged in his back. I squeezed my eyelids shut as tight as I could, bright colors dancing before me, and tried to pull myself back as men died around me.

Finally there was silence, save for the sound of heavy breathing. A gloved hand caressed my cheek, sticky and cold.

"Saya, my darling."

The skeletal visor of the *kai talan* hovered over me, a white tree bursting from the mouth. With his signature nonchalance, Favian unclipped his mask and smiled down at me, brushing back his blond hair with a blood-streaked glove. How did he know I was here?

"Oh, you think I trust you, my little bird?" he asked, reading my thoughts. He sniffed as one of his *kai talan* pummeled the body of the big, pig-eyed soldier with his boot. The Marauda leader was also crumpled against a tunnel entrance, black tears leaking from his eye sockets. Ugly sobs gushed from my throat, high and young as the boy Three. Favian pulled me onto his shoulder, stroking my hair. I held myself in the street urchin's body, reverberating.

"Shhhhh, shhhhh now . . ." Favian whispered. "My little bird in a cage . . ."

I remembered something about you then, my lost boy from the dream: how your arms felt around me as the stars of the universe danced across the surface of the ocean. *I'm sorry I stopped dreaming about you. I just can't bear to dream about anything ever again.*

You have probably forgotten me, as I have forgotten myself.

* ✦ *

I returned from the past with a sickening jolt.

Another little boy called Salerio grinned up at me expectantly.

"You saw the Traveler?" My voice came out shuddering, the past catching in my throat.

✦ 4 ✦

ANDREAS

Old Time

GALLOPING THROUGH THE RAVINE PATHS, I could soon make out the sloped thatched roofs of our hidden hamlet between the trees. Wild grass covered the earthen paths, dotted with paper lanterns and clay sculptures. On a hillside beyond the village, the dome of the Temple of Beginnings winked, the bronze circlet embedded in the stone catching the sunlight. The village was home to some hundred, the last remaining people of the Second Sun.

Zahara charged over the winding road toward the ceremonial bronze gates decorated with concentric circles carved from oak. I steered Zahara into the village past red-stained walls toward Rosana's homestead. Under its crumbling thatched roof, the reed doors were nailed shut. I dismounted and stalked around it, peering into the threadbare interior, calling for her. Only emptiness answered my voice. In the stables at the back, the family donkey brayed at me. I cursed myself for letting her ever be persuaded by the rantings of the mad giant Melasquez.

With Zahara I raced back into the village, cantering past women carrying vegetables to market in their sleeveless white gowns, heads bowed, and leaped over groaning drunkards. I shouted for Rosana, but they all avoided my eyes, and I grew ever more fretful.

I pursued returning farmers in their patterned tunics and fruit merchants carrying tangerines and honey and chased kids playing naked in the streets under the colored prayer flags of yellow, gray, and white. Each piece of cloth hanging between the thatched houses was emblazoned with the concentric circles of the Temple of Beginnings, adding to my unease.

None would commit to Rosana's whereabouts. There was an evasiveness to their answers, even from the children who seemed to somehow intuit I was bad news. Spying the Strange Tales Tavern, I dismounted and ducked in.

Hunched at a corner table was the sturdy farmer Abrahash, father of Seren, one of Melasquez's original *mayaa*. Once she had been a devotee at the temples, before she'd recruited Rosana into the service of Melasquez, I suspected. Now both she and my fiancée tended to the giant's filthy beard as he slipped deeper into the madness that had gripped him since he opened the Rift.

Abrahash's bristly mustache drooped so low a strand of it marinated in his beer, a mushy pot of wild boar before him.

"Abrahash!" I shook his shoulder, and he turned to me slowly as if underwater. "Have you seen Rosana? Was she with Seren?"

The bags under his eyes bulged as he blinked and studied the wall.

"Do you truly believe the Fates will save us, as the giant promises?" I swore savagely.

Abrahash hawked and spat. "You saw him before he became a giant."

I nodded. Little more than a beggar and tinker, a nasty drunk and a doomsayer when the moods descended on him.

"If the Marauda return to end us all, then so shall it be."

I didn't bother to argue with him.

The faithful of the temples were incurably fatalistic. They believed time was dreamed by the World Trees in a circle, over and over like a merry-go-round, the same events repeating eternally in the same pattern. My interpretation was different.

I believed our paths were the World Trees' search for meaning. Each time the world began and ended in the dreams of the trees, the conscious universe learned about itself and what it meant to be alive. The World Trees' dreams were an exploration on a course charted by us. The trees dreamed our lives as a means of understanding themselves.

But mine was an old interpretation. Now most people of the Second Sun believed it was pointless to contest what would happen. Regardless, another beginning and ending of the world would happen. The story would repeat in a cycle. So why bother to fight it?

"Is Melasquez truly mad?" I let my suspicion hang in the air.

"He wrecked his laboratory. Took us near fourteen men to stop him." The balding man grunted with satisfaction, rubbing his thumb over his fingernails. "He don't eat no more, mutters crazy talk of time. Ever since the Rift, he brought out that accursed sickness for all of us." He trailed off, his mustache drooping back into his gray beer. "The Marauda come? So shall it be then, heh . . ."

During the last full moon, they'd tied Melasquez to the Black

Tree he'd used to open the Rift on the outskirts of the village. Some swore it was a black Fate, a harbinger of the inevitable end of this world and the beginning of another. They'd used the tree cutter's ropes and sailor's knots, and the women had built a shelter over his head to protect him from the wind and the rain. The serving women had begun tending to his ginger beard, which had grown past his feet, and washing his massive wasting body as he refused to eat.

"Where is Seren? Have you seen her?" I pressed him again.

The father shrugged, snorting phlegm, and swore that if I didn't leave him to forget in peace, he would stuff a goat so far up my ass I would be braying.

I mounted Zahara in disgust and cantered beyond the hill toward a little stream and a familiar cottage on the outskirts of the village. The filly threw a gangly shadow over the wooden gate. I unlocked it and slapped Zahara twice on the rump. She knew where home was. I wasn't so lucky. My cracked toe still stung from my precarious climb.

Inside the gate were olive trees, and in the grass, the faded red balls my father had brought me from a faraway land. Azalea bushes grew untamed up the back of our cottage, and the garden was spotted with wildflowers of snow white, yellow, and purple. Maybe I should come back more often. My mom's rocking chair had spiderwebs between its rungs. She wasn't weaving that cursed black shroud for once.

"Where's your papa?" she would always ask me, even though he used to disappear for months at a time, ever since I was a small boy. She knew I couldn't answer. Still she asked me, until I took it as an accusation. She still loved him, so much so I didn't think she'd seen me since he left us for the final time.

I remembered it like yesterday. It was right before the Dreaming began, a day of strange pale green light and lavender clouds sailing across the sky. My father promised us that day it would be his final expedition. Perhaps he had finally told the truth, about that at least. My mother just wanted to weave the shroud she'd seen in her Dreaming, pretending that if she completed it perfectly, he would return for her. And yet somehow, despite how the years had passed, she never finished it.

I checked on the garden by the brook. I had brought her exotic plants and flowers I found in the forest every now and then: orchids, nightshade, cacti with blue blossoms on their spiky little heads from the Uncharted Lands. Sometimes she planted what I gave her; sometimes she didn't. She had tended the nightshade, and there was more structure back here. I knocked on the back door.

"Mama?" I knew she wouldn't answer. My hopes that she had abandoned her ghastly shroud dissipated. She had retreated even further into herself, cocooned in her room with her obsession.

I ducked as I entered through the low doorway. The house was clean, the floorboards brushed. My father's room with all his spare ropes, gloves, and compass was locked as always. I hurried down the hall, into my old room.

On the table was a small sketch of a girl's feet swinging above that beach, stars mirrored in the sea. I'd burned the last of my savings on the skillful work of one of the priestesses at the Temple of Beginnings. I'd been meaning to throw it away if ever I married—I couldn't think about it. My mind ran back to the cliff and those pitiless, slitted eyes of the beast that waited for me at the bottom.

Why had I even asked Rosana? Was I mad, as Heron implied? Perhaps I wanted to help someone so I didn't have to deal with myself all the time. Perhaps something in me understood she didn't need me to say I loved her. I would never be able to say that to anyone. Was it so bad to just want to be like everyone else after losing you, girl of my dreams?

+ ✦ +

Even if she seemed like an obedient temple girl, Rosana always had a secret teasing in her smile. She often wore eggshell-white shawls, wrapped her ash-blond hair, and decorated her fingers with henna. She daydreamed and would answer you as if from a distance in the middle of a conversation. She painted her lips auburn and powdered her cheeks, and I always wondered what she was thinking about. But her different-colored eyes—one cyan blue, the other green as mint—made one feel she was not made for this world's pain.

I used to see her at the market when I sold wood or furs. I never spoke to her much until her papa came past during last month's full moon, and I blurted out of nowhere that I'd like to court her. She glared at me in shock with those unusual eyes, and I saw in her fright something that pricked my heart. It had been a long time since I had wanted anything.

We started seeing each other once a week on strictly controlled occasions, always with one of her parents following no more than ten steps behind. We got along well, both of us appreciating being quiet with one another. She was the only person I could be silent with, who didn't ask questions and to whom I didn't feel the need to justify myself.

Then two weeks ago at the Summerswerd Festival, when her parents weren't looking, Rosana took my hand briefly. We were watching three children playing hopscotch, the clash of cymbals egging them on in the temple square. Neither of us said anything, but we both knew she had accepted me. It was a big moment. Perhaps I'd finally let go of things.

But one thing I couldn't let go of was her attachment to the giant, Melasquez.

"Why do you pamper him?" I'd tried to keep my voice free of accusation. The bushy-haired children had made the temple square into their playground, rich with music, shrieking, and the smell of roasted walnuts.

Rosana didn't say anything. I knew she was forbidden to tell me of anything that had passed between them.

"To you, is he the savior?" We sat down on a stone step together, in the shadow of the temple dome, a little away from the noisy festivities.

"Was the Marauda's retreat a coincidence, my dear?" she demurred, keeping her eyes down.

"I think there's something wrong with that tree you tied him to." I tried not to offend her. "Did you notice how much bigger it got after the Dreaming?"

She didn't answer, just clasped her hands with their henna twirls together. I knew she believed the tree was sacred, not a harbinger of the end but perhaps an incarnation of the World Trees, the Fates themselves. Where she once used to spend every morning in the Temple of Beginnings listening to the First Mothers, now she spent them with the giant, kneeling beneath the dark tree under the colorful canopy of fabrics, recording his pronouncements and teasing out the knots from his tangled beard.

"Melasquez had a brother. Where is he?" I pressed. I couldn't help myself. The giant's little brother had contracted consumption and met his end before the Marauda arrived, though none had seen his grave.

She watched the kids brawl and squeal as the priestesses chased after them, her expression even and sure. "He is a very great man, perhaps not of this earth. He will change the world." Her parents returned from a stall where they were buying spearmint sweets, and she would not speak anymore of it.

Her acceptance of the way things were calmed me in the end, and a wordless bond grew between us. That night, I helped her cook rabbit and potato stew for her family, and I saw how beautiful she really was. She was alive when she laughed with her sister, Channa, and everyone complimented her cooking in that warm homestead. She liked taking care of things.

After a thirteen-hour ordeal shoveling cow dung for her father's potato farm, it was agreed we could wed. Our wrists were entangled on the lakeshore in the presence of the Elder Pan, her parents, and a First Mother, Rosana's face veiled in gossamer white. We were instructed to contemplate our vows of binding for this time and any other.

My mama had attended the betrothal by the lake briefly and didn't say much. She bowed her head, murmured "Fates' blessings upon you" to all the right people, and left early. I think she would have done likewise regardless of my choice. That evening, I climbed one of the largest of the granite walls in the Passage of Ravines without a harness.

I winced and rubbed my wrist at the memory of the binding. I had to tell her before I left. I owed her that much at least. I pressed the sketch of the girl on the swing beneath the stars into my satchel without looking at it. I was afraid it would begin to replace the real memory. What would I have left then?

In preparation for my audience with Melasquez, I stripped, then donned a bone-white shirt with a fern-green pattern and the bangles and necklaces of my profession as a forester. The room was otherwise bare. I'd moved all my belongings into my cabin in the woods. Viciously, I strapped my injured toe and then found the tiny mirror.

Dragging my fingers through my beard, I saw how shredded and sunbaked I had become free-climbing the valley cliffs, able to hold my entire body weight with my fingers alone. I had grown a mane like a lion. I chuffed at myself now, raising my chin in defiance, my starburst green eyes flashing. I belted my ceremonial dagger, used to take animals into the next life if they were injured or caught in my traps in the forest.

Promise me. The whisper of my Traveler's voice reverberated through my heart, faint as a life I'd lived as another person.

I strode to my father's room. "Mama?" I called again. She would never give me the key. I kicked the door open, and it crunched as dust sprayed from the rafters. Particles floated through the light that leaked between the curtains.

My father's maps rolled and fell onto the floor, unfurling. On the desk were scattered pencils, a pair of goggles, gloves, and a cracked compass. I grabbed a climbing rope from the shelf and looped it swiftly into a lasso, stuffing it into my satchel. The man who wanted to be the greatest explorer in the world had gotten lost and never come back. He never would.

I charged to my mother's bedroom door next. I lifted up my fist to knock. My hand hovered endlessly, as if stuck in time.

✦

I strode up the earthen road that wound through the outskirts of the village to where they'd tied the giant at the edge of a ravine. The sun had barely moved, an orb burning in the sky, heat rising from the crumbling ground. It seemed as if the forest itself had retreated, the trees slinking away as I left our hamlet behind me. I chewed the inside of my lip, head down, trying not to clutch my bag.

You're here to ask for your fiancée! I reminded myself. *Be proud!* My instincts were difficult to fight. I felt combative and was trying unsuccessfully to calm down.

Strewn across the path were scraps of rusted metal, springs, and broken armor. As I walked, I saw shoulder plates, nails, beams, bolts, all piled together senselessly. There were steel leggings, pipes, wood, and even disturbing doll faces attached to iron skeletons. The Fates only knew what the giant was playing at.

The wind-up toys he'd made before his gigantism began were famously useless, fizzling into trash at first try. He'd hawked them in the village square, moaning to anyone who would listen that automatons would change the world. Rosana had bought a few out of pity, rusty spring-driven contraptions that resembled self-propelled carts.

His grotesque size only heightened the villagers' reverence for him. The blacksmith was obliged to send him metal for his schemes. As I continued down the earthen road, I came across signs of his larger experiments, discarded wagons and winged boats. He'd build these before they'd tied him to the tree for good.

The scrap heaps of metal and wood now were shambling walls around me, twisting up to the ugly tree perched on the cliffside. Beneath it sat a hulking figure trapped in rope, his head hanging low. No other plants grew around, but a few stray dogs and goats pawed the reddish dust. The forest stood away from the Black Tree, as if keeping its distance.

Two serving women, his *mayaa*, were seated on wooden boxes in the path before me. Their cream-and-rose skirts rippled in the wind. One of them I recognized as Seren, Abrahash's daughter. A shrine of candles, relics picked from the giant's beard hair, and wine stood between them. The giant had leached followers first from the temple faithful. Then his influence expanded to the credulous. Always women. The only ones who had seen the Rift, the portal of light that had once cracked open in the earth beneath the tree.

Both *mayaa* in their organdy boots rose from their wooden boxes. "Beginnings' blessings," Seren greeted me cordially. Both women's expressions were vacant. I noticed hoofprints in the dust. Heron's horses. They seemed to be expecting me.

I was surprised neither protested the dagger at my hip, given my history with the giant. Seeing it as a form of respect to visit the giant in formal dress, they didn't even check my bag. Although Seren hadn't, other *mayaa* had seen me drunk and boiling with black rage, restrained by three of the village guards from flinging them aside and demanding an audience with the giant. Seren offered me wine in a clay cup. I took it carefully.

"He speaks directly with the Fates."

"Thank you, *Seren*," I said, deliberately using her name, as if it could jog her out of her dreamy formality. "Have you seen Rosana?"

The former honey seller did not respond. I'd bought her products more than once. We'd had full conversations together about the weather, her lazy husband, her honeybees, but all of this she seemed to have forgotten in service to the giant. Both Seren and her junior curtsied as I passed them, as if it were a royal gathering.

I scowled. What was all this pomp and ceremony? The man had been a drunk and a failure not so long ago.

A hundred yards away, the dark tree reared, its leafless branches grasping at the sun, a web of dark roots clawing down the back of the ravine. My palms were sweaty, my breathing skittish. I adjusted my shoulders and marched down the earthen path. I suddenly hoped Rosana was not there at all.

As I neared, the Black Tree seemed even larger than before. It was gnarled and ominous even in daylight, with branches thick as a man's legs, as if an oak had been flipped upside down, the underground root systems reaching to the sky. Its roots ate down into the sides of the ravine, which dropped off sheer and deep.

Under the contorted shadows of its branches, the giant's bald head hung as if asleep. His orange beard covered most of his belly. Flies buzzed around the rope that bound him to the trunk. Up close, it was easy to see the knotted scars where he had wrestled mightily to free himself from his bondage—thank the Fates he had not succeeded. He was over twenty feet tall, with a bald head and a potbelly, arms that hung like an ape's, and a perpetual expression that swung between concentration and futility.

In the chaotic days after the Marauda occupation, he'd been dragged from his shack into the courtyard where the soldiers had assembled us. A monstrous, fat-bellied, blubbering freak that took twenty men to control.

They had chained him and thrown him among the rest of us assembled in the mist. At first, we'd been just as horrified as our jailors at his monstrous growth. But when the Dreaming had come through the Rift, we'd all seen dreams that had merged with our waking worlds. It was only strange that his had persisted. As had mine. As if we were linked in some way.

"You need not fear the future hmmm, Andreas son of Revanan," he rumbled as I approached, "for it shall decide your past."

My heart pounded in my chest. *By the Fates, control yourself, man!* The giant was talking in circles already. "Where is my fiancée, Melasquez?" I countered, my voice wavering despite myself. My cheeks flushed.

"The one you love hmmm?" The giant mouthed the word, tasting it with simian emotions, chewing on it. "Love, love, love . . ."

I clutched my knife tightly, surveying around me. His *mayaa* had retreated back up the path into the heaps of metal and broken inventions. There seemed to be no one around, not a sound carrying from the village behind us.

"You are a fraud!" I hissed, louder than I had intended. "If you refuse to open the Rift to save us, I will hang you from that tree like the old stories of the Beginnings!" I bounded forward and threw the cup of wine up into his face. It bounced off like a toy, splashing a bloody streak over his chin and dribbling down onto his fat belly. It seemed as if his head moved in sly interest. Red droplets ran down his protruding lips, dripping into the dust.

"What is your offering thennn?" the giant asked, rolling the words in his mouth again. His narcissism had grown with his swollen flesh. Now he wore his vanity like a crown.

"Open it!" I cried. "I will do whatever you ask of me! For if you do not . . ." My voice faded up into the canopy of boards and brightly colored fabrics that protected him from the sun, then out beyond the cliff face shadowed by the tree. From my pouch I withdrew my father's climbing rope. I twirled the lasso, visualizing looping it over his bald dome.

"As the Fates foretold, so you have offered," the giant boomed.

I faltered, the noose's momentum falling into the dust.

The giant began laughing maniacally. He smelled of sweat and oil. "The future is already decided!" he shrieked.

"My future is ours to decide!" I fired back.

I didn't know if it was the angle of the sunlight, but the fabrics above had begun to look ghostly, like a mirage. The giant raised his neck, his adamantine eyes clear as an alpine morning. Just as quickly, they clouded again.

"You claim to be the savior who speaks with the Fates, but I see you just as lost as any other!"

He chuckled and then giggled at my accusation, unusual coming with that booming voice. Hiding behind his size, smoke and shadow!

"What is your price?" I roared, stepping forward. The Black Tree loomed over us, its curved branches blotting across the roof of the sky. I shook my head to clear my vision. An unearthly gray-black mist had risen from the dirt, coiling around the giant's feet.

"The Rift goes where the Fates dream." Melasquez touched the tip of his tongue to his upper lip. His mustard-colored teeth were each the size of my hand. "And this Fate"—he lifted his chin up—"has already dreamed you will return her to us."

My mouth hung open. Every time I had broken through the *mayaa* and forced my way to him, I had found him like a mountain, unresponsive and stinking of despair. And yet now he seemed to discern my deepest intentions. Had he said that the tree had told him what I would demand before I had even spoken?

"You wish to find her? Your dream girl?" The giant leered at me like an orangutan with his oversized lips and filthy carrot beard. "So, find your Traveler and bring her back to me. It is her you seek, not Rosana."

"That will save the village?" I frowned. A second sun had

appeared in the sky, a burning black eclipse from another world. Melasquez was silent, his head tilted as if he was listening to an unknown voice. The mist curled around him, pouring over the side of the cliff like a waterfall.

"Commit the heresy the Marauda hunt us for." The giant was suddenly melancholy, muttering and squinting into the distant sky. "Taste the fruit of the Travelers, those who walk across time and starlight . . ." Streaking across the heavens beyond the Black Tree's branches were hundreds of shooting stars, like burning angels across the ceiling of the world. "And I will reopen the Rift to the forbidden way." He hunched in on himself, dipping his massive head down in subservience as if to a voice in his head.

But I was too busy staring up in wonder at the fire-streaked sky, unable to move. At my feet, the ground opened to release light, sublimely pure as if issuing from the center of the earth itself. It formed the shape of a man, legs splayed as if falling, one hand outreached in desperation, as if grasping for something. This was the Rift!

With shaking hands, I undid the lasso and wrapped it swiftly around me like a belt.

"Return with your love, Andreas son of Revanan . . ." The giant had begun to babble, his voice increasing in pitch and volume. His features had hardened as if into fossil; veins of black like marble shot through his forehead as he fixed me with his ungodly stare. "And let us create a new time together!" His voice echoed strong and terrifying as he spoke these final words.

I sucked the air into my lungs, my vision spinning as the light from the Rift burned into my eyelids. I was afraid. But though I couldn't untangle the giant's riddles, this was my only way back. Back to you!

From behind the tree, a figure emerged like a ghost in white robes, gliding over the burnt-orange dirt. Rosana's hands were clasped in prayer, only her lips visible beneath her gossamer veil. She knelt down in the mist next to the giant, coating her knees in dust.

I staggered. My mouth moved, but I could not speak. She held her smile, full of the mysterious knowledge she'd always withheld from the world.

Forgive me . . . I mouthed, trying to speak. With both hands, Rosana raised her veil, and a tear glistened in her eyes. But I could not interpret its meaning. Her smile held with its secret as the sparkle ran down her cheek. Was it real or another impossible illusion like the sky? I grabbed hold of my satchel and stepped forward. *Forgi*—I tried to speak but the words would not come.

Gently, she shook her head.

And then, as if in a dream, I found myself lowering my body through the mist onto the light. My arms rose, clutching for an unseen hand, and my legs splayed, as if suspended. The light held my weight but seemed to sink slightly. I shivered as above me, the day split the sky in half, the twin suns burning in both night and day.

My body began tingling, and a humming started in my ears. The giant's visage loomed along with Rosana's shawl, the Black Tree's branches eating into the sky. Day and night swirled into one another, deepening into patterns of exquisite colors, vortexing into the sky as the mist covered my vision.

I felt suddenly on the verge of understanding the language of colors, the meaning of each swirl pulsating with significance. I sank into the swirling portal with the giant's bargain ringing in my ears.

Down, down, down into a bright echoing, as if the ground

had swallowed me whole and a vast nothingness lay beneath it. Turning, I saw a puny outline of blue sky in the shape of the reaching man.

Then I plummeted deeper into darkness until it was total, and the everlasting swallowed me and all sound and space. There was only a sense of vibration, the rhythms almost a song, their beats alive with meanings I couldn't quite grasp.

It was at once familiar and immense. I quickly lost my sense of direction, even of up and down, hugging my knees to my chest, with a humming in my blood like the strings of a harp. Slowly, the space around me began to form into a fine mist. Moisture prickled my skin.

I cannoned into a substance that seemed to suction in and welcome me. The landing was forceful and then gentle as I slowed and was brought back to equilibrium. I found I did not need to breathe, the pulse in my ears and the humming in my bones growing in intensity.

There was a crowd, a living presence. A warmth began in my belly, and I swallowed the liquid into my lungs. Incredibly, I could breathe, and I did not breathe alone. For an instant, I was everyone, countless lives flashing before and within, and I gazed into the face I had before the world was made and forgot it within that instant.

Then I sensed myself rising upward, buoying in a current. The tip of my nose and lips broke the surface, and still I did not need to breathe. I lay in an open sea, ears under the everlasting waters, sounds muted by the rhythms of the waves. The lights from the purple and green galaxies above reflected and flowed through the ripples around me, through my body itself, and into the depths. I couldn't tell if I was in the sea looking up at the sky or in the sky looking down on the sea.

In the strands of myself that were still there, I understood this place. This was the Dreaming. Above were branches made of light, the limbs of a tree growing out of the star-studded canopy. They looked so elemental and alive they seemed to comprehend me back. I heard the voice, like my own, like the voice of everyone.

Of what do you dream?

"Of her!" I shouted up into the branches, my voice soundless in the sea.

Eat freely of what is given.

There was an echo, an impact, and bubbles under the water. The ripples reflected across the sky. To my left I saw a strange white fruit, like a message in a bottle, bobbing and twinkling in the waves.

I reached out and picked it up, a ripe fruit dripping with star water. Was this the forbidden way that Melasquez had spoken of? I brought it to my lips and bit into its crunchy white flesh.

For the briefest of seconds, I remembered kissing you.

It tasted like love.

✦ 5 ✦

SAYA

New Time

I SNAPPED BACK INTO THE PRESENT. Salerio was grinning at me, breathless.

"Something's wrong with him," he reported. The Traveler? Of course, the child was confused, fanciful. He'd evaded the dream tax and so his imagination leaped to the wonders of the world.

His little sister was still staring at me, a tiny frown crinkling her forehead, when I heard the heavy metal knocking echo from the other side of the dome. "Can we help him?" the little girl asked. "People from other times need help too!" Salerio's wick of pale hair was shaking with excitement.

"Children, whatever you do, do not speak of this. To your friends. To *anyone*. Do you understand me?" I wasn't sure they were old enough to fully comprehend, but I had to control information flow. I would have to make a decision quickly. The sun was going down. Perhaps they would dream of this tonight. Even if it was fanciful—especially if it was fanciful—the roots could still take it to the capital, and even before the Dreaming Curfew was over, the *kai talan* would be here to complicate things.

"Stay here," I instructed the orphans, picking up my robe and hurrying back inside. I marched through the dome, shooing away the curious children who popped their heads in from outside. Then I strode down the aisle and toward the exit.

The main door of the temple was down another long, tight passageway. Dusk was approaching, and the lanterns that lined the long hallway had not yet been lit. The only reddish light was coming from under the door and through the keyhole. As I neared, the iron knocker banged once more. I stopped to compose my face into a neutral welcome. Then I placed my hand on the rusted doorknob and swung the thick wooden slab open.

Outside, the sun was dipping beneath the mountains, silhouetting a bent figure at the top of the temple steps.

The so-called Traveler was nothing like I had expected.

Before me knelt a purple-and-gray, muddy, muscular mess with its head bowed. It was dripping. The tunic, boots, and bangles and necklaces it wore were in a style I'd only ever seen men wear in illustrated books.

The apparition offered me a hand unlike any I had ever laid eyes on. Its fingers were thick and preternaturally strong. The topmost joints were gnarled and powerful, fingerprints eroded from years of gripping harsh surfaces, calloused and leathery, palms supple. These were hands never to pick your pocket or fix your jewelry. They were the products of trials weathered and the physical prowess of their bearer. They were hands more animal than man. I was afraid at first to touch them.

"Hello, First Mother." Its voice was masculine and gravelly, as if it was not used to speaking, yet surprisingly gentle. Its greeting was in the old manner. And it waited, politely, for my acknowledgment. There was a kindness to it that I trusted, which never happened to me, and my instincts convinced me that the Traveler was a mere man.

I placed my hand in his.

At the touch of his skin, a ripple coursed through my body, igniting my entire being. The splintering of the changeling reverberated inside me, and for the first time since I could remember, I was free of the pain. I could breathe again. It was as if I had been carrying a weight that had crippled my movements for so long I had forgotten what it felt like to dance. I shivered in relief.

He raised his eyes to meet mine, fierce, dark, arresting—a shocking starburst of green against his mud-caked face with its mane of soggy hair and mangled beard. Who was this man? I could not speak. Our eyes locked. My heart pounded in my chest, excitement rushing through my body and into my lower belly.

I spoke automatically. "Can I help you?"

He did not respond.

I repeated the question. He seemed to have trouble talking. All I could hear was his breathing. His hungry eyes penetrated my skin and left me raw and defenseless, as if my disguise had melted away under the heat of his gaze.

"Are you looking for someone?"

He still did not speak. Was he an idiot? To my disappointment, he slowly removed his hand, and the rush dissipated from my body. Even then, the pain of the changeling did not fully return. Despite his lithe appearance, he moved as if underwater. He began digging in the matted bag that was slung over his shoulder.

I controlled myself and looked at him more closely. The old patterns under the mud, the foresters' glyphs on his tunic, were odd. There were no more forests on the Floating Lands. The lush woodlands didn't survive the Day of Rising, when the crescent-shaped landmass rose into the sky. Unable to adapt to the elevation, they were cut down to make way for the quarries that built the citadel. He wore a necklace with a locket and leather bangles, unfashionable and odd. It didn't make any sense.

Could Salerio have been right? The fact that it was even mildly plausible meant it could be my way into the Last Men, I calculated instantly. I just needed to play this charade right.

"I am looking for . . ." he managed.

"Yes?"

Still on his knee, he removed a piece of paper from his bag, unfolded it, and showed it to me. I was so distracted by his animalistic eyes obviously assessing me I could hardly look at it. It was a charcoal sketch of a girl's feet on a swing winging out from the center. The stars in the sky were reflected in the ocean before her, and the two mirrored each other so perfectly you could not tell if the ocean was the sky or the sky was the ocean.

"Who is she?" I demanded. There was something familiar about it.

He swayed slightly, as if unsure himself.

"Are you going to faint?"

He continued to stare intensely. I felt heat rising between us. Why was he on his knees like this? My head was swimming in a way I was completely unused to. He seemed confused too—he must have been having the same feeling, I was sure of it.

He finally recovered enough to say, "My dream girl . . ."

Crows above circled and cawed, interrupting us. A column of

dust was rising and moving rapidly up the old town road toward us. It was the Guard, or Fates forbid the *kai talan*, bearing down the mountain pass.

The man down on the ground seemed unaware of the danger, observing the column of dust as though it was simply the wind. My assignment was known to a very select few. I would not allow them to derail my best chance at finding the secrets of the Last Men and uncovering the Traveler's true purpose.

"Get up!" I snapped at him. He rose to his feet with visible effort, and I realized finally how big he was. "Hurry, you idiot!"

He stood still and just stared at me like a large, confused cat. I looked over his shoulder at the column of dust and grabbed his tunic, tugging him into the passageway and closing the door behind us. I could feel his chest, how muscular it was and how small I was next to him. The pulsing started in my stomach again. In the dark, narrow passageway, we were closer together than was comfortable. The rush throughout my body took my breath away. And I knew nothing about him.

"Get behind me. Do not say anything. Do not move." *Was he looking at my lips just then? Get those thoughts out of your head, Saya! And what is this feeling in my body?*

He obeyed, ducking past me and down the passage, bracing himself against the wall. I had a few moments to compose myself. I could feel his physical presence behind me in the dark hallway. I stroked at my hair only to realize I didn't have any to adjust. Was he a pervert to be looking at an old woman like this? Ugh!

I needed to find out more about him. As soon as possible. My nose wrinkled at the scent of him—strange, almost woody. Not the unpleasant stink of oddly colored mud. It was musky, sandalwood and amber, green and orange. A natural perfume that reminded me of sunset in a deep forest among the sweet smoke of lanterns.

Within seconds I heard the crunch of wooden wheels on the loose stones of the ruined square below. The spring-powered vehicles moved surprisingly quickly, like wind-up toys. I heard at least two sets of boots clanking up the steps. That was good; it was probably only the Guard, ordinary foot soldiers of the Regent drawn from the common folk, not the forbidding *kai talan* inquisitors. But was it a random inspection? It was at least three hours before the Dreaming Curfew.

The iron knocker clanged, sharp and urgent.

I checked my shape quickly. Yes, I was still wearing the First Mother, thank the Fates. I was uncharacteristically spooked. I took a breath to steady myself and opened the door in no hurry, adjusting my body to a dignified bearing.

"We couldn't live without ya famous soup, First Mother!" exclaimed the guard, placing a cocky hand on her hip. She had spiky red hair and an inquisitive snout like a mink that wrinkled when she spoke. I pegged her as bossy.

Her colorless military jacket with shapeless shoulder pads reflected the Floating City's dwindling imagination. Where once it would have sparkled with burnt-orange insignia, now it was at home among the forgotten dirt of the crumbling city. The cheap, durable trousers and cape embodied the pragmatic leftovers of the once proud defenders of the Tree.

Her brazen tone didn't fool me. The way her hand strayed to play with the hilt of her blade told me she was also nervous. She was smiling at me from under her cap with small ivory teeth. She had ferrety cinnamon eyes and even larger ears. At the bottom of the steps was the wooden police racer, its wheels raised and still spinning with tendrils of pungent blue smoke.

The second guard was puffing his way up the stairs. I pegged him at little more than seventeen, overgrown for his age, with a roly-poly figure and bowl haircut that screamed new recruit. He had patches of sweat on his back, and his uniform looked too big for him.

"Mother!" he babbled. "Mother!" To my shock, he threw his blubbering form onto me, embracing me in a hug that was as smelly as it was touching as I sank into his squishy folds. "Heeheehee!" he giggled, pulling me tighter. The first guard snorted and tugged him away by the back of his cloak.

"Get off her, slug monkey! We here on official business!"

After squeezing all the air out of me, the fat boy stepped back, a cheery gap-toothed smile pasted across his face. Siblings. The new recruit had the same red hair as his companion, except curled, and the same jug ears and cinnamon-brown eyes, too. His nose was sunburned. "I'm hungry!" he announced, as if it were his birthday. The sun was dipping beneath the mountains, and the wind was picking up, licking at their capes.

"Could ya be more obvious, Gellie?" quipped his sister. But her look wasn't as friendly as his. She held on to her cap as the wind tried to drag it off her head into the thorn bushes.

"You are always welcome," I replied. "Always welcome."

The sister gave me a quizzical look. My tone must not have reflected the depth of their relationship with the First Mother. I needed more information, and quickly. Gellie was looking at the temple appreciatively and sighed. I placed my fingers gently into the First Mother's steeple shape and set my features to calm concern.

"Mother, as you may have figured, this be not a social visit." The sister's fingers drummed on the hilt of her blade. She winced and glanced away for a second. "Look, are you to tell us or not?"

"Perhaps inquire after my health first?" I said archly. It was a gamble, but it succeeded. The brother's cheeks went shiny red, and his sister's wince got even worse. She took off her cap and started rubbing the back of her head, the spikes of her hair popping up between her fingers.

"Of course. How—"

"We miss you!" blurted out her little brother. "Me and Reece miss your stories!"

I smiled at him. My hypothesis had been right: He had been an orphan himself.

"Growing up is not for everyone, Gellie," I observed. This delighted him, and he was about to speak again when Reece cut him off. She seemed frustrated. I couldn't help but feel I wasn't reacting quite as she had expected.

"You look good, First Mother, and yeah, it's true we miss you like mad, especially Gellie. But let's get . . . look, gee . . . there's been a dream collected—from the folks down the mountain pass. People doze off pretty fast now, you know, especially when they see things that have never been seen before . . . like, um . . ." She trailed off and then started going again like the city spiral train. "Anyway, one of them dreamed of a person appearing through a crack in the earth? Like a light? Uh . . . If they know they can get favors, they try to sleep it off as soon as . . ." Reece's delivery was speeding up. She was justifying herself to me.

"Where are the *kai talan*? Will you bring them to this place of peace?" I asked. I put admonition in my voice.

She shook her head quickly. "You know we'd never do that to you, Mother, never! Fates forbid." So she believed in the ways of the Beginnings. "But dreams like this be serious, Mother. Serious!" She cupped her hand over her mouth and said more quietly, "Have you heard of the Traveler?"

"We will take care of you, Mother!" affirmed Gellie.

"What is your plan then?" I asked the duo. This seemed to completely stump them. They shared a look. Had I made another mistake? At that moment, I could have sworn I heard a swish of movement from behind me, and I bit back a curse. Then Gellie brightened.

"We believe in the Beginnings," he intoned, as if it was a rallying cry. With his index finger he drew a circle on his chest. I had no idea what it meant.

Both of them stared at me expectantly.

For a moment I was at a loss. But I quickly calculated the risk. If I got it right, the connection would solidify. If I was wrong or rebuffed Gellie, Reece would know there was something wrong. I couldn't have her getting pushy and discovering more until I had control of the situation. There was no choice. I had to guess.

"We believe in the Beginnings," I repeated, drawing the circle on my chest. I kept my hand slow and confident.

Both of them relaxed immediately. What had I committed to?

"We find out what happened, and we take the information into the Skala Mines," Reece said, lowering her voice and tracing the circle on her chest while trying to peek over my shoulder. "There be someone I know, and this fearful burden be off our hands, if . . . ?" It was a question. They were looking for my approval.

If the Traveler was real? She could not be serious. And the mines? That was a forsaken place, deep under the Sentinels in the Outer Rim. It was crawling with Miners, hopeless souls who plumbed the depths of the earth for artifacts that could ignite their dreams once more. It was also home to those who had become Forgotten, drained of all their deepest dreams until they were little more than shadows. There was no one in the Skala Mines who could help take this burden off our hands. Unless . . .

"You know what I say, right?" Reece prodded.

Unless they had a contact with the Last Men. The unquenchable rebellion I aimed to uncover.

I nodded slowly. Instead of releasing, the tension only mounted.

"Return. After the Dreaming Curfew. We must leave as soon as possible. No one can spot you," I enunciated slowly and clearly. "The moment more dreams are distilled, the *kai talan* will conclude something came this way." I paused for effect. "I will not put you nor the children at risk of becoming Forgotten."

Gellie suddenly looked afraid. Clearly, the poor fool had not realized the forces at play. Reece's ferrety front teeth chewed on her lower lip.

I stopped for a second to evaluate the brother and sister. Could I trust them not to make a mistake? I could suddenly hear my heart beating loudly in my ears. Salerio. His sister. The others. He would never draw another monster again, never dream of another monster, because he'd have already met all the monsters he would ever meet once the *kai talan* were done with him.

"Now, the Traveler will pose as an escaped Miner," I stated slowly. "You are depositing him back where he belongs." This would provide adequate cover for the operation. Escaped Miners could be unpredictable and dangerous, and it was natural that the Guard would recapture them, even after Dreaming Curfew. It was the best plan I could think of on my feet, and I hoped to the Fates it would work. I felt the edge of the moment slicing both ways.

Reece swallowed hard. "The Traveler?"

"Yes," I said. "This may be our chance to return all the dreams we fight for, Fates willing." For this gamble not to come crashing down, I would need to convince the stranger in the hall behind me to play along. It was even more crucial now that I win his trust and extract as much intelligence as possible.

"Not good, not good!" blubbered Gellie.

"Gellie, my child. You are a man of the Guard now," I said sternly.

"Yes, Mother," he sniveled.

"Go now and come back on foot as soon as the curfew begins. There is a young woman named Ciana I need you to escort. She will accompany the Traveler. Let none see your return!"

Gellie saluted me, and Reece put her cap back on.

"Who is Cian—" Reece was tougher than her brother.

"There is no time!"

She wrinkled her nose like a mink and seemed about to say something.

"Go!" I commanded, pointing my finger at them the way the First Mother had pointed at me. I noticed a chip in the purple fingernail polish.

That seemed to bend their last resistance. Gellie turned immediately and hurried down the stairs, followed by his sister, who trotted more slowly, deep in thought. The fat recruit grunted as he cranked up the springs of the wooden vehicle, the sweaty patch on the back of his shirt growing. The wheels began spinning again, whirring blue smoke as they wound up and hissed into release. Reece looked up at me one more time from under her cap and raised an uncertain hand in farewell.

I placed my hands into the steeple. "May the Beginnings guide you," I said, as the wheels ground the dust once more into the sky.

✦ 6 ✦

ANDREAS

New Time

I FORCED MY EYES OPEN. MY vision hurt as though I had never used it before, stinging and swimming in the rosy-yellow light. I huddled with my hands wrapped around my knees on heated cobblestone in the shadow of an immense tower that blotted out the sky.

So quickly, the memory of my passage through the Rift was disappearing. I forced myself to grab on to your taste, faint on my lips, but you slipped away with the waves, fading like the Dreaming you had come from. I ran my tongue over my mouth again and again, but you were gone.

My grasp of space was groggy. My eyes narrowed in the sun as I blinked at the tower above me, dumbly trying to estimate the size of it. A mile wide at least at the base, I decided—a living canopy dark with veined cobalt. Disks surrounded the base, fortified with towers and keeps, supported by roots and stone buttresses at the lower levels.

I sat up. It was a tree with a castle spiraling around the trunk, minarets gleaming ivory and pink.

My clothes were caked in stinking charcoal mud, hanging thickly and weighing down my hair. Tendrils of smoke were still rising off my body and my father's exploring rope. Was this the Village of the Second Sun? The buildings were older and larger and more broken than I had known them to be. My ears popped, and I heard the hissing of the vapor escaping.

Through my hair, I glimpsed a family running across the edges of the deserted square, a mother and father holding the hands of a small boy between them. They wore shapeless ash frocks, not the patterned shirts of our people. As his parents dragged him around a corner, the boy looked back at me, his face blank. They were gone before I could confirm the accuracy of my senses.

I rolled to my knees, groaning and dragging my satchel with me. The stone buildings were ancient, dilapidated. Next to me was a crumbled fountain, weeds celebrating all along its fault lines. Tough grass broke through the cobblestones, and a grumpy wind was blowing. My bag and my knife were still with me. I glanced around and gritted my teeth against a wave of nausea. The immense tree was still there. It couldn't be real.

I picked myself up and stumbled toward the nearest stone dwelling, trying to find my equilibrium, dizzy and gulping air. It tasted thin, like the atmosphere at the very peaks of the mountains. The fiery rose light was harsh, and I had to shade my eyes, coughing into my armpit. As a climber, I recognized elevation sickness, and I crouched down against the brick for a while to let my body acclimate. I knew the terrain yet couldn't comprehend the broken city around me. None of this made any sense.

It appeared I was in the Village of the Second Sun—not so far above sea level. And yet I was in another world . . . another time. A door slammed in the street behind me.

"Hello?" I swiveled. My voice echoed in my ears, reverberating like the hum of the portal. I shivered at the memory of my passage, trying to clear my mind. *Keep moving.*

I got up and walked down the dusty street, sticking to the burgundy shadows, glancing up at the boarded windows. At one point I heard running footsteps up ahead but could not move quickly enough to catch them. I knocked on splintered doors, bewildered by the lack of care or curiosity. I sensed eyes on me, perhaps from above, but I didn't spot them. I glanced behind. I was leaving a dripping trail of purple-gray mud, still smoking.

As I turned back, I recognized a structure of spotted metal winking on a broken hillside. The traditional haven of wanderers, the Temple of Beginnings with its bronze circle. I felt eyes on me again, a certainty in my forest senses prickling. There! A crone in a window above, hunkered over herself like a hyena, her boggled eyes both pleading and bankrupt. She closed the curtains.

"Greetings!" I shouted up at her. I laughed, incredulous and more than a little nervous. A muddied man steaming with wisps of smoke, wandering through the street, and no one pays it any attention? I began to doubt the certainty of this reality. The thought made me stronger.

The Temple of Beginnings lay among the ruins of what had once been a thriving prayer ground. Where I remembered a square surrounded with wheat and high grass, now horned weeds fought among each other for territory. It was and was not the same square where I had walked hand in hand with Rosana while her parents were distracted by a stall of toffee apples and mint sweets.

"Is this the Dreaming? Or something else?" I wondered aloud.

Even the idea of it brought a stinging surge of anxiety. I crushed it with force of will. I needed to be clearheaded and focused, like when I was on the wall of granite. Empty. Pure. Suddenly I hoped the beast would appear again. Anything for a familiar face, even if it was the ugly mug of that murder poodle.

The cold wind blew from the west, as it never had in my experience. I rubbed my hands together, feeling the grip strength that had saved my life on more than one occasion. How many fingertip pull-ups had I done to train myself to trust my body's ability?

My nose twitched where Rosana's hair had tickled it as she had leaned into me in her shawl. We were again watching three children playing hopscotch like frogs. A fiddler danced with them with cymbals jingling on his boots. They appeared just a few meters from me in the present, as if my sight and my memories had been seamlessly overlaid. The giddy music tickled my skin, raising goose pimples. The phantoms giggled and ran into the thorns, disappearing through a broken doorway.

Rosana's ghost emerged from within my body, turning to beckon me onward to the temple with arms decorated in henna. Just as quickly, she faded into the sunlight, taking the sound of the dancing cymbals with her. I was rocked by the lucidity of it. Like a living dream, memories intermingled with the now. Birds from another time dipped and chirped over my head.

I smelled the roasted walnuts; saw temple devotees cross-legged and basking, sunlight gleaming from their bronze circlets; watched naked children with overgrown hair tumbling and wrestling, all shimmering like mirages. It was overwhelming, and it made me angry. *Don't think, Andreas. Keep moving.*

Cleaning as much of the mud from myself as I could, I strode into the center of the deserted square. By reflex I brushed aside the colorful prayer flags that once hung between the stalls. They turned gossamer and merged into the red-sandstone light.

My forest instincts tingled. I crouched on the balls of my feet and squinted toward the temple. Two kids were looking at me with owl eyes, and before I realized they were real, they scrambled away, the boy leading the girl—who was clutching her teddy—up the temple steps and around the side of the dome.

Sighing, I took my hand off my knife handle. The living memories were gone. The square was only ruins now, long abandoned to the elements. Above me, a column of steps led to a rounded door, the entrance to the circular temple.

The dome was cracked, as if pulled apart by the webs of black roots and branches with baby-blue leaves that emerged out of the hillside itself. Where once the temple dome had been encircled by a bronze band like the circlets of the devoted, now the dark root held it in its clutches, digging into every crack and crevice. I tightened my father's rope around my hips, hoping for my determination to strengthen.

The strange westerly wind bit into my cheek as I tried to shake the pitted mud from my hair, but it was hopeless. I stepped my way through the ruins, kicking caked dirt from my boots, climbing over the weeds to the bottom of the temple steps.

Suddenly I felt an overwhelming desire to go home. I didn't need to be tramping through this unknown world. I could be safe in my bed, accepting a solitary life in the mountains. But there was no way back. Something tugged me onward, the invisible string.

I climbed the steps and thunked the bronze knocker, heard the clunk echoing, and waited.

Behind me, the ruby sun hovered above the gray and purple Sentinels. I'd never seen it that shade of crimson. And rising above the dome of the temple was the monstrous tree with the spiraling castle I could barely look at; it was so preposterously unreal.

An elderly priestess wearing a pebble-gray robe and a bronze circlet opened the round door. She had cropped white hair that sharply contrasted with her dusky skin, a round face, and rough hands from years of manual work. Stern eyes. No-nonsense demeanor. I knelt at her sandals. There was a small rash that ran up her inner foot. Her toenails were purple as an orchid.

"Hello, First Mother," I said, greeting her formally, offering her my palm in the traditional gesture. The First Mothers provided shelter to those from all walks of life. I was hoping this would still be the case, given my appearance.

I waited several seconds. The wind blew restlessly into my mane. Then it seemed that all time condensed into a single moment, that the world stopped moving. I was aware of everything, the almost soundless rustle of her robe, my heartbeat pounding, the crinkle of dust in my nostrils, caked mud pulling the skin of my cheeks.

The moment she touched my hand, it was electric.

I looked up and saw an old woman no longer. Before me now was a radiant young woman, her face blooming with wonder. Her hair was streaming colors like a rainbow, flashing through shapes, her eyes magnetic blue, green, lilac, orange, black, and furnace red. Her lips ran like an oil painting through every shade and depth imaginable; her features created and destroyed themselves in an instant. It was as if she were the universe itself, dancing through possibilities, in all the pain and beauty of becoming.

In all my life, I had never seen anything so beautiful.

"Can I help you?" she repeated, her lips dazzling me. "Are you looking for someone?"

Finally I found my tongue, thick and clunky in my mouth. "I am looking for . . ."

"Yes?"

As if in a daze, I removed the sketch of the girl's feet on the swing from my satchel and showed it to her. Her hair shimmered like an opal of white soundless brilliance, and I could hardly respond. She demanded to know more, her mouth moving but the words reaching me from far away. There was a terrible tingle deep within my chest, like a tug to an unseen world.

"My dream girl . . ." I managed.

She snapped at me, glancing over my shoulder, then grabbed my tunic and dragged me into the passageway with her. The door shut behind us, and we were close. There she was even more breathtaking, her lips a blur of escalating golds, silvers, and prismatic blue, her eyes glistening like the chest of a hummingbird and settling into violet, her skin coalescing into caramel.

"Get behind me. Do not say anything. Do not move."

Feeling ill, I collapsed in the gloomy, shrinking corridor behind her. The first few times I'd ascended a mountain too fast for my body to acclimate, I'd gotten similar symptoms—fatigue, headache, shortness of breath. But after years of climbing in the Passage of Ravines and even higher in the Sentinels during my wanderings, I was conditioned to fast ascents. The Temple of Beginnings was not far above sea level, for Fate's sake! I could only put the feeling down to that bizarre journey through the Rift.

It was more than the elevation. I rested against the rough stone and held my palm up. The life lines were tingling from where the

Mother had touched me, the energy spreading up my arm and into my chest and belly. I closed my eyes and massaged my temples. The radiant colors and shapes of the female figure were imprinted behind my eyelids like an afterglow.

Like the eyes of the beast, came a quiet voice in my mind.

I shook my head. What I had seen underneath the Mother was different from the memories in the temple square. It was as if she was *becoming* right before me, a person being created before my very eyes. But when she had dragged me inside, her form had ignited again. As she pressed me against the wall, it had stabilized into a slender honey-skinned woman with blazing eyes of violet and orange and shoulder-length hair streaming through colors. It was as though when we touched, another self had burst from within.

Was it an illusion? She had felt real, her flesh warm and electric against me, and when her lips had been so close to mine in the cramped corridor, had I felt something between us? My imagination was running with confusion and fanciful images. I gritted my teeth and pushed through, trying to make out what the voices were saying outside.

The three seemed to be old friends, but there was something off about the pauses between the Mother's responses. It was clear to me that she was no First Mother and that these two had little notion of it. What she was, I had no idea. I'd never seen or felt anything like what had passed between us, and I could tell it had affected her too, unexpectedly. And when she had pushed me against the wall, had we really . . . ?

I tried to unscramble my thoughts. It was undoubtedly another side effect of the portal, like the phantoms in the square. . . . But if it was just me, why had she reacted with the same surprise?

The Mother seemed to be negotiating the terms of my escape.

But to whom or where they were taking me was a mystery. They kept referring to the mines. To my knowledge, there were no precious minerals under the Village of the Second Sun, much less a mine. Ours had been farming country for generations. Then I heard them repeat the words "the Traveler," and my heart thumped louder. Could that be a coincidence?

Of one thing I was certain: I didn't like the sound of a Dreaming Curfew. It had echoes of Marauda occupation in my own time and made me even warier of this world. And I had little faith in the two outside, who were obviously being manipulated.

I glanced behind me. In the light of the temple entrance, two saucer sets of eyes were poking out horizontally, one on either side, each face almost as filthy as mine. I recognized the scruffy boy and girl who had spotted me in the square. I stuck my tongue out at them.

They squeaked and ran. But only moments later, they appeared again, shyly peeking out on either side. Keeping my ears on the conversation outside, I pulled an even sillier face, like a drunk, cross-eyed lion. It was the same one my mother had warned me would stay forever if the wind changed directions. That seemed to get rid of them. And it made me feel a little brighter.

The Mother swung the door closed and plunged us into half darkness. I had recovered enough to stand. The low ceiling made me worried I would bump my head and make a fool of myself.

"Well?" she demanded.

I didn't know what to say. She had just planned my escape from the temple, as if I was in danger. And yet she was not at all what she seemed. We just stood there. A delicious smell had drifted into the corridor, sweet and rich and smoky. My stomach rumbled noisily. I hadn't realized how hungry I was. I heard giggles behind me. I swiveled with my hands clawed, and the kids bolted with a squeak.

The Mother was looking me up and down. She didn't look at all pleased. It was odd to see her now as the stern First Mother who had opened the door to the temple, and I couldn't shake the feeling that this was not her true self.

"Frightened of me too?" I grinned.

"Frightened by how stupid you are."

Ouch. Just as I was thinking of how to respond to that, I felt the children sneaking up behind me—not two but five sets of feet padding quietly like cubs. As they neared, I roared and turned around, scattering them. For a moment I considered chasing them, but the tiny girl with her teddy was frozen in place like a baby rabbit, her eyes huge and shining. I crouched down in front of her. Maybe I had overdone it. Had I been living in the wild too long?

I pushed aside my mane to reveal a smile I hoped was reassuring. "Don't worry, my lovely little one. It's only mud."

With her dusty-blond fringe and a minute nose, her gigantic eyes took up most of her face. She sniffed, clutching her teddy.

"I am no beast. See?" I placed my finger on my nose and crossed my eyes. Then I pretended to be dead, making a silly grunting noise as I pushed myself over by my nose until I fell onto my backside.

Her brother raced toward us up the corridor, wielding a broken stick. Seeing me fallen, he leaped onto my chest and swung his sword right past my nose. "Surrender at once, creature!"

"I surrender!" I cried in mock distress. He placed the stick at my throat like a blade. I turned my chin up to see the Mother grimace in exasperation.

"You are my slave now, beast!"

"Do not slay me." I held up my hands in defeat. The other kids had gathered at the end of the corridor to witness my surrender.

"Apologize to Lady Flower Pot."

"I apologize, my lady," I said with a glance at the little girl, who was hiding behind her teddy.

"Apologize to Lord Salerio." He pushed the stick against my throat, his feet balancing precariously on my chest.

"I apologize, my Lord Salerio," I said gravely. "I will serve you and your lady until my last breath."

This seemed to satisfy him. He retracted his stick and placed it in an imaginary sheath. Then he held his arms up in victory and the kids behind him cheered and clapped.

Above his head, I noticed a blue streak inside the dark root that ran along the ceiling. It danced through the corridor root system, disappearing up into the temple dome. *Will I truly find you in this strange world, my lovely Traveler girl?* I wondered.

"Off! Off!" The Mother shooed them away. "Let's get this monster some food."

"Rawrrr!" cried the little boy, running off with Lady Flower Pot and Lord Teddy in tow. The rest of the kids cheered and danced around him as he held up his stick sword.

I rolled onto one knee, the last of the altitude sickness clearing, and regarded the First Mother steadily from under my eyebrows. There she was, a formidable old woman, just as she had been before we had touched. It was impossible, surely. Or was it?

She was giving me a grudgingly benevolent look, like a mother forgiving her favorite wayward child. My stomach growled again at the mention of food, and I winced, sending the triumphant kids into another fit of giggles. Her expression softened even further. I didn't buy it.

"I thank you for your hospitality, but now I must be on my way," I said from below her. There was a moment of shock as my decision registered, but she recovered quickly.

"That is not advisable." She folded her arms and planted her feet. "You have put us all in danger by coming here." There was no doubt I was to believe I was in trouble.

"Then I'll leave." I rose fluidly and took a step toward her. She did not budge even a little. Though she was a stout old woman, I towered over her. For some reason, my heart was jumping around in my chest. If she was afraid of me, she wasn't showing it.

"Don't take another step." She uncrossed her arms. "Only a fool would leave after curfew." She steepled her fingers into the gesture of the Mothers and laid out her logic. "If you are caught, which you will be, there will be consequences for us all."

Ignoring her steely tone, I edged closer, barely two feet away, my head brushing the roof. "Or maybe . . . *you* will get caught?" I suggested quietly. Now up close, I could study her features. I could sense the iron behind the resolute elder, and I wondered where it came from, whether it was manufactured or real.

There was the tiniest of pauses but almost no change in her stern and tightly bound lips. "You may not understand the danger, but I have to protect those children."

She was completely believable, and I could not doubt her sentiment. Still, I . . .

"Don't take another step," she warned, implacable.

I did it anyway, reaching out to push her aside.

I hadn't been surprised often in grappling, but the speed at which she used both hands to yank and twist my wrist caught me completely unawares. Maybe I was naive, or maybe I had wanted it, but she had me in an armlock before I knew what had hit me.

This time I felt rather than saw the blaze of color tingling outside my arm, because already she had forced my face down with the pressure. While I was trying to get a look at her, she twisted my arm behind my back and yelled "Back! *Back!*" marching me down the corridor.

"Ouch!" I yowled.

"Don't be a child," she scolded, wrenching my wrist higher.

"Ow!" I yowled again. She was far stronger than she looked.

As we emerged into the temple dome, the kids spilled apart, looking on with horror and delight. And from their reaction, I knew immediately they did not see her as she had appeared to me in the doorway. And yet I could have sworn I had felt her image begin to morph again when she had locked my arm.

We must have looked quite a sight, a granny manhandling a filthy young man almost twice her size. I yelled "Ow!" one more time for dramatic effect and winked at Lady Flower Pot and her rescuer. Both kids covered their mouths, one with his hand, the other with her teddy.

"Get ready for supper, all of you!" the First Mother commanded, meaning business. I rolled my eyes at them and the giggling got louder. "Do it now or no supper for any of you!"

They scattered almost as one through the wood pews and out a doorway on the other side of the dome, squabbling and chattering furiously among themselves. Lady Flower Pot held the stick sword above her head with her proud brother following.

Two aproned and well-meaning women had emerged from the exits, no doubt attracted by the commotion. They reminded me a little of Atta, the farmer's daughter—the same chestnut hair, long lashes, and ironic twirl to their lips, except not as pretty and much sturdier.

"First Mother, what has happened?" the younger of them asked.

"This *beast* is joining us for dinner."

She released me. I stumbled, then straightened, breathing a

theatrical sigh of relief and rubbing my wrist sheepishly. My stomach chose that moment to growl like a fiend again.

The elder of the two women stifled a smile. "But surely he must be bathed first."

"Take him to the showers," said the First Mother, dismissing me.

The younger cook approached me timidly and gestured to the exit. I could not resist glancing over my shoulder at the Mother one last time. Where I expected fury, I found her intractable. She hid her emotions well, I noted. I would be advised to learn more before I made any further moves.

I wiped my filthy hair from my face and followed the serving lady deeper into the temple. Where this story would lead I could not tell, but I did not like the look of that dark root that had spread throughout the dome. Was it just my imagination, or did it seem to be watching us?

✦ 7 ✦

SAYA

New Time

AS I WATCHED THE STRANGER'S muscular back disappear down the corridor, I took satisfaction in not letting him see my frustration.

He was infuriating, stubborn, dangerously insightful. Somehow I felt he knew I was not the Mother, but how had he discerned it so quickly when I had even managed to fool those like Reece and Gellie who knew her intimately? I needed a change.

I turned to the serving woman next to me, surprised to see a dreamy look on her face as her eyes lingered in the same direction as mine. She was married and middle-aged, a rural housewife with walnut-brown braids, long lashes, and a sweet disposition. But that look could only mean one thing.

"What are you looking at?" I snapped.

She came back and shook her head, embarrassed. "My apologies, Mother. It's just I have not seen a man of such . . ."

"Don't let me hear it," I growled menacingly.

She ducked her head, but I could tell I had not changed her thoughts in the slightest. "Shall I prepare the table? Will he be served?"

I fixed her with a stare as her cheeks reddened. "Control yourself," I admonished.

"I wasn't the only one . . ." she mumbled under her breath.

"What was that?"

"Nothing, Mother, nothing."

I would need to make her pay for this. "Not only him. A lady who is visiting us, Ciana, will also be joining, although I will not be taking supper," I continued, speaking slowly to make sure she absorbed what I was telling her. "The time has come for me to join the Life Praise in the *sai maran* for exactly one week, to pray for the safekeeping of the children and to reconnect us with our Beginnings."

The housewife's eyes widened in awe at the mention of the sanctuary of dreaming, and she clasped her hands over her apron.

"I shall leave it to you to assist them in their preparations. They will depart with the Guard shortly after curfew." I paused, pointedly. "There is danger here. Do you understand?"

"I understand, First Mother." She bowed obediently.

I briefed her carefully on the mechanism inside the wall of the Mother's residence that led to the secret passage. I questioned her to make sure she understood she should open it in precisely a week. I then dismissed her and made my way out of the dome and past the kitchen with its mouthwatering smells. As I crossed the grass on the way toward the Mother's residence, I saw from the corner of my eye the stranger in the waterfalls that doubled as the temple showers.

He had taken off his shirt. I could see every muscle of his taut upper body in detail. The tie of his pants had loosened and they were hanging low, exposing the lines of his lower torso more than necessary. Thank the Fates I looked away before he could glance up.

I entered the Mother's residence and closed the door behind me perhaps too quickly. I leaned against it, sighed, and bit my lip, then caught myself. What was this stupidity? He was a tool, nothing more. I hardly knew him. I needed to stay objective, or this whole mission would crumble in an instant.

I approached the mirror on the wall once more to examine myself. The First Mother looked back at me, almost perfectly replicated. How had I raised his suspicions? I had answered his accusation unflinchingly. Yet for some reason, I felt it was less an accusation than a game. I ran my hands through my short-cropped hair and over my wrinkled face and braced myself for the pure pain of the changeling.

But it did not come.

The First Mother shook and distorted, but the agony of the change did not rip apart the tiniest pieces of me, as it had since I began the process years ago. Instead of ripping me apart, I felt as if it were pulling me together, toward a shape I had long abandoned.

For another split second, I was staring into that lost girl's violet eyes, her pain raw and unmistakably mine. Then I shut them tightly and shuddered, fighting the surge of grief within me, as Ciana's form overlaid my old self and cloaked her again. I had imprisoned my original shape inside me ever since the day I had escaped my glassy prison only to step into another cage—the shape of someone else.

I opened my eyes fearfully and to my relief saw only Ciana staring back at me, looking innocuous with her freckles and dimples, luminous blue eyes, white dress, and sandals artfully recreated from my imagination. I tucked a lock of golden hair over my ear.

"May the Beginnings protect you, First Mother," I whispered.

I spent a few minutes clearing my confusion, rehearsing my character, my gestures and demeanor. The sadness to Ciana that was so endearing came easily, but I saw more than a hint of self-pity and anger in it that I recognized as my own. When I was satisfied I had eliminated it to the best of my ability, I gathered myself and turned to the door to make my way to the supper table.

I stepped out onto the withered grass. The sun had dipped below the mountains now, and the serving ladies had lit the lanterns. And despite myself, I could not resist looking across the yard toward the waterfall.

He was still there luxuriating in the water, his eyes closed, as if undergoing a spiritual experience. Finally clean, every inch of him lit up red-gold and gleaming in the firelight from the kitchen doorway. My eyes traveled everywhere they should not have. He was huge and beautiful, untamed like a panther, his hair long and thick and hanging down to his shoulder blades. And slung casually over the low wall were his clothes, along with the bag containing the sketch of the girl on the swing before the stars. I focused on his clothes first; they would surely draw suspicion.

Hurrying back inside, I opened the Mother's closet. Miners wore little in the heat of the earth. We would both need appropriate rags, but I could find nothing that fit, and clicked my tongue in annoyance.

Then the sketch jumped into my head again in a flash of déjà vu. Where had I seen it before? And hadn't he said it was his dream girl? I needed to see it again.

I snuck out the door again and immediately ducked down,

moving toward the cliff face like a burglar. I crept sideways along the rock wall, taking care to make as little sound as possible. My heart was pounding—annoying since I had taught myself to be calm under pressure.

This is foolish, a voice in my head was saying. *Why risk your second disguise? There will be another moment.* But then I was already close to his bag with the sketch peeking out, I could hear the water hitting his skin, and I could actually see the girl's feet dangling from her swing. Who was she?

I crouched down on my hands and knees and could not resist reaching out—

Something moving incredibly fast snatched my wrist, swallowing it whole. The hand led all the way up to a firelit arm of pure muscle, and above, this giant of a man, gleaming wet with eyes of blazing starburst green. I could feel the drips of water falling from his hair onto my skin, and a shaking within me. The changeling was responding to him, I was sure of it, and with everything I had I strained to keep Ciana's form together.

As he held my hand, his expression shifted from annoyance to glee, an infuriating smile spreading over his lips under his beard. I stared up at him murderously.

"Let go of me," I said, Ciana's voice even higher than usual.

"Nice to see you again." He grinned.

"I was instructed by the Mother to make your clothes suitable for the journey," I managed to say. *What did he mean by "again"?*

"Oh?" he said. His smile got even wider.

"Yes, and I wanted to be discreet so I did not see . . . this—you—" I actually stammered. I couldn't look at him. My cheeks were burning. *Keep it together, Saya!* I was still on my hands and knees.

"You could have asked."

He still hadn't let go of my wrist. I was absolutely powerless in his grip as Ciana. There was extraordinary strength in his fingers, but also control. He was taking care not to hurt me. He was looking at me curiously now. The suspicion cleared, and only fascination remained on his face, his mouth slightly open. I wasn't sure which was worse, his suspicion or his scrutiny.

"They need to be ripped—the clothes. It's hot in the Skala Mines. The Mother said you may not agree and that I should . . ." I was rambling. *It's okay, it's fine*, I reassured myself. *You are in character.*

"Like this?" He let go of me and, in a show of tremendous strength, ripped his still-wet pants at the thighs and his shirt in half. I turned my back against the low wall and suffered my own foolishness while he finished the tearing up and dressed, looping the rope around his waist last. I could not believe how embarrassed I felt, but at the same time, I wanted to laugh. I played with my hair hotly to find something to do.

He hopped over the small stone wall and tucked the sketch securely in his bag. I found the care he took annoying, as though he was mocking me. Did he discern my intentions? He was so hard to read. And that image of the girl on the swing, I could have sworn I recognized it.

"Are you joining us for supper, lady?" he said gallantly, slinging the bag over his shoulder and offering me his hand. He was unbelievable.

Ignoring his offer, I got up and stormed off over the grass. *Urgh!* This was so stupid. I could not believe how I was behaving. I was angry at myself as much as him. I needed time to cool off.

I met the youngest serving woman in the kitchen, where the aroma of warm food and fresh herbs made me immediately hungry. This must be the famous soup Reece and Gellie were so enamored by. My taste buds were already tangled with the scent of hot tomato, roasted onion and potatoes with rosemary and thyme, garlic, eggplant, sweet peppers, and homemade bread. The serving woman led me to the dining hall, where the places had been set for fourteen at a long table. The room itself was more of a hallway lined with empty bookshelves, perhaps once a library.

I chose a place at the end farthest from the door, near the fireplace. The elder housewife, Elena, the younger woman informed me, was rounding up the children and would join us shortly. As she left to fetch the food from the kitchen, she brushed up against the Traveler coming through the doorway in his ripped clothing. She squeaked and scuttled away. He took a place at the table farthest from me, but every now and then he would glance in my direction. I kept my eyes furiously on my plate. The silence was excruciating, the only sound the crackling of the fire in the grate. He began to drum his fingers on the table, each tap driving irritation up my spine.

After a small eternity, the sounds of raucous children rescued me as the orphans began pouring in. Seeing Salerio, I brightened and waved to him. He waved back but, unbelievably, sat next to the beastly stranger.

His sister, Lady Flower Pot, took her place next to me, placing her teddy on the chair alongside her, while I fumed at her brother's betrayal. She gestured to me conspiratorially, cupping a hand over her mouth. "He loves you. But you know how he is with 'monsters.'"

I forced myself to nod and gave Salerio a withering look that he pretended not to see. Instead he began to mimic the stranger's posture—slouching, both hands on the table, drumming his fingers—watching his monster for any change, which he instantly mirrored.

The rest of the orphans scrambled to their places, showing an equal amount of curiosity for both me and the new arrival with open-mouthed looks, whispers, and giggles. The Traveler's response was mostly amusement. I did everything not to meet his gaze. I really wished he would shave in the way of the Marauda so I could see his face better.

Then the food arrived, piping hot and irresistible. The bread was handed out starting on our side of the table, one chunky piece to each child, including Lord Teddy, who got half of Lady Flower Pot's. The children stared at their bread like puppies, but none of them touched it.

I sneaked a look at the time walker. He was fixated on the incoming loaf, drooling over each chunk being served while his fingers drummed on the table. His mouth was slightly open. I watched his tongue lick his lips. When his piece arrived, he snatched it off the platter and stuffed it into his mouth. There was a collective gasp. He chewed loudly, making small moans of pleasure that excited me. It was only when he was about to take his third bite that he stopped with his mouth open. All in the room were staring at him. With everyone watching, he still could not resist taking one more bite, chewing sheepishly under our gaze, trying to look as innocent as possible.

Elena started laughing and soon everyone joined in, the kids giggling and pointing at him. Then everyone began tucking into their food. Even Lady Flower Pot was smiling and she tugged my arm and pointed. But I was stony faced and still staring murder at the stranger. He seemed to be continuing to feign ignorance. The young serving maid—I overheard her name was Tabitha—came to collect my bowl for the soup.

"Oh, how I envy you," she whispered in my ear.

"Huh?" I almost snapped.

"He can't take his eyes off you." She held her wrist to her forehead dramatically.

I frowned and stole a glance at him. It was true. Now that he'd gotten over the bread, he was watching me again. I cursed Ciana's childlike beauty, wishing I could give him a meaner look. Oh, I had some looks that would turn him to stone, that would blister the skin off his body, boil his bones . . .

The soup distracted me from my violent fantasies. There was no conversation across the table, just the joyful sound of wholesome food being devoured. The children were happily dunking their bread in the soup and slurping loudly from their bowls. The stranger too was drinking from his bowl, holding it with two hands. Salerio watched and copied him. I delicately cut my bread the way I had since childhood, taking pleasure in the little white squares. Lady Flower Pot offered her teddy some bread and then ate it in little pieces for him. Elena and Tabitha gossiped hotly, flashing looks at the stranger.

It felt cozy, almost like a family, and I felt my walls begin to come down. I even offered Lady Flower Pot's teddy some of my food and she let me pretend to feed him. I caught the Traveler looking my way again, and for once, I didn't glare at him. This moment having dinner together with everyone, with the children, was honest, despite everything. It had been so long since I had something good like this in my life. That realization hurt me with a brutal whimsy, and I did not want the evening to end. Lady Flower Pot used her teddy to thank me and I smiled without needing a character for the first time in ages.

We heard a gonging as Elena tapped the ladle against the thick soup pot. "Ahem!" The kids kept babbling among themselves but she kept gonging until they quieted down. "Ahem, children!

Children and welcome guests," she began again more formally. "I have some important news. The Mother has returned to the Life Praise. For a full week she will commune with the Beginnings in the sanctuary of dreaming, and wishes a speedy and safe journey for our guests . . . whose names are . . . ?"

She looked at us expectantly. I stood and he did likewise. Finally, some manners.

"Andreas."

"Ciana." *Andreas . . . interesting name.* It was an old name, not used often anymore.

"As Andreas and Ciana journey together to find their true selves in the protection of our friends under the earth, let us all join together in a moment of prayer to wish them Fate's protection."

What did she mean by "true selves"? I wondered. *And "our friends under the earth"—does this refer to the Last Men?* Perhaps, as I had theorized, this temple was a recruitment center, a protected place for orphans where they were spared from giving away their dreams to the Tree. The children's expressions ranged from somber and stoic to frowns and raised eyebrows. Only Andreas did not show a hint of confusion.

The children all closed their eyes with the serving women. The stranger—Andreas—was staring right at me. I couldn't read his expression, but I felt it was hostile. I simply closed my eyes and hoped he would do the same. I needed a plan.

"Thank you," Elena said, breaking the silence.

Andreas seemed to have accepted the news with perfect equanimity. Did he *know*? What could he have meant by his earlier comment "nice to see you *again*"? I needed more information about him; it seemed he understood more about me than I did of him, and that unsettled me. I had little time; the Guard would return shortly. I stood up.

"Hello, everyone. I am grateful for the blessings, for both me and Andreas. Thank you to the cooks for their delicious soup and bread. Let us toast your skills." I held up my clay cup of water. We all moved our cups in a circle and then drank together, except the Traveler, of course.

"I want to let you all know that I spoke to the Mother before she entered the *sai maran*, and she wanted you all to know that she loves you very much. She cannot wait to return and be with you again." I had everyone's attention now. "And she warned that if any of you misbehave, there will be trouble!" They smiled with me, the connection strengthening. "You need to be strong this week. It will not be easy. But I have faith in you all. Especially you, Salerio. My brave monster slayer. Take care of everyone for me, okay?" A hint of emotion had crept into my voice and I let it stay there. "And now I have one final request from the Mother. A game."

The children all began oohing and aahing and the serving woman Tabitha clapped her hands with delight. Andreas was watching me more carefully, his expression still unreadable.

"Andreas and I are dressing up as Miners tonight!"

The oohs and aahs grew louder. The Miners were bogeymen to these children, who had been told tall tales of them escaping from the mines and eating little boys who did not do as they were told.

"For this game to work," I said, looking at Andreas, "we need you to help us get dirty!" The kids started yelling and shouting. "Let's go, everyone!"

I got up from the table, holding Lady Flower Pot's hand. All the children followed us out of the hall, much to the consternation of Elena. As I passed Andreas, I leaned down and brushed his forearm.

"Come on, time traveler," I whispered in his ear. I didn't know if it was true, but it would either intrigue or spook him enough to follow me.

Trailing the horde of raucous kids, I strode into the firelit yard. It was pitch dark now, with the first stars starting to flicker in the sky above. The serving women followed, and I held my breath. The kids were all gathering up handfuls of dust and mud around me. For a second, I thought I had miscalculated.

But there he came, moving fluidly and powerfully, his grace restored by the meal. I suddenly felt intimidated in a way I hadn't earlier. His mood had darkened and there was a latent energy in him now, coiled the same way it had been when he knelt before me on the temple steps.

The children parted for him and he came to stand next to me in the firelight under the stars. Behind us we could hear the rushing sound of the waterfall. I cupped a hand over my mouth as Lady Flower Pot had done and leaned into his ear, leaving my hot breath on his skin. Ciana was no old lady.

"Just trust me." And when I felt the almost imperceptible nod of his mane, I turned to the kids and said, "Let it fly!"

Shrieking with glee, they pelted us with dirt and mud, jumping up and down and throwing it into the sky, spattering each other as much as us. The joy was infectious. Andreas and I exchanged looks, and I reached down for a big handful of mud.

"Wait!" he protested. But it was too late—I smacked the mud right into his face like a cake. It dripped off him and he looked at me aghast. And then he reached down to load his own shot. I yelped and ran, and he chased me until he caught me against the wall of the waterfall and plastered my face with muck. For a second we were close. I could feel his body almost on top of me and there was a sudden tension in the air. Everyone stopped. My world narrowed to just us, just a bit too close together.

"You monster!" I shouted. He grinned and bolted.

"Ciana, Andreas." It was Elena. "They are here."

I realized then that my smile was genuine, tinged with the sweet ache of nostalgia, and I savored it for just a moment longer. I watched him peel the disappointed children off him. This happiness, stolen from the real Ciana, contrived and not real, was the only warmth of its kind I had felt in years. My prison doors were open, if only for a moment.

The pain of the changeling had not returned. Nevertheless, I calculated I had barely two days to return to my cage or it would begin to tear me apart. He saw the look on my face and came toward me as if magnetically. "Do I scare you?" he asked as he approached. He held up his hands like claws and was about to make a stupid face when I put a finger to his lips.

"Your eyes are what scare me. And what the Mother told me about you." I needed to set the parameters, make him understand the risks. "The Miners have forgotten their dreams. Your eyes have too much light in them. You must hide it, or they will take it from both of us."

He pulled away. My finger was humming again, that strange warmth spreading through my body from mere contact with him.

"I won't let anyone take the light from you," he said suddenly, but his next words were sharp. "But what do you know of *me*?"

"Enough to know you have no idea what is out there," I snapped back, his naivety frustrating me in kind. Or was it something else I needed to know before we left together? "The Mother tells me you are searching for your dream girl."

He did not answer at once, and a moody glint came into his

eyes. We both heard the heavy clang of the bronze knocker. I could feel Elena's anxious gaze as she fretted on the doorstep.

"Do you love her?" I demanded, stalling.

"I would die to see her one last time." He did not break my gaze.

"But do you love her?"

"I would die for her," he repeated. "Isn't that enough?" His mood had darkened to anger. I had perhaps pushed too far. We both heard the bronze knocker clanging again, this time louder and more urgently. He was stubborn, angrier than he even knew.

"I don't know where your dream girl is," I said, trying to keep the sarcasm out of my voice, "but where we are going, they might."

"Ciana! Andreas!"

"Will you come now?" I softened. His starburst eyes were flashing, energy inside him coiling, darkening, and I realized that deep within him were powerful emotions barely contained, perhaps that he did not truly understand. I could not wait for him.

Elena was in the doorway to the dome with my travel bags—packed with biscuits, apples, and bread—twisting her apron. Tabitha was herding the kids into their quarters, trying to keep them calm. Andreas picked up his own bag with whitened knuckles.

"You look handsome," I told him, "but you need one more mud cake in your face."

He raised his eyebrows at me. I gave him my best and most dazzling smile. The bronze knocker came again, a hint of panic in the rapid speed. Above us the stars glinted, clouds moving across the moon as a hint of wind caught and played with our filthy hair.

"Coming!" I cried sweetly to Elena and skipped toward the kids, blowing them kisses and quick farewells, bowing to receive my own bag from her. I felt rather than heard Andreas follow, saw out of the corner of my eye him ruffling Salerio's hair and bidding goodbye with a quick, wordless bow to Lady Flower Pot. And then we were striding together through the dome and down the corridor toward the exit.

"Fate's folly!" I cursed, tugging at my filthy dress. I had just realized the quality of the material was far too high for a Miner. I had no time, nor the privacy, to modify the disguise right in front of him. I tried to tear the material, but it was surprisingly tough when wet, and suddenly I felt his hands on my back, ripping through the dress like butter, exposing my back to the night. He crouched down and savagely tore the lovely fabric from the hem, revealing my legs while at the same time paying them no mind.

"Sorry," he said curtly.

"Are you?" I fumed.

"Sorry for these kids . . . that you are not who you seem . . ." he replied harshly.

He gripped the door handle and tugged it open.

✦ 8 ✦

ANDREAS

New Time

L ONG BEFORE THE PALE GIRL with the luminous blue eyes had smiled her invitation for an alliance, hands holding demurely to the hem of her skirt, I knew I was being swept along in a momentum I could not control.

It was not only the turn of events, made worse by my lack of understanding of this new world. It was a pull toward this impossible woman that I could not pin down, like a tide dragging me out to sea. Already, I felt myself committed beyond my comfort. She skipped ahead of me, delighting the orphans with kisses on their cheeks, as if she were dancing over the surface of a pond.

First the Mother and then Ciana. Her true self lay beneath the surface, revealing itself at the slightest brush of our skin. That tingle had begun again as I caught hold of her, younger, vulnerable, looking up at the night sky as if begging for escape.

She was a shape-shifter.

I had heard tales about her kind since I was a child. In the stories they were called faeries of the Uncharted Lands. My mama had explained to me in a rare moment of sharing herself that faeries were not the carefree sprites of the tales. They were creatures whose dreams could come true and who had wished with all their hearts to be real people, not the lost spirits they truly were.

They only played at being people for a short time, but if they could not find a person to love them, they were doomed to live alone and invisible forever.

Mama had grown wistful when she told her version of the story, then returned to the expanse that had always separated us. It took me a long time to understand she too felt herself to be a lost spirit whose dream could never be real. And like all things for her, this had nothing to do with me. Like everything, it had to do with her love for my father, which had never ended despite his disappearances.

I remembered watching her knitting her shroud on her rocking chair in front of the fire, waiting for his return, a woman frozen in time. I hated that shroud, how it consumed her frail body in its deathly embrace. She would stare out of the window past my plants at the moon, as if my father was there on that distant world waiting for her. It took me many years, and many bruises, to realize there was nothing I could do to save her.

Sometimes, gazing up at the moon from the isolation of my cabin, I wondered if I was just like her, waiting for someone to save me too.

But even if I couldn't save Mama, there was something at least that I could do. I could bring my Traveler back from this fraught world, where people feared the light being taken from their eyes, where children were in danger and the gargantuan twisted tree blotted out the stars.

If this truly was the future, I wanted no part in it. If I could find my Traveler and bring her home . . . but I had no idea how to do it, or even how to return if I did. I cursed myself for letting my anger lead me once again, and my chest felt the tight band of its leash. Why had Melasquez not told me the way back? Why had I not even thought to ask?

Once again the fury that filled me was boiling over, the same as when Ciana had interrogated me about the dream girl. I marched behind her, at a loss for how to control it, knowing that somehow she had worked out my journey through the Rift.

"Fate's folly!" she swore, tugging at her lace dress, figuring it was too fancy for a Miner even caked in mud. Despite myself, I smiled at the incongruity of that slender girl's foul mouth.

I watched her struggle with it, and then in a delicious sweep, I ripped it right open, exposing her back. The aghast look on her face was priceless. Hadn't she crept up on me in the shower? I knelt before her and destroyed the fabric with efficiency. Touching it felt odd, dreamlike—even her clothes did not seem entirely real.

"Sorry," I said, hiding my pleasure at her shock.

"Are you?" Her eyes stung with self-righteous anger. A game that had no basis. I was tired of playing with her.

"Sorry for these kids." I dropped all pretenses. "That you are not who you seem." And with that, I wrenched the door open to the temple steps. The force almost threw the mouselike body of the soldier clinging to the knocker off her feet.

The red-haired woman let go immediately and backed away, rebounding off the girth of her fat, round brother. Reece and . . . Gellie, I recalled, from overhearing their conversation. She had already drawn her blade and I tensed. The streets were deserted. Dreaming Curfew, I remembered.

"So you're the one who's going to get us killed?" Reece brushed herself off and swung her torch directly between us.

I squinted and said nothing.

"Do you think the travel baked his brain?" she asked her brother wryly.

I tried not to react to that. Then Ciana emerged from behind me and Reece's mouth popped open.

"A princess!" Gellie blurted out. Ciana dipped a tiny curtsy, charming even with her muddy face and ripped clothing.

"And this be Ciana? That girl Mother says seeks refuge?" Reece shone the torchlight onto her. It lit up her pretty heart-shaped face in an angelic glow and she lowered her eyelashes, as if afraid.

Reece was having none of it. She looked Ciana up and down, scrutinizing the ripped dress and her slender legs, which she crossed as if embarrassed. "Match the descriptor of the spy, don't she?" she mused. "Can't say Mother was exactly herself . . . earlier . . ."

Gellie wasn't listening. He seemed to be entranced by the sight of Ciana. But his sister's fingers looped the blade around her wrist with a dexterity I didn't like the look of. Ciana edged closer to me as if by instinct, and I sensed that her shock was real. I watched Reece's fingers tighten on the handle, feeling the thin blade of the moment could slice either way.

"She's with me," I growled. I cocked my head at Reece and grinned. Maybe a good fight was exactly what I needed.

"He speaks!" Reece turned to Gellie, who had snapped out of his stupor at the tone of my voice. He seemed to be offended by what I had said. Not that I cared.

"The Mother entrusted her to my care." I stepped between the guards and Ciana, letting them observe my defensive stance. Whatever she was, she was my best chance at finding my Traveler girl.

"Okay, big guy, okay, no need to get aggressive."

Gellie pulled his sister back and fronted up to me. He was shorter but much wider than me, made mostly of fat, with a lower center of gravity. His pig eyes stared up at me with a mean, childish look. I waited, silently daring him to make the first move.

"Oi, she your girlfriend?" he blurted.

"No!" both Ciana and I exclaimed at the same time as I took a step backward, almost knocking her over.

"Hmmm, okay!" Gellie relaxed completely. "So tell Gellie about where you traveled here from. Do all live in caves? Eat rock soup?"

"Gellie, not now," Reece sighed, exasperated. "This is not the time."

"Is everyone hairy? Your sister, she has a beard?"

I was about to get angry again when I heard Ciana's musical laughter from behind me. Her laugh had a lonely melody, as if the memory of her had already been forgotten. "The Spy and the Rock Muncher!" she sighed, shaking her head.

Why did I suddenly feel foolish? And at the same time, protective.

"Are we not the playthings of the Fates?" she mused, looking up at the heavens.

And then, the future hanging in the balance, I followed her gaze to see a streak of burning fire across the sky. It was bigger than any shooting star I had ever seen, soaring through the darkness like an angel falling from heaven, its tail cutting across the top of the world. I had to turn around to see the full length of its luminescent silver tail, and in its wake, the impossible—a crack of blue dappled with clouds, daylight from another world.

"By the Beginnings," I heard myself say.

Reece peered at me more closely. "He really is a Traveler from another world, isn't he?"

"You've never seen it before?" Ciana asked.

I was only able to shake my head. The blue crack in the sky was closing slowly as the glowing ball of light cut its way across the heavens. "We must hurry if we aim to be undiscovered! Everyone will soon be coming out of their homes to witness this," I said.

"No, they won't," said Reece. Still, she looked around gingerly.

"But it's incredible. How could they not . . ." I trailed off, glancing to Ciana for support.

She looked at me with empathy, as if she did not want to hurt me. A sadness I could not grasp shadowed Reece's and even Gellie's faces too. "At least we are saved," Reece recited, like a mantra, to no one in particular.

"No one will be coming out to see it. It has lost its value to them," said Ciana. "But you are right." She looked at the siblings. "Please, trust in the Mother's judgment. She believed in giving everyone, even the least likely, a chance at a full life." She cupped her hands on her belly protectively.

It took us a few seconds to grasp what she was implying.

"You are with child?" Reece narrowed her eyes. There was a moment of shock for all of us.

"I ran from my husband because I would not bring this child into this world. A world where she could not dream of a better future." Ciana stated it matter-of-factly, but the pain in her voice was unmistakable. "My daughter deserves to dream. She deserves it! She deserves it," she repeated. She wrapped her arms around her thin body and sat down, choking up.

Even though I knew, or thought I knew, that this story was fiction, I could not help but be affected by it. There is truth and power in a performance if it comes from real pain. The despair we sensed was that. And against her better judgment, I saw Reece feeling it too. Gellie, for his part, looked heartbroken.

Reece looked from person to person and then swore violently. "By a Fate's butthole! You better not make us regret this!"

With a flick of her spiky red hair, she agreed to take us. Gellie followed his sister without question. I didn't have the heart to scowl at Ciana for the performance; instead I took her hand and picked her up. She hid her face from me.

We started on our way across the crumbling city on foot, going down the hill into the valley, traveling in single file through the sheltered back roads. The looming canopy of the Black Tree swallowed up the shooting star and the last of its tail. In its wake, the blue crack of sky closed once more into darkness. Then the night was complete, and we were lit only by the light of Reece's torch as we crept through broken cobblestone streets past dilapidated homes. Were these the descendants of my kind?

Curtains were drawn; roofs sagged under the weight of neglect. I did not see a peek nor sense a single glance. It was eerie and surreal, and the city seemed to hum in a strange blue afterglow. My vision adjusted, and I saw lines of this same bluish light, streaked with shapes as if alive. There were thousands of blue veins, running up above the roofs. The ghostly lines led from the village all the way up into the layered canopy of the Tree, twisting along the black roots.

"What are those?" I whispered into Ciana's ear as she walked in front of me, pointing at the ghostly images.

"Quiet!" she hissed.

"Those. What are they?" I pointed insistently.

She looked at me angrily over her shoulder, and I hushed. Did she not see them?

Perhaps she did not hear the music either, the songs that were rising from the homes. I could hear them, tales of my time, the tasteless waters of the soul. Perhaps my head was still scrambled from the jump, but I thought I heard echoes singing from far away.

Was this the Dream Curfew that they had spoken of? And were these truly dreams rising up from each home and being pulled along the roots toward the Black Tree? It reminded me of what had happened in the Village of the Second Sun in the aftermath of the Dreaming, where I had felt our dreams were being drained and forgotten more as time moved on, and how the Tree only grew larger with each passing day.

I watched the bobbing head of Ciana, outlined dimly in the blue light, as we walked through more crumbling back roads and eventually wound our way down to the streams. Reece was leading and Gellie followed, climbing over vegetation and broken walls where necessary. Ciana moved well, athletically for someone so willowy. Her long legs stepped effortlessly over the old walls.

She glanced behind her frequently, as if to check I was still there. It became a game between us, her eyebrows asking the question, my grim smile answering it.

But the game faded when I realized we were drawing closer to the same stretch of tiny houses where my family's cottage had been. I avoided looking for the thatched roof, the green window frames, the canary-yellow daffodils, white wildflowers, and lavender in my memory. I felt a knot of anxiety in my chest tightening as we got to our old street. I stared at the ground, adjusting the bag slung over my back, retreating into myself. I had not even bothered to say farewell to my mother. If Ciana noticed my discomfort, she did not say.

"Andreas," Ciana whispered. "We're here."

When I glanced up finally, the sight before me was not at all the ruin I had expected in the old village. Instead, we stood before a stone head twice the height of a person, gaping open-mouthed. Through the mouth was the entrance to a vast building. The visage was so massive it seemed almost godlike in the half-blue night. And I recognized the sunken eyes, the heavy brows, the apelike protruding lips and curled beard.

Melasquez, the giant, incarnate in stone. And from his forehead rose the Tree like a sickening totem, its branches spread across his massive skull.

So, you did it, Melasquez, I thought grimly, standing in place for a second as the others entered the mouth. *You were the savior you always claimed to be.* And for a moment, I felt a stab of fear. Had he manipulated me? Had I given him everything he had ever wanted?

Then another thought occurred, and a sudden excitement came rushing over me. I must have made it back! I must have returned with my Traveler! I must have found her—for how else did we escape the soldiers of Marauda who had come to exterminate our people?

I was destined to find her. I had already found her. I looked around me. The slender shadow of Ciana danced before me like a half-remembered impression.

As my eyes adjusted to the lack of light, I saw the sloped building we entered was connected to a spiral of scaffolding that climbed upward toward the castle. It was an unbelievable architectural feat, and my eyes followed it all the way up into the first rung of the Black Tree.

"Rock Muncher!" Reece hissed from between the giant's teeth.

I ducked my head into the stone monstrosity. Inside we stepped onto a platform that sat alongside a track on which stood a series of connected wooden carts, and at one end there was a cylindrical compartment topped with a strange funnel shape. It was the most advanced cart system I had ever seen, but there were no animals, sails, or water to propel it.

"Can't believe we are putting our lives on the line for this primitive," Reece said, shaking her head at me as I studied the strange device before us.

"That we can agree on," Ciana said.

"Look, Rock Muncher, it's a train," said Reece. "We can move the breadth of the Floating City within half a day. I bet you don't have any of these in your pigsty village."

"Floating—?"

Ciana grabbed my arm, and I shut up as we boarded one of the carts. I followed Ciana to the back. There was only one seat—a simple bench opposite the window. We were forced to sit together, barely a foot apart.

"Big surprise, big surprise coming, Rock Muncher," gurgled Gellie. "Hold on to your butt hair." He smirked as he and Reece left to the front. Ciana sighed and shook her head.

"Who made you pregnant?" I asked her. She stared sideways at me and made a disgusted sound in the back of her throat. I smiled as she crossed her arms and stared out of the window. That suited me just fine. I crossed my arms and did the same.

There was a moment of silence, and then suddenly a bluish ball of light ignited on the ceiling of the train, illuminating everything. I jumped—where was the firelight coming from? And then the whole compartment lurched forward, and I lost my balance, grabbing tightly on to the wooden bench.

Ciana covered a smile with her hand. A frightening screech sounded from the front. My astonishment shifted from the glowing blue suns on the ceiling to the landscape outside, flashing by at a faster and faster rate.

"We need to stop, our heads will explode if we move faster, people weren't meant to move—"

Ciana kept shaking her head, and I could see she was laughing at me. "Rock Muncher scared?"

I gripped the seat with white knuckles as if I were climbing a granite wall, thinking I would fly backward, saying nothing. I had pictured myself dying as a hero. Not like this. Not like this. I closed my eyes, waiting for my head to explode.

But nothing happened.

After a while, I opened one eye gingerly, sure that I was already dead and had not even felt it. A river was racing past peacefully, sparkling in the moonlight. The cabin was completely stable. Ciana had even stood up and gone to the window. Careful to keep my balance, I joined her, walking in exaggerated steps. She seemed deep in thought. I followed her gaze.

In front of us was a wall of cloud, thundering, churning, flowing, crackling, rapids set perfectly on edge, never remaining in the same place. Sometimes it oscillated along the ground; sometimes it retreated. We weren't going toward the Tree. We were going away from it.

The train sped over the polished silver tracks, cutting through the mist like a bullet and curving to follow the river. I heard the sound of thunder booming, saw the bright flashes. How could there be lightning this close to the ground?

"Don't worry, we are safe," Ciana said, as if reading my thoughts. "This train has a conductor."

I had no idea what a conductor was, but she seemed irrationally calm, given the tempest pulsing before us. Truly, the world had changed so much I did not even understand the weather. As a forester who had lived at the behest of nature, I suddenly longed for the deep silence of the woods, where the rhythms of slow and ancient cycles had seeped into my bones.

I glanced backward along the track. The monstrous tree was now behind us, shrouded in clouds. Lights twinkled through the city, perhaps of the same style as the glowing suns within our train cabin. Had Melasquez's dabbling with the Fates changed the very nature of this world? Thunder rumbled around us, shaking the cabin ever so slightly, and the orbs above us flickered.

"You might as well get comfortable. We are going through the night." Ciana sat back down on the bench and leaned her head back. The outsides of her arms were dotted with goose pimples. I had ripped her dress with a bit too much gusto, and a chill had settled into the cabin.

After a while, when I felt stable, I came to sit next to her. Outside, a drizzle had begun to patter against the roof. There were a few more flashes, rumblings, and then we seemed to pass through the storm. A silence settled between us as we listened to the rain and the rhythmic chug of the train wheels.

Both of us were tired after the hike and the intensity of the day, and at the prospect of all that lay before us. She began to hum gently. I listened for a while, and then slowly, like the mist parting, came her song:

Dragon, dragon, come and go
As your heart lost in the flow
Find your tail and time will show

Her voice was sweet, lilting, and full of a sadness that filled my chest when she grew silent.

"I like the way you lifted it at the end, but I can't remember where I last heard it," I said.

"Don't be silly," she admonished me softly. "No one sings the song like this except me. Get some sleep," she said and closed her eyes.

I stared out the window next to us. The fog was lifting. I watched as slowly the outlines of the mountains began to appear, and then the moon, gigantic and mysterious, and then the stars, so close you felt you might be able to reach them. I sighed and looked back at her. She was asleep, or pretending to be. I looked back outside.

Where are you, my Traveler? How will you find your way back to me? If I return with you, will all of this come to pass once more?

I looked back at Ciana. Her mouth was slightly open, hair fallen over her face. She was tilting slightly toward me. I shifted uncomfortably on the tight bench. The train angled as it went around a corner, and her slim neck tilted farther, with her body following. I tried to edge away but there was nowhere else for me to go. Second by second she leaned closer to me, until her cold cheek rested gently on my shoulder. I raised a hand to push her off, but then I noticed the goose pimples again and stopped.

I had expected the same igniting of color and shape when we touched, but the effect was much softer tonight. It was like a deep inner glow, the melding more tender as she changed. Her hair shortened into delicate strands of chiffon white, and her skin darkened into honey. Her eyelashes thickened and her body too, still slim but stronger than Ciana's, less girlish, so curved and feminine in the ripped dress that I was forced to avert my eyes. Her waist was tiny, but other things were not.

I stared straight ahead for a while, then dared another look. Her face no longer held that innocent beauty she used as a mask; it was harder, with a stronger jaw, puffier lips, striking eyebrows, freckles. Hers was an unearthly, wild beauty that belonged to a race of people

I had never heard of. I watched her sleep on my shoulder. Was this her true self? And why was I the only one who could see it?

The rain had stopped, but for a while now, I had noticed the sound of falling water, a sound that was growing louder and louder but did not make sense. The river that the train was following led past the base of the Sentinel Mountains in the world I'd left behind on the other side of the Rift, and there were no waterfalls along its path. It filtered down from a number of tributaries among the peaks. But as we rounded the corner, I saw an astonishing sight. To the left of the train tracks, massive waterfalls cascaded down into the night, falling off the edge into . . . nowhere? The moon, enormous, lit up the rushing waters. Unbelievable! It was as if we had reached the edge of the world.

I pushed Ciana gently off me and half stumbled over to the opposite window. The tracks ran along the edge of a landmass humped with the smaller peaks of the Sentinels. We were curving away from a waterfall that roared into the open night, falling into nothingness. Beneath the plunging waters were entire clouds and, farther below, hundreds of feet down, the tiny winking lights of what must have been other villages and cities.

It felt like free-climbing, when you reach for a hold that seems certain but vanishes beneath your fingers, and for a moment, your life hangs in balance, about to tumble. As though I could slip off the edge of the world right down into that vast darkness.

I don't know how long I stood there, struck dumb by the miraculous beauty of it, trying to process all I had seen that day. Slowly, my thoughts coalesced, broke apart, reformulated into something close to sense. So this was Melasquez's new world. This Floating City was our future, far above the clouds, safe from the Marauda Empire. The mad giant had managed the impossible once again with the Rift we'd opened. Our people had escaped! Which meant . . . I must have found my Traveler and brought her back to him. And yet here I was still searching for her?

A story I'd heard in the Strange Tales Tavern popped into my mind. Somehow in all the confusion I had not recalled it, but it rose now in my memory. The tale of the Traveler. A man finds an arcane tome on his doorstep. To his astonishment, it describes how to create a portal into another time. After years of furious study, he succeeds in opening the portal and travels back to the moment he received the tome. There, he leaves the instructions on his very own doorstep, for his past self to find.

The story had perplexed me, for it seemed to have no meaning other than a head-scratching paradox. But now I found myself in a similar circle! A time loop!

I had traveled in time to the future to find my Traveler girl. I had found her, then returned to the past to create the same future that would allow me to find her and return once more. Like the story of the Traveler, I myself was stuck in a loop of my own making!

How will that affect the delicate balance of things? I wondered. Was this a natural ring in time, where the world ended and began on its own terms? Or had I traveled "the forbidden way," as the Marauda called it, a heresy that could break apart time and space? The image of that comet slicing through the night stars, opening up a window into a blue, daylit sky, flashed through my mind.

And it was as these thoughts were musing through my head that I saw the first of the ghostly warriors falling through translucent rubble, and then another tumbling through crumbling crust beyond the edges of the world. And then it was an entire army in full battle armor.

Marauda soldiers, their crimson *V*—symbolizing their vow to live in the present—embossed on yellow flags. The glowing figures were plummeting now by the thousands past the waterfalls, the earth cracking apart under their feet. Horses and men disappeared into the empty beyond as the city rose into the sky. And between them all was the mist I had seen in the Dreaming, that evil sentient mist whispering and clawing around their bodies.

I sat back down on the bench and breathed, my hands cupped over my face. The ghosts I was seeing were not illusions; they were memories. It was the story of this land, like the children dancing in the prayer ground and songs I had heard in the streets when I first arrived. Memories cascading through time, overlaying like the rings inside a tree, from the heartwood to the bark.

The fabric of time and space collapsing, then pulling apart.

What was this future I had created? I sat down next to Ciana in bemused exhaustion. My head spun and slowly I drifted away, pulled down into the comforting darkness.

✦

"Remember when I asked you if I could escape?"
"Yes."
"Even if this is imaginary?"
"Yes, you said all your dreams will come true."
"Look. The fireflies agree."
"With?"
"That question in your eyes."
"I didn't know it was there."
"I'm the only one who can see it."

I woke with a slight jolt as the train came to a stop. I could feel Ciana's head against my shoulder and warm breath against my arm. She must have tipped once more in her sleep. I shifted uncomfortably, and she shook herself awake, jerking away in sweet shock.

Her disguise melded quickly back, eyes shifting from violet to innocuous blue, shimmering into the maiden I had sensed and seen in the temple. I looked away to hide a weird sense of disappointment as she winced and rubbed her eyes.

"Are we there yet?" I asked as she looked bleary-eyed out the window, the early morning sun streaking over her face.

The Miners' town was built along the river, where waterfalls cascaded over the edge of the world. Sunlight dazzled and twinkled on the water, turning the spray into beams of gold. Above the mist was a rainbow, arching over clouds. A sight like that sings to the spirit, and in that moment, it felt as if we were the only two people in the world.

"Almost," she murmured. Her voice was humbled. Our eyes locked, and I sensed in her a profound yearning, a yearning mirrored only by the one in my heart. The feeling was so sudden that I panicked and fled to the window on the other side.

The view on the other side was not nearly as enchanting. The town itself was encircled by mountains, but the architecture was a flat sprawl of square stone houses, each identical to the last, without the break of a tree line or open paths. The stone was an ugly fossil color, but even bleaker to me was the haphazardness of the dwellings, the lack of distinguishing features. Above it all hung a dreary mist, umber and yellow.

This had once been Skala, a mountain town of stilted houses—famous for their tradition of catching river eels using horse heads, and for their bards, and in particular the ballad of Aiyan, the white dragon. The singers had been inspired by the olms—the pale cave salamanders—that washed into town after heavy rains. Everyone had been convinced the white mudpuppies were baby dragons, and the myth had only grown from there.

"The people of Skala have been drained of dreams worse than most," Ciana said from behind me. "Those who live in the mines are even worse off. They can hardly remember themselves, and they only harbor hate for those who took their dreams and memories. They wish for the world to forget them too. You and I need to become as they are, bereft of our deepest desires."

The train started up again, and soon we were departing back along the waterfall and turning slowly into the leaden gray mass of homes. "The loneliest sky is the sky above slaves," Ciana said, as if quoting, "for they do not look up."

She had seated herself back on the bench, looking through her travel bag for breakfast. I went back to the other window for a last glimpse of the waterfalls. Once again, a memory of times past overlaid my view of the road that ran alongside the tracks. A parade of ghostly figures danced down the waterfall road, waving rainbow-colored flags and celebrating. Thousands of excited people danced through the streets, and behind them children flew white kites shaped like dragons, flocking in the air. As we rounded the corner, the squalid stone of the present swallowed them up.

More flashes of the past came in their place. Dimly through the smog I saw a city rising. Raised homes and tree houses with aerial walkways and the warm glow of fires from circular windows. Everywhere, children flying dragon kites, even from the topmost branches of their own homes. Fireworks, ghostly in the sky. Celebrations everywhere. But as the wind picked up, the fog gulped the bright memories away, until all that was left was the hopeless squares, identical hovels as far as the eye could see.

I settled back and watched the landscape for signs of life. Stray dogs wandered the streets like shadows. Finally, there rose a distinguishing feature: a platform, like the one we had departed from the previous night in what was left of the Village of the Second Sun. It was a squat rectangle with that giant stone visage upon it, Melasquez, and in his mouth, a squadron of black-garbed soldiers in steel armor and skeletal masks.

"Uhh . . . Ciana?"

She cried out in alarm when she saw them. "Your bag, we must throw it!" She snatched my satchel from under the bench, racing to open the opposite window.

"No!" I shouted, catching her arm as she dangled it over a ditch filled with trash. The train rumbled to a jolting stop and I pulled her closer to keep balance. Once again, I felt the exciting heat of her, her flashing violet eyes, the gorgeous igniting of a soul into existence. We both heard steel boots clang up the steps up front where Reece and Gellie were.

"You will not forget your dream girl's toes surely, since you love her so?" she taunted, holding my bag out.

"Please, it's my only memory of her," I struggled to explain. "I have nothing else . . . please . . ."

The hardness in her eyes softened, swirled with confusion. We both looked down at the same time and saw the handle on the outside. Swiftly, she pushed me away and looped the strap over it. We heard doors clicking, the sound of marching boots. She retreated to the corner, about to speak. Then a masked soldier appeared in the cabin door window, the silver branches of the Tree on his mouth like a skeleton.

The door screeched open.

✦ 9 ✦

SAYA

New Time

I WOKE UP AS IF RISING from another world. For a split second, I was so gently floating that I wanted to fall back into the embrace of my dreams. It felt so comfortable, that warmth; it felt right. But then I snapped awake, suddenly aware, and jerked away from him, embarrassment hot on my cheeks. His eyes sparkled and I couldn't look at him. I winced and rubbed the sleep and the flush away.

"Are we there yet?" he asked, and I mumbled an answer. I still felt clumsy, with one foot in and one foot out of this world. So many memories had surfaced while I slept, things I had forgotten, an old self I thought buried long ago in a cage, a rush of the aching past. And for a sweet moment I wanted to tell Andreas everything, for it to be real again.

This was what I wanted to remember.

I grew up in a desolate village of thirty people in the Uncharted Lands. The story goes that my father found me in a basket coming down the river. He was a fisherman, and had never caught anything of importance his entire life. He never expected this little abandoned cherub.

As he lifted me from the steaming green water, I was perfectly calm, tiny and ethereal. I looked extraordinary: violet eyes, honey skin, silver-white hair. He immediately took me for a faerie who would bring him good fortune. I stared up at him seriously, regal and otherworldly, and reached out and squashed his nose. Then I yawned and fell asleep cradled in his arms.

He brought me home to a childless wife, who at first believed him. The other kids of the village were fascinated with me. They called me Lil Rainbow, because every now and then my hair would run with color as we played naked in the mud. They cheered for me as I learned to walk and my father cheered too.

I was happy for a while, then. But as I got older, I began to feel more and more distant from everyone else. One day when I was eleven, a boy kissed me to see what the big deal was. Gossip spread among the fishwives that I would steal their sons. The other kids began to bully me, and my mother would bemoan my father's failings to anyone who would listen. She could not bear children, and she blamed him or me alternately.

I had one friend, though, a girl named Emery, with chocolate skin and hair like spun sunshine. I loved her. She was clever, feminine, confident. Everything I wasn't. I was boyish, awkward, and shy. I modeled parts of Ciana on Emery, I think, so I could pretend to be her for a while. But when Emery sensed the boys' fascination with me, their love-hate obsession, she grew distant from me too.

I liked to wander in the desert alone, daydreaming or sleeping, collecting cactus sap or knitting blankets and pillows. In these days, I lost my rainbow coloring and became pale and transparent as the wind. On the exceedingly rare occasion strangers came into our village, I was spirited into the hut and hidden by my mom for longer periods, for fear they would mistake me for a ghost.

All my life I slept dreamlessly. But on my seventeenth birthday, I dreamed of the moon. And stepping down from the stars, I found a boy. That boy knew I was lost, but still he wanted to come with me. That boy made me believe I could fly away and escape all of this.

And as soon as I did, I never saw him again. But because of him, my life changed forever. When my foster parents sold me, it didn't matter, because my dream came true and for a precious moment, I was free.

I hadn't thought about these old days in a very long time. The memories were too painful. But this sweet surrender to the past could not match the steel-toed reality of the present as the masks of the *kai talan* marched back into my life.

I shook myself back to the confrontation in the cabin with Andreas, listening to the boots stomping their savage tirade. *Wake up, you weak and worthless fool! That pathetic self is dead! And you will be with her soon if you believe in her again.* I bit back more vicious curses as a masked figure slid the door open.

I was shocked by the agility of the network. Since Favian had been given the mandate to hunt Last Men, resources had grown. Even here, in a remote station at dawn on the Outer Rim, a whole squad of *kai talan* stood ready. Or perhaps it spoke merely to his level of ruthless ambition.

The infamous interrogator Herodin, Favian's own father, had been the first to experiment until he'd perfected the draining, the involuntary taking of dreams by force that had weaponized the *kai talan*. The old zealot had died on a mission to the Flat Lands, chasing Marauda spies; he'd caught a foreign disease and passed away in an unnamed cave. A pointless death in an unending war. His son preferred a different legacy.

Favian wore the ominous war dress of his order, not a glimpse of human flesh on him. Braids of dark steel glinted beneath his robes as he strode toward us with his gauntlets clasped behind his back. His mask had the menacing roots of the Tree branching from his mouth along his cheekbones and around his eyes, to symbolize that he spoke with the Regent's authority. But to many, it looked more like the bones of a skull.

I had dreamed again of the boy who had set me free, who had given the gift of hope in his poem from the moon. It was so vivid; it felt like a memory—it felt real. I had not seen him in so long, and my heart stung when he reappeared to me again. He had saved me before. Would he save me now? No! I could not afford such fantasies with the *kai talan* on top of us.

I had not prepped Andreas for an interrogation—he would be discovered easily.

Shouldn't I denounce him to Favian as the Traveler immediately? If I didn't say anything and it was found to be true, would I be locked back in my glass cage, left to wither to dust for my disloyalty? And what of the Rock Muncher next to me? I stole a look sideways. The girl in his dream he had mentioned . . . Could it be . . . ? No! I could not allow myself to hope again.

The inquisitor regarded us with his hands behind his back. He seemed to be waiting. Then he sat down and crossed his legs, sliding off his mask and hood.

"Ah!" Favian grinned up at us, rubbing his gauntlets together. His blond hair with its blue wave was streaked back severely. He was gaunt, heavy bags under his bloodshot eyes. He was under soul-crushing pressure. "It is not often I have a conversation like this. My name is Favian, a pleasure, and what are yours?"

"Ciana," I replied flatly, clasping my hands together and making myself as small as possible. "He has forgotten his."

"Ah! A common affliction among the Miners." Favian flicked a friendly glance at Andreas with his inky pupils. The time walker was hunched over on the bench, his filthy hair and forearms glistening in the morning light. "You have my sympathies indeed. Your dreams must once have been great. May I ask you a favor? Do you have any snacks? I am feeling extremely peckish."

I picked up my travel bag. Inside were apples, cookies, and a flask of water. I held out an apple to him. He nodded up at me enthusiastically, holding out both hands in glee. I stepped over and dropped the fruit into his palms.

"Thank you, thank you!" he said, taking a noisy bite into the crisp skin. "Mmm! It is most delicious. My compliments." He regarded both of us brightly for a second. "I regret to intrude on you so early this morning, but may I interrupt your journey?" He took another bite, loud in the morning quiet. "I am quite aware that you are not the bogeymen they make Miners out to be. It is most lonely out here."

I nodded slowly, noticing Andreas was still frozen. *Come on, you fool. I told you, you have lost all dreams, not all common sense. Follow my lead!*

"While I am familiar with Miners," said Favian, "I have no way of knowing if you are familiar with me."

I nodded and noticed with relief a slight shake of Andreas's head. He was trying to give as little away as possible.

"Excellent! And are you aware of the job I have been ordered to carry out in the Floating Lands?"

"Yes," I said, allowing a hint of trepidation. Favian's attention was drawn toward weakness like a knife through butter. He smiled pleasantly at me and took a bite of the apple. He looked at Andreas then.

"Please, tell me what you have heard." We could hear the crunch of the apple's flesh as he chewed. "Please." He waved his hands in a welcoming gesture to Andreas. I placed my eyes on the skeletal mask on his lap, waiting for the end.

"I have heard that you hunt those who believe in the Traveler . . ." Andreas's voice was devoid of all emotion, thank the Beginnings. He had been paying attention.

"How sophisticated! The Regent could not have said it better himself!" Favian seemed delighted by this. He munched on his apple, looking from one of us to the other, the tension thickening.

"As pleasant as it is to break our fast together, may I ask what you request of us?" said Andreas eventually. A mistake, too politely phrased, far too brazen. Favian seemed to become even more cheerful.

"I am aware of how pleasant it is, do not mistake me! It is in fact a personal issue. I am nostalgic." Favian got up and went to the window, where we had slung Andreas's bag. My heart leaped in my chest. *Please*, I begged the Fates, *don't look down.* If he found the drawing, the very presence of artwork would eliminate any pretense, and I had no excuse ready for it.

"It has been a long time since I have met someone who lived in Skala, so many leagues from the original Village of the Second Sun. Indeed, I am from this town too, and in earnest I wished to escape as much as you did. I cannot blame you." Favian examined the apple core. The dirty leather pouch with its secrets was right beneath his gaze. "In fact I am not even going to ask why. It is obvious." He sighed.

"Like you, I grew up with nothing. And I wish to share some boyhood memories, as the morning is cold and my fellow soldiers look down upon me." He bit the core in half, letting the pieces fall to the floor. He stepped on them and turned to Andreas. I let out a tiny breath. "Tell me, what do you remember of this town? The homes were not always as they are now, correct?"

"No, they were not," Andreas replied, hunched up in a ball, his hair falling over his shoulders. "Would it be okay if I too have a snack?"

"Of course. The lady is not hungry? I do not wish to be rude." Favian's smile was lavishing itself upon us. The end was near. My mind was racing. I would never be thrown back in that cage. Maybe I should betray Andreas, before it was too late.

Andreas needed to back down, but clearly it was not in his nature. I examined his fierce jaw lit by the sun, the fine wrinkles that had played around his eyes with the orphans. He was a difficult, beautiful man, inside and out. I looked away bitterly, unable to imagine the husk he would become.

Then he began to describe the Miners' town. Impossibly. Before the Tree's tax hikes, before even the reorganization, reaching all the way back to the Day of Rising. It was all I could do to keep my shock from showing. His descriptions were straightforward, vivid, and detailed. I watched Favian absorb his stories, fascinated.

"There were many kites. The boys would run down behind them along the waterfall," Andreas finished.

How could he have known any of that? My gaze was drawn down the corridor. Through the door window, I saw Reece and Gellie looking back in sheer terror. *Kai talan* surrounded them, armored elbows securely wrapped around their necks. He must have been from Skala, and yet . . .

"Aha! You are so correct!" Favian exclaimed. "You have made me so happy. What memories, yes?" He clapped his hands. "Well, I guess that should do it . . . But before I go, do you have another snack to share with me? I am still so peckish."

Andreas reached into my bag and handed him a cookie.

"Thank you, ah!" The skeleton took a bite. "This too is scrumptious! And I wish my stories were so clear as yours. Do you remember the big red kites that celebrated Our Day of Rising, praise be to our Regent?"

"The kites were white. Shaped like dragons."

"You are so correct! Wonderful days." Another unimaginable detail. Favian was devouring the cookie. "Remind me, what was the name of the street you lived on?"

Andreas said nothing. The seconds ticked on. Favian's smile began creeping back. He scratched his chin with a black gauntleted finger, tilting his head like a bird.

Slowly, Andreas spoke. "I don't remember."

"You don't remember." Favian stopped scratching, putting his index finger up as if he had an idea. "I remember! You used to live down by the . . ." He stroked his chin, frowning. "No! I've forgotten again."

By now, the air in the cabin had thickened into a cauldron. Outside, Reece was shaking her head in despair. Gellie looked as though he could cry. My mind was racing for an answer, racing, racing.

"I wronged my mother," Andreas announced. He hunched over, running clawed fingers through his matted mane. "And I ran away. But I cannot remember our family home. I cannot remember and I don't know why."

"Mothers! Our most precious relationships," Favian said very quickly. "What happened?"

"She blamed me for my father becoming Forgotten." Andreas hunched over farther, shaking his head.

"But you cannot remember your own street?" Favian peered at him maliciously.

"It was taken away. By someone like you," Andreas growled.

"This is most unfortunate," said Favian, stepping forward, crouching, and balancing on his heels before his prey. "Your dream must have been to return home. It is indeed a worthy one! For home is what gives us the wings to fly." He took both of Andreas's hands and fluttered them in the air, smiling sidelong at me.

Black ivy twined around my neck, climbing into my heart. I felt myself once again bound and spread-eagled on the table, wings pinned with carmine nails, a brace squeezing on my forehead, morphine on my tongue as the glinting surgeon saws came for me. My breathing was constricted, the gruesome scars invisible but still pulsating beneath my disguise.

But like the shadow of a man he was pretending to be, Andreas did not react, letting his hands become puppets for Favian's show. The bastard let go and stepped back.

"There is one more thing I wish to share with you. It is a gift. A poem, a beautiful poem about hope. The feeling ignites this scroll and we have an enchanting light." Favian unfurled a thin scroll and handed it to Andreas. His hands were shaking ever so slightly in excitement.

I truly hated him then. The poem was mine, given to me, and it had saved my life. I had not seen it since the day I had escaped my prison, but I knew Favian had been using it during interrogations to incriminate his victims. Anyone who felt even a glimmer of hope while reading it would cause the words to emit a faint blue light, as if it had been charged by that day it had saved me.

The color drained from Andreas's cheeks as he read:

What is love?
To offer a hand
In a secret forest
To crack the shell

Of your own understanding
To let go of fate,
To leap without feet,
In the keen light of the moon
In the presence of all things
To always know
I want you, forever.

Favian's fanatical gaze was fixated on the scroll. But mine were fixated within my heart. This was the poem the boy from my dreams had sent me in a lantern across time and space. I knew it—I knew it in my soul. He had saved my life that day, high above the clouds when I wanted to give up and fall into the sea, into nothingness.

The words Andreas read were words that had saved me. But the scroll did not glow, not even a flicker of light. And while I should have rejoiced at our escape, all I could feel was sorrow.

If the poem was written by the boy from my dreams, it could not be Andreas.

"It seems you truly have lost your dreams, if they ever had any hope . . ." Favian snatched the scroll back, peering at the thin paper, and held it up to the light. "This makes me nostalgic, it truly does." He shook his head and looked up at the ceiling. "Truly nostalgic," he repeated. "I wish to dance now. Will you dance with me?" He turned to me and offered his hand. "My lady?"

Like an automaton, I took it. My handler put his arm around my waist. "I miss the dance of my people!" he said to Andreas. He led me in the steps, and I followed, awkward and wooden. The dance culminated in a spin and he caught me as I dipped back toward the ground.

"We will expose the Traveler," his lips whispered in my ear. He drew me back up and held me tight against him, examining my reaction, squeezing my shoulders. My heart leaped in terror. I managed to let only a short breath escape, and it could have been in surprise. He evaluated me with his black, inky eyes and then pulled me close again, his breath hot in my ear. "Lure them into the Maiden's Tower."

With that, he let go and stepped back. "That was wonderful. I bid you farewell, indeed. Farewell." He threw his hands up and marched out of the cabin.

✦

As we sat in the aftermath of Favian's departure, so many feelings were rushing through me. I had been so close to betraying Andreas. Yet he had made me remember. I wanted to tell him everything, to say all these memories out loud to see if they were still true. To see if it was him. But it couldn't be.

My friend, my love, my poet, I miss you, I thought as I looked at him. *But you cannot be him, because he wrote me that poem and you felt nothing when you read it. I don't even know if you are a Traveler. You know so much and so little. And you are much angrier than my love ever was. I taught him better than that.*

"Do you think he knows who I am?" Andreas demanded. I could see that he thought I had betrayed him.

"Who are you, Andreas?" I asked him.

"Who are *you*?" he snarled back. I didn't blame him. Favian was upsetting. "You asked me to come with you. I covered for you with the Guard! When are you going to start being honest with me?"

"You were only pretending to be a victim of the city, Andreas. But I truly am. If I don't bring down the Regent, I will be its prisoner forever."

"You *are* pretending! Show me your real self, under the disguises, under the stories you tell yourself!"

I did not know what to say to that. No one had ever demanded such a thing of me. In fact, they preferred my disguises. So I just looked at him.

Reece and Gellie interrupted us by stumbling into the cabin. The man-child was visibly shaken. *That makes two of us, Gellie.* Reece was hiding it a bit better.

"We're leaving," she rasped. "I never want to see a *kai talan* up close again."

"Are you proud to work with these people?" Andreas roared.

"They told us to come to the capital," Reece said. "Something big is happening. All of the Guard is being called up to the castle. We have to go. Come on, Gellie."

"Wait! We need to know who to contact," I said quickly.

"Meet the Canary at the Gate. That's all I know. May the Beginnings guide you."

"Meet the Canary at the Gate," I repeated.

"Bye, Rock Muncher. Bye, Princess," muttered Gellie.

"Thank you!" I called after them.

"I hope to never see you again!" shouted Andreas.

"You live in a cave!" shouted Gellie.

"Your mother has a beard!" Reece shouted back.

Andreas scowled.

"Stop sulking," I snapped. "Don't you have a dream girl to save?"

"That poem . . ." he said, and it seemed as if he was on the verge of telling me something.

"Yes?" My heart fluttered.

"Nothing . . ." He got up, shaking his head, and collected his bag. "Let's go."

⋆ 10 ⋆

ANDREAS

New Time

WE DISEMBARKED FROM THE TRAIN in silence. Ciana gestured toward the tracks heading into a mountain cave, and I marched off without a word, grinding my teeth. An intense heat was growing in my chest, like a leash tightening around my heart.

Where in the Fates had that *snake* gotten my poem? It *was* mine; it was my handwriting. How had it survived?

I wanted to shout but instead kicked a nearby rock, crunching my toe against it, and swore. I tried to balance on one foot while holding the injured one but fell on my butt. Ciana rushed over, holding her finger to her lips.

"Is that a smirk?" I managed through gritted teeth.

She smiled, but underneath it she looked devastated. Something had affected her during that encounter. It was as if her core had caved in and now her spirit was being dragged under. Could the poem too have traveled across time? Across worlds? My tiny floating lantern in the Uncharted Lands had traveled into the reflection of the moon—could it have brought my poem here into this time?

Ciana slowly pulled my hands away from my throbbing toe. I watched her ignite into a different person at the touch of our skin, a striking, radiant beauty with rainbow hair and eyes that flashed through soft colors. I would never get used to how breathtaking she was, I thought, as her hair gently settled into lily white. Her lips parted too with the sensation and I felt the impact in her physically. We locked eyes then for a long time and neither of us wanted to look away.

Wordlessly, she began to wrap my toe roughly in thin strips of fabric ripped from her dress.

"Ssss!" I winced and glanced away. She was not the only one who had been affected by the near miss in the train. I felt an old wound in my chest too as I recalled the words of the poem.

To always know
I want you, forever.

The worst moment of my life. The moment I had to say goodbye to you, with a fisherman on the last river on earth, your lantern disappearing through the rainbows in the mist. I had watched the only person I had ever loved float away into the moon, the same place you had come from. Never to return.

"Where is that poem from?" I asked. Her hands paused, stopped suddenly. Then she pulled away.

"It's mine," she said coldly. I watched her turn back into Ciana, watched her mask come back.

"You wrote it?"

"I found it."

"Where? When?"

"A long time ago, in a place very far from here."

"Where did that maniac get it then?"

I felt her pulling even further away. The silence grew between us. "Ciana?"

She got up, ending the conversation. I had no choice but to follow. The railway tracks ended in a cave at the foot of the mountains. At the end of the tracks, one of the floating orbs hung above a steel doorway. Ciana rapped on it twice and the door slid open. She glanced at me. I glared back at her.

"You wish to descend?" a hooded voice asked from behind the lock.

"As the Fates will it," replied Ciana, looking at me. "We crave the black."

"As the Fates will it," the voice echoed its assent, and we stepped in. An ancient, gray-robed man stood inside a steel cage. He appeared to have been weeping, but the tears were made of an inky black substance. They ran down his cheeks like spider legs.

"To which depths?" His voice was like sandpaper.

"Take us down to the Halo," Ciana said.

"To the Halo," he echoed, pressing a stone button. The whole cage shuddered and then began to descend. I folded my arms and chewed the inside of my cheek, a bad habit I'd had since I was a teen. I hated caves. It wasn't claustrophobia. I just preferred climbing up, not down.

"If you abandon someone you love, do you think it is forgivable?" I said suddenly. I wasn't sure why I said it; it just popped out. I could have been thinking of my mother, whom I had left with not even a word. Or the girl I loved in the dream, whom I had abandoned. Just like my father had me.

"Forgiveness starts with honesty—you could try some of that," Ciana said. When I didn't reply, she asked, "Any plans I should know about?"

Again I didn't respond. I just looked at the ceiling and watched the passing stone.

"I should never have come here," I sighed eventually.

"I should never have come here either," said the ancient man.

The comment was so incongruous, so unexpected, that both Ciana and I snorted. For a second, the old man's face cracked into the glimmer of a smile. Then the cage traveled deeper into the cave.

"Don't go down there without me, okay?" I said to her after a while.

"Are you worried about me?" she replied.

"It's not like that."

"Sounds like that."

The cage clanged to a halt at last. I folded my arms more tightly and examined the ceiling.

"Thank you, ancient," said Ciana, touching him lightly on the arm.

"Thank you, friend," echoed the old man, bowing his head. He sounded as though he actually meant it. I wondered how long it had been since he had smiled. "May you find the black you crave."

The cage opened and we stepped out into the cavern. It looked like the inside of some gigantic creature, ribbed like a whale's gullet, lit by a string of dull orbs on the ceiling, splitting into two pathways. I missed the open sky already.

"Is this where you take all your boyfriends?" I asked Ciana.

"The Halo is a circular band of tunnels. We will take the left route. It's closer to the Gate. We will have to pass through a large cavern. There may be Miners on the way. Do not talk to them. If they ask, we are seeking the black."

"I'm seeing enough black as it is." I shook my head, taking the lead.

"What kind of Rock Muncher is scared of caves?" she said from behind me. A hint of a smile ghosted over my lips.

It was surprisingly warm in these caves. The orbs above us did not seem to be reliable. As they flickered, I wondered how long it would take a person to go mad down here, lost in darkness so thick you couldn't see your hand in front of your face.

"What made the ancient cry like that?" I asked after a moment.

"He was trying to recall dreams he has forgotten. It's called weeping the black. He is addicted to the tears of the blue flowers." She paused for a second, and then continued. "They grow along the roots of the great Tree above us. When Miners discovered that the flowers would weep with the moonrise, they began excavating along the roots. Where once they were looking for artifacts to trigger dreams, now they seek only the abyss of the Forgotten that comes at the touch of tears."

As we walked, Ciana whispered to me of the Floating City, a miracle made possible by harnessing the dreams of its citizens. To avert a catastrophic fall from the sky, every man, woman, and child in the Floating City needed to contribute. In the lands above the mines, the Regent had cultivated the root systems that reached into every home, harvesting the dreams of those whom it had saved from the Marauda forces on that fateful Day of Rising.

Moreover, she told me that those who did not pay the tax were seen as selfish and mean-spirited toward their neighbors. In time, this disdain multiplied and anyone who did not contribute was despised and scorned, and the city brought legal measures against them. They were banished to the mines or drained to join the Forgotten. And the Regent grew more secretive and paranoid.

In the investigation of people's hopes and intimate terrors, the Regent employed a network of spies. The most feared was the Sifter, an ancient crone who bathed in the dreams of our people, collected in the gargantuan roots at the base of the Black Tree. Wading through the distilled unconscious of the city, she aimed to not only uncover betrayals before they happened but mold the very future itself.

For the ordinary citizen, there were the mouths of the stone visages of the giant, strategically located throughout the city. Inside were holes where malign or benevolent people placed their accusations. Slowly, these changed the spirit of the people.

The Regent would make grand, rambling speeches from the balcony of the palace. He said that to relinquish their dreams was to make them safe from any further threats from the Marauda, because the dreams kept the city afloat. The Tree would not accept these offerings unless they were given willingly. And as the impact upon people became clearer and clearer, more and more refused.

Chief among them were the Last Men, who began among the Temple of Beginnings. They sensed the reverence for the Beginnings fading from this world. They believed that the people of the city were losing something vital to the Tree—not just their appreciation for art, culture, and song, but their very souls.

Dissent spread from the temple pews, and harsher measures were taken. Heavier taxation, the Dreaming Curfew, the *kai talan*. And then finally, the draining: an involuntary surrender of dreams through exposure to the addictive extract from the blue flowers of the roots, the black tears.

The tears—the very same weapon the Regent had used to defeat the last armies of Marauda who had risen with the Floating City, now turned upon the people it was designed to keep safe. Tears extracted from the blue flowers, flowers that wept with the moonrise. The image, that strange blue gleam in the moonlight, took me back to the first days of the Marauda invasion, on the night the Dreaming began.

Old Time

IT WAS THE NIGHT AFTER the Marauda had lined us up for the Vow. They'd whipped and beaten us. Made us scream to never walk the forbidden way, vow to live in this time and this time alone. And Melasquez, with his rictus grin, stared up at the stars as he intoned the words like a prophecy.

I slept fitfully that night, my back stinging from the pain, slipping in and out of consciousness. Suddenly, I was snapped into the world by gigantic temple bells bonging at a vast distance.

I scrambled to the window. My first thought was, this was it— the Marauda were coming for us. Villagers were stumbling through the streets in the blue and blackened night, looking upward into the sky with gaping mouths.

I ran to check on my mother. She lay in her bed, the fine wrinkles around her eyes glistening like spiderwebs in the pale light of the moon. All my efforts could not raise her from her deep slumber and I feared for her life.

Again I heard the bells ringing, ringing. But there were no bells in our village. Scared and disoriented, I opened our front door onto the porch. Two of our neighbors, the Reddevns, were standing in the middle of the road staring at the stars. I followed their gaze skyward.

Above us in the clouds I saw a galleon, ghosting through the night on unseen waves. It rode across the moon, its sails blown by an invincible wind, rocking and dipping and surging as if caught in a storm, and then disappeared into the darkness. And from that moment, I do not recall going back to sleep, and yet I awoke the next morning as if from a dream.

Wearily, I dragged myself to the window. The drizzle had continued; the heavy fog descended into the courtyard. I spotted the Reddevns huddled exactly as they had been the night before, gazing up into the heavens, cowering together. I went outside to them and whispered bashfully of the galleon.

"Can you not see it?" they asked, pointing up into the overcast sky. "It churns in the storm."

I backed away slowly, shaking my head. Unease settled in my belly. I turned down the path that led out of town to check on the Marauda camp.

"There are two lovers aboard!" the Reddevns called after me, making me frown. As I marched down the path, the village was silent, the mist licking the windowpanes, rubbing its muzzle along the glass, seeming to breathe as it cloaked what was inside. It curled around my ankles like something alive and I wanted a way out of that ugly sentient fog. As I neared the village gates, I saw they were unmanned. They hung open, the fog curling between and up the sides, seeping over the lanterns.

The walls of thorns the Marauda had erected hung eerie and barbed. For some moments I stood before the gates, the mist whirlpooling into them, unnaturally, like a mouth swirling smoke. The Marauda soldiers were camped beyond. Something old in me warded me off. I turned toward the better part of town, in the opposite direction of my home. The mist had only worsened. Navigating through the swirling ocean of pale shapes, I saw a naked body huddled in the road, its white skin gleaming and wet like a ghost. It was Heron, curled in a fetal position, sucking on his thumb, cradled in the mud.

"Heron!" I shook him. "Golden Boy!"

Heron opened those scintillating blue eyes of his, as if seeing me from a long distance. He seemed unsure of his surroundings. I gripped his hand, pulling him up and wrapping him in my cloak. I glanced around. A lone Marauda sentry stared at us through the mist like a statue.

"*Zabibti Mai*," he said groggily, still holding on to my clasped hand. *Brain the size of a raisin*, in the old tongue.

I stared at him, concerned.

"I was having strange . . . dreams, my friend." He looked at me, his golden hair flashing as if from the sun, causing me to glance around wildly for the source of light. His voice, usually so incisive, was shaken and he was covered in sweat.

Heron held his hand up into the mist, as if shielding his eyes, adjusting the cloak I'd given him. "By the Fates, it's boiling." Sweat dripped from his brows.

"By the arse of the Fates!" I exploded.

He turned to me in surprise and indignation. Just as he was about to admonish me for speaking ill of his faith, I squinted at the Marauda soldier, who stood like a stone sentinel with his yellow cape and black helmet beneath a leafy gray-green tree.

"How's the weather today?" I shouted at him.

"This northeasterly is the devil himself," came the sneering response. And indeed, his cloak was ensnared by an invisible gale, licking at the cloth like water: the wicked wind from the east that swung across the icy seas from the Marauda Empire. We both noticed it at the same time—that the tree above the soldier stood silent in the gale, its leaves unmoving, while his cloak billowed like a thing alive. Heron waved his hands before his face.

"Am I still dreaming, my friend?" He squinted up into the sky. "I swear there are twin suns burning down on us."

I grabbed his arm and ducked my way toward the Strange Tales Tavern.

The fog had risen to waist height now. I cursed descriptively and Heron swore to me that the day was windless, insisting the second sun was surely only a hallucination. I heard the edge to his voice. He was unnerved. That made two of us.

"Andreas," he said, grasping my shoulder, his voice lucid once more. "Leah . . ." His elfin wife, the lovely daughter of the Elders. She only tolerated our friendship because she pitied me and knew I had once desired her. Heron had won her—it hadn't even been close.

"No matter what it takes," I growled at him. I reached out my hand, and we clasped arms.

We searched frantically that day. From the weavers to the baker, our whole village was locked in a strange stillness. The fog seeped in everywhere, making visibility nearly impossible. Heron was sweating, but at least he could see clearly in the bright and burning world he was living in.

I could not be certain in the mist, but time seemed to be spreading out within the endless gray. All the sentries had abandoned their posts, making me suddenly wonder if the Marauda we had chanced across was real.

"I saw her," came a small voice. We looked up. Around nine years old and downcast, a little blond boy was wearing a ripped shirt several sizes too big for him with holes in it. His lip protruded. He had emerged from an unlikely circle in the fog, backlit by a red glow. A white bird stood just behind him, elegant on a single leg. "She's in the well," the boy said.

"Thank the Fates!" cried Heron. He grabbed my shoulder, and we ran together. I looked over my shoulder at the strange boy, but the mist quickly consumed him. I could have sworn he looked like the younger version of Heron himself.

The well was on the outskirts, beyond the thorn barriers the soldiers had begun erecting. Aware we were in forbidden territory, I tiptoed through the fog, circling like a hunter. But Heron simply sprinted ahead of me. I heard him skid to a stop on his knees in the gravel. He grabbed the stone walls and called down into the well.

"Leah? Leah! Leah, my heart!"

I heard no response. Sensing no Marauda, I picked my way through the thorns toward him, a sinking feeling in my stomach. Heron leaned so far over the lip he was at risk of falling in. I looked down too and waited as my eyes adjusted. There she was, her legs splayed beneath a soiled pink dress, one hand on her belly. With the other, she played with a blue flower that gleamed enigmatically in the dark.

"Leah!" I cried.

"My heart!" shouted Heron again.

Finally she looked up at us, a beatific smile upon her lips, her tawny hair plastered over her brow.

"I saw our unborn children at the bottom, Heron." Her voice was dreamy. "I came here to take care of them."

"What are you saying?" he cried. "Andreas, rope!"

And so I ran. I cannot describe the thoughts in my head as I raced back through the barricades into the village, my skin nicked by hungry thorns. The mist had thickened and it seemed alive, filled with ghostly figures and creatures that ran alongside me. The blood pulsed in my veins.

In the old mill, I scrambled to find a rope in the nests of hay. When I found a sturdy horse noose at last and wrapped it around my waist, droplets of blood from my scratches formed and leaked onto the strands. I stepped out of the entrance to the mill, and I heard a scream from my right. A soldier ran at me with his blade drawn.

"You travel the forbidden way!" he screamed. "You break the world!"

Before I could defend myself, he sprinted right past me into the village as if pursuing something none of us could see. I gripped the rope around me and ran. Trying to shake off the prickling on the back of my neck, I returned to the well as quickly as I could.

Heron was still trying to talk to Leah but simply shook his head at me. I looped a climbing knot and tossed it down, bracing my frame against the stone wall.

"Leah, my heart! Tie this to yourself," Heron begged as the rope sailed down toward her. Leah held her belly and smiled up at us. "I love you, Heron," she said radiantly from the bottom of the well.

"I'll go," I grunted. He nodded, unable to look at me, wiping away tears. As I began to loop the rope in swift, practiced movements, an emanation began in the mist. Soft light rose from the earth, circling around the lip of the well, blossoming up the trees, twisting around their branches. Blue flowers began to bloom, bursting into life along the strands of vine. Heron scrambled to the edge of the well. The glow was coming from Leah's stomach, and blue flowers blossomed all up the walls of the well, coiling in circles of eerie light.

"Bring your family home, my love," Leah sang up at him, cradling her belly.

We got her out, in the light of those blue flowers. And in those strange days that I would later call the Dreaming, they would appear wherever she slept, blooming between the floorboards around her bed, curling around her pillow and her tawny hair. Leah never explained why she had gone into the well, only saying that the Fates had blessed their family.

A week later, she gave birth safely to twin boys with eyes the same shade of blue as the flowers.

※

New Time

"THE BLUE FLOWERS YOU SPEAK of . . . that you call the tears. They grow in these mines?" I asked Ciana in the oppressive darkness.

She brushed against me, uncomfortably close.

"Yes," she answered, her eyes wide, reflecting the round globes embedded in the ceiling. With her girlish features, she looked otherworldly in the gloom, the unnatural light dancing over her glistening skin. "In the roots of the Black Tree."

"What is this place?" I asked, keenly aware of the depths of my ignorance.

I was about to speak again but she shushed me. "There are more than Miners down here. Marauda, and worse."

My foot bumped against something in the gloom. I looked down to see a femur with what looked like teeth marks on it. "Care to specify?"

"Shh," she whispered, overtaking me. "Keep moving."

Up ahead, there was an opening in the rock filled with orange light. So far, we had not seen a living soul, but I had a feeling that was about to change. We crept along the rock slowly, taking care not to make a sound, until we were right up to the opening.

Ciana looked first. I waited. Her whole body seemed to have frozen.

"I never knew there were so many . . ." she whispered.

I peeked in to get a look for myself.

The opening led to a cavern filled with thousands upon thousands of writhing bodies. All were wet with a shining black substance like oil; they squirmed, reached, and crawled through it, stretching toward the cavern's roof.

And above them, tens of thousands of blue poppies sprouted from the root systems on the roof. Each gleamed blue and wept the poisonous black liquid onto the writhing mass of bodies. The cavern was lit from all around by thousands of candles and there was a soft moaning sound, an air of sickening ritual. As it drained through the mass of bodies, the black tears were sifted into pumps that would take it to the surface, likely all the way to the capital.

They were the same blue flowers I'd seen in the well with Leah.

I grabbed Ciana's hand and drew her stricken gaze away from the horror. She seemed so disturbed, so frightened, that when we made it away, I could not resist pulling her into an embrace. I felt that delicious light ignite within her, felt her whole body responding. Her hands resting on my chest changed, lengthened. We held each other for a second, until I realized that she was genuinely blazing and that it seemed to have caused a stir within the cauldron of bodies.

"Where is the Gate?" I whispered fiercely, my heart thumping.

"Just up ahead." She looked up at me then. She was so gorgeous, vulnerable, begging for an escape. It took everything in me to let go of her. Listening to the cavern, we hurried for a few hundred feet away from the mass of Miners. I could feel the sweat beginning to soak into my ripped clothes as the tunnel curved on and on, featureless.

Then a flash of light made me cover my eyes. Crystal stalactites spiked up from the tunnel floor like monoliths, reflecting our image back at us like mirrors. We looked frightened. In between the crystal structures was a huge doorway carved from stone.

The Gate.

"This is the last passing spot for the Forgotten on their way to the depths. When they can no longer recognize their own reflections, then they are truly lost," Ciana whispered. I could see no guards, not a soul in sight. Carefully we moved closer through the sea of crystal, toward hundreds of fragmented reflections.

"Meet the Canary at the Gate?" I repeated, looking at her.

She shrugged, still breathing hard, shaken by what we had seen in the cavern. We made it to the spikes of crystal, and she sank back against one, hiding us from view.

"I think so . . ." she said.

"I'll scout ahead, see if I can see anything." The look in her eyes told me everything. "I will never abandon you. Never. Do you hear me?" She looked up at me as she had at the cavern, and my heart tugged. "Stay put."

She nodded. She did not look well. Did she believe she had a hand in creating this? Or was it something else?

The tunnels curved on ahead, widening into a much larger space. I crouched and began to run lightly, sticking to the shadows. I heard something drip and skidded to a halt. A single malignant black droplet landed right in front of my toe. I glanced up. There were hundreds of blue flowers all over the ceiling. The same blue as the eyes of the children. *Oh, Leah, Heron, what happened to you?*

Shrugging off goose pimples, I spotted a series of holds that had been carved up the right side of the tunnel and ascended to the roof, maybe for collection purposes. I climbed up easily, grateful to be out of range of that black rain. I climbed sideways and upward to gain a better view of the tunnel for some fifty yards.

That's when I heard voices.

Below me I saw umbrellas emerge. There were at least twenty of them, moving across the gravel—mostly dark colors, until the final one. It was bright yellow, unmissable in the depths of the mines. The yellow Canary.

"Meet the Canary at the Gate," Reece had instructed us. Was this yellow umbrella our contact for the Last Men? I clung to the tunnel wall, pressing my body against the rock high above them. Their voices carried.

"Not to tempt the Fates, but could it be the real Traveler?" asked one of the umbrellas. The voice sounded young, barely a teenager.

"What has happened has already happened," dismissed the Canary, as if it was of no consequence.

"I'll be wagering it's the pretty blond spy," said another.

"The traitor?" the first umbrella murmured in awe. "The Magister gave the sentence. She will be tossed to the Flat Lands."

There was an uncomfortable murmur among the men.

"This is a war," cut in the Canary, "for our very souls."

I needed to get back to Ciana.

"The others are coming up the other loop. Tread carefully, brothers," said the Canary.

Black droplets plopped onto their umbrellas, running down the fabric in spidery tears like I had seen on the ancient's face. I scrambled sideways, using all my climbing experience to clamber down and get around the curve before they saw me. Back on the ground, I set off running toward the Gate.

I couldn't see her as I rounded the corner, and my heart squeezed. It couldn't be, it couldn't be. I skidded behind the crystal, the sound of marching boots echoing just around the corner. Thank the Fates she was there! She grabbed me and swung us both against the rock.

"Shh!" She pressed me against the mirror rock and I saw our reflection behind her in a thousand thousand refractions of light.

"You need to show your true self!" I quickly said. I felt her breath on my neck. Her scent.

"What do you mean?" she asked. I took her hand. I could feel her skin against me, lingering, and despite it all, butterflies in my stomach.

"They know you're a spy!" There was something so familiar about each of us, but we didn't know each other at all. And in that moment, despite the urgent feet approaching, I felt alone, nervous, excited. *Why can't I stop thinking about you?*

There was only one thing I could think of to do.

I kissed her.

I felt her whole body ignite like a flame against me in beautiful despair. The hiss of the boots surrounded us.

"Do you see?" I said, showing her, holding her face in both hands, hoping against hope she would show her real self, not just to me but to everyone. She stared at her reflection in the mirror crystal, and for a split second I thought I saw wonder.

Then the bags came down over our heads.

✦ 11 ✦

SAYA

New Time

THE REBELS MARCHED US INTO a cart of some kind.

My body was tingling, the effervescence of the change-ling moving within me. At the same time, I was badly scared and disoriented, trying to remain calm as the cart wheels began screeching. Andreas and I were shoulder to shoulder, the rope chafing our wrists. The murmurs of the men were muffled, barely audible through my hood, to not draw the attention of the Miners.

I had found them at last. The Last Men. But at what cost?

Ciana had fallen off me; her lips, her body had melted in an instant. I felt myself, the girl I had buried and whose gaze I could not meet in the mirror. Without pain, without recrimination, alive and breathless. And stable somehow, not breaking apart as she had been for so long. For the first time since I could remember, I was not yearning to be another with all my heart. Could Andreas have seen my real self beneath my disguise? Had the kiss . . . No, I refused to think about the implications of that.

The cart squeaked through the caverns. The men were disciplined and mostly silent. Their silence was more frightening than any jeering. We entered a lift and I felt us rising. Andreas was against my shoulder, big, solid. At least I knew where he was. At least I was not alone. If this was to be my final moment, then by the Fates, it would be with him. He had given me this gift. If I was to die, at least let it be as myself.

The lift screeched and there was the sound of iron bars opening. "Release," came a curt voice, and someone gave a sharp pull at my bound hands. My knees scraped on the iron lip of the cart as I scrambled out of it, and suddenly I felt us being separated.

"I will find you . . ." Andreas yelled and then I heard a thud as he struggled and was winded.

"Sister," came the curt instruction. I was dragged in the opposite direction, stumbling after my captors. I could hear my pitiful breath in my ears under the hood as fear rose in me. The fear of being imprisoned again, of losing more of myself slowly each day. Wilting into nothing.

I heard the squeak of steel hinges and then I was pushed to my knees. The rope was unwound and I coughed as the dusty darkness was pulled from my head.

"Fates, she's beautiful . . ."

"Shhh!"

They were both behind me. The cage clanged shut.

"Why are we doing this? She's clearly a faerie!"

I did not dare turn around.

"Shhh!"

There was the sound of the key turning in the lock, and then they left me there, in the dark. I coughed, rubbing the back of my hand across my mouth. The moon shone giant through a tiny barred window, reflecting off the jagged rock walls. I blinked. We had returned close to the surface.

My eyes slowly adjusted. The only light was a pool of quicksilver from the moon that poured in through the bars. All was quiet. I sneezed as the shadow of a moth danced against the rock. Its wings vibrated in the stillness, stretched gently in the night air. I stood up and the scars running over my shoulder blades ached as I came closer. But the moth flew away into the moonlight, rising through the beam of light, through the bars, and away into the dark universe.

I fell to my knees. Imprisoned. I had promised myself. Never again.

And the years came rushing back in a torrent. Withering in that glass prison. Unable to accomplish anything, unable to grow, unable to have memories. Meaningless days turning into meaningless weeks and then into meaningless months with my soul becoming stagnant. Everything I loved, every choice, every freedom, the recipe of me . . . wilting.

And I felt myself falling once more, the changeling splintering my being from within. I leaned my head against the wall, trying to pull myself back together. Even the stars looked as if they'd lost faith. Disintegrating . . . Remembering . . .

The moth floated once more before the prison bars and then disappeared into the light of the moon.

A memory of another face—lit by the unearthly light of a free sky—floated into the expanse.

Alia. Jailor. Friend. Confessor.

The moon shone on her face, heartbroken with hope and fear,

her dusky skin a few shades darker than my own. The fierce nostrils of her thick nose flared. Our skin, the complexion of the unnamed people of the Uncharted Lands, was painted gray in the pale light, and her waist-length braid whipped in the evening air.

Trembling, she had opened the intricate lock of my domed cage. The insignia of the Black Tree on her breast hovered before me. The claustrophobic walls of the castle loomed, and the scent of open air was on my tongue, electric with terror.

"The route," she hissed. Her mouth closed in a frown, betrayal choking her almond eyes. Duty had once meant everything to her, hardened her, protected her like the uniform she wore. I nodded, shaking. She blinked and we stared at each other then, the depth of an unknown future between us as our lives tossed in the dreams of the World Trees.

"For the love of Fates, I will never forget you," I whispered. Her jaw jutted out, tears streaking like quicksilver into the gravel beneath her boots. We hugged for the first and last time.

Behind her, she'd arranged the sliced apples and watermelon of my dinner in the courtyard, scattered artfully from the fallen tray. She offered me her wrists, glancing over her shoulder and up into the battlements as I lashed them with a flowered vine. She winced as I pulled the binding tight.

"Fly, little bird," she said through gritted teeth, her slitted eyes hot with anger. "Fly far away from here."

I took two steps and hammered my fist into her face. She reeled and sprawled out backward, her braid swinging out into the night. With lightning-fast movements, I bound her feet.

"Quick, little bird," she whispered, her voice breaking. "The moon shines so bright tonight." My furtive movements cast spindly shadows into the courtyard.

I touched her cheek, wiping the last of the quicksilver from her eyes in farewell. Then I powered forward through the doorway.

And with that, I was running. I half crouched, sand crunching beneath my bare feet, ducking into the shadows beneath the walls. My hands felt, reached, searched. Frantic, I glanced back to Alia's prone body. Her legs kicked right. I continued to the right, fumbling until I found the pebbled wedge to the secret door at last.

I stumbled from the hidden doorway into the silence of a bramble garden. The hedges of the palace maze were shaped like living creatures in the night. A whispering quiet descended. A distant dog barked. There were seven doors leading to this oval where I now stood. Six of those led to new mazes that eventually returned to this identical space. The secret path, the seventh, led to another maze of oval chambers, layered upon the first. And so I began singing, the lyrics my guide.

> *Oh world, where will you take me?*
> *Left and left and right and left.*
> *Oh world, where will you lose me?*
> *Right and left and left and right.*

This was the song Favian had once stopped to listen to, fallen asleep to, my voice a lilting, hushed whisper as my feet floated up and down on my swing in my cage. In his arrogance, he'd assumed it was an ode to my long-lost self. Instead, it had masked the lyrics to my escape.

The lyrics were on my lips as the last door of the seventh maze led me into the palace itself. Another hidden opening slipped into an arched corridor filled with armored suits and tapestries depicting the Black Tree and the Day of Rising. Glancing left and right,

I tiptoed along the hallways of the silent suits, down some stairs, past what looked like bedrooms with door-shaped windows and balconies, and by servants' quarters.

It was late. The moon had already risen.

The limbs of the Black Tree seemed to follow me in the hanging artwork. Freezing at the sound of giggles, I ducked behind a tapestry as a couple of young maids scuttled past, my bare feet peeking out the bottom. The heavy fabric was dusty and I desperately resisted the tingle in my lungs. As I slipped out, I realized I was hopelessly lost. Without you. I heard shouting, hounds barking, raw splinters in the night.

I raced onward, blindly, opening a door to a balcony and embracing the rush of darkness. Open air! Stars! I breathed in, cold lungs filled with freedom and fear. There were bobbing torches, men coming down the walls on the right. I was near the royal bedroom, layers of cultivated gardens beneath me. And before me, the entire world.

I stared into the empty helmet of the suit of armor next to me, its gaze serrated by a visor. And for a terrifying moment, I wanted to grab its ceremonial weapons and rush into the Regent's quarters and . . .

No, you must run!

I sprinted across the lush lawn, my bare feet on grass for the first time in years. Hunting dogs barked, alert fires sprang up in the distance, and my lungs burned. I ran through the gardens, past a startled guard who shouted and waved his torch at me. I vaulted over him and grabbed ahold of the hanging vines to swing to the veranda below. When I hit the ground, I rolled, terrified, then sprinted on, ducking past trees and onto a path lined with poplars, the moon shining gigantic at the end. I heard the dogs unleashed behind me and the arrows whizzing past my ear, thudding into a trunk. I zigzagged down the pathway toward the observation deck, dancing between the trees, the first hints of possibility aching inside me.

Searing pain grazed my calf as I ducked back into the trees, and then a dog hit me in a rolling ball of teeth and fur and hot pain that sank into my forearm. I kicked and screamed and grabbed for a branch, tearing it off just as the dog released my arm and leaped at my throat. I wrenched my body aside and sprinted back into the open, the snarling fury behind me, running and running. Just as I made it to the low wall at the edge of the world, for a split second I hesitated and turned.

The soldiers aimed their arrows at my heart. The hounds thundered down on me.

I saw you, a night moth fluttering in the moonlight.

I let myself fall backward.

As if in slow motion, I watched the arrows flying past the spot where I had been, as I plummeted off the edge of the Floating City. The wind rushed into my hair, covering my eyes and lifting my arms. The lights of the castle disappeared away from me, and the air held my body in a cushion of weightlessness as the branch fell from my fingers.

For a moment there were only misty clouds and vast ocean, the moon peeking through as it had in my dreams with you, my love. Peaceful, and I almost let it be. But then from my back came the gift you gave me. Wings, my love, wings not just of hope but real wings—the wings I wanted to show you again after the night we lost each other. The wings I had dreamed of since I was a little girl who wanted more than anything to feel hope. Hope for love. Hope to fly away into a new world, on wings made from my very dreams.

I never dreamed of you again. But now I felt the powerful caress of them, reaching out of my shoulder blades and stretching out into the wind, rolling and effortlessly cutting through the night sky, gliding through the great expanse. And then, that glorious sound, the whooshing beat as I stretched my back, drove my wings down into the air, and rose into the night sky, into the moonlight. The beating sound of hope in my heart, taking me away from here, away from everything and back to you.

I wished you were there with me to see it, even with your furrowed brows and burning heart, so alight I called you Angry Boy. It was all your doing, in the end. You ignited something in me. It was beautiful. You made my dreams come true.

It didn't last, of course. Without you it never could. My strength was diminished from years in captivity. I tired quickly over that dark sea; I was far weaker than I knew. And when the automatons came after me, I was not ready to fight their mechanical endurance, the steady thump, thump, thump of their spinning blades, closer and closer. I grew so tired in that desperate flight across the clouds. It was only fear, in the end.

They neared, the automatons casting out their hissing nets, the spinning copters powered by the ingenuity of my captor, the Regent. I dodged and dived through the searchlights and the mists of the sky. My lungs burning in desperation, I flew straight up, higher and higher and higher.

I felt this everlasting loneliness overtake me, Angry Boy. I thought maybe I would make it to the moon—back to you. But the portal you had opened into our dreams was closed now and I was so tired. You weren't coming back for me. I had no reason to keep flying anymore. So I stopped, all the way up there near the stars. I was ready to fall into that obsidian sea, forever, without you.

And that was when I saw it. Your lantern, coming down out of the moonlight. Floating down to me, its flame impossible and tiny. I knew it had come from our dream together. With the last of my strength, I pushed upward with a final burst. Before the nets closed on me, I found what you had stitched to its base. I found your poem.

They dragged me away through the sky, the net clutching me and my wings, abrasive and rough on my skin and feathers. But wrapped in secret, I had your poem. By snatching the light of the moon between the shadows of the net, I was able to read what you wrote me. Even then, even caught like an animal in a snare, I felt it for the first time in years.

Hope.

You were still alive. And you still loved me. You would love me forever, as we had promised each other wordlessly, in this world and any other. Even if you could never say it.

That was why—as they dragged me across the night, back to the castle and back to my cage, the nets tangled painfully in my wings—I held your poem to my heart. That was why, I thought, it glowed with the light of the moon even now, even in the hands of a snake like Favian. It was the light of the hope you gave back to me. The hope that my wings were made of.

They cut the cord and dumped me from several meters up. The impact took my breath away. The first face to cut my net open bloomed out of the night. Alia. My best friend, jailor, and trainer and the one who had helped me escape, who had made life bearable behind those unbearable bars.

It was Alia who, with cold anger, manacled my legs and arms. Alia who, with the other guards, carried me like an animal back into my cage. The same Alia I'd taught to sing to woo her unrequited love. It was she who threw me back into that hole in the ground and cursed me with the other pilots, and she who turned her back on me after that. For what? For the crime of being caught? Or for her part in catching me?

I was breaking apart again.

+ ✦ +

I believed in dreams once. Believed they could come true. But I also learned that when the Fates gave you a dream, it was never the way you wanted it.

When the defenders of the Tree captured me fleeing through the clouds above the ocean, they threw me back in my domed cage. I found myself lying spread-eagled on a table, staring up at the sky I'd never touch again. My limbs were bound with leather straps, cinched tight, my wings pinned to the floor with blood-red nails.

I couldn't even feel them anymore. Maybe I no longer believed I had them. They rippled weakly, searching for a night wind. Morning blushed across the heavens, pink and gold from a horizon far beneath my sight. Lonely stars still winked through the glass dome of my cage.

Voices were getting nearer. Wind chimes tinkled in the breeze as the pass-coded door to my prison was unlocked and opened.

The beaded cushions that had once formed my nest were scattered around threadbare carpets. The fountain Favian had gotten me for my birthday trickled among the shimmering gray ferns. I had no tears left to join it. Some women cry easily, their tears like the fragrant rain of a sun shower. Others cry hard, all the loveliness of themselves collapsing. I was the latter sort, and the valleys of my tears had already been written across my heart.

Alia got up and approached me from the swing to my right. Overhead, the blue jays, red-crested turacos, and pheasants roused from their sleep by the newcomers spun, hooting across the roof of the cage. Naomi, the peacock, hid shyly beneath the drooping sunflowers, their yellow faces turned to the ground.

"Saya. Please." Alia struggled to keep the fury from her voice. "Drink it." She came to stand next to the table, as she had since I had first been tied to it. I turned my head away from the vial of dark liquid she offered.

"Did you know I am a girl whose dreams come true?" I said to the sunflowers. "And once, I dreamed of love?"

The men pushed their way through the ferns, and I heard the clinking of tools in leather bags. I remembered that scared little boy I'd found in the forest. And that frightening creature he'd become.

Alia's lips twisted. She caressed my cheek, digging her fingers behind my jaw and pressing the vial against the corner of my mouth. "Saya! It will help with the pain."

"I created a boy in a dream, or he created me, I can't tell which." I turned my head to face her, a smile breaking over my lips. "He gave me my wings."

Alia held a palm up to the approaching men, the vial still in her other hand.

"Do you know what they are made of?" I asked. No matter what they had done to me, I had never told anyone where my wings had come from. I'd always said they were a miracle.

Perhaps they were.

In the gentle pull of the surf, as the water at our ankles glowed with phosphorescence, I'd led Angry Boy into the ocean. The wings had emerged from my back in joy, from the light he gave me within, when we made love for the first and only time. Before I could no longer stay in that dream world. Before this one pulled me back.

I looked at Alia, at the shadowy outlines of the surgeons behind her waiting in the ferns. The birds flew above us, calling to each other in distress.

"My wings are made of hope."

"Little bird, just drink!" Alia hissed, glancing behind, her nostrils flaring.

I opened my mouth. The taste of the vial was revolting and my body nearly brought the liquid back up. Alia held my jaw shut. I couldn't see her through the black lights under my stinging tears. I heard the men clanking their bags of surgical equipment under the table.

"Butchers!" Alia spat.

I opened my eyes for a final glance upward. There was Naomi, my peacock. She floated across my vision. The last of the stars were gone. My vision began to swim and I began to see the Black Tree, its branches merging with the sky.

"I can't watch this." Alia stepped backward, turning away from the table and slamming into the shoulder of one of the goggled men, the one with the hooked nose and beard of speckled gray.

"Meat monkey!" he grumbled, threatening her with a saw, its teeth glinting in his fist. I closed my eyes, trying to imagine the sparkling ocean, fireflies dancing above the surface.

"Incredible specimen!" The other surgeon approached the table, running his hands over my wings in wonder. He was older, with a goatee and an elegant bearing, but his gaze was just as cold as the other's through the green goggles.

"Ever dreamed you could fly?" The first grinned beneath his walrus mustache, tearing off a strap of plaster with tobacco-stained teeth, ignoring me.

"Maybe, but it was probably taxed to the Tree many moons ago." The elder surgeon strapped my mouth shut. I screwed my eyes until more colors floated beneath. Blues, greens, and reds, sparks of yellow. A brace tightened over my forehead.

"The Floating Lands barely have enough dreams to stay in the sky." The surgeon's voice was filled with clinical curiosity. "Can you imagine what dream we'd need to lift off?"

I heard the wind chimes tinkling. The teeth of the saw bit beneath the bones of my shoulder blades, and red filled my eyes.

"We'd need a miracle."

I love you, Angry Boy. You and your beast.

Dream of me as I once was.

ANDREAS

New Time

As the hood was pulled down over my head, rough hands pushed me into the dirt. Efficiently and silently, our captors forced my arms behind my back and tied my wrists, the cords biting deep. But I hardly felt it. My mind still swirled with the heat of the kiss. I couldn't believe it, not only her and who she had been becoming the moment our lips touched, but me too, the swirling change in my chest, intimate and terrifying.

We were thrown together into a cart of some kind and I was grateful that I could feel her next to me for a moment. My cheeks burned under the hood as the cart wobbled precariously. My shoulder crunched into the iron and I snapped into reality.

The dusty sweat, the claustrophobic fear, the shifting center of gravity, the cart rising as we entered a lift of some kind. Bars, then we were dragged from the cart. I sensed them pulling us apart and instinctively I lashed out, kicking at a shape and hearing the air whoosh out of him.

"I will find you!" I cried out to her, wrestling at my bonds and ripping a man off his feet. A boot caught me in my chest, but I kept swinging around wildly. What were they doing to her?

"Stop!" a rebel hissed, but I wouldn't. Wooden poles thundered into my back and thighs. Each strike brought crippling pain and an old, terrible rage that simmered and bled. At last I crumpled, panting. There was a short pause, then a drag at the rope, forcing me to try to stand. "Please," the rebel asked again, breathing hard.

Was I letting this happen, leaving again without trying? A coward? The pain thumped with the same red beat of my heart, like a cordon around my chest. And as they pulled me onward into the darkness, my thoughts turned black and murderous.

Under the hood, I imagined ripping the chain from his hands, throwing men against walls, smashing rib cages with my shoulder. The madness took me and I roared with all my heart, sprinting in the direction of the chain in a ball of power. I felt legs, and I uprooted them, lifting the body and driving it headfirst into the ground. There were arms around me but I was seeking the chain, and I found it as boots pounded into my ribs, kicking the air from my lungs. Another blow landed on my head. But I would not let go of the chain no matter the cost. And quickly, the thumping darkness of the boots faded into the red mist.

My last thoughts were about the girl I had lost. The hole in my heart. I remembered only the beginning and the end. Just fragments, evaporating like the dreams they were, disappearing out into the universe . . .

✦

Like everyone else who'd experienced it, I found that my memories of the Dreaming were not clear or connected in any ordinary way. All I could recall was that in the days after we'd rescued Leah from the well, I'd begun to be possessed by ugly dreams I could never remember afterward.

In the days before I met you, that awful sentient mist had curled around the hamlet and through the trees. And for the first time in my life, the forest had changed. Its mighty silence was no longer peaceful. Instead, I felt a strange pull from the murky depths that both repelled and drew me.

One evening, in the jumpy heat before a storm, there was a pounding on the door. Opening it, I saw two Marauda soldiers in full battle armor, the storm air licking hungrily at their capes. Behind them, a nervous man was shaking, his arm wrapped in a blood-soaked bandage. The wound looked fresh.

"This is Raknik. He is one of my orderlies. You are the hunter Andreas?" The captain did not take off his helmet. He seemed elemental, his hand over his sword pommel. Enormously powerful, a dangerous man.

I nodded.

"He is attacked," he said, not using past tense, as was the Marauda way. "A man-eater. The first incident of its kind here, I am told?"

I didn't say anything. I just studied the wounded man.

"The beast springs on them, him and his horse together. There is not much left of the stallion."

I listened without emotion. But within, I felt a hint of an old dread stalking me, as if I had always known this day was coming, like the gaze I felt within the forest.

Behind the captain, I saw a drunk soldier wandering into the woods. I ran to catch him and managed to grab his arm before he stepped beyond the tree line. He swore violently and tried to swing at me, but I ducked and grabbed him in a bear hug.

Behind me, soldiers came running, drawing their swords. But I continued to stare out into the forest. I could feel it, staring back. The man wrestled against me, but I held him easily.

"No one goes out—the beast owns the forest!" I flung the drunken soldier to the ground.

The men began to reply but I shushed them with a hand and stared out into the night. The wind blew, rippling through the leaves. Deep within the trees, the shadows began to move, shuffling through the dense thicket. The captain came to stand with me. The tall grass in the forest began to bend and sway in the wind, making odd patterns. I exchanged a glance with the captain.

The pattern seemed to be making its way across the grass toward the path. Then it seemed to stop. Around it, the wind continued to deceive the eye. I felt it swirl, cold and hard against my back, as if pushing me toward the pathway. I continued to stare at the spot where it had stopped. The man I had thrown to the ground began to shiver. The captain grunted. Around his throat I saw a necklace of vicious fangs, some as long as my fingers.

He noticed me looking. "With my bare hands." He grinned, showing me his death grip. The wind blew again and his smile died along with his words. "You have good instincts." He patted me on my shoulder and gave me his spear before marching away.

That night I waited in the clearing just beyond the southern edge of the forest. A horse stood by nervously. The wind tinkled the bell around its neck, the sound seeming to linger in the air. And I could not help wondering: Was this the same bell that had woken me, the sound growing bigger and bigger as it traveled into the past, echoing back from this moment? I could not tell, but the thought unsettled me. A circle in time. The future affecting the past.

I held on to my spear and waited. It was impossible to get comfortable. I could not find an easy way to hold my weapon. The hours went by slowly, my eyelids dipping. The bell would wake me, but the fatigue soaked deeper and deeper as the night ran on into the morning. My eyes, against my will, started to give in to the fatigue, battling and drooping closed . . . and drooping . . .

Two yellow eyes stared up at me, right beneath my tree.

Startled, I awoke, fumbling for the spear and nearly dropping it. But there was nothing. Just the forest moving in the night and the horse with its bell, echoing in my memory. The beast wanted me. I could feel it.

That was when I heard the screaming. I leaped down from the tree and sprinted toward the Marauda camp on the edge of the forest. The terrible sounds grew louder. As I neared, soldiers began erupting from their tents, crying out and running. I saw a shape sliding across the ground at tremendous speed.

It was the captain, gliding along the ground headfirst as if being pulled by some monstrous force. It was so dark I could not see what was dragging him. He was going faster, his cries weakening, and then I saw his body flip, rising magically over the encampment wall, all six feet of the barricade.

None slept that night. Or perhaps we were all already asleep.

I went with the soldiers in the morning, following the cawing of the crows. We found him in an area of white grass, the stalks flecked with blood. So lovely, you might have said, in any other world. There was a patch in the middle that was blood red. Something was moving. The beast had licked his skin off so it could drink his blood and then feasted on him, starting with his feet. Just wings swarmed on him now, crows cawing at each other in the pale grass.

The soldier I had prevented from entering the forest fell to his knees in shock, in despair, as if he had seen something beyond imagination. That night, the beast killed again. Two dead in two nights. The soldiers told me there was even less left of him than the captain. No regular beast would be hungry again so soon.

"I will kill the creature," I told everyone, repeating it to anyone who would listen, shaking, trying to get control. "There is no reason to fear!"

A drunk soldier laughed in my face. "It is no normal beast. You are dying, a fool thinking he is a hero. Is this what you want?"

I lived in fear of sleep, that something black and angry would come upon me in the night. But as the night fell, I heard its terrible sound. It wasn't roaring; it was weeping.

I woke up with blood all over my chest. I checked for a wound and found nothing. And suddenly I emptied myself, tears pouring down my face, my body racked with sobs.

As the creature continued to hunt us, those soldiers who remained began to take out their vengeance against the people of the village. They blamed us for the man-eater. I heard them one day and from my window saw them dragging Heron and some of the other men from the village in chains.

"Heretics! You must be stopped!" a soldier shouted.

"The world is breaking!" howled the drunk. He took a swig of wine and poured it on Heron's face. "We must make a sacrifice!" He gripped Heron's chain and all ten of them were dragged into the forest, down the path.

I knew I had to follow.

It was easy to track their sounds in the thick woods. The forest was my home and I knew its paths. I moved downwind and silently, lithe as a beast myself. I could even smell the foul alcohol, the fear in the air. I hated the fire they brought with them.

As in a dream, I was not surprised when I looked down at my hands to see giant claws still flecked with blood. The creature and I were one; we had always been, two sides of the same person. I quickly closed the distance between me and the group. Then with a ripple of terrifying speed, I pounced into the soldiers, grabbed the first man by the throat, and flung him against a tree, where he crumpled like a rag doll.

An incredible roar came from my throat, with an echo that could be heard five miles away in the night. They ran from me, and my claws ripped at them, slashing, smashing their tiny bodies and spears with deafening fury, slapping them aside so fast they could not follow it.

The soldiers kept coming, faceless and wearing my father's boots. I filled the clearing, towering over everything like a nightmare. I knew then why I had come.

I bit a fat one's neck in two, killing him instantly, the blood sweet in my mouth. Crazed destruction was within me, and that terrible lonely weeping sound came from my throat. The huge darkness inside me tore at my bones, but more and more came, all of them with my father's boots. Right as I was about to pounce upon a soldier, he said, "I love you, my Little Explorer." I was midair when his sword drove into my heart and my claws ripped into his throat. In agony, I threw his body against a tree.

I felt another spear enter my back, and that soldier too said, "I love you, my Little Explorer." I turned and smashed his armored face, but then another spear was thrust into my chest. I reared on my hind legs, slashing at them. I was surrounded, but I knew I would never stop until they killed me, and they would never stop until I destroyed them all. And so I howled with all my bleeding heart to the moon.

That was when I saw her.

Coming down from the moon.

Stepping down from the sky through the stars, as if on puddles of water.

Tiny delicate feet, a gossamer dress.

White hair, curling at the ends like ocean foam.

The first snows falling into an everlasting silence.

Each intricate flake danced gently through the air. Time itself stopped. The light of dazzling stars shone behind her, and the rush of wind moved through my hair. I wished more than anything I could remember, just remember her face.

"Why are you fighting yourself?" she asked as daintily as her tiptoes touched down on the ground.

"I'm fighting our enemies!" I could speak again.

"You're only a little boy," she replied. It was true. The blood was gone, and my voice was tiny and high. I looked around for Heron and the others, but they were nowhere to be seen. The soldiers too.

"Who are you?" I shouted in fury, but my high voice sounded weak and afraid in the vast forest. She seemed sad, as if that question hurt her more than I knew.

"I'm not sure yet." She shrugged. She turned to go and I saw her disappearing, fading like a memory of the future.

I heard marching boots, thousands and thousands of my father's boots. I knew at that moment if I did not follow her, I would live and die as a beast, alone in this dark forest for the rest of my life.

"Let me come with you!" I called to her, my voice a man's once more.

She looked back at me then, smiled, and held out her hand. She was the most beautiful thing I had ever seen.

"You can stop fighting now, Angry Boy . . ."

New Time

SO STRANGE, THOSE MEMORIES FROM the Dreaming.

The giant's vengeful grin to the heavens as the Marauda forced us to say the Vow. That sentient mist that curled through the village. Finding Leah in the well with her blue flowers and future children. The beast that haunted me, that became me. The gossamer dress descending in the moonlight.

I remembered all of this, and then I found myself again with a hood over my head, waking up to the savage dust of this new world. Like the beast I became in the Dreaming, I had followed my pain into the forest of the unknown, hoping to slay what haunted my heart and return a hero. But instead here I was, bleeding and broken in the dark belly of the world. I had made so many mistakes.

My greatest was losing her.

I did not resist when my captors came in and poked at me. Perhaps they would put me down now, like the ugly beast I was.

⋆ 13 ⋆

SAYA

New Time

I T WAS YOU, ANGRY BOY, who gave me my dream of hope.

But once you left me, it all fell apart.

On the day I awoke from our last night together, it was early dusk. I was younger then, and you had set my heart free to be younger still.

I woke my parents in the early morning, standing at the foot of their straw mattress, my immaculate white wings stretching from my back in the light from the window. They had come from our dream together, and yet they were real.

I felt like a miracle, pure and clean and purposeful in a way I had never felt before. I knew that you lived in my dreams and that your love was the gift that gave me permission to fly. I was grateful to you, whether you really existed or not.

But my parents did not see it like this. They recoiled from me. As I went to hug them, they scrambled to escape me, shouting and making signs to ward off evil. I did not understand what was happening; I was filled only with love at that moment and the gift you gave me.

They wrapped me in bedding and hid me in the wagon. As I lay in the darkness, they discussed what should be done with me. I heard footsteps, and my heart lifted, a faint glow coming from my wings. But as they removed the blankets, their faces loomed above me like strangers, hostile and afraid. I heard my mother's voice telling me to stay there, to not come out ever, that she was taking us to the capital to start a new life.

We traveled for days on bumpy roads, skirting the main highways. The whole time, I heard only whispers. My mother would not speak to me. She tapped on the wagon to let me know I could reach up for the dried fruit or hard bread she left there. I slept fitfully and did not dream. It was hot and I cried often.

On the third day, she finally removed the covers. The sky was the most perfect blue you could imagine. Just a single cloud floated above me.

"Wrap yourself!" Mama told me. "All of it! Get out, come out!"

Covered in layers of thick horse blankets, I stumbled out of the wagon. She did not help me. I blinked. We were in a field of red poppies, the sun shining brightly. The field was scarred with gigantic crevices, like a dragon's claws had cut into the earth, and beneath us, concave cliff faces dropped into the vast Flat Lands below. We were on the edge of the earth.

"I need to collect food nearby. Stay here!"

"Mama, please look at me!" I said miserably.

"Stay here! Do not take off the blankets!"

So she left with the wagon, and I waited, as I have always waited to dream of you again. The sun was beautiful and bright, and a cool, brisk wind softened the heat and made the poppies dance. I lay in the warm grass and played with their petals and watched the little bugs wander on their unknowable journeys. I saw a pair of purple dragonflies floating over the field, dipping and pirouetting with each other through the wind.

I waited there. I wanted to tell you that I flew away from my life in the desert. That my mother was taking me to the city. That I would start a new life thanks to you.

I'm still that young girl, waiting for you, wanting to fly away with you, clutching at real hope for the first time in my life. But now, all I can see is that same girl saying "Mama? Mama?" and the night getting colder and lonelier. I see her crying, shivering, falling asleep next to the giant crevices in that field of poppies, wrapped in her wings and those layers of coarse blankets.

My mother did come back. She woke me up in the night, distraught. "Oh, my baby, no! Oh no!" She wept and hugged me.

I was so grateful as I hugged her back. I was so happy that she still cared about me. "It's okay, Mama," I whispered through my tears as I clutched her to me, feeling her body racked with sobs. "Don't cry. It's okay, I forgive you."

A steel gauntlet pulled us away from each other. I had not seen the soldiers, who stripped the blankets off me first in horror and then with wonder. They dragged my mother away from me. My wings bloomed outward, ethereal and glowing in the night. I stretched them for the first time in days with a whoosh and saw that they had grown even more wondrous than I could imagine.

"Quickly!" barked a young lieutenant with blond hair and inky black eyes. The soldiers clamped the manacles around my wrists.

"No!" I cried as I traced the chain to the wagon. My wings began to beat with fearsome power, driving the soldiers back with gusts of wind.

"The Regent pays handsomely for miracles," I heard the young lieutenant say, dropping a bag of tinkling coins in my mother's hand. Favian watched as his men grabbed at my ankles and dragged me back to earth, his eyes dark with ambition. Bound and chained, I was taken to the castle and to my cage.

From the day they locked that ball around my leg, I stopped dreaming of you. After they took my wings from me, I thought I'd never dream again. But I did. I dreamed with all my heart to be anyone else.

In the days after the operation, branches of agony crawled through my back with even the smallest movement. I lay on my side or my stomach, refusing to eat.

The bones of my skull, near the temples, had become sharply defined. My cheekbones cut deep lines like valleys that ran to my hard and hungry jaw. My violet eyes were cavernous, ridged under my once delicate brows. Radiant light, made from my agonies, streamed from my eyes. As time went by, I found a luminous, transcendent beatitude in the torment and silence of myself, a bliss that cracked and broke in my desperate longing to change my life for another's.

"There is only madness and love left in you now," Alia told me. Trying to persuade me to eat, she would look at me as if I was at once fearsome and immensely pitiable. Her last resort was holding my nose and forcing soup into my mouth. Each day ended in both of us begging or sobbing. I could not sleep, so Alia smuggled me vials of the dark liquid she had first slipped into my mouth during the operation.

It was the only thing I asked for. And I always asked for more.

My life was a haze for weeks as I healed and starved. Awful plasters were wrapped and rewrapped around my back and ribs. I could hardly move. My lashes fluttered as I watched the blue jays, red-crested turacos, and pheasants fly across the dome of sky with hatred and longing. On secret nights, I held Naomi the peacock and cried myself to sleep, the sobbing racking me until I reopened the wounds, rivers of blood leaking down my back.

After months, I would finally limp to the swing they had built for me among the ferns that decorated my domed cage. On that one evening, Alia had brought me a mirror to show me what I was becoming.

It was the first night of the *changeling*.

In the clearing where my carpets and pillows nested, pieces of myself glinted in the shards of the shattered mirror. I had refused to look at my wretched image and broken it violently the moment Alia had left. Off to one side, I floated back and forth on the swing, listening to the booming pops of fireworks overhead. I pushed myself higher and higher. In the lull of gravity at the top, I could almost feel the sensation of flying.

Almost.

I stared up at the bright lights of the celebrations arching across the sky. Balls of gold, green, and red exploded across the heavens, bursting free of themselves. A few seconds of transcendence, and then they disappeared forever, as if they had never existed.

I slowed, digging my heels into the dust. From the plasters around my wasted body, I pulled a vial of liquid and glugged the bitter potion until my vision clouded over. Wind chimes and fountains tinkled in my ears. I envied the dark night sky, its everlasting nothing. I had been having dreams of not being myself. Of not being anyone, of being nothing at all.

"Happy Day of Rising," came a sibilant, confident voice. I jumped. I heard hands dipping into the pools of water behind me. Favian could sneak up on you even on your best of days.

My captor circled around me.

He ran the water on his hand through his close-cropped blond hair, water from the fountain he'd gotten me for my birthday. Droplets gleamed from the new blue streak he sported. In his other hand he held a bottle of wine, an opener, and two cups.

I examined him through murky eyes. He wore riding boots and a slim leather jerkin with a high collar and black leather gloves. Behind his eyes was cold, naked, incomprehensible hatred. It was mesmerizing. Strangely, it made me feel ashamed.

"Wondering why I'm not out there?" He smiled at me with his perplexing malice. The birds were silent, cowed by the boom of the fireworks.

I gave no answer, but he continued anyway.

"I abhor days like this, darling," he said flippantly, hiding the darkness inside him. "I prefer to listen to you sing, but you don't give us your voice anymore." He put the wine and the glasses down and took the opener in his hand, kneeling in front of me to pour the wine. Naomi the peacock padded in the ferns behind him, curiously poking her head out.

"Oh world, where will you take me? Left and left and right and left," he sang softly. There was a hint of black irony in his voice. Did he know? He had bags under his bloodshot eyes, a grim spatter of stubble, a quirk in the corners of his smile. "A man can hope." Favian offered a glass to me.

I stared back at him from the ruins of myself, shrugged, and downed the acidic, stinging red wine. Immediately he took back the glass and refilled it, his hypnotic black eyes gleaming.

"I got a promotion." He grinned at my nonresponse. "Inquisitor of the *kai talan*." He toasted himself with jaunty grace. "Almost my father's position." He handed me back the drink.

I glugged the burning liquid. Again, Favian refilled it. I'd heard the story. His father had died on a pointless rock in the Flat Lands, a fanatic chasing Marauda ghosts. Naomi padded out from the ferns, raising one delicate foot at a time.

"Boo!" Favian cried, and the peacock bolted back into the ferns.

"The war goes badly," the new inquisitor continued, gesturing grandly with his cup. "The black rain continues to fall on the Flat Landers. The Marauda have declared it the end of times. Perhaps they are right!" The fireworks cracked above us. He saluted them.

"And yet we cannot eradicate the resistance of our own people. The Last Men, I'm sure you've heard of them. Almost impossible to locate, never mind *infiltrate*." He stopped and inspected me closely. "The Regent will have me join the Forgotten if I don't deliver every last one of them."

I laughed in his face. He watched me for a while, then suddenly his laughter joined mine. Our cackles echoed up into the dome, a wild, ugly sound.

"The Regent is somewhat obsessed with you," Favian managed at last, wiping the mirth off his mouth. "The miracle, he calls you." He swirled his wine while pacing around my small enclosure. "The girl whose dreams come true." He reversed direction and paced the other way. "He says someone is coming for you, but your rescuer will only return you to him. Thoughts?"

Through the dimly lit halls of my mind drifted cracked, faded images. Angry Boy. Old, broken dreams. Everything was shattering, the pain of staying together too much.

"Oh Saya, my bird in a cage." He swooped in to cup my chin.

For a moment, I felt he would kiss me. Instead he held the wine up to my lips. I drank, the wine dribbling down my chin.

He pulled it away and swigged down the last of it. "Maybe one day you'll sing again," he said, almost goading me. Did he know I'd used my songs to escape?

The fireworks exploded, setting themselves free to die in their own light among the stars.

I wanted to be anyone, anyone but myself. The cocktail of painkillers and wine made my head swim. My vision clouded as I saw him turn to leave me. I felt the dreams rising in me, that frightful need to disintegrate, to burst apart like the sizzle of light in the sky and disappear. Something ignited inside me, a burning, exploding fury that broke me apart.

I imagined Alia, her dusky skin from the Uncharted Lands, her whiplike braid, her slitted almond eyes, her compact stance and wide cheekbones, so sturdy and strong. The way she wore her uniform like protection and the duty that held her straight. If only I could be like her, a trooper who marched forward no matter the cost!

I felt myself *change*.

Favian stopped.

The air around the enclosure sang with strange, frightening vibrations, and the birds squawked and flew in distress.

"Saya?"

"Saya's not here anymore," I called to him in Alia's raspy voice, drunk and high on the pain. "Can't you see?" I stood up shakily, Alia's braid swinging down my back. "I have *infiltrated*, just as you asked!"

He squinted, hesitant, then stepped closer, shaking his head in wonder. "Saya! You are . . . a miracle," he whispered. I saw the fireworks reflecting in his light hair with its blue streak. It was like every particle inside me was splintering, like the fabric of me was ripping. My legs gave out.

I braced myself, watching as the skin and shape of my own fingers overlaid Alia's. I cried out in confusion, suddenly grasping what was happening to me, another voice coming out of my mouth as I was pulled apart.

"Saya," Favian said, standing over me and cupping my face up to him as it shimmered between my own and Alia's. "You're perfect."

His hypnotic eyes gleamed with ambition as he kissed me, my face shimmering between selves.

+ ✦ +

That was the beginning of the changeling: my need to not be myself, made real. The longer I was away from the last place I had felt my wings, the more unstable I became. And now, without the will to hold myself together and weeks without having returned to my cage, I could hardly hold my disguise as Ciana any longer.

Footsteps snapped me from my reveries.

Wiping tears from my eyes, I tried to put away the pain coming from the scars on my back. I retreated into the shadows under the barred window, vibrating with the changeling. The shredding was nearly unbearable. I looked at my hands. They were transparent, splitting apart, as if I was seeing double. Two selves overlaid each other, like ghosts from a past life.

The footsteps neared. A silhouetted figure cast long shadows in the firelight, shadows spiking like wings from the back. But it was not some imagined figure I saw in this new prison on the edge of the mountains. In the firelight, a face flickered that I never thought I would see again.

It was Alia.

I crouched in the gloom, hardly able to believe my eyes. My former friend and jailor was stiff, slightly hesitant, the burning torch casting theatrical shadows on her face. Her dusky skin from the Uncharted Lands was black and red in the flickering light. Her frank and exaggerated features, her flat nose with its aggressive nostrils, looked older down here in the dark.

She was in an unmarked military uniform, the armor she hid herself behind. Was she here to set me free again? My arms were shaking between different skins, my nails changing colors before my eyes. I could even feel my heart vibrating as if it too was growing.

"Saya?" Her voice had an edge to it. "Little bird? Could it be? By the Fates!" She was the only one apart from Favian who had seen me like this, the only one to recognize it—changing, my entire self begging to be another, shifting in real time. She'd seen me after they'd taken my wings, and it was she who discovered how I would become unstable within weeks of being kept from the memory of them, who made sure to bring me back to my cage to recover.

She knew that without anything to hope for, there was nothing worth keeping myself together for.

She'd seen me before that too, taken out to pasture like a circus freak, painted and decorated for the clapping crowds. She'd held the chain around my neck, forcing me to fly for the aristocrats of the castle, if only for a few stunted seconds, barely lifting into the air. And then she'd returned me to my cage, shivering, begging.

I could not speak. I just stood there, shaking, and then finally released a muffled scream as I pulled myself back into shape. I was still in my original self, somehow. It was Andreas's kiss; I just had to remember his kiss, and I could keep it together. Alia thrust the torch through the bars so that the light finally reached me. She gasped and held her hand over her mouth.

"What are *you* doing here?" I managed to say.

At my tone, her face hardened. She dropped her hand from her mouth, abrupt as a salute. She placed the torch in an iron holder and clasped her hands behind her back, her braid swishing like a long, prehensile tail.

Her unflinching almond eyes measured me, the same eyes that had forced me, held me, set me free. And there she stood, conservative, tough, dark skinned—just like the tiny villages in the Uncharted Lands we grew up in.

"Your partner told the leader you were a Marauda. That you are seeking asylum. That you met in the Skala Mines." She was speaking to me like I was a report.

"He had nothing to do with it! He is innocent!" He wasn't as stupid as I had thought. He didn't deserve this. I wrapped my arms around myself, my voice shaky.

"He said the same about you. That everything was his fault and that you should be freed." Alia was impassive, any concern she might have had herself hidden beneath her uniform.

I tried to breathe. Why would Andreas risk his life for me? "He was just my way to meet you, to get to you," I managed.

"You're the blond, aren't you?" Alia sank the blade in. "Why are you here, Saya?"

I was shaking again, the changeling flashing within me. My hair cascaded down my back in ivory waves, spreading onto the ground. All the color had bleached from my skin, hair, nails, and eyes as it had within my cage. The scars on my back ached like the day my wings were taken. I shrank into the corner, hiding my tears from her. I was falling apart again.

"Why are you here, Saya?"

"To feel . . . hope . . . again."

And I felt then, like a physical weight, the time and history between us. The moment replayed: her unlocking my cage, terror and trust in her eyes. Then the burning shame, the frosted fury, as I was caught and dragged from the sky. Her bruised face was purple and swollen where she had let me punch her. She was the one who locked my cage, closing the barred door of our relationship forever.

"The changeling . . . is it getting worse?" Had some humanity finally made its way out of her uniform and into her voice?

"I can keep it together," I gasped. "You're with the Last Men now?" I pulled myself together. I needed information. I had to survive this.

"I'm with the innocents." Alia shook her head slowly and frowned. Once before, she had defied her duty and set me free. Had I underestimated her courage? "Have you seen what's down there in the mines?" she asked.

The writhing horror of bodies clamoring over each other in the tears was fresh in my mind. "Yes," I replied.

"It's gone too far. I don't like what we are becoming . . . what we have become. I can't save Favian. He's become a fanatic, just like his father, obsessed with the Traveler." Finally, Alia appeared, grabbing the bars of my cage. "I found your cover in his files. Did you know he's . . ." Her voice trailed off. She knew about Favian draining the First Mothers, about the dreams he'd taken in the Regent's name. "This place needs to end. I don't care anymore," she said bitterly.

And when the girl loved him
She danced along the clouds.

It was the first song I had taught her, and I sang it now. The one she used to sing every day outside of Favian's quarters. The song that had made him see her, but never love her. Her eyes lit up with memories between us, sweet and bitter.

"You still sing like a bird in a cage. Oh, Saya. I haven't seen your real face since I . . ."

Since Favian had secretly recruited me after watching me shift into another self. I would have taken anything then, because I was broken—wishing with all my heart to be anyone, anything else, my wings taken from me.

"I thought I buried that girl." I got up, limping painfully into the light. "But Andreas, the man you met. He made me remember."

"Who is he? Is he truly the Traveler?" Alia was shaking her head. "He seems to have . . . known our leader in the Flat Times."

"I think he might be . . . Angry Boy." I had the changeling more under control now, my body less transparent in the firelight. But now I saw it clearly in Alia: pity.

"The boy from your dream is a fantasy, Saya."

"Then where did my wings come from?" I almost shouted. It was too painful to go on and I collapsed again in front of her. She let go of the bars and stepped back. "You need to get me out of here."

"I can't do that." Her hands were behind her back again, the armor of her uniform straightened back into place. "I don't trust you, Saya. I don't know who you are anymore."

"I'm me, can't you see?" I cried, holding up my hands to her. But they betrayed me, translucent, shifting in color.

"It's not you, Saya. Look at yourself. You can hardly hold yourself together."

I could deal with Alia's fury. But not her pity.

"You've been pretending to be someone else for so long . . ." she said, "you've forgotten who you are."

"Alia, please!"

"Remember what happened last time I helped you?" She picked up the torch, tears glistening in her eyes. "It only brought more pain." And then she marched off, as if unable to even look at me anymore.

*　✦　*

I lay in my new prison far beneath the earth, watching the particles rising off my palm like specks of moon dust. Soon the rest of me would follow. I was curled up in a pool of moonlight in the center of the small cell, my face streaked with the shadows of the bars.

Slowly disintegrating.

"I'll join you soon," I said to the moon.

Behind me, I heard footsteps. A key fitted into a lock. Turning. And then they came for me.

I flung my leg out, slamming it into their ankles, and turned like a wild thing on the floor, grabbing and dragging at the sandaled foot. The man fell heavily with a shout of surprise, and I was on top of him in an instant, an elbow at his throat and about to jab my fingernails into his eye.

It was him. Andreas's fierce starburst eyes of green and hazel looked back at me. One hand gripped my forearm and his other held my wrist as I lay mounted on top of him. With his touch, I felt warmth spreading through me, the particles settling, a pulsing heat in my chest and between my legs. I removed my elbow from his throat, panting, but he didn't take his hands off me. I was very aware of my legs around him and the delicious pressure I was up against myself.

"Hey," he said.

Our faces were almost on top of each other, my breasts brushing his tight shirt. My eyes flicked to his lips. How in the Fates did he get here?

⋆14⋆

ANDREAS

New Time

LYING IN THAT CELL, I fully expected my captors to finish the job they had started with their boots. Perhaps I even hoped they would finish off the ugly beast I was inside. That was the kind of wound that wouldn't stop bleeding. Instead, they loitered outside my cell, leaning against the bars. I heard the sound of a match, smelled the raspy scent of tobacco. It tingled in the back of my throat, mingling with the dust and coppery blood.

An older man spoke first, amused. "Here."

"I don't get it," a young voice replied, anxious. The same teenager from the mines. "The Magister is a holy man. His purpose is pure! He will bring down the Tree and set us free of the black parasite!"

"I second that," agreed a third, his guttural Skala accent as apparent as the wicked smile I could almost hear, "but . . . you knows he used to be *kai talan?*"

"Wha . . . ?" The lad started coughing as he inhaled and spluttered at the same time.

The veteran grunted as the Skala man dropped his punch line. "Until his wife and children was drained. A special dream they had!"

The kid kept coughing as I heard the veteran take a drag of the pipe. "Did he have a hand in it?" the younger man managed.

My throat was tingling now, almost uncontrollably.

"It was her dream of blue flowers that gives children to the Tree!" the Skala man baited, savoring the boy's reaction.

"No one knows the truth but the Magister," the older man growled.

I didn't know why but a sick feeling of dread curdled in my chest.

"Shh!" the Skala man cried as my stomach clenched and shuddered, the cough bursting from my lungs. He unlocked the door to the cell. "He's a lightweight like you," he jeered at the kid.

"Careful now, son," the veteran said to me. "Let's not have you wriggle like an eel on us."

I dragged myself to my feet as they took up their positions, two behind, the veteran in front, still smoking. The bag came down over my head again. We marched for a while and I quickly lost my sense of direction as I limped alongside them. Dreams becoming real. Women giving birth to flowers. Men becoming children. And me, becoming the beast I was inside. Finally I heard the sound of a massive door opening.

"Take off the hood."

The boy swept off the darkness and I blinked as the Skala warrior yanked on the iron ring of a great door. He wore a windswept jerkin and his hair was braided. Tattoos of horse heads and dragons ran along his gnarled forearms and up his right cheek. A short blade was strapped to his waist and he appraised me like a farm chicken.

The one I called the veteran was wide waisted and thick necked, bulging from his blue robes, with cauliflower ears and a graying widow's peak. He regarded me with a curiosity that belied his toughness, knuckle-dusters on both hands.

"Fierce lad," he said, with a hint of approval. "Are you truly the Traveler?"

I glanced behind me at the boy and saw a dark-haired and callow youth of barely sixteen with an air of regret about him. He smiled at me like he wanted to be friends, which made me frown, and I pegged him as a runaway.

I didn't answer.

Disappointed, the Skala man dragged me forward. "Let him see what we fight for," he said. There was pride in his voice.

"We call ourselves the Last Men, for we are the last men with souls," said the veteran.

I winced my way into the cavern with the boy behind me.

Within, the huge cave was sculpted like a cathedral with sweeping staircases and stained glass windows built into the ragged stone. The air smelled musty and old, full of secrets. Through an archway to my left was a wing full of bookcases upon bookcases, tilting and uneven. Another to my right held broken statues of men wrestling with dreamlike figures, ancient armor, and columns inscribed with forgotten languages. And all around us in the central hallway were paintings and portraits that seemed alive upon their canvas, interspersed with cracked vases. The richness and abundance of life, chaotically collected and displayed.

I shook my head in wonder as my gaze traveled up to the stained glass windows. Light cascaded through them, casting green, gold, and reddish beams through the air. On the ceiling nearly a hundred feet above was a circular pattern representing the rings of the universe, shaped like a cross section of a tree. At the center, where the World Trees lived, was the Dreaming. The ring of time that represented our own sparkled in gold. Had I traveled through that center to another point in our circle in time, into the future?

Straight ahead at the end of the central hall was a grand staircase flanked by heavy stone archways, and at my feet, along the central path carved through all these treasures, was written in great letters:

We believe in the Beginnings.

I was marched up the staircase, unable to believe that such a place existed beneath the earth. At the top of the stairs was a long carpet with a mystical maze decorated with golden birds. The path then led to an arched corridor lined with sculptures, dramatically posed men and women grappling, slaying, and being overwhelmed by fantastical creatures. The trio led me past them.

Finally we came to a gigantic wooden doorway and emerged onto a balcony, looking out into the expanse of a cave. An old man sat in a simple wooden chair with wheels on its heels. His misty gray hair was tied in a topknot in front, while the back cascaded into intricate braids with silver charms and flowed down the back of the chair.

The trio deposited me on my knees behind him. I winced and waited for him to speak. The air smelled sharper here, clearer.

"Tell me, friend, do you believe you are free?" His voice was rich with suffering, a severe baritone that softened at the end of his sentences, as if sighing. He seemed to have been contemplating the vast darkness of the cave and its stalactites. I saw now as I got closer that they were mineral deposits, faintly green.

What kind of question was that to your prisoner? Unsure how to answer, I gave the religious interpretation. "The Temple of Beginnings teaches that our choices are the dreams of the great World Trees, the Fates."

"And do you believe you are free to change the Fates' dreams?" he responded almost immediately, his voice again dropping off on the final word. A learned man, their underground leader, curator perhaps, or philosopher-king. The conversation had the feel of a sparring match, a dance with deadly consequences.

"We do more than change them. We create their dreams with our decisions."

The trio behind me bristled. What I was professing contradicted the old ways. The old man turned his cheek slightly. I didn't care anymore. If they wanted to destroy me, so be it. I'd hit back.

"Or perhaps, as the temples teach us, our decisions have already been dreamed for us. We simply discover them." With effort, he began turning his chair. The guards began to step forward, but he waved them off with an elegant gesture. "But of late, I myself have been wondering if indeed this orthodoxy has been broken . . ." He paused. "Your irreverence, it reminds me of . . ." As he turned, I observed his elegantly combed mustache, his decorated beard, the silver circlet around his brow, the swans on his sky-blue robe and scintillating blue eyes that could only belong to . . .

"By the shaved balls of the Fates!" I gasped. The Skala man behind me drew his blades and I felt the veteran looming.

The old man leaned forward, squinting over his mustache. "... Andreas?"

"Heron!" I cried out.

"It is I, the immortal Heron." His sunken lips split into an unlikely grin that crinkled his whole face.

"You're uglier than I remember, and even more uptight," I said. The veteran behind me pulled my head back and I felt a keen blade thrust to my throat.

"If I throw a stick, will this animal leave?" Heron asked, laughing. With a gesture, he waved the men off, and they let me go, not bothering to hide their reluctance.

"I didn't mean to offend you, but it was a welcome outcome," I replied. From the look on the veteran's face, he wanted more than anything in the world to stab me.

"*Zabibti Mai.*" *A brain the size of a raisin.* Our old joke, and we shared a grin.

"Oh, my friend, how I've missed you," he murmured, and there it came again, the rich weight of an unknown history. "What to make of you, a Traveler at this time?" At the name of the Traveler, the tension in the room thickened.

The nervous, dark-haired boy unchained me, excitement burning in his cheeks.

But I couldn't help myself, seeing Heron again like this. "Where is Leah?" I blurted.

The trio's tension told me I had overstepped. His twinkling eyes hardened and I saw glimpses of the young leader I had known, shadowed by the sorrow and compromise of a life lived in power. Was he the Magister I had overheard them gossiping about?

"My friend, you were right about Melasquez. He was a parasite. But it took me too long to see it." His voice cracked with bitterness. "Take me to the hallway?" he asked, recovering himself.

I took the handles of his chair and pushed him down past the sculptures in the corridors. The guards trailed us at a distance. What had happened to his family? Where was the Golden Boy I remembered? I was afraid to ask. He did not speak and my gaze lingered on the twisted torsos, the faces contorted in triumph and desolation, a vast surreal army of creatures all around us.

"I have never confessed this to any man," he said softly, "but perhaps the Fates have brought us together for a purpose."

I waited as he gathered himself, his voice soft as wind slipping through white birch trees.

"When the city rose, I joined the leaders in elevating the giant to Regent. When the magic weakened over time, I became one of the *kai talan* who did their duty. But the price . . . the price was . . ." His voice wavered and broke.

I stopped and knelt in front of him.

"I wanted . . . I gave . . ." He looked at me, and I saw my friend's withered mouth twist in agony. "Leah's dream of children. The blue flowers. To set an example. The Black Tree took that dream and . . ."

An image came upon me of his beautiful twin boys, naked and writhing, bathed in inky tears in the pit of bodies in the depths of the tunnels, their eyes the same blue as the poppies that grew around their mother. Forgotten.

"Now the Tree has flowers of its own under the mines, and Leah and the boys are . . ."

I hugged him. His bones felt skeletal and brittle in my arms, his wispy gray hair tickling my nose. The guards behind me bristled but stilled. Together we nursed the horror of it, and I cursed myself for once believing his love for her had faded.

"My friend, I searched for you in vain for decades," Heron said after a while, waking me from my reverie and removing my arms. We had stopped before a titan of a sculpture, a man splayed with his arms and legs in a perfect circle, holding around him a great serpent swallowing its own tail. "Tell me, why did you go into Melasquez's Rift?"

He looked up at me, his eyes piercing, their grief sharpened to a point. Something inside me sensed danger.

"The giant told me if I returned with my Traveler girl, I could save the village," I said. Heron nodded sagely, as if he had just confirmed a theory. "Wait. What do you mean, you searched for decades?"

I realized then what had been staring at me all along. "I never returned."

Heron pressed his hands together and touched them to his mustache, measuring me from under silver eyebrows. "You started all of this, Andreas." He watched me closely. I could not hold his gaze and retreated in confusion. "It was you who gave the giant the miracle that raised the city. You may not have returned, but you sent something back through the Rift. A dream so powerful, it lifted us all into the sky."

I felt my body go numb. "My Traveler girl?" I managed.

"Yes. You found her. And because you found her once, you will find her again. And all of this will happen again and again, for eternity, unless we stop it!"

I opened my mouth, but he cut me off, his eyes gleaming with a haunted light.

"Let me tell you a story, *Zabibti Mai*, from back home in the Strange Tales Tavern." Heron opened his palms, a wilted gesture of benediction. "It is one of our people's most ancient tales, that of the First Traveler."

His index fingers pointed at the heavens and he circled them as he spoke, the bracelets around his forearms jingling softly in the cave air. "A man loses his daughter in a tragic accident. A frightened horse rears in a storm and kicks her in the temple. Obsessed with saving her, this man spends decades researching the means to travel through time using the arcane arts. One day, he succeeds in opening a Rift into another time, arriving minutes before the accident. The storm is fierce, and in the lashing rain the man hurries to the town square where it happened. As he nears, he sees his daughter for the first time in the street, from beyond the grave. He leaps into the street and cries out, waving his hands to get her attention. She turns toward him, and his sudden appearance startles an oncoming horse, causing it to rear. She never sees the hoof that ends her life."

"And so the Traveler causes the very accident he sought to save her from," I finished the story for him, trying to keep my emotions in check. Had he just told me I was destined to die? I couldn't help glancing at the sculpture behind Heron of the naked man holding the snake devouring its own tail, his eyes raised to the heavens like a martyr. "It is a paradox, Heron. Was his travel not caused by the accident? Or was the accident caused by his travel?"

"Exactly so, *Zabibti Mai*." Heron joined his fingers together again, a wizened ancient in his wooden wheelchair. "The man caused his own escapable fate. And so it is with this new circle in time you have caused. By delivering your Traveler back to Melasquez, you have created a paradox in time. It is why the sky breaks."

The comet. The incandescent splitting of day and night.

"It is why the Marauda were right," Heron continued. "The forbidden way of the Travelers . . . creates loops that are never meant to exist."

The accusation of the mad soldier during the onset of the Dreaming came back to me: *"You are breaking the world!"*

"Enough philosophy!" I felt my temper rising, like a neglected beast raising its shaggy head. "Where is she, Heron?"

"The Regent holds her. You delivered her to him."

"I will never!"

"Which came first, my friend, the accident or the travel?" Heron countered.

I could not answer him.

"You gave him her dream, a dream so powerful it lifted these lands into the sky. And now the Tree feeds upon us all."

The wings on her back, arching like miracles as we made love in the turquoise waves, fireflies dancing around us. Hope that would one day lift her into the sky.

"These dreams must be returned to us!" Heron's voice came to a honed point, and under his grief sang vengeance.

"You speak of the Traveler prophecy?"

"I do! It is *my* prophecy." Heron saw the familiar rage flickering and feebly held his hands out to me. "Listen to me, Andreas, finding her is not just your goal but ours."

I just stared at him and the guards once more drew their blades.

"We must rescue her so you can never take her back." My friend's voice cut me like a rapier, his luminous blue eyes keen with suffering and intelligence. "So this future never happens again."

With a sickening lurch, I understood. It was me. Everything—all the pain in Heron's voice, Leah, his boys, all the writhing bodies in the pit, all the blank-eyed children of the village, all the combined suffering of this entire world—had been started by me and completed by my returning with the very girl Melasquez had requested!

If I had never come up with my grand, stupid idea of finding my dream girl, none of this would have happened. I turned away and held my hands over my face. "Fates' folly!" I whispered.

The chair creaked as Heron leaned forward. "Now tell me. Who is the girl we found with you?"

I froze at the question. Scrambling, I said the first thing that came to mind. "She's a Marauda. A refugee. She did nothing wrong. You cannot punish her." *The resistance was working with our old enemies?*—a guess I was staking her life on.

"You were kissing her?" The amusement in his voice was a lie. I was suddenly aware of the two guards who stood before me and saw that the Skala man had not yet sheathed his blade.

"I cannot explain it, Heron, but . . . I think . . ."

He waited patiently, lethally.

"I think . . . she is *her*." I turned to confront my ancient friend in his wooden wheelchair.

"How could that be?" he asked instantly, his eyes widening. "You forgot everything about her but for the tiniest details."

"I would know her, in this world or any other," I said helplessly. But would I? I had seen a girl change like no other, felt a vibrancy responding within me that rose dimly like a long-forgotten dream. But still, I had not recognized her; I had not seen her. What if I was wrong? With all my heart, I struggled to remember her face as she came down from the moon in that forest, her feet making puddles in the stars.

"It cannot be," Heron said slowly, "because the Last Men already know where she is, and it is not here."

The Skala behind me spun his blade casually, flashing in the stained glass light. Heron evaluated me, all the warmth in his piercing blue eyes forgotten, and I saw now the leader whose decisions had burned out the exuberance from his soul. Now it was only the harsh calculations of power, and I realized that he was seriously considering imprisoning his closest friend and had been during our entire conversation.

"Magister Heron." It was a woman's voice from behind us.

I turned to see a short, compact soldier with her hands behind her back. She had the deep dusky skin of the Uncharted Lands. How long had she been standing there? Had she overheard our conversation?

"We have the ambassadors' blessing."

Heron flicked his gaze to me and back to her. Then he nodded. More soldiers came from behind her, bringing an ornate trunk emblazoned with the red *V* of Marauda. The woman looked at me from slanted almond eyes and back to Heron.

"I'll allow it, Alia," he said.

She opened the trunk with a flourish, her dark braid whipping around her like a tail. Inside were two sets of ornately embroidered clothes, outfits for both a man and a woman. The colors were regal—royal red and gold—with layers of accessories, powders, and makeups, the vicious hallmarks of empire. The officer picked up a splendid red jacket with a high collar and gold along the inner lining, splashed with a single dark *V* patch that had been smudged downward.

"The blood is their way of wishing us good luck," Alia said wryly, the bronze bindings of her braid twirling in the cave light. She had a strong jaw, fierce nostrils, and a grappler's thickness to her neck and shoulders.

"By the Fates, our path is set." Heron seemed suddenly exhausted by the weight of what he had said, like a man going to war with the knowledge of how many he would send to their deaths. "Andreas, you must excuse me," he said, suddenly frustrated. "I have a rescue to lead."

I watched him being carried on the shoulders of his defenders. How the roles had reversed. Now he sought to rescue my girl and I was the helpless one. But whatever happened, I felt a surge of pride in him. My friend had done well, the future be damned.

The officer continued to regard me with suspicion. Ignoring her, I placed my hands behind my back and strolled down the corridor past the sculptures, examining them. She followed at a distance. I transferred my gaze to a mural painted across the walls, a grand, exquisitely detailed fresco. It depicted the second Marauda invasion. There were the soldiers, camped on the beaches of the Eastern Shore a mere five miles from the village, their yellow tents glowing with fires like a thousand crimson eyes.

Behind them, warships docked in the vast oceans, the ice chunks having melted during the summer in the gulf between our lands. The *V* of the Marauda standards flowed proudly in the wind, and below, the general in black steel stood upon pelts of bear and wolf. My eyes were drawn to the empty eyes of a helmet lying at his feet. These were the men who had come to destroy my people, for the heresy I had committed. For walking the forbidden way. In their minds, was there any greater honor than to save the world from breaking?

In the next panel, the soldiers rode up the Western Road into the wild of the ravines where I had climbed. The general proudly sat mounted on a warhorse, his mustard cloak billowing on the summit of a hill, his arm pointing bravely to our distant village. His soldiers marched into black-gray mists that reached from the ravines all the way to the Sentinel Mountains. The back of my neck prickled at the sight of the mist, curled in strange circles like ring mail, possessive, almost sentient.

In the next panel, chaos. The entire panel was set at an angle, as if the balance of the earth had shifted. Horses reared, ears flat, eyes darting. I could almost hear the whinnies, the Marauda shouting in fright as they were thrown from their saddles, weapons scattering. And around them, the cataclysm, a monstrous crack growing like an evil grin, cutting a massive semicircle through the ravines. It spread through the forests, the ground shifting as if the earth was reinventing itself. Gusts of dust vortexed from the fissures, billowing upward and blocking out the sun.

And then in the next panel, the landmass as far as the eye could see was elevating, cracking and lifting upward, black reams of earth and rock towering before the soldiers' cowering gazes, higher and higher. An upside-down mountain, the scale of it impossible. Boulders crumbled and fell, crashing into the crater. The inverted mountain floated as if a god had dug its foundations from the earth and lifted it on invisible palms into the sky.

Soldiers were scrambling back to avoid the grotesquely massive hole, craning their heads upward in holy terror. Others stared vacantly, unable to think, unable to respond to the cataclysm, their cheeks wet. Others seemed to slip slowly into catatonia, while still more ran, dodging falling debris. In the sky, black specks with yellow cloaks plummeted downward like rain. And once again, my gaze was drawn to a helmet of shattered steel, its single blank eye gazing.

"What is the name of this painting?" I asked, speaking with difficulty.

"It is called *Our Day of Rising*," Alia replied from behind me.

I turned around. She was observing me carefully, her hand not far from her blade. I walked back toward the trunk containing the two outfits, and she let me pass, ensuring I never got too close.

"What is this trunk then?" I said gruffly as I neared the chest. "We are working with the Marauda now?"

Alia frowned at my impertinence. "Since the land rose, they

believe they have been forsaken by their gods. I don't blame them. We have all had to reevaluate our worlds."

I rounded the chest. Inside, a regal red jacket was splayed open, the dark V-shaped stain on the inner lining. The same *V* they'd painted on the doors of our village, that they'd placed before us when they'd whipped us. It looked like blood.

"We vow to live now and now alone," I whispered.

Instinctively, I reached out to touch the stain. As my fingertips brushed the blood, the world swirled into red and darkness, lights moving at impossible speeds. I felt disembodied, floating, flung through time and space. The redness blossomed, moved, bubbled, and my vision cleared.

I saw a room with high windows, bookshelves, wolf-pelt carpets, and burning fires. Within it was an elderly man with a hand planted on a rich wooden desk. He was dressed in an immaculate mustard coat with swirls of gold, clean shaven in the way of the Marauda. He looked shaken.

In his hand, he was holding an invitation. It was elegantly penned on a scroll, stamped with swirling wax, and I could see that the insignia was the Black Tree. What was this vision? A memory of the man whose blood stained the jacket?

"We are invited. To the Floating City," the man said, hunching on his knuckles over the desk.

From the other side of the anteroom, a fierce woman with a garnet on her forehead and silver hair strode toward him, her crimson skirts flowing like petals. Her eyebrow lifted in disdain. "For?"

"Surrender."

Were these the ambassadors? The woman's lips twisted as she held his cheeks and pressed her forehead against his. The first rumbling of thunder came from the distance.

"I defend you against anyone and anything," the old man growled. Behind him on the walls were drawings of him: countless duels, all to the death, beginning with the *sai maga*, the ritual challenge at the couple's wedding. From his hip, the old man drew his blade, flipping it expertly and slamming it into the wood.

"Take my soul," said his wife angrily, caressing his face, "that we may follow each other in every world, in this present or the next." From the pocket of her dress she took a ribbon and twisted it around their wrists, binding them together, much as Rosana and I had once been bound, so long ago, on the banks of the river near the Village of the Second Sun.

"The vows of our Entangling." The old man grinned painfully.

Light flashed through the high windows in his office. Outside, rumbling began once more. His wife kissed him on the lips, searching, slowly drawing out his passion as she gripped the back of his head. Though they were old, their love still burned fiercely. The famous Marauda sensuality, even in the face of defeat. She dragged herself back with a charged breath, her mouth curling in contempt.

"We accept," she told him. They gazed at each other then, as they heard the first droplets of black rain begin to patter against the windows. To my horror, the vision took me to the windows. In the sky above this Marauda city were halos of clouds. They were the same black-gray hue as the mist from our village, the same curling ring mail that I'd seen in the mural of Our Day of Rising.

There were whoops and cheers resounding through the city as from every doorway came naked bodies. I could make out their glazed eyes, hungry and yearning. Hundreds stampeded into the black tears that fell from the sky, splattering their bodies as they danced.

The sound of their rejoicing was the sound of the world ending.

+ ✦ +

I was flung back into my own consciousness, my hand recoiling as if singed by flame. I felt the blood singing in my veins, burning with significance.

"Hey!" Alia's frown hovered over me, swimming between spaces. *"Hey!"*

I shook my head, surging to my feet, pushed her aside, and ran down the corridor of sculptures, past the terrible mural, and back into the main hall. I saw Heron on his wooden throne, paused before two advisers speaking urgently.

"Heron!"

He did not turn.

"Magister Heron!"

With the unfolding of an ancient, spotted hand, he silenced the two before him.

"I know the Marauda will be invited to surrender," I said, panting. The advisers' faces reverberated in shock. "That's your plan, isn't it?"

"Spy!" hissed Alia behind me, drawing her dagger and crouching into a fighting stance, the north-south defense. I didn't have time to be surprised as to how I knew that. I turned back to my old friend.

"Send me to the palace as the Marauda ambassador, Heron! I will find my dream girl for you!"

The bearers turned Heron around on his wooden throne. He held himself stiffly, harshly, his icy eyes penetrating. Once again, my freedom hung in his hands, and we both knew it.

"How?"

"You just told me," I snarled at him. "I already found her, or all of this would not have happened! The Fates will take me to her again!"

Muffled shock went through the advisers once more. Even Alia, I could sense, seemed flattened.

Heron alone had not reacted, except for the papery skin around his wrinkles, which seemed tighter and more translucent. "And your compatriot?" he asked.

"She is a Marauda herself. Who better than to play my wife?"

Heron smiled grimly. Whatever faith I had been banking on, his lay not in people any longer. I was reeling from the impact of the ambassador's memories and felt my will weakening.

"Alia, go interrogate her." He slingshot the order. "Make sure she is not Ciana of the Outer Rim."

"Sir!" Alia protested.

Heron stared icily at us from atop his wooden throne. For a second, I thought he would change his mind and send me back into the prison. Then he laughed, a short, harsh bark. At his signal, the bodyguards carried him down the stairs.

Letting out a deep breath, I nearly fell. But Alia pricked her dagger into the small of my back and pushed me toward the corner of the room. I was heady, still trying to process what I had seen, what I was seeing. Before us, more than a hundred fighters gathered around a vast map of the crescent-shaped Floating Lands laid upon the floor. The generals crouched, awaiting the Magister as I collapsed in the corner of the stairwell.

"Stay put," hissed Alia in my ear, giving me one final prick for good measure and then disappearing down among the soldiers. That was fine with me. My system was in shock. I felt as if I had experienced another person's life. The ambassador's experiences were fading slowly, replaced with my own perspective, layer upon layer.

Still, some flashes continued, but there were new images now: duel after duel, slash after parry after stab after disemboweling, every form of attack, every counter and thrust, every hour of grueling training. A first kill at thirteen. Rising through each challenge on the back of another's body, the blood-soaked path to a political career among the Marauda.

I watched blankly for some time while the generals gesticulated and moved wooden pieces around the map, Heron overseeing them in a high wooden stool. A part of me desperately wanted to believe that none of this was my fault. I found myself staring up at the ceiling, at the concentric circles like the rings of a tree. With the knowledge I had now, how could I possibly allow this to happen again? I could not lie to myself.

Slowly I began to take in what the Last Men were planning. And as I listened to their intricate strategy to take down the Floating City, it was clear it had been years in the making. They all knew they were facing overwhelming odds, and many of them would die. But while they spoke with clarity about almost every aspect, voices rose over one crucial detail.

"You don't really know where my dream girl is, do you?" I called out, standing with difficulty.

There was a deafening silence as all the heads in the hall turned toward me.

"Who is the tramp?" growled one of the generals, to muffled anger.

"A friend of the Magister, yet he remains so young?" another said scowling.

"The Traveler?" Whispers threaded through the crowd like spider silk.

"By your own reasoning, Heron," I shouted, shuffling forward, "Melasquez will show me to her."

The generals began to shout back at me in fury.

"I'm the key. You know it's true!"

"Silence!" Heron roared and pointed up at me. "I should have you thrown to the Flat Lands!" His finger began to shake slightly. "How do we know you will not repeat the past?"

"We can choose a different future, Heron. The world does not have to end like this." I gestured to the museum as I continued advancing into the center of the hall. "Is this not the truth of the prayer that we stand upon? A new beginning?"

I moved toward Heron and his soldiers clustered to block me. But he waved them away and I approached his wooden throne.

"All of this, Leah, the boys, the black rain. It is at my door. Whatever you did, whatever I did, I can't bring them back." I reached out my hand. "But we can make sure it never happens again."

"Andreas, you did not return." Heron's voice had no give in it.

"I know," I replied. And finally, I saw the tears in his eyes register with the tears in mine. Slowly, he leaned down, and his ancient hand clasped mine, as it had done so many times before in a different age.

"We believe in the Beginnings," he said, tracing the sign of a circle with his finger on his chest.

"We believe in the Beginnings!" roared the soldiers, repeating the gesture. The museum reverberated with their cry, the prayer echoing through the collected memories of our people. I held his hand and, for the first time in a long time, felt hope surge through me. Maybe, just maybe, I could do this. I could save everyone.

"Magister."

In the roaring excitement of the crowd, Alia had returned. There was a kinetic energy to the room now, and Alia did not quite understand. She waited dutifully for Heron's attention, which was slow to come among the ruckus. She stood patiently, repeating herself until finally he turned to her.

"The girl we captured, the stranger's compatriot. She is no spy."

"Is she Marauda?" Heron's intellect scythed into my fears.

"She looks like no one I've ever seen," Alia responded. Heron looked at me, and I knew he was wondering if she truly was the girl from the Dreaming.

"Will she work with us?"

My heart jumped. Alia looked pale. I couldn't meet Heron's gaze. Everything hung on the solid officer, with her braid whipping behind her. I wondered what Ciana had said to her.

"I believe . . . she will," Alia said at last.

Heron closed his eyes. I let out a breath I didn't even know I was holding. *Thank you, Alia, thank you!*

"Then may the Fates guide us," Heron said, cold and certain as an arctic wind.

✦

I asked Alia to take me to Ciana, and with Heron's permission, she guided me back out of the museum hallway and through the great door with its iron rings. A servant asked me if I wanted to eat and mindlessly I requested the soup Ciana and I had at the temples, with no crusts on the bread.

Then I followed Alia through the winding caves, the same way I had come blindfolded, in silence. Fatigue was setting in and my ribs ached where the boots had landed. All I could think about was Ciana. I could tell from the slope that we were heading to the surface. We stopped before a padded steel door. Two guards nodded to Alia, handing her a torch that burned the angles of her nose into sharp relief.

The steps were uneven as we ascended up into the dungeons. At the top were three bleak cells, the bars cold and rusted. Alia turned to me with pursed lips, gave me a set of tinkling keys, and gestured to the second. I trembled slightly as I approached. I couldn't see anything within except for a pool of moonlight streaked with bars of shadow. I unlocked the gate and stepped inside, blinking at a shape crumpled on the floor. I stepped toward it, about to speak and . . .

Something hit my ankle, knocking me off balance. The shape spun and gripped my heel, flinging me upward. My legs flipped into the air and I landed hard on the stone, a shout torn from my lungs. An elbow drove into my throat as the prisoner mounted me. Instinctively, I put my arms up to defend myself and . . .

Ciana.

She looked down at me in disbelief. As always when we touched, I felt the brightness in her igniting. Her hair glistened into white, her pale skin coalescing into honey. Her eyes swam from damp red into violet, gleaming with tears, incandescent like feathers of a bird catching the sun.

My hand was around her wrist as her forearm pressed against my neck and I didn't let go. I had surprised her and she was almost feral. Her legs were around my hips, her belly pressed against mine. There were only the flimsy rags she was wearing between us.

"Hey," I managed gently. Her eyes flicked to my lips and back.

"Everything okay in there?" Alia's voice arrested both of us.

Ciana jumped off me, rolling into the shadows. I rose too, dusting myself off. The officer stepped into the doorway of the cell, two guards and two servant girls behind her. Ciana was glaring at her with naked hatred. What had gone on between these two?

Alia refused to return her look, holding open the door to the cell. "Hurry up." She turned on her heel.

I went over to Ciana and offered her my hand. She shivered

and looked up, all the violence melting from her. Something had shaken her deeply.

"It's okay," I told her, pulling her up. She was so fragile in that moment, vulnerable, delicate. Suddenly she hugged me tightly. I stroked her hair as she buried her head in my shoulder.

"You found me," she said into my chest.

"Follow us!" Alia ordered from outside, her voice strained.

I took Ciana's hand and together we walked out of the cell. I could feel the relief shudder through her as we stepped out into the tunnel.

"Let's go," said Alia, her voice softening at last. She added to the trailing servants, "Make sure they follow the procedure. No deviations."

Ciana said nothing the whole way out of the cells.

She didn't let go of my hand.

Alia led us through tunnels upon tunnels, and I felt as if my feet were about to fall off. Finally, we stopped outside a small doorway made from richly carved planks of hardwood. As the doors opened inward, a soft scent wafted through, a blend of patchouli, praline, red berries, and vanilla, celestial, delicious, and voluptuous.

The scent led us into a long, narrow room lined with niches where small candles had been placed. Two more female servants awaited us with scented towels. I looked at Ciana and finally she let go of my hand with a tiny, embarrassed smile. I held the towel to my face, inhaling deeply after a small sigh escaped me. I rubbed the grime away, all the dirt and fear of the last two days, and put the cloth back into the wooden bowl.

We were ushered through another doorway, where the servants who had brought us here were waiting with unfurled ribbons. Around us were colorful soaps; rich, gleaming oils; liquids; hundreds of bright crimson roses; and buckets of hot, foaming water that wafted with the heavenly scent that had drawn us inside.

"Give in to your senses, lord," the woman said, kneeling and offering me the ribbon. When I did not react, she stood and began wrapping it around my eyes, blindfolding me.

"Please relax, lady," I heard the other say. Then I felt two sets of hands gripping my clothing. I grunted in alarm, my ribs protesting as they pulled off my shirt.

"We will clean you now," I heard her say, as hands stripped off my pants. I heard a small squeak, telling me they were doing the same to Ciana. "I am sorry, lord and lady. We must follow instructions."

I stiffened when the warm sponges first touched my bruised ribs; the foam dripped over me. I winced as they poured the hot water over my shoulders, the scent rushing up my nostrils, guilty and sensual.

"This is the gift of Illana, the forbidden roses of the Sentinel Mountains." The effect of the flowers was a numbing warmth spreading over my aching body, the magical heat unlocking the muscles of my back, the pain of the harrowing journey melting away.

"Uhhhhhh . . ." I heard a deep sigh of pleasure next to me, and inexplicably the blood rushed to my loins. *No!* This would be a terrible time for that! I was exhausted, and yet . . . *Go blank, mind, go blank!* I took a deep breath, praying to the Fates for mercy.

Thankfully, it was granted.

I felt the relaxation course through me like a wave. The essence of the roses was as magical as they had promised. I surrendered to the warm water, the delicate heat through my hair . . .

My mind conjured an image of Ciana, blindfolded in the steam, bubbles dripping from her body in the candlelight, arms raised above her head to hold her hair, lips slightly open in pleasure . . . I heard a muffled giggle, and my cheeks burned in shame. I prayed to the Fates that the bath would end quickly and with a towel.

But instead, I was asked to take a forearm. The soles of my bare feet padded across bamboo sheets as before me I heard a gentle bubbling. I felt another rush of sensation, my whole body hot and aching. Were these flowers only for healing or for other things too?

"Please enter the spring, lord and lady." The servants guided us into the water, my feet gripping onto small stone steps. I felt petals parting around my ankles and the scented bubbles running over my legs and then over my chest. Then came the sound of footsteps retreating and a door closing.

I felt Ciana swimming softly, searching for the limits of the pool. Reaching out my hands, I could feel the pool around me was small and rounded, made of natural rock. I heard the soft lap of the water coming near me and stopped exploring immediately.

"You can take it off now, Andreas," she said softly. Her voice was breathy, flushed.

I removed my blindfold. Ciana's hair was slicked back, her collarbone glistening. Moonlight cupped the top of her breasts, the rest of her hidden by the dark bubbles. The hot springs were dappled with red petals and open to the night on our left, the stars shining down upon us. On our right, a muted red glow came from embers placed in urns.

"It's beautiful," I said. I had almost said she was beautiful. She seemed to smile, but I could not be sure in the dark. A night moth floated in from the night and danced above us, then fluttered away into the stars. I heard the dark liquid swishing with her underwater movements, the moonlight dancing over the little waves.

"My name is Saya," she said. "My . . . real name."

"Saya . . . Saya . . ." I tasted the name twice. It brushed along the tongue and lifted. I liked it. I liked that she had told me.

I rubbed warm water over my beard and tried to remember my Traveler girl's name, but I'd forgotten it, of course. Only fragments remained, sensations, evaporating like mist—how she made me feel, not even her name. It was like being tormented by memories of a previous life, one that both was and wasn't mine. I knew nothing about her, and I couldn't help myself. "Who are you, Saya?" I tried to keep the question as gentle as I could.

"The girl whose dreams come true." She dipped her head backward and soaked in the water, her long arms making delicate ripples in the light. I watched the light glistening on the curves of her breasts.

"A faerie?" Faeries dreamed of love. But why was I thinking this?

"I'm not sure." She sighed and lifted an elegant leg out of the water, then disappeared under.

The way she said it, it was familiar. Wasn't this the same thing the girl from the dream had said? Suddenly, I panicked. What was coming toward me under the bubbles? But then she appeared, a safe distance away. I let the moment hang between us, let the hot bubbles massage my body as I surrendered to the warmth and closed my eyes, just breathing and letting go.

"You came back for me," I heard her say after a while, her voice thick and heavy.

"I told you in the caves I would never abandon you." I felt the water moving and opened my eyes. Now she had drifted close to me, within arm's reach. I could almost sense her under the water. I could see her sad, beautiful smile, see the crimson petals on her chest.

"What did you mean down there, 'show your true self'?"

What I had said, right before I had kissed her. Why was she

remembering it? Right now, right here? She was drifting closer. The bubbles ran up my body and hers, popping gently and insistently between us.

"I've always been able to see you. Just like this." We were so close now. I could feel her brushing against me. "From the first moment we met."

The door opened, and the servants came in. "Your dinner awaits."

But instead of moving, Saya just stayed there, looking over her shoulder at them. She turned her dazzling eyes back to me, alive with mischief, the magnetic aching driving me crazy.

"We are coming," I said, unable to hold her gaze.

"Did you peek?" she said.

"When? No!"

"Liar," she said. "Don't. Move." She ran her hands over my eyes, closing them. I heard the water dripping from her as she walked up the steps into the clothes held out by the servants.

I kept my eyes shut, grateful to cool the throbbing pressure between my legs.

Once she was gone, I levered myself out of the fragrant water. Although my loins still tingled, I had myself under control. Still, the vision of her dripping in the moonlight lingered. I slapped myself a few times on the cheeks before I took one of the robes waiting for me. Once we'd exited the pools, one of the servants knelt and then led me back to our room. My heart rate rose again as I knocked on the door.

"Come in," I heard her voice say softly.

I slipped inside. There was a king-sized bed with white curtains hanging from the bedposts, carpeted floors, and the ambassadors' chest. A table glinted with plates covered with steel domes. I saw the glimpse of her thigh slipping between the folds of a cream robe as she lit a candle and adjusted her hair in the mirror.

I strode to the bed, pulling off two pillows and reaching underneath for the extra quilt to set up on the floor.

"If you've lost your appetite, I think I have it." She was amused as she walked past me. She sat down at the table expectantly, crossing her lean golden legs. "I can't be held accountable for what I do when I'm hungry." She shrugged, taking off the steel lids. "Oh . . . how?" she muttered, bemused.

I saw the bread then and smiled to myself. They had cut off the crusts, just as I had asked them. "I noticed in the temple, with the kids," I said, laying out my blankets on the floor. "That's how you like to dunk your bread in your soup."

I sat down opposite her, taking the lid off my meal. She took a strand of hair and tucked it behind her ear, unable to look at me. I grinned in satisfaction. Got her on that one. Slowly, shyly, she raised her violet eyes to meet mine.

Together, we would journey into the unknown tomorrow, and who knew which stars would guide us home?

·15·

SAYA

New Time

. . . *I* WAS THRASHING IN THE *heat, my fingers twisted, gripping the gossamer sheets around me as the ship swirled and rocked on the waves. I raised my hips and arched my back, trying to make it stop, but it was only building as the swells crashed and rose. Then I fell out of the bed.*

Thunder reverberated, and I could feel the intensity in the air seeping into me. I got up as the ship swirled, and held on to the cabinet for balance. I could see myself in the mirror—my lips puffy, lipstick smudged, cheeks flushed, long white hair falling in waves down my honey shoulders and back, tickling me. Beads of sweat tingled on my chest, sliding downward.

I gasped and ran out the door as he came after me, grabbing and tearing the fabric of my dress. I turned to hit him, but he was on top of me, my thigh wrapping around his hip, his lips on my neck, lighting the electricity that surged and tingled between my legs as the ship bucked in the storm.

I gripped his neck, aching to surrender. "No!" I shouted in fear as the ship rocked. Moaning, I slapped him and twisted free. I felt my dress rip; his foot had stamped the fabric to the floorboards, and my breasts and nakedness were free to him as I ran . . . He caught my arm and pulled me back, his hands possessing me from behind, one around my throat. His lips pressed against my shoulder. Warm salt water sprayed across our bodies, and pleasure parted me, slipping over me, rocking as the tidal swell built inside me.

But I could not take it, and I elbowed him in his stomach and ran once more toward the ladder, then scrambled into the sky. The winds were gale force, swirling my hair and spraying me with warm ocean surf, the ship like a toy within the whirlpool drawing us deeper and deeper. I turned to see him emerge from the galleon's hold, muscular and lithe. I backed into the mast and cried out as he grabbed me.

"We are sinking," I whispered into his mouth as his warm tongue took us swirling downward. My legs wrapped around his hips as he hoisted and entered me with a ferocious hunger. The pressure sucked inward into ecstasy while the ship fell apart beneath us into the pumping foam, leaving me gasping as my wings burst forth from my back . . .

"Saya! Saya! Are you all right?" Andreas was shaking my shoulders, his green eyes wide with alarm. He was shirtless, his hair hanging loose, the gold morning light casting him in sharp relief. And way too close. He had shaved like all Marauda men, and finally I could examine his big jaw, the fresh stubble.

"I'm fine! I'm fine," I said and clutched the sheets against me. I was sweating, my chest still heaving. And between my legs . . .

"Okay," he said, removing his hand quickly. "Thank the Fates! You were . . . changing colors in your sleep and . . ." He was acting extremely awkward.

"You were watching me sleep?"

He couldn't look at me, and I saw the heat in his cheeks. Oh, no way! Did he know?

"No, I . . ." he mumbled and retreated back toward the table. The morning light was coming from a secret porthole I had not seen last night, bathing the lace curtains in a gentle glow. I could see his wide back through the gauzy fabric. And I couldn't stop looking.

When I was more sure of myself, I got up and went to the mirror. My hair was a tangled mess of white, but my skin at least was glowing. I smiled, mischievous, radiant, a little puffy maybe because . . . I bit my lip and winced. I was still delicately throbbing down there. But once more, not a trace of the changeling . . . somehow. Everything miraculously in order. I fixed my hair. Calm now, and lovely. "Nice to see you again," I whispered to my reflection.

"Saya?" I loved the way he said my name. I loved that he knew it—so few in this world did. "The Marauda, they . . ."

"Have certain traditions," I finished off. I approached him as he fiddled with the buttons on his ivory dress shirt, elegant but too tight for him. "To duel those who insult our union." That it was a barbaric custom didn't stop me from teasing him that he'd need to fight for us. I looked at the muscular hunch of his shoulders, wondered what it would be like to run my hands down his back.

"It's not just that," he said, still fiddling with the button.

Oh? He was thinking of it too. The infamous public passion of their people. "Relax. Think of it like a job."

He turned around, his big fingers helpless with the button. Gently, I pushed them aside and slid the smooth wood into the perfectly shaped hole. I could feel his energy, dark and submerged, holding itself back.

"We have to practice," I said, resting my hands on his chest when I was done, looking up into his eyes, lingering in the green depths of him, starbursts flecked with warm hazel. I put my hands around his wide neck and swept them up into his hair, around the nape, and he wrapped his around my waist. I ran my fingers up his scalp and tilted my lips up to him, pressing my belly to his pelvis. Our gazes were locked, afraid of what might happen, daring it to happen, begging for . . .

He kissed me, and it was long unsatiated, slow passion building between us, overwhelming, hands gripping and pulling. I was breathless, his low, deep groan sending me into a frenzy. And then the kiss slowed, becoming tender and more vulnerable, exploring tongues and mouths, opening gently to one another, and deep within the changeling, a joy alighted in my body that danced in colors like a rainbow. We pulled away together, and I rested my forehead on his cheek.

"I wanted . . . to ask you . . ." he said, his voice husky, his hands traveling over my shoulders all the way to the small of my back, tracing me protectively. "What are these?"

I realized then the lines he was drawing on me. My scars. He must have seen them at some point last night, or this morning. In my disguise as Ciana, he wouldn't have.

It's him! It must be him! He's Angry Boy! But why doesn't he know me then? He doesn't remember I had wings? Angry Boy gave them to me, so it can't be him . . . Why didn't he respond to the poem? It doesn't make sense!

I stepped away. Maybe I should tell him. But how could I? I looked into his confusion, his bewilderment, and felt the same within myself, and it infuriated me. Suddenly I hated him for making me feel vulnerable.

"A long time ago, I was naive enough to hope . . ." I shut down, pushing past him to the trunk of clothes. I distracted myself by exploring the elements of my disguise, holding up an exquisite red velvet dress. "But now I know I will never escape."

I selected lacy white underwear, pearl earrings, a gold tiara, and the makeup box and took them to the mirror, then drew the curtain and stripped off my robe. Anyone who made me feel weak was my enemy.

The undergarments were too big for me, but as I pulled them onto my body, I opened myself to the pain of the changeling and melded myself to them, building the shape of me layer by layer. "I will always be in a cage. The scars are my proof."

"You need to be your true self. No matter the cost."

It was amazing how free he was of all encumbrances. He would do what he wanted no matter the cost, no matter what anyone said or told him. He was himself, unapologetic, wild and true, however destructive that would be to himself and others.

"Even prison?" I turned to look at the ragged oyster-white-and-pink rips in my back, the stitch wounds even now barely seeming to hold them together.

"Not being yourself is prison."

"Even dying?" I glared at myself over my shoulder.

"Doesn't lying to yourself every day feel like you're dying?"

I hid the scars with the undergarments and examined the fit in the mirror, molding to my disguise, the changeling ripping me apart inside, a million tiny tears. And through the pain, a little voice in me spoke. The voice of a young girl I hadn't heard in a long time. "What if you could? What if you really could?" she asked.

If I stayed close to him, the changeling wouldn't kill me. I didn't need my wings back. We could run away together, escape to the Outer Rim, into the ground, maybe even to the Flat Lands, maybe . . . I saw glimmers of her then, the girl who had stepped down from the stars in her dreams and rescued that boy from himself. A girl filled with hope, the same hope that made wings bloom from her back.

But then I remembered, and all the resentment for the deep emotions I could not control inside me glistened in my eyes.

"You have to go back." I snapped open the makeup box and ghosted my face in foundation, blanking out my features. Whoever was looking back at me, her purple eyes looked frightening, alien. "To your time. With your dream girl." Why did I do this to myself? It was the whole point of this mission, the whole reason for him being here.

There was silence.

"Magister Heron says all this has already happened. And I did not return," he said flatly after a while.

"So why are you doing this?" I drew the eyeliner in sharp black wings, overlaid with smoky shadows with hints of smoldering purple. "Are you trying to get yourself killed?"

"If I die for others, isn't that a worthy cause?" He sounded angry.

I blinked twice at the mirror. This was not the first time I had seen him like this. I remembered him in the Temple of Beginnings: *I would die for her. Isn't that enough?* Why was he so eager to give his life away? Did he, on some level, think he deserved it?

"Andreas, whatever it is, you have to forgive yourself," I replied quietly, setting the makeup back on the cabinet. I hated him for being so irrational, but still I didn't want him to . . .

"It's nearly time to go. Are you ready yet?" he growled.

"Read your brief," I snapped back at him. "And let me get ready." He was unbelievable, blind to himself, stupid, and egotistical. A typical man.

I went over the plans in my head as we had together last night, contouring my cheekbones and trying to calm myself. It was a simpler problem than Andreas. Then I clasped the necklace and placed it over my collarbones, testing the fit.

It was an interesting approach. The resistance believed that the biggest weakness in the Floating City lay in its beginnings—so typical of the faithful. Almost a parody.

Exactly how the Day of Rising had happened was the most closely guarded secret on the Floating Lands. No one except the Regent himself and perhaps the Sifter, the ancient seer who bathed in our collected dreams at the base of the Tree, knew what truly launched us into the sky. The Tree itself was too immense to destroy. And while the Magister's theory of returning dreams was a fascinating idea, it could go so wrong.

The plan was twofold.

First, their intelligence told them that Andreas's so-called dream girl was in the Maiden's Tower. Using distractions during the official surrender ceremony of the Marauda ambassadors, they would secure the automaton bays and break into the tower. The scale of the infiltration told me there were many more spies inside the castle than either Favian or I had realized.

"Draw them to the Maiden's Tower," I remembered Favian hissing in my ear on the train. No, they were doomed. I teased my hair with a comb and then began twisting it into a crown braid, letting some fall over my cheeks and the rest cascade over and between my scars.

The second part of the plan relied on the Regent sowing the seeds of his own downfall. Posing as Marauda ambassadors, we would gain an audience with the Regent and invite an introduction. If indeed Andreas was the Traveler, the giant would bring him to his "dream girl" to restart the time loop.

But once we had this confounded girl's location, we would launch a signal flare hidden in Andreas's boot. Alia would swoop in to our location with backup, then we would kidnap the girl and escape. And perhaps our dreams would be returned to us. Faith was their biggest folly—the idea that the Regent himself would offer her to us.

If indeed this girl was the miracle sent back to the past on Our Day of Rising, what was to stop the Regent from killing Andreas and forcing her return anyway? Who was to say it hadn't already happened?

It was a suicide mission, a foolish gamble.

One final look in the mirror. Perfect on the surface. But underneath my disguises, all the layers of me . . . fear. But for the first time since I could remember, I was more worried about someone other than myself.

✦ ✦ ✦

It was a biting morning outside. Puffy clouds floated on the back of a crisp wind, the fresh blue of the sky welcoming my heart after so long underground. Vines camouflaged the opening of this long, flat cave, and I tried not to see them as prison bars. For now, they hid us from view.

Alia was waiting for us in the cave entrance, dressed in the black tunic of the Tree's corsairs. Other resistance fighters stood ready nearby. They whistled and clapped when they saw us. We walked through the curtain of vines and out into the courtyard together, the streaks of sunlight catching the resplendent red velvet of my dress. A sumptuous crimson wedding train swept along the ground behind me, and beside it, my sleeves reached all the way to the floor, the scarlet material embroidered with sparkling glass beads and red crystal. The white lace collar's deep V-neck opening dipped almost to my belly. Golden filigree flowered from the red velvet bodice of the dress, and pearls tinkled from my ears. From my neck hung the golden chain of the Marauda that signaled I was married, and finally, a ruby sparkled between my eyes.

If I wanted to be a princess for a day, I would be one, the Fates be damned.

Beside me, Andreas looked magnificent, although I refused to tell him that. He wore a deep mustard tailcoat with an embroidered pattern of gold oak and palm leaves down the seams, which gleamed down his chest, cuffs, and back, resplendent in the sun. He'd shaved in the tradition of the Marauda, and now I could see his face, acutely handsome and intimidating. The high red collar round his neck glinted with scrolls of gold leaf, and the crimson *V* of the Marauda was embossed on his right breast. Tight white breeches and supple leather riding boots completed the outfit. He was carrying both our bags.

I curstied, and Andreas did an awkward bow. The soldiers cheered and whooped.

Alia greeted us, all business. "Ideal flying conditions, Your Excellencies. We'll dip under the city and come up through the cloud banks on the other side, cloaking our approach. They'll be waiting for us at the palace."

"Flying conditions?" asked Andreas, alarmed.

"How did you think the ambassadors got here?" I said tartly. "A ladder?"

"I'm not getting in . . . that." He dropped the bags and pointed.

The automaton looked like a squat boat with skis attached. Instead of billowing forward, the sails around its mast were shaped like disks, spiraling up in a corkscrew pattern. Inside was a complicated spring-loaded system with a series of wheels and a lever, which, when twisted, would spin the corkscrew sails round and round and lift the craft up into the sky. The *Interceptor* was painted in blue along the starboard.

"You didn't tell me he was such a wimp," Alia said to me. From beneath her guarded gaze and her corsair's uniform, there was a hint of the sisterhood that had once bound us. Andreas glanced at us in shock, as if there was something he was missing. There was. Alia might have left me in that cell, but she'd vouched for us. In truth, my heart ached to forgive her. But Andreas would not be so lucky.

"Will you load the baggage, Rock Muncher, or are you royalty now?" I said. He walked tentatively up to the automaton, approaching it as if it would attack him. The soldiers helped him with the bags, trying to reassure him. He did not look convinced.

"You recovered," Alia said. We both looked after Andreas, meaningfully.

"Thank you." I meant it.

"It's good to see you again," she replied. "To really . . . see you." She used her chin to gesture to my outfit, but I knew she meant more than that. We shared a smile, and I was grateful. She followed my gaze to the ship.

"The *Interceptor*," I said. The same one that had caught me. I'd have recognized it anywhere.

"It will have a new story this time." She turned to leave.

Suddenly, I felt nervous, jumpy. "Alia!"

She turned with a look that said, *Don't make me regret this.*

"Favian told me," I said. "They *want* you to go into the Maiden's Tower."

Her jaw tensed, her posture stiffening as her armor came back up. "When I see that flare, just make sure you're not the one closing a trap," she replied.

I cursed under my breath. She still did not trust me. I should have used the term *us* instead of *you*. And I shouldn't have mentioned my relationship with Favian.

I saw her again, crestfallen against the bars of my cell.

"How did it go, with the song?" I had asked.

We'd been practicing for weeks. Alia had a soft, haunting voice, so unlike her hard exterior, the uniform of duty she wore even on her days off. "He came to sit next to me on the second day. Do you know what he said? He said it reminded him of our beautiful bird in the cage." And then she had turned her back on me.

I mounted the steps of the automaton, watching Alia strap herself in on deck. I put the images of the nets that had once hung from the craft out of my mind. *Forgiveness only goes so far, Alia. But if I can embrace you, can't you do the same for me?* With the rebels' help, I climbed the ladder to our seats below deck.

Andreas was pale faced and staring out of the open doorways. "Won't we . . . fall out?"

"Ugh," I said, forced to sit next to him. The soldiers began cranking the spring, and soon there was too much noise to speak. The mast began to turn, and the sails began to corkscrew, faster and faster. Andreas's knuckles went white.

And then that magical feeling, the joyous impossibility of lifting up and above the earth and rising and rising. Oh, Fates, how much I missed this! Andreas had his eyes squeezed shut. I elbowed him. He saw my expression and just looked miserable. It had been so long!

And that was when we popped off the crescent's edge into the glorious freedom of the day. The morning sun danced through the clouds, and we were far and away and turning, turning, and then the entire magnificent miracle of the Floating City came into view. The great Tree was cloaked in clouds, the metropolis sprawling beneath it and winding in layers up the trunk. Below us were the mountains, the train track now tiny, and now all the waterfalls were visible, sparkling, spilling over the edge of the land.

We looked down on quarries and mining craters where once the lush green forests had stood; the snow-swept caps of the Sentinel mountain range, almost purple; the plains and wheat fields and fog banks. And all roads led to the great Tree, towering above it all, with its circular layers of twinkling lights and tiny homes.

And then we dipped below, into the clouds, a rush of gray gulping us from view. I hoped Alia knew what she was doing. The visibility was now close to zero—one mistake and this fragile machine would take us all the way to the Flat Lands. *Just breathe. Trust her. There is nothing else to be done.*

"I never thought I would fly again," I said.

"I preferred our date underground," he grumbled. It made me smile.

I took the time to prepare myself, deleting my emotions, submerging, drowning myself to embrace that fearless woman I had made in the depths of my mind. Nika, ambassador of Marauda.

When we finally broke from the clouds, twenty or thirty automatons awaited us, flying the black-and-silver flag of the Tree. They flew close enough to identify our craft, and with a short salute they fell alongside, escorting us up the gargantuan rock face of the city and up over the edge. Up close, the Tree was even more monstrous than I had thought possible, blocking out the sun. Was it still growing? Were we falling each year because it was getting physically too heavy for the city?

We rose farther, above the sprawling homes. I spotted a few people far below us glancing up at the fleet of automatons trailing black flags, but of course, they quickly went back to their business with barely a hint of curiosity.

Then we were above the first ring, where the wealth of the aristocracy gushed from mansions and balconies. We climbed higher, to the second ring and the palace that surrounded the Tree in an elegant spiral of minarets ever climbing to the tips of the great door, the only way into the Tree itself.

My heart quickened. The last time I was here, it was as a circus animal.

Next to me, Andreas took a deep breath. I took pity on him and squeezed his wrist. He didn't let go as we approached the landing strip, a balcony lined with poplar trees leading into the heart of the palace, which reared a hundred feet into the sky, built into the trunk above us. Awaiting us was a small procession of lords and ladies dappled in the court fashion of blues, blacks, and silvers, flanked by the plate-armored palace guards.

Alia took us in smoothly, landing with the same precision as she had a hundred times. Wasn't she nervous in the least? "By the hairy arsehole of Fate," Andreas mumbled, making me snort. I began unstrapping. He followed my lead. This was our last moment together, as ourselves. Who knew what the future would bring?

I turned to him, fixing a displaced strand of hair. "Remember, Ambassador." I looked up at him. "I am yours, wife in body and soul." He nodded, nervously. "We are partners, no matter what comes."

I took his hand and we walked toward the ladder. The angle of the light was falling, the particles of dust hovering . . . It was just like my dream this morning. But there was no time to think of coincidences. He held the train of my red dress, and I emerged as elegantly as I could. Alia was waiting for us at the ship's rail, and beyond that I could see the balcony lined with trees—the same balcony where, barely a girl, I had fallen backward, arrows whizzing past my heart.

"Are you ready?" Alia whispered.

As one, we nodded.

"Lords and ladies of the court, may I introduce His and Her Excellencies, the Living Edge and the Jewel of the East, the Overseers of the Karaka, the Burning Keep, son of Viruc and daughter of Hella, Ambassadors Viruc and Nika of the Marauda."

"Claim me," I whispered. He held me possessively around the hip. Alia let down the ramp, and we descended into the burbling crowd. I held myself tall and proud, chin high, grateful for the simple slippers I had chosen underneath the dress. There was a tinkling of applause and champagne glasses rose.

A foppish man with oiled gray hair dyed blue at the temples and a silver suit awaited us with hand outstretched. Ambassador Marlow. The ladies simpered, gloved hands over their mouths and richly powdered cheeks, waving fans. We were causing quite a stir. I stepped down onto the same balcony where they had almost killed me and haughtily ignored Marlow's offered hand. Andreas followed my lead, glaring at him. Smoothly, he retracted it in an elegant circling gesture, as if inviting us in.

How long had these rich survived on the dreams of the poor? I recognized some of these parasites and stared them down. As each in turn looked away, I wondered if they could imagine I was the same emaciated girl who had once been paraded before them, fluttering a few meters above the ground, a chain around my neck, all pigment lost from being kept in that barren cell. Now I stood before them radiant in royal crimson and gold, sensual and invincible.

Seated at the wall I saw the veiled abaya of the Sifter. The ancient crone had her hands crossed on her lap, the veil hiding her expression. But she leaned forward, craning her neck at us, as if in distress. What was she doing here? I wished she was still in her web of pooled dreams in the spine of the Black Tree.

"Your Excellencies, you are most welcome! How was your journey? I am Ambassador Marlow. Please." He gestured and a young serving man offered us both glasses.

I looked at Andreas hungrily, and he nodded. Together we took the glasses and in a single sip, downed the liquid. Andreas thanked the ambassador, who seemed to be taking everything in stride.

"You are so young!" he said to me. "And you have reached great heights already. Your lords must hold you in the highest regard."

I smiled archly. He tried a different tack.

"What do you think of the view? Most splendid. Your first time above the Flat Lands?"

I remember you, Lord Marlow, you bastard. The same man who dressed me as a chicken and made that poor frightened girl dance and fly before his guests as they threw eggs at her.

"I dream of flying," I replied, in the present tense of the Marauda. "Free from all the cruelty of the earth." I stared into his oily eyes.

"Even the thought of it raises up the soul," he assured me. "Please, follow me."

Every eye was on us as we walked between the poplar trees. The hounds barked relentlessly at me, the silver-armored guards clutching at their leashes, dragging them back as they whined and growled at my scent.

"We know that the bond between husband and wife is the most sacred in your culture. So to honor your people and reaffirm our commitment to the terms of our peace, we wish to offer you our biggest honor." By "peace" Marlow meant unconditional surrender. "The Entangling of your fates."

"We are likewise honored," I replied. A deceptively simple diplomatic ploy—a reaffirmation of our marital bond, in the tradition of our former enemies. Or perhaps, now our rulers. It was clever. Marauda couples saw the ceremony as sacred, and the Entangling was one of the very few traditions our peoples shared. Perhaps they'd received word the ambassadors' anniversary was due and leaped at the opportunity to salvage bonds on our day of surrender.

Still, the hypocrisy of it was like acid on my tongue: aristocrats amusing themselves with the old ceremonies, while the people of the city starved themselves of their most sacred dreams. I was never more certain these strange and sparkling creatures were not paying their due tax. Andreas took another champagne. We had to be careful. I looked around behind us for the Sifter, but she had disappeared in the wake of the crowd.

Marlow led us on the cobblestones toward a stone archway. A delicate garden spread out before us, the rest of the palace towering above, a castle built into the very flesh of the Tree itself. It was a succession of colossal multistory structures built into the trunk, supported by stone buttresses and connected by countless arching stairways. High walls with gatehouses protected the castle beneath the Tree's coat of arms, and within were courtyards and living quarters for servants and aristocrats. The keeps had steep orange gable roofs and were decorated with countless sparkling ivory turrets and chimneys. I could not help but trace my old escape route in my mind, tower to balcony to stairway.

As we passed under the archway into the garden, I heard gushing excitement as Marlow presented Andreas to a coquettish gang of gorgeous young countesses, each breathlessly introducing themselves and trying to outdo the last. *The bad guy is a celebrity, huh?* I stared murder at them as they pretended to ignore me.

A cold voice suddenly sliced into my awareness.

"Your Excellency! A moment!" It was Favian, jostling forward between the lords. Dressed simply, he was surprisingly handsome in his blue tunic. He looked gaunt, purple bags under his eyes, his usually immaculate hair swept back, blue dye faded at his temple, a shade unkempt for the court. I knew him well; he was hiding his shock, flustered for once. Well, did he expect me to return broken and begging for my wings, crawling back to him with scraps of information? I ignored him.

He had injected himself roughly between two lords who were in the midst of admiring my dress and what lay underneath. He didn't care. His whole demeanor burned with urgency.

But before he could speak, I pointed. "Is that not the famed Warrior's Tower?"

He frowned, his mouth slightly open.

Yes, Favian, I'm trying to tell you. Not the Maiden's Tower, the Warrior's. That's where the Last Men will be. "It is essential to the architecture of the palace, is it not?" I said, trying to push home the misinformation.

Run, he mouthed suddenly. I felt a spike of anxiety in my breast. I tried to keep walking, but he snatched my hand. "Please," he begged, out loud. I stared into his inky eyes. Was that fear? Concern? It couldn't be.

"Take your hands off my wife." Andreas's big frame stepped between us, and his muscular fingers engulfed Favian's wrist. And then he twisted it, forcing Favian to his knees.

A gush of thrilled twittering came from the ladies. I heard the steel of the armored guards, but Marlow stilled them. Favian looked up at Andreas, and I saw the fetid glint of hatred in his eyes. One thing Favian could never forgive was being outwitted. Did he recognize him?

"I beg of you, my apologies, my most humble apologies, Your Excellency," he hissed from his knees. His pupils were almost hollow, with an ugly hypnotic gleam. Andreas released him, and the room released a collective breath. The palace guards marched to stand over the fallen *kai talan*.

Marlow quickly stepped in. "Please forgive us our rudeness, Ambassadors. We are most unfamiliar with your ways, but this is not acceptable. Please, allow me the honor of fixing this slight." He looked at Favian as if he were a worm. My handler hung his head, refusing to acknowledge it. And on we marched, leaving him there in the dust. The guards picked him up by the underarms and escorted him away.

What was he playing at? Public humiliation in exchange for what? Was the resistance planning something they had not told us? I could not shake the expression in his eyes. He was scared for me. And I remembered again his plaintive cries in the tunnels after he had hit me. *"Saya! Saya!"*

Marlow led us through the stone archway into the palace garden, along a pathway winding through a corridor of cherry blossom trees draped with luminous crystal moss, the lush grass carpeted with petals and arching bridges over burbling streams. Lit candles hung from the branches like faeries, and drifting scents of berries and pear mingled with rich white musk. We could hear the gentle strumming of guitars; the light wind brushed my hair, and the petals fell gently through the morning light around us.

We came to a clearing where a crowd of aristocrats and soldiers were assembled before a seating of simple wooden chairs. In the center, an altar of flowers overlooked a dazzling turquoise lake, the water rippling with pink blossoms that pirouetted through the breeze and onto the mirrored surface. The ethereal forest reflected perfectly on the aquamarine liquid, which flowed from deep underground.

"May love and a lightness of spirit follow you all of your days," said Marlow, gesturing for us to walk to the altar.

I felt Andreas's gaze on me and I met it carelessly. His usual brooding countenance was looking inquiringly at me and I felt swirls of myself. *Don't look at me like that, you fool!*

He took my hand and we walked up to the altar as the guests took their seats. A small, peanut-eyed girl with flowers in her hair was waiting for us, smiling a gap-toothed greeting from beneath the altar decorated in pink, white, and fern. Her cheeks were chubby and she wiggled from side to side to prepare herself. Then she opened a book and read in a high, sweet voice, her delivery fluent and pure and full of an unlikely understanding.

"We are gathered here today to witness the binding of this man and this woman beneath the everlasting constant, before the namelessness we call Fate but which has no name, the void without essence, the origin of now, the gate to the eternal, before and what is to come, in this world and all others.

"May love and a lightness of spirit follow you all of your days," she said as she turned her eyes to us and invited us forward.

We faced each other, the strangeness of the situation suddenly hanging between us.

"Repeat after me," said the little girl.

I met Andreas's gaze coolly, willing him a calm head. But I could sense his discomfort; he was avoiding my look.

"I that is tethered to thee, you are my light," said the little girl expectantly. I reached out my hands and he took them.

"I that is tethered to thee, you are my light," I began, and Andreas followed with me after a slight pause, his voice gravelly and tight.

"That which guides me to more love than I've ever known," the girl continued.

I saw his chest swell and felt an odd tingling in the air. The dark repressed emotion, that coiled electricity of him, was affecting me.

"That which guides me," we said to each other, "to more love than I've ever known." A tiny snowflake landed on his shoulder, magical, impossible in the ethereal sunlight.

"Take my body, that we be one."

All around us, the flakes were falling among the petals and through the trees. The wind was picking up, swirling my hair.

"Take my body, that we be one." The dream from this morning came again into my mind, him against me, him inside me against the masthead, me whispering into his mouth, "We're sinking." He was getting tighter; I could feel it.

"Take my spirit till these lives rest."

The crowd murmured. Andreas glanced away from us, back in the direction we had come from. In the distance, opposite us, the comet was splitting the daylight of the sky; its tail cut across the morning blue and opened up the blue-black night, glistening with constellations and, deeper than that, a purple-and-teal universe swirling in its wake.

It was coming right toward us.

"Take my spirit till these lives rest," we said together, watching it. The crowd was standing now, turning to look at the miracle. The comet was beginning to arch over our heads, over the top of the Black Tree.

"Take my soul, that we may follow each other in every world, in this present or the next."

Tornadoes of snowflakes and pink petals were swirling through the forest. Andreas and I looked at each other then, and I felt him whole and complete—in his eyes sweet, raw hope—and the honesty of him crushed me, destabilized me.

"Take my soul," we said, and I felt the emotion igniting in my chest, overcoming me, "that we may follow each other in every world, in this present or the next." We spoke together as the comet continued its journey over the Tree, the stars twinkling and the universe vibrating in its wake before folding back into the blue of the morning sky.

"I love you," said the girl.

Our lips froze. The petals and the snowflakes danced around us, locking us together in the moment. "I . . ." All eyes were on us, and I found myself waiting for him, with everything in me, just as I had so long ago in my dreams: a young girl waiting for the boy she loved, the hope of her life unfurling in wings that fluttered expectantly like a butterfly's. Waiting to tell him that I loved him.

But she never dreamed of that boy again.

"I love you," I whispered, and kissed him. The crowd erupted in cheers of awe and celebration. His lips were flat but as I pulled myself against him, I felt him awake, felt his mouth open, his tongue against mine, his arms around me. In that kiss I felt all of his pain, his desperate aching for forgiveness.

I forgave that boy, that beautiful angry boy who broke my heart. Andreas. I forgave him because he gave me hope. *So you too can forgive yourself, for whatever you are carrying inside.*

I couldn't breathe; I was losing myself in him, as if time was stopping, breaking, carrying us away . . . When we came apart for air at last, we continued clinging to one another, gazing deep into each other's eyes. And then I saw his lips beginning to move, beginning to open . . .

Two soldiers appeared out of nowhere and grabbed our forearms. The little girl held a thorn like a fang in her hand. Swiftly, she ripped a cut into each of our wrists, mine first and then Andreas's. We hardly had time to react as the soldiers pushed the two wounds together, making them bleed into each other. Quickly, the little girl bound them with a bandage made from pale vines and flowers. She held up our tied hands proudly to the onlookers, and I felt a tingling heat as the binding emitted a faint glow.

"We now pronounce you Entangl—"

"I challenge it!"

A cold voice rang out in the clearing. Together, we looked down the aisle. There, flanked by four skeleton-masked *kai talan* keeping the palace guards at bay, was Favian.

"I challenge it," he called again, pointing his finger at Andreas. "I invoke my right!"

"Why would you press a fight against our ally?" Marlow stood from the second row, his voice low and venomous.

"She must be championed!" Favian gestured at me, the wind blowing the petals diagonally.

"Even though they are under the protection of the Regent?"

"By their law, I invoke the *sai maga*. It is my right."

"Then, if your own blade is not turned against you, you will have to answer to the Regent himself."

I recovered enough to speak. "You cannot do this, Ambassador. We come here in peace!" What was Favian doing? He had told me to run yet now picked a battle that could reignite a war?

"Do not interfere," Marlow rebutted me over his shoulder. "We too follow the old laws of your people in the Entangling. It is the last of our ways." I heard a glimmer of sadness in his voice, saw the stiffness with which he held himself in his silver tunic. The old man knew this was a mistake, but there was honor left in him. Perhaps he was not so craven. But this was not the time for him to rediscover his dignity!

"Kai talan!" I called to Favian. He glared at me, all the festering ambition that drove his fanaticism behind his eyes. But there was something more too, the same look I had seen when we landed. A glimmer of fear, a protectiveness I would not accept. My wrist still stung where the little girl had drawn blood and bound me to Andreas in the cloth. "Touch him and your father's death is worthless! The violence will never end!"

"Nika . . ." Andreas pulled my attention. I turned my fury on him, but his green eyes with their starbursts were somber, gentle even. He was pressing something into my other hand.

"And now you must be silent!" cried Favian at us.

Opposite me, the man whose blood was mingling with mine seemed eerily calm. "It's okay," he said, closing my hand on the package. I could not understand him. The little girl began untying us, and kind hands pulled me back. The binding fell to the floor, the white flowers dotted with crimson blooms. I picked it up and held it to my breast, hiding what he'd given me in the same motion.

It was the flare.

The crowd stood and moved the chairs, forming a circle in the clearing as Andreas was separated from me. Was he saying goodbye? No! I pulled free of the soldiers and ran to him, hissing fiercely into his ear. "Beware! His knife is poisoned with the black tears!" Before I could say more, I was dragged away by the palace guards.

The music had stopped, and with it the wind. The trees now stood silent, no longer whispering with their petals. Favian was looking at me in the oddest way as I asked him with my eyes, *Why are you doing this?* I saw his gaze shift to Andreas, saw the corrosive hatred that sucked all the nobility from him.

"You will never take her back. Do you understand?" he said to Andreas. Favian stepped into the ring, flinging off his tunic into the crowd, then stripping off his shirt. He stood whiplash lean and lethal, his forearms crisscrossed with scars. Was this it? What Heron had predicted? That Andreas would die before he could send his dream girl back? It couldn't be!

How had the *kai talan* seen through us?

Favian was frowning, disturbed by my mention of his father. I would not have used such a personal weapon if I weren't desperate. It would make him hesitate. But did I want that? Did I want to see him bleeding out on the ground, a victim of his own misguided ambition? My handler took up the mask of the *kai talan* and placed it ritualistically over his face.

The alternative was far worse.

Andreas took off his tunic and shirt and bound his hair, sending ripples into the crowd. Marlow offered his knife, but he declined it. He instead took from his hip a knife made in the old ways of the village. Some in the crowd recognized the ancient artifact as priceless, thrumming with memories. It was one of their own. But it was not a combat weapon; it was a hunting knife, with no guard to trap an opponent's blade. An excited energy trickled over us.

Andreas walked bare chested and alone into the ring, wearing only his white leggings, with the climbing rope he'd brought all the way from another time wrapped around his left arm. His feet were bare even of the supple riding boots for better purchase on the uneven ground. There was a single droplet of blood—mine, his, or both—on his thigh. How skilled must a fighter be to not sustain even a single cut in a knife fight? I did not know of Andreas's training, but I could see from the muscular frame, the hardened bone, that it was not his first combat. He did not look afraid; he seemed . . . so calm.

Was he willing to die for me?

I must stop this. I'd already planted some hesitation in Favian; it might slow him. If only I could believe the Fates were on our side. *Think, Saya!*

The Marauda vied for political prestige, defended insults, and even settled common scores with duels like this. Any man who had risen to the level of an ambassador would be an eminent killer, with a litter of bodies to prove his rank and his wife's honor. It should cause further hesitation, and yet Favian looked supremely confident.

He knows! He knows Andreas is no ambassador!

Carefully, Favian released his black blade from its sheath and stepped into the ring. The poisoned weapon seemed to absorb the sunlight, deepening the shadows in the overhead trees. The crowd hushed, and a frightful suspense descended over the clearing. With the coiled rope wrapped around his left arm and the ancient knife glittering in his right hand, Andreas's lightly sweating body looked poised to spring. Every eye in the crowd was on him and Favian.

Favian began sidling right along the edge of the ring. Andreas crouched and waited for him, looking strangely distant, as if on automatic. It was an unconventional stance, more that of a wrestler than a dancer, with both hands forward, in contrast to Favian's elongated fencing form, his blade the farthest thing from his body.

"May thy beginnings be ended!" Favian called out the ritual challenge from behind his skeleton mask, the roots of the Tree branching from his mouth. Andreas did not respond. Each had his thumb pressed tightly along the back of his blade, drawing every advantage from the flexibility of the wrist, in a struggle where the space of an inch could mean death or life.

Fear coursed through me. All my hopes hung on a few milliseconds. If Andreas was touched, even a scratch, he would join the Forgotten. I would never know what could have been. Anything could tip the Fates now—a cough, the deceptive shadow of a falling petal, a variation in the light.

Favian let out a high-pitched scream and lunged at Andreas's eyes. I stifled a cry. But where Andreas had stood, there was only empty air, and Andreas appeared right next to Favian. *Now!* I screamed in my mind.

Andreas's motion was vicious and instantaneous, pummeling Favian under the armpit and then locking his arms around Favian's neck. He picked him up, driving him off his feet, and thundered him into the ground, neck first. The impact drove the air from the stunned *kai talan*'s lungs, and the squeeze tightened like a vise. Favian's arm was locked against his own head, feebly hanging on to the knife, as Andreas's back constricted in a coiled hunch.

But then I saw Favian's knife turning slowly over in his stiffening wrist, the point turning, aiming for just the slightest scratch on Andreas's head. Suddenly Andreas let go, pulling away and staggering back, disoriented like a sleepwalker. My heart leaped into my chest. Had the cut already landed? Were the tears taking him already?

"No!" I gasped.

Andreas looked around the forest as if seeing it for the first time. Favian cradled his throat.

"We come here to surrender," Andreas said, as if from a long way away. He rewrapped the rope around his arm, looking as if he wanted to sheathe his weapon.

Favian spat and got up, shaking his head, and settled back into stance. Warier now, he stalked around Andreas, who seemed to be staring at a fixed point behind his back. The murmuring of the crowd was growing louder; the court ladies had their hands over their mouths.

Again Favian attacked, his inky eyes glowing, his body a blur in the flecked light. Andreas stepped aside and parried the blade with the climbing rope, catching the knife arm and twisting, but he seemed to forget midway what he was doing and let go without driving his blade home.

Again Favian attacked, and again Andreas parried with his roped arm, stepped, and . . . hesitated.

And again.

Each time, Andreas's opening was plain for all to see, but he pulled away at the last instant.

"Is he toying with him?" Marlow asked me, unable to believe what we were seeing.

Now the two figures circled each other: Favian with his blade long in front of him and tipped slightly down, and Andreas with his hands behind his back, his head tauntingly forward and a distant look on his face.

Again, Favian pounced, this time faking left and ducking to the right where Andreas had been dodging. But Andreas lunged forward to meet him, a scintillating straight riposte that stopped the gleaming steel within an inch of Favian's eyeball. The *kai talan* slashed desperately upward, but Andreas's arm was gone, behind his back once more. It was as if he was moving in a different time altogether.

Favian backed away and ripped off his mask, eyes wide and staring, studying Andreas in mounting fear.

"Do you yield?" I cried out, stepping into the ring. The soldiers did not stop me.

"Hah!" Marlow replied to the right of me. The crowd murmured. "There is no yield. The *sai maga* is to the death. To surrender is to join the Forgotten."

Favian backed off, the realization now creeping over him that this was no untrained warrior but a graceful killer who had no choice but to send him to his grave in humiliation.

I sensed the shadow of desperation on his face. *Now is when he is at his most dangerous*, I thought. *He's desperate and can do anything. He sees himself dying pointlessly in a war without end, just like his father. The fear that I planted in him has come to maturity.* I felt a terrible pity for him.

The crowd began to shout and bay. *They think he is toying with Favian*, I realized, *with needless cruelty.* But beneath it, they were thrilled by the drama of the spectacle.

"End it," Marlow muttered.

Andreas pressed the fight now, circling but not attacking. He sensed the realization in his opponent. He was waiting for the terror to build, for the pressure to break Favian inside. Waiting for that desperate attack that would open him up.

Andreas circled Favian as I watched from inside the ring. I could see it in my handler, in the way he was looking at me, as if his last request was for me to accept that repugnant question in his eyes. When I did not respond, when it became too much for him, he attacked.

With disdain Andreas parried, leaned right, leaned left, and slashed a bright red blossom across Favian's knife hand. A short scream of pain, and the poisoned blade dropped to the floor. Andreas kicked it aside casually and began to march forward. The gleaming point of the hunter's knife pressed forward relentlessly as Favian scrambled away.

But then I saw, just to his right, one of the *kai talan* bending down to pick up the knife. As his leader squirmed backward, holding his bloodied hand, I saw the *kai talan*'s mask turn to Favian, to Andreas, and then back to me. He whipped his hand back behind his mask, holding the knife by the hilt with two fingers. Andreas looked over his shoulder as I shrieked and ducked.

I heard a scuffle, screams of excitement and fear.

I opened my eyes. The bone-masked *kai talan* was crumpled on the ground, blood pumping from his neck. And above him was Andreas with his back to me. And clean through the hand of the arm wrapped in rope was the poisoned blade. He looked over his shoulder at me, and from his eyes I saw a single black tear leak and run down his cheek.

He fell to his knees.

Favian recoiled like a snake and then grabbed at Andreas's knife, which had fallen from his listless fingers. He scrambled to his feet and took my partner by his hair.

"*Kai talan* Favian, stop!" shouted Marlow, holding back the guards who'd pushed forward, weapons drawn. "He has joined the Forgotten!"

I saw Favian's hatred burning, his mouth twisted with the thrill of vengeance. The crowd was stricken with horror by the sight of the black tears. Horror that could quickly change to anger.

"You have won, you fool!" cried Marlow. "You may now claim her!"

With a quick flick of his eyes to me, Favian returned to himself. Then, casually, he tossed Andreas's head aside. The time walker drooped sideways on his knees. Favian ripped the poisoned blade from his hand, not bothering to wipe it before placing it back in his sheath.

"I saved you," he said, marching up to me, reaching for my arm.

I slapped him as hard as I could and ran, in which direction I knew not. The crowd erupted.

"Saya, please!" I heard him calling in the maelstrom. "Saya!"

· 16 ·

ANDREAS

New Time

THE MEMORIES OF THE AMBASSADOR sang in my blood.

My opponent backed away, gaping like many before him. They always looked this way in the end, peasants or princes, soldiers or milkmen, brawlers, infighters, or artists. It was as if I were watching my body in third person, like a dream overlaid on another. Oh, this delightful dance of death, played to music that was only a distant memory, strumming to the steps of another world. I had tried to fight it, pulling back at the final sweet moment of release, but when I heard Marlow's words, the spirit in me rejoiced.

No one would take her from me, I affirmed.

I dodged his last pitiful attempts effortlessly. He was predictable, broken, exhausted. I defanged the snake, slashing two economical cuts in his knife hand and kicking aside the poisoned weapon. A straight riposte to the throat was most elegant. As I discarded the last of the resistance, free for absolute focus on the killing stroke, I saw my mistake.

I saw the subordinate's arm whip back and I dived with my roped arm outstretched. My left hand went numb; I rolled and came up spinning, slicing open the neck arteries of the masked coward. He melted, his eyes wide in shock, as a veil descended over the crowd. The clearing went quiet. Black roots like veins of darkness sprouted up from the ground, spasmed into the sky, and poured into my chest.

I turned for one last glimpse of her, the last thing I would ever see. She looked so beautiful when she cried.

Old Time

IN THE WARM BLACK COCOON, my eyes opened.

I was in my old body, this time a passenger within myself, a living memory. It was a dream I'd dreamed so many times. Myself as a young man, my voice wavering in the darkness of the predawn.

"Papa?"

My father stood in the doorway to my bedroom, holding a lantern. The candlelight streaked his rugged face with patterned shadow. With his long beard, expressive lips, and broken nose, he looked like a crumbling statue, as if the light always hit him at unflattering angles. He came into the room, his heavy boots thudding on the wood, bringing with him the smell of forest dirt, charcoal, and pine. The snow had melted on his thick wool cloak, forming cloudlike stains.

"My Little Explorer." His pet nickname for me. Once, it had

charmed. Now it smacked of resentment. He went off exploring, leaving me and Mama to be lost.

He put the lantern on the side table and sat heavily on the stool, wine sour on his breath. He tucked the quilt around me with his rough, calloused hands, hands that I'd once wrestled on the couch, his manner always more in need of gestures than words.

As he was about to speak, his hazel eyes lit up, sparks of brown and green starbursts. His bushy eyebrows furrowed and through his thick beard he blew the sound of the northeasterly, the wicked wind that came from over the Marauda seas. And with that sound, I knew he was leaving us again.

"Last time," he said, holding his finger to his broken nose. He blew out the candle and my nostrils prickled with the sweet smoke. I felt him there in the darkness, his size, like a mountain. "Never. Again."

I was about to wake, to scream and rage, to fight him like I always did, to shame him. But this time I didn't. I felt his presence rise and stride softly across the room.

"I love you, Papa," I moaned, the words coming unbidden from my mouth.

"I love you, my Little Explorer," he said like a statue in the doorway.

From another world, I felt them coming, the roots crawling over the ceiling and walls and into my dream of him. They exploded inward, spasming like spider legs, and writhed toward Papa. I looked on in horror as the roots poured into and through his chest, my mouth open in a soundless scream. Veins crawled across my vision, blinding me.

I felt myself floating into a great expanse, a space without measure, my tiny arms grasping but catching nothing, a small boy adrift in an endless sea. I saw others floating alongside me, other faceless bodies, shrinking and spinning in the dark. I tried to call out to them, but all I could feel was the expanse, the eternal peacefulness of myself giving up all my pain, all my desires, all my needs, all of myself.

Drifting . . .
A drop.
Like a tear hitting a pool.
The sound rippling.
Breathing.
Red.
Ripping.
Rebirth.

+ ✦ +

Through blood and light, I came back into another memory, my body singing with essence once more. I seemed barely myself, hollow even as my formlessness gained form and my consciousness awoke as a passenger in another.

My eyes recognized the patterned flags of red, white, and green in the Village of the Second Sun. My arms were robed in white, cradling groceries, hands decorated in lovely henna swirls and a chain ring linking thumb to forefinger.

I was slow to formulate language, ducking my head as I returned from the market. But as I smiled and exchanged a laugh with Atta, the farmer's daughter, I understood. It was Rosana's life I now inhabited. My fiancée's memories flowed in my blood—somehow she had returned me from the abyss of Forgetting.

I watched from within as Rosana nodded a few more shy

smiles, ambling along the beaten earth road through the center of town. She aimed to make vegetable stew for the family tonight with onion and butternut. Naturally, her mother would ask her again, "Rosana, why aren't you married?" She was relentless. Rosana would distract the old lady with all her many hours spent at the Temple of Beginnings, and her mother would hush.

From this I dimly understood that the events I was watching had happened before we had met. Rosana sighed. It was impossible to tell her mother that all the suitors her parents had picked were boring. But she knew she would need to choose soon. They could not support her on their meager income. Her mother meant well.

Rosana saw the inventor Melasquez in his usual spot on the corner, perched on a wooden box, his potbelly swollen, his apelike arms hanging in futility. She had bought a few of his wind-up toys for her sister Channa. They were ingenious, but they broke quickly. This time, he was fiddling with an almost human-looking contraption, a doll but with wind-up parts, next to him on a ragged blanket. It was creepy, made of scavenged metal or stolen parts.

In the living memory, Rosana paused to purchase a self-driving cart from his mixed collection. "My dear, why do you continue to build these things?" she asked. "You need not live in that squalid shack." The cart looked flimsy, but she felt sorry for him. He looked hungry.

"Mhmmm of course, it is to save the world!" He rubbed his balding red hair and gesticulated wildly. "Look, look how it has a mechanical memory." He wound up a key in the back of the doll's head, but it collapsed. "It will work perfectly! None of our poisonous dreams, no hate, bias, anger, or pain." He seemed unaware that the doll was broken. "Wouldn't you want to be like it, just forget everything? Save yourself from the burden of it all?" he asked Rosana plaintively.

She had smiled kindly at him and wished him good luck. It did not seem that time had been kind to him.

He was even more ragged than usual today, his threadbare cloak ripped, his sandals in need of repair. He was hugging himself with his lanky arms, his belly swollen, his scraggly carrot beard streaked with dirt and early gray. He seemed to not have eaten for a long time, and his breath smelled of sour beer. She wished that this man with almost nothing would not drink himself into oblivion.

"Mhhmm the Marauda will return! I have seen it!" he cried out, climbing atop a wooden box in the middle of the street, gesticulating to everyone who walked past as he rocked himself with his other arm. "Why won't you listen?"

Rosana saw Heron and his band of friends rounding the corner, laughing and joking with rowdy good spirits, punching each other's arms. Immediately she had a bad feeling about it.

"We must flee!" Melasquez screeched.

"From what, you mad fool?" said one of the bigger boys, taken aback. An Elder's son, thick, tall, and pimpled.

"The Marauda! They are coming for us!"

"We have not seen a Marauda in generations," said Heron coolly. "Come off it, Jost."

But Jost, the pimpled one, stared up into Melasquez's haggard eyes. "Are they coming to break your toys?" He smirked.

Melasquez's mouth was open, but no words seemed to be coming out. Finally a thin, weak squeal emerged.

"Stop stirring troubles, by the Fates." Jost booted the wind-up toy over.

"My treasures hmmmm!" Melasquez dived on top of them, protecting them with his body.

Jost raised his boot, but Heron stopped him. "We will leave you alone, but only if you stop fearmongering. You don't need any more attention, Melasquez," Heron reprimanded.

"Please, only I can save us," he whimpered, crawling up to Heron and grasping at his legs.

"Get away from me!" the pretty young man cried in revulsion. Jost pushed Melasquez roughly to the ground, where he lay mewling.

"Stop!" Rosana cried, running in between them. She could see by the hot flush in Jost's cheeks that he very well might have pushed her aside too. "Heron!" she appealed.

The blue-eyed boy took a step back and shook himself. He put a hand on Jost's shoulder.

"You shut your doomsayer mouth, or I'll be back to shut it for you," Jost said through his teeth at the pathetic figure Rosana shielded. She heard the crunch as his boots stepped on the iron parts that lay strewn on the road.

Rosana watched the boys leave, pushing each other and making fun of Heron, crawling up to him like Melasquez had and laughing. She turned to see the poor man shivering, frantically trying to collect the screws back into his dilapidated bag. The doll's face was cracked.

"Would you like something to eat?" Rosana asked him. He gathered his scraps and broken parts to himself and nodded. She gave him an apple and he ate it in big, hurried bites. But halfway through, he stopped, gulped hard. With effort, he put the other half into a pocket in his cloak.

"Thank you, thank you," he said. "I . . . am . . . not myself . . ."

"Let me take you home, my dear," Rosana said, helping him up. They walked together through the village, drawing a few stares. But she didn't care.

"Please hmmm. Don't tell my brother about this," he said. Rosana nodded. Together they made their way down the winding road that snaked its way through the outskirts of the village and into the forest.

They came to his shack, which lay precariously on the edge of a cliff, and she saw sadly that he had been fortifying it with wood, nails, and scavenged parts. Around it, the many stray animals he collected mewled at him. He took from his cloak two soiled and stiff crusts of bread and broke them apart, feeding the dogs and cats and baby goat. He kept a separate piece for a mangy monkey that held out its hands like a beggar.

"How do you know the Marauda are coming?"

"The tree told me," he said, "in a dream." She smelled the alcohol on his breath again. He was notorious for getting thrown out of taverns, a nasty, malicious drunk.

Rosana hesitated to follow him inside, but then she heard from within the excited voice of a young boy. "You're back!"

She followed Melasquez into the shack. It was a workshop, covered from floor to ceiling with dusty books in old languages, artifacts, tools, and rusted metals, leathers, and chemicals. The only light came from a small window at the back, which shone down on a cot where a little boy with bright, fevered eyes was smiling at us. Rosana had seen complexions like that before. Consumption.

"How did it go?" The boy's voice was filled with hope.

"Magnificent," cried Melasquez, handing him the remaining half of the apple. "The self-driving cart amazed every man who set eyes upon it! The Elders agreed that it will save the world from all labor! They said it is the greatest invention since the compass and will discuss more tomorrow!"

"Whoa . . ." said the boy, munching on the apple, his eyes wide. "Can I come?"

"If you're well enough," Melasquez said, stroking the sick child's wet hair, puffing out his chest to appear as proud as possible. She saw the tree then in the corner, its black root wrapped around the little boy's wrist.

"I dreamed you will be a giant!" said the boy, staring up at his brother with delirious eyes.

✦

The world swirled into darkness once more, shifting and moving, leaping and changing. And another vision came upon me, as suddenly as the first. But my mind was working now, and I evaluated the meaning of what I had seen.

Melasquez's own brother had dreamed he would be a giant. Was the first dream the Tree had consumed that child's, as it had taken Leah's dream of blue flowers to make children of its own? And taken Saya's dream of hope to elevate the land into the sky?

When the world came back to me once more, there was chaos in the village. The time and place had changed. It was a hot early evening. Pack animals were everywhere as people shoved their belongings into wagons. Children cried, and the multicolored flags lay torn and trampled in the mud. I remembered this day myself— the day the Marauda first returned.

My fiancée's fist hammered into the shack door. I saw from behind her eyes again.

"Melasquez!" Rosana stepped back in frustration. "We cannot run." The words of Elder Yan at the village council echoed in her mind: *They outnumber us by the hundreds and block our escape through the Sentinels.*

"Melasquez!" she shouted again. "I need your help!"

There was no response. The thought that he might already be dead raced through her mind. He could have leaped off the cliff face behind his shack. Bottles lay scattered at her feet. Perhaps he had drunk himself into oblivion.

"*We* need you . . . to save us!" Rosana knelt down at the door. The walls of the shack had extended upward and seemed taller somehow. It was hopeless, stupid of her to come here. How could this madman be of any use? She should be helping her parents hide their few possessions or plan an escape route. She should . . .

The door squeaked on its hinges, slowly swinging open. Rosana heard something large stir behind it. She did not move; she was so frightened. As the chaos and the shouting continued, a scruffy little dog trotted past her and jumped into the shack. And it was followed by other strays, cats and dogs, monkeys, even mice.

She took a deep breath and pushed the heavy door fully open. As before, it was dim inside, filled with the smell of rotten books and fungus. She coughed and held a hand over her mouth. A thin streak of light beamed diagonally across the room.

"Melasquez?"

"They have come, haven't they?" His voice was deep and booming, so unexpected that she froze in fear. It came from the darkness, and I felt a huge presence there. The strays were flocking into the shack. How had he known?

"Is this the will of the Fates?" Rosana asked him. She heard something hunched and gigantic shifting in the gloom.

"Mmmhmm, the Fates have no will. Their will is to know their own meaning, and so they dream our lives. I would know. I have met one." There was a rumbling chuckle and Rosana felt dread in her breast. "Behold with your own eyes."

Her vision was adjusting as Rosana came closer, and in the dim light she could see that the roof was no longer made of rotting boards but a veined pattern of dark living wood and, above it, an indigo canopy of leaves. The broken parts of discarded automatons littered the floor, cracked doll faces staring up at her.

"This tree is one of the Fates?" Rosana saw it then, a freakishly swollen foot with thick strands of hair sprouting from each massive toe. She gasped and backed away.

"Surely, you see it now! The Fates dream us into existence because they feed on us! They feed on our dreams because only *we* can choose new worlds!" Melasquez gave the despondent sigh of a man misunderstood all his life, pointlessly explaining himself. "And now I have found a Fate that will allow *me* to choose a new world, a new *time* . . ."

She heard the screeching wonder in his voice, and she realized that he actually believed what he was saying.

"If we travel the forbidden way, it will . . ." Suddenly he groaned and clutched his forehead. There was a thick black mist rising from the floor, swirling around the hem of Rosana's skirt, consuming the broken dolls.

"Where is your brother?" she shouted, frightened of him now.

"This Fate will save us, Rosana!" he roared, clawing at his face and stepping forward into the light, pointing at the misty carpet between them.

Opening between us under the tree was a light shaped like the body of a man reaching, as if falling. Inside it was a constellation of stars, a vortex of light dipping into impossible depths. The Rift!

And above it stood Melasquez, but not as she had ever known

him. He was huge and hunched, his mouth open, ragged face enormous, swollen and distended, his limbs thicker than any man's.

He towered over Rosana, a giant.

✦

As the visions swirled and changed once more, their meaning became clearer. The monster had given his own brother's dream to the Tree, to become the giant the little boy idolized him to be. A despicable crime, but only the beginning of his reign. For the giant already knew the Black Fate was feeding on our dreams. It was growing in the new time, fed by not just our dreams but the Marauda's too. So why had it needed us?

Had I been its unwitting pawn in choosing the forbidden way of travel? Beginning the new circle of time from the moment my teeth had sunk into that fruit it had offered in the Dreaming?

The visions coalesced once more into color and space and time, and I became embodied. I breathed the air once more as Rosana and could do nothing but watch the memories play out.

My fiancée now sat at Melasquez's feet, sewing. Above her, the bright sunlight came through the canopy of colored cloth the *mayaa* had built for him. This would have been months after the last vision, for now the giant had been enthroned and bound with ship rope in his madness. He leaned against the Black Tree, his head drooping, mumbling to himself, pulling at the huge knots that held him fast. Rosana wondered if he had eaten today.

Seren came to Rosana with water for Melasquez. She thanked her, and the former honey seller curtsied, her syrupy eyes thick with adoration. Rosana turned to the giant, climbing carefully up his thigh. His baldness was worsening, the last of his red-orange hair falling out.

"If you will not eat, you must at least drink," Rosana said, placing a tiny hand on his barrel chest. She felt his lungs breathing. In and out, like cave winds. Above them, birds circled. She should bring his strays to him today, she thought. They always cheered him.

"They will come back," he muttered. "The Marauda will return."

"And you will save us again," Rosana said, running a hand over his cheek.

"How can I?" he cried. "The tree is not speaking to me!"

"Hush now," she said.

"It is still hungry mhhhmm! It wants more, more than I have to give!"

She looked into his eyes, into the deep madness within him.

"What does it want?" She thought of all of our futures. Me. Her parents. The village. Everyone she knew and loved.

"It wants dreams, not of the present but of the future too." He looked at me in desperation, glugging down a bottle of wine as if it were a toy. "It wants the dreams of all eternity."

New Time

Drifting . . .
A drop.
Like a tear hitting a pool.
The sound rippling.
Breathing.
Red.
Ripping.
Rebirth.

A great presence, green in my belly, comforting, wrapping, like a seed, falling into the void, from the before that was, a nameless, a gate, a harvest.

I awoke, gasping in air, bolting upright. Two wrinkled hands were on my bare chest, gently pressing me down. I let them, sucking in air in hoarse breaths. The air smelled like fern, earth, and sparkling rainwater. The hands stayed there, ringed in silver and henna swirls, nails white as a dove, and beneath the fingerprint of the index finger, a wet oyster of blood. Their owner knelt in a pool of luminescent turquoise, draped and veiled in pale jasmine white.

"Hush . . ." she said, taking her hands off my chest and dipping the bleeding finger into a small cup that floated in the substance of the pool. "Hush now."

I could hear a faint dripping sound echoing through space—real or imagined, I could not tell. I had been laid in a natural wooden groove that rose from the glowing liquid like a bathtub, my legs hanging over the side, ankle-deep in an aquamarine substance that somehow didn't feel wet. The small room was itself a semicircular hollow of dark living wood, its wrinkles curving and growing like waves around us. Coral-pink ferns poked through the crevices.

The overlay of memory began to settle, sinking into my mind as I came back toward myself. Still, everything looked strange and unfamiliar. I examined my body. My hand ached with the wound, but I was otherwise unharmed.

"My dearest Andreas . . ." Rosana undid her veil. I could not believe she was real. Surely she was just a projection of memory? But no, those multicolored eyes, startling cyan blue and mint green, could be none other's. The years had been kind to her, but the ravages of time on her cheeks and arms still shocked me.

"I'm . . . sorry . . ." I strained to speak.

"Perhaps I should say the same." She sucked on her finger gently. She'd painted her lips lilac instead of the auburn I remembered, and her silver-and-ash-blond hair was cut short around her shapely skull. "Shh now . . ." She stroked my arm, encouraging me to rest.

"You . . . and the giant," I managed. She squeezed me and did not say anything for a while, retreating into herself. But when she came back, she was much firmer than the mousy girl I remembered.

"I am sorry. For not telling you, dearest," she said eventually, holding my arm. "I did not think you would understand." Her throat was pale as a ghost, stained with the blue veins of time.

Here she was, my former fiancée, the girl I had abandoned to chase a dream. The woman I had intended to marry to escape myself and my broken heart. The woman I had thought would accept a life without love but instead had sent me across worlds. Had she betrayed me? Or had I betrayed her?

"How did you bring me back?" I asked, my feet in the warm turquoise liquid.

"Long have we been searching for an antidote to the black tears," she said quietly. There was a solidity to her, a dignity she had never found with me.

"We? You and Melasquez caused all of this!" I sat up, pushing her hands off me.

"I serve the Fates," she demurred, crossing her palms on her lap. Ripples ran through the glowing liquid around us.

"What does that even mean?" I cried.

"That our paths are not ours to choose." Her multicolored eyes glinted.

I made an animal noise of annoyance in my throat. It was pointless arguing with her theology. "What happened to his brother?"

"He was the first to be Forgotten," she said sadly, "but there have been many more since."

"We need to fix this, Rosana! Find the Traveler." I clutched at my father's climbing rope that lay on an outcrop of wood. "Go back into the Dreaming." Saya's face suddenly flashed into my mind. Did that snake Favian have her?

Rosana said nothing. Her air of mystery had not left her. I was about to speak again, but she put her finger to her lips. I restrained myself and we communicated without words as we always had. This was her way of telling me to stop being so headstrong and abrasive, to still my nature and listen.

"Did you know this Black Fate exists in the Dreaming with the other World Trees?" She gestured around us. "It is creating this new circle of time in its dream, for it was the Black Tree's fruit that you tasted."

Dimly, I recalled the crunchy white flesh melting in my mouth, the taste of it like kissing my dream girl for the first time, bright and pure, disappearing into her. The forbidden way. A trap to create a new time together, all this pain. My stomach clenched, as if I'd swallowed a pellet of blood and guilt coated in clay and fur.

"Can we stop it? There must be a way back into the Dreaming!" I cried out. She said nothing, but again the question teased in her smile. "Or will we repeat all of our mistakes again and again, forever?" I tried to stand up.

"Did you ever truly love me, Andreas?" she asked.

I could not answer. All I could see was Saya's face, those beautiful, devastating tears, the last thing I remembered before the black veil descended.

"It's okay. I knew. But . . ." She smiled that secret, enigmatic smile that had captured me so long ago. "We made my mother happy."

I had no answer for her.

"Come, there is something you should see."

She got up from her knees, her draped dress making ripples in the turquoise liquid, beckoning me to follow her deeper into the Tree. She led me barefoot down a stream that trickled over hundreds of tiny waterfalls, running over and between the grooves in the wood. There was an immensely fresh and heady wind, first pushing us forward, and then pushing us back. I touched the wall, running my fingers along the knots in the wood. It was firm, warm.

Was the Tree breathing?

We came to an opening shaped like a vulva where the liquid cascaded into an unearthly aquamarine basin that swirled with pale eddies and currents. Bright pink vegetation grew along the walls and grape-colored vines hung from a ceiling too far up for me to see clearly. In the center of the pool was an oval bubble of translucent green resin the size of a cabin. Above us, bird wings fluttered, and there was the trickling sound of the liquid flowing into the basin, but it was otherwise silent, the silence of secrets.

"Follow me," said Rosana, grasping the vines and stepping daintily down onto a node of wood just below the surface. The vines too were warm to the touch. Was it just my imagination or did they curl around my hands, giving me easier purchase?

Using the nodes as stepping stones, we made our way to the bubble of resin. Almost invisible in the gummy resin was an entrance, and she beckoned me in. In the oval room was an elevated hump with a dip filled with knitting materials, like an organically formed table. Rosana wafted toward it and gently climbed on top, sitting cross-legged, beckoning me to settle opposite her. She gathered her knitting to her knees, an obsidian-colored cloak that cascaded down to the ground. On it was a white dragon flying in a circle, consuming its own tail—a depiction of Aiyan, the Eternally Blooming. She took up the two needles in her hands and laced the threads together with finality.

"There is someone that must be found, my dearest Andreas." Her voice floated, inscrutable in the strange green cave, her lilac lips pursed in concentration. Her hands began knitting faster. She was finishing off Aiyan the white dragon, stitching in the teeth. "A great explorer. Perhaps the greatest who ever lived."

"I'm tired of riddles, Rosana," I growled. "Just tell me!"

She crisscrossed the needles, looping the thread around them, completing the scales of the tail. Then she looked through the glass-like walls of the resin cavern, as if listening to the water-falls, growing sadder, older, and more vulnerable. "I have long sifted through the dreams of our people . . ." She was so small, like a child. "I found something. A first cause, the beginning of the loop." Using scissors, she cut off the final strand of her work, then stood up with difficulty, folding the cape on her lap. I didn't like the color of it; it was somehow familiar.

"What is it, Rosana?" I almost shouted.

She placed both her hands on the finished cape, then touched her forehead. Then, folding it carefully over one arm, she limped past me toward the entrance of the glassy bubble. I chewed furi-ously on the inside of my mouth.

Out beyond was the vast pool of swirling aquamarine eddies. They were ever-changing, pale shapes coalescing into half-recog-nizable forms and then dissipating, almost alive, falling from the oddly shaped holes in the Tree. Were these the liquid memories of our people, our collected dreams?

Rosana reached up, and the grape-colored vines came toward her. As she touched them, they spiraled around her wrist, running down under her arms. I felt rage burning inside me. I wanted more than anything to destroy Melasquez, to stop this horror from ever happening. I needed to find Saya and escape this cursed loop.

"I felt something . . . in the space between time." She paused, her eyes suddenly swelling with the fear and hope of a true believer. "I can't describe it . . . a living presence . . ."

"I felt it too," I mumbled.

We locked gazes, baring ourselves.

"May the Beginnings guide you," I said, breaking the silence. "And I am sorry, for not loving . . ."

"Hush . . ." she said with a smile, and handed me the vine. I watched it curl around our wrists, along our arms, entwining our waists. "When will you learn to accept yourself?" She ran her finger gently down my cheek. I let out a breath. The gleam in her eyes disappeared as suddenly the vines lifted her away, up into the darkness.

"Wait!" I cried, reaching out instinctively. But she had already gone.

I pulled down on the vines and they wrapped, held, and responded, lifting me up too. In the rushing darkness, I heard the fluttering of startled birds, felt the weightless fright of helplessness. I accelerated, faster and faster, the air rushing and roaring in my ears, the gargantuan being breathing around us as we rose ever higher at a terrifying speed.

Just as I thought the vines would fling us into the sky, I saw light, thick golden streaks of it beaming down. The vines pulled me out from the enormous hollow trunk and flung me into the canopy. The size of it struck me with awe, a dome bigger than a city, gnarled branches wider than five roads put together.

There were flocks of robins and starlings streaming in

ever-changing shapes, the chatter of velvet monkeys, clans of chimps with babies on their backs. Yellow and blue butterflies the size of my hand floated past me, and harpy eagles called from their nests. Droplets of sunlight dappled my cheeks as the indigo leaves of the canopy swayed in the rushing winds.

The vines pulled me to an immense black branch that diverged in two, and then gently uncoiled from my body. Rosana was waiting for me at the fork. I rubbed my chest with the heel of my palm, shaken by the journey. From our vantage point, we could see not only the canopy above but down through the branches that spread many miles around us.

Below us was the tiny palace with its minarets, a few puffy clouds floating nearby, and the city built around it in circular rings. Beyond, to the horizon, we saw the gray-purple snowcapped Sentinels and, encircling us, the very edges of the miraculous floating landscape. I could not believe I had been on its perimeter just this morning.

"The speech should already be happening," said Rosana. "And I believe this is the moment he will show it."

"What?"

"The way this story ends."

·17·

SAYA

New Time

I'D NEVER FELT SO HOLLOW.

Not even when I had lost color in the cage, my skin and hair nearly transparent, and I felt the wind could blow straight through me. Not even when I had wanted to let myself fall from the uncaring sky into the ocean.

Even now I had myself, the gold of my body, the violet in my eyes, the hunger in my bones, the peace that settled around me without warning in secret moments with him. I wanted, needed, rejoiced in this shape of me and all the living colors that wanted to burst into the hollow space of my heart. But there was nothing, only dust blowing through me.

There, in the grove among the pink blossoms where we'd spoken our love to each other. Turning to see me, the last thing he would remember. A single black tear running down his cheek. Andreas, Forgotten.

Nothing could bring him back.

And now I was seated in a gilded chair on the palace dais with Favian. Of all the cruel jokes the Fates had played on me. I stared at the moon in the cerulean sky without seeing. Beneath our feet were plush blue carpets decorated with silver leaves, and hanging from the balcony were flags embroidered with the bone-white tree. Diagonal steps and smaller podiums crisscrossed the view before us. Behind, gated layer upon layer, were the walls of the palace and the keep that housed the throne. Outlandishly dressed aristocrats kept stealing glances at my naked devastation, but I didn't care.

Beneath us, the trumpets sounded, and more soldiers paraded past us in the courtyard, taking their place in formation. Then came the speeders, the spring-loaded vehicles of the Guard.

On our far right was the stone spiral of the Maiden's Tower, and its twin, the Warrior's, on the left. I let the tears run, wondering whether Gellie and Reece were in that crowd. The flare Andreas had given me before his duel with Favian was tucked snugly against my inner thigh.

Did it even matter anymore?

Here came the hated *kai talan* in their masks. They stood in formation and saluted their leader, seated beside me. He stood and returned the salute. The pink patch on his cheek gave me a tiny satisfaction, shaped as it was to match my hand.

I hope you got the boys and girls out, Reece and Gellie, I thought, *before these sick parasites got there.*

Then came the automatons, flying through the sky in intricate formations, trailing blue-and-white smoke. *Is that you, Alia, in the* Interceptor? *Perhaps you should catch me again before I jump?*

I glanced idly behind me, saw the ladies staring, gossiping hotly. But really, I was noting the four palace guards behind them, one at each exit. The one closest to me was almost my height, a hard-nosed peasant, balding, dark skinned, with a foul-tempered mouth that habitually chewed tobacco. He was affecting a bored look and holding the ceremonial pike casually with a shade of insolence in his eyes. Him.

I glanced over my other shoulder, expecting to see the same snickering court ladies with gloved hands over their powdered mouths. But they weren't looking at me. An expectant hush came over the crowd around us. They were looking past me over my shoulder to the grand balcony just above.

"I tried to warn you," Favian whispered again. "That bind connects you through time!" He kept trying to explain that the giant wanted to bond me to the stranger in the Entangling, but the moment he mentioned Andreas, I'd struck him.

The parade stood ready, the eerie silence interrupted only by the scream of a chimp coming from the black containers. I turned away from Favian to follow the gaze of the court ladies and saw Marlow appearing grandly in the sunlight.

"Ladies and gentlemen, armies of the Tree, people of the Second Sun! I present to you our Prophet of the Floating City, our Savior of Our Day of Rising, and the Inventor of the Great Automaton Revolution, your Regent, Melasquez the Giant!"

The parade erupted into cheering. There was no doubt the giant was loved among his true believers. Perhaps they had given away everything else in service of survival, burning away the last of their doubt.

As Marlow retreated, I watched the Regent's massive hunched back emerge onto the balcony, his apelike arms that swung nearly to his knees, his belly that could not be hidden by his golden robes. His bald head winked in the afternoon sun. He had always refused to wear a crown. He was a custodian, he said, not a king. He was followed by his *mayaa*, serving women wearing discreet skirts of cream and rose.

He waved to the crowd with one disproportionate hand and the cheer intensified. He basked in the response, glancing around at the gathered lords and ladies, a smug smile on his drooping jowls. Was it just me, or did his gaze seem to linger on my location? It was rumored he was going blind. Was this because his brows had grown so heavy they cloaked his eyes? He drew his hands across his chest and signaled for silence. Again the eerie hush pervaded the parade.

"People of the Second Sun! We are saved!" he roared, holding his arms out benevolently. The crowd erupted again, cheering and stomping. He crossed his arms, and they fell silent.

"In the shade of the great Tree mhhhmm. In the presence of the ambassadors of Marauda. In the presence of our great automatons and protectors. I come to share with you my final testament."

He held his palm out to the sky. "Let us begin!"

There was a flurry of activity in the crowd.

"Let us ask ourselves now. Why do we stand free while apes are housed in cages?" the giant boomed.

The soldiers stood in rigid formation, but I could be sure some were as uneasy as I was.

"You may think it is because we are smarter than they are. Because we have souls, we are special, we are chosen by the Fates," bellowed the giant, hammering his fist to his chest. But then he leaned forward.

"I ask you now, if it was us and them on a remote island, who would you bet on to survive? Them, of course! One chimp against one man, the man is weak hmmm. But what about thousands of

men against thousands of chimps?" He grinned, showing missing teeth at the corner of his hairy lips. "They would scatter! They
would be slaughtered!"

Was he drunk or insane to be speaking like this?

"These creatures must know each other intimately, for it is only
through knowledge of another ape that they can know the other is
trustworthy. But does each soldier need to know every other soldier
in an army to work together? No." He held himself together, paus-
ing for effect. "I say to you mhhmm, we rule because of our dreams."

A murmur went through the crowd.

"A dream of a shared nation. A dream of peace! In this world,
we are the only creatures that create and believe in dreams! Dreams
are not real. Yet if we all believe in the same dream, we all have the
same rules." He waited again for effect, building momentum. "So
hmmm, here is a dream for you. The people of the Village of the
Second Sun will discover the forbidden way. If we don't destroy
them, we will all be punished."

The crowd roared in anger. He turned and pointed his massive
finger directly at me, his hooded brows darkened by shadow. I felt
the gaze of the entire procession suffocating me, the hairs on my
neck tingling.

"The Marauda all believe in this dream. But it does not exist
in the real world. It is a story, like everything else they believe in.
Where is the nation of Marauda? Is it real mmmm? Can you point
to it?"

The crowd booed and jeered.

The giant held up two massive stacks of paper notes in his monstrous hands. "This is their money. Is it real? You cannot wear it or
drink it. They say this paper is worth more than food. A stranger
will kill you for it."

He threw the money into the crowd and they roared in approval. The notes fluttered in the light wind, the tiny red *V*s of Marauda falling away.

"Just as they tried to exterminate us for the lies of a corrupt and weakening empire!" he roared. The crowd was building into a frenzy.

"But how can the Marauda muster armies to kill us without their false dreams?" the giant said scornfully. "Hmmm, how can there be killings of entire peoples, the horror of war, if they are not all under the same spell of this story? Theirs is a dream from which they will not awaken. But we have awoken them!"

The crowd bayed and he let them.

"We rained the black tears on the Marauda when they stood ready to slaughter us," he shouted into the troop of rumbling soldiers. "We have taken their dreams from them hmmm, driving them from the very edge of our Floating Lands! And yet even now, I can tell you that their poisonous stories live on." He crossed his arms and the crowd fell silent. "Stories that will raze our beloved city to the ground."

As he spoke, he looked skyward. Directly above him, a shining light had emerged from the distant canopy of the Tree. It spiraled and dipped toward us, twirling and spinning. As it grew closer, an anxiety began to grow inside me. I felt the changeling begin to shred the particles of me from the inside, starting at the hollow point. I clutched myself, bending over in pain. Favian tried to touch me, but I shrank from him.

"We feed our dreams to our sacred Tree, that it may guide us," the giant said into the canopy of indigo branches.

Around the light, a dark cloud had begun to build, swirling into a forbidding vortex. A nervous muttering went through the aristocrats. As the light drew closer, I could almost make out a figure inside it, held by a thin line that leashed it to the Tree.

"So I have come to you with my final testament," the giant said, finally taking his eyes off the strange weather formation and opening his arms benevolently. "For this world to be saved, not only we but also the Marauda must sacrifice their dreams. We must give everything!"

As he spoke, a series of violent explosions went off in the Maiden's Tower. The crowd gasped as the tower began to keel over and then it collapsed like a toy house in the dust. A shiver went through the air, like spider cracks across a sheet of ice.

"Let us all give our dreams to our Fate. Let us all be saved!" the giant cried as the sky rumbled and a black cloud swirled above us.

A single black drop hit the carpet right in front of me, sizzling slightly as it hit the silver material and sank in like glutinous oil. As I looked up in horror, I could now see the shining figure clearly. A single, invincible outline in the eye of the storm.

She had wings.

✦ ✦ ✦

Favian grabbed me, flipping an umbrella over us and blocking the giant from view. There was chaos and screaming, a mass of legs and skirts. I heard another sickening droplet fall, then another and another. I couldn't move. The pain of the changeling was ripping me apart.

"Saya!" Favian was pulling me toward the exit, bodies buffeting us from all directions. I couldn't do this anymore. I couldn't *be* anymore.

I got hit by a shrieking woman and then I saw someone grab

Favian's umbrella and his grip loosen. I ducked under a lady's dress, black rain dribbling around me as I crawled through the forest of legs, my body shivering and flickering and turning into that of a thick peasant. My nose flattened, my hair grew in black and coarse, my legs became stumpy, and my clothing restitched itself into the palace garments. As I stood up on my powerful, stocky thighs, I caught Favian's desperate glance scanning for me, a streak of blood running down his forehead.

The rip of the changeling was burning in my every vein but I fought and elbowed my way through the crowd ruthlessly. They were trampling each other, fleeing into the palace courtyard and then into the safety of the drawing rooms. I stumbled, making my way down a less crowded corridor, away from the cries of terror. Slumped beneath an oil portrait was one of the young countesses who had been giggling at Andreas. Black tears poured down her beautiful cheeks as she stared sightlessly at the ceiling.

I turned to look behind me at the black rain falling into the courtyard. A massive stone visage of the giant stared back at me, his mouth open, his bald dome dripping sizzling tears. I ripped my shirt off as I darted away from the crowd, checking myself for any touch of the black.

Had Favian saved me?

I raced down a corridor, past palace guards running in the opposite direction, my legs unsteady. One of them grabbed me by the shoulders, shouting at me, but I pushed him off and kept running. Tears streamed from my eyes, each falling like a sparkling rainbow as the changeling ignited, ripping open the old scars down my back.

You cannot bear to be yourself because that winged girl in the sky is you. She is you!

You have to escape.

I screamed, my voice half-man, half-woman. A guard saw me from the other end of the corridor, and I screamed my pain at him, too. He turned and ran as if he'd seen a ghost. The walls flashed with prismatic light, and it was then that I saw it: a room on my left that I recognized, the door tilted open, with a balcony overlooking the palace maze.

I pulled myself together and sprinted toward it, unheeding of all around me, then vaulted over the balcony into the sunlight. I landed and rolled, panting. I glanced up in horror, but the black halo of cloud was behind me. And the winged girl, leashed to the Tree . . .

No!

I ran to the entrance of the maze; I went left, right, left, like a homing pigeon. I had memorized this route, rehearsed it countless times in reverse. It was the same escape I had used that night, the night I had almost been rid of myself forever.

Seven doors opened to this hedged oval. Six led to another maze that returned, deceitfully, to the same oval; the seventh led through another maze to a second oval chamber identical to the first. And within that second chamber was the hidden door, the latch concealed in the brambled ferns. I gripped and pushed. And pushed. And then I opened it. In the center of the courtyard was a glass dome and, around it, walls many times the height of a person.

My cage.

I heard voices squabbling, male and female.

"We can't just sit!"

"D'ya wanna get demoted again?"

"I'm hungry!"

"Slug monkey!"

The voices were coming from behind the dome, and just within view were mops and buckets of soapy water. Complaining, the janitors crunched toward me on the gravel. I ran on tiptoe toward the dome, my whole form shaking.

Just as their footsteps rounded the corner, I ducked into the tiny doorway. *Why did you come back here?* My hands shifting, I fiddled with the wooden spring lock comprised of letters on circular rings. I thumbed them desperately, trying to unlock the combination. What was the password? I had forgotten. I heard their voices again, louder.

"We should be helping people!"

"Hold your horses!"

Aah, yes! Then I remembered. The song I had sung for the children.

Dragon, dragon, come and go
As your heart lost in the flow
Find your tail and time will show . . .

The tale of the white dragon Aiyan, the Eternally Blooming. I spun *Aiyan* into the disks as the arguing drew closer, praying the lock would click open. It didn't. Of course! They'd changed it after I'd escaped! I felt myself disappearing, my arms becoming almost transparent. I was suddenly afraid my fingers would go right through the lock.

I heard crunching on the gravel, saw the janitors' backs to me, a fat man-boy and a shorter redheaded woman in shapeless overalls. Both were shading their eyes as they listened to the commotion. They were about to turn when another explosion went off in the distance, forcing them to the ground. The fat one reached out to hold the other protectively.

I was fiddling feverishly behind them. What was it? Favian's father, what was his name? It wasn't coming. Why would it be that? Something simple, simpler! *Come on, Saya!* What was the price of being saved? The giant had said it! *Dreams.* The lock clicked and opened, and I slipped in.

This dome, my home, my prison for so many years. Once filled with fountains, plants and swings, blue jays, red-crested turacos, pheasants, and even Naomi the peacock. My gilded cage of sunflowers, light, and windchimes, my nest of cushions, all gone now. What was before me instead, from the roof above to the ground below, was the black root dappled with blue poppy flowers, and beneath, sleeping in rows of tiny beds, like cherubs, were children. Around each of their wrists twined the black root, the cloying, sweet scent of opium clinging to the air. And from their wrists, the roots twisted and retreated, glowing faintly in blue, sucking toward a central pedestal.

And on that pedestal were my wings, mounted, gleaming, alive. Dripping the black tears. The wings Melasquez himself had ordered sawn from my back as I lay gagged, face down on the surgical table, passed out from pain.

Those wings were my true prison, the trap I could not leave for more than a week or else the changeling would destroy me. Weaponized and black, dripping corruption. Still alive, moving weakly as they sensed me. But did they know me? Had they forgotten?

I saw again the shining figure, leashed to the Tree, invincible in the eye of the storm.

My mind was reeling, splintered and flung wide into the unknown. Floundering among those alien stars, I ricocheted into Andreas's story of the First Traveler. A man traveled through time to save his daughter from a tragic accident, only to find himself the perpetrator of that very accident. A thought had stuck in my mind, a yawning question: When his future self returned to the past, were there not two of him? Both past and future self?

Was that winged figure . . . me? Was I the prophecy?

Was I the Traveler?

✦ ✦ ✦

"Mama?"

I blinked. One of the children in my old cage was groaning as if in delirium, twisting in his cot.

"Mama?"

I came closer. It was Salerio, the warm caramel of his eyes open and unseeing, streaks of ash on his plump cheeks. Next to him was Lady Flower Pot dreaming peacefully with her thumb in her mouth, Lord Teddy snuggled under her arm. The cloying opium smoke drifting from an urn next to their bed stuck in my throat. Was he hallucinating? I had no idea who I was at this moment. I was everyone, no one, disintegrating.

"Mammaaa!" His cry broke my heart. He reached toward me and then fell back, tears bulging from his unfocused eyes. I was breaking apart. But I heard him; I heard it in him.

And I pulled with all my strength for Ciana. I knew she was there. I knew she had been inside me for a purpose. She was here for Salerio. Not for the wings, not for the nightmares, not for the years of wilting and waste. She was here for the children of tomorrow, for those who had a chance for a better life.

And I found her.

I shifted: her long golden hair cascading down my back, her elfin features, her freckles, her pure blue eyes, her dainty limbs, her delicate, sweet sadness. The same white dress, the flower in my hair. I ran to the children's cots, crying their names to wake them, but they were insensible. I clawed at the roots on their wrists, dragging with all my strength. They only gripped harder, constricting, but I would not let them. Nothing would stop me. I bit and ripped at them. I shrieked at my wings, and slowly, gently, they let go.

"Salerio! Salerio!" I pulled his little body into my arms. He stirred dully, blinking up at me, his lips opening but not forming any sounds. "Don't you remember me?" I laid him down. "Lady Flower Pot!" I cried out and cradled her head, stroked her dirty-blond hair, pulling Lord Teddy from her underarm. "Who is this? It's Lord Teddy!" Her lids fluttered open and closed, her pupils unfocused. Tears blurred my vision.

"Remember the First Mother? Our friend the Traveler, he was covered in mud? You are the slayer of monsters! Remember! Remember?" I was crying, shaking them, pleading with them, but it wasn't working. I started singing.

Dragon, dragon, come and go
As your heart lost in the flow
Find your tail and time will show . . .

"Princess?" an astonished voice blubbered from behind me. "What is she doing here?"

Over my shoulder I could see the two janitors, Reece and Gellie, brandishing their mops like spears dripping foam. I could hardly hear what they were saying.

"You came back," came a little voice. I looked down at Salerio, at his mashed cumulus of pale hair, and I thought my chest would burst. His vision had cleared, filled with a need that tugged at my heart. "You came back to be my mama?"

"Oh the Fates! Thank you!" I cried.

"Lord Teddy needs soup," whispered Lady Flower Pot, cradled in my other arm.

I cried for happiness, uncaring of what happened next.

"Princess."

I felt Gellie's wobbly hand on my shoulder. I couldn't stop crying. They were going to be okay!

"It is good, good," he said, hugging us into his belly.

Reece kept her distance, her arm over her nose, brandishing her mop. "Are you done? She's a spy!"

"We need to get them out of here," I seethed back, holding on to the children.

"Gellie can't believe we was cleaning this!" Gellie shouted at his sister.

The mousy redhead winced, glancing around at the children in their beds with a sick look. "I still don't trust her." Her voice wavered.

"You caused this!" I told her the ugly truth. "You led the *kai talan* to the temple!"

Reece paled. I clutched Salerio and his sister to my breast, crouching, helping them stand. Gellie didn't seem to process what I was saying.

"You led our people to ruin! You're the spy!" Reece fired back.

"No," I replied, "I am the signal."

From the strap on my thigh, I took out the flare Andreas had given me in the grove, our signal to the Last Men that we had found the Traveler.

"The Magister trusted me to find the key to bringing down the city. The Traveler." With Salerio and Lady Flower Pot still at my side, I moved toward Reece, holding out the flare for her to take. "And I have found her."

"Where is she then?" Reece barked.

I closed my eyes and reached inside, into the scars on my back. I felt again the moment the saw broke the bone, the moment they left my back forever. And that first stretch, that glorious first beat, in the sea in the Dreaming, with the great tree above me stretching into the universe, the fireflies dancing.

Will we ever find each other again?

My wings responded to my call, flaring outward, the black tips arching all the way to the ceiling of the dome. Gellie stumbled in fear, and Reece backed away. The wings framed me as I stood with the children before her.

"She is the figure in the sky!" moaned Gellie, moving protectively closer to his sister.

I held the flare out to her. "Reece, will you trust me?"

✦

The bright smoke rose into the sky in puffy orange balls.

Inside the luminous vapor, Reece waved the flare, the tip burning a stinging red. Behind us, Gellie was shepherding the children, who blinked, yawned, gaped, or wailed in confusion, awakened from the opium fumes to the sight of tangerine clouds.

"Has Lord Teddy ever flown before?" I asked.

Lady Flower Pot sucked her thumb, holding her plush toy tightly at her side, a burn mark on his paw as if he'd tested the embers in the urns. "He went in his dream," she said in alarm as the beats of the chopper pumped through our eardrums.

I shaded my eyes from the sun, spotting the silhouette of the ship.

"Is the dragon coming to save us?" Salerio's tiny fingers dug into my hand as he tried his best not to hide.

"Yes, the dragon is coming. And you are being so brave." I squinted at the *Interceptor*'s sails cutting a cylindrical opening in the orange smog. The craft's landing blasted our hair backward, sand particles stinging our skin as the captain expertly navigated the chopper into the narrow courtyard. The loud whirring of the sails slowed, the wooden springs hissing with heat.

"Gellie, get the children on board," I instructed over my shoulder. "Reece, tell the captain to meet me inside."

They both acknowledged their orders, slightly in awe.

"Be safe," I whispered, kissing Salerio and Lady Flower Pot on their plump cheeks, pushing them toward the automaton. The little girl ran back to hug me.

"Will we ever see you again?" asked Salerio, unable to part from his princess again. Behind their backs, I saw Alia dismount, fixated on my blond hair, her other hand on her weapon.

"Remember our song. *Heart lost in time, and found again*," I murmured in their ears, ruffling their hair. Reece was blabbering to Alia, who nodded and ushered the kids in without taking her eyes off me. I met her accusation without flinching.

I turned on my heel. If my jailor wanted this fight, let us have it in my cage.

+ ✦ +

They were still beautiful.

Black-tinged feathers, iridescent with stolen memories, humming with forgotten music and the darkness of the root. Calling to me.

My wings.

I always believed that losing them was why the changeling ripped and scratched at my bones. The disintegration, the pulling apart of the tiniest fractions of me, was repaired when I returned to the cage in which they were taken, if only for a few blessed days. Losing them was why I desperately needed to be someone, anyone else, wasn't it? Wasn't it?

That shining figure, invincible in the eye of the storm. My second self.

The scars on my shoulder blades prickled. I heard the click of the door and didn't turn. I didn't care if Alia knew I was the blond spy she had sworn I was not. I had told her not to go to the Maiden's Tower. The structure had crumpled like a child's toy, explosions knocking out its vertical supports, trapping everyone inside. The ambush had been sprung. If she believed I was the one who led them into it, so be it.

"I tried to warn you," came a cold voice from behind me. It was not Alia's. Favian!

I spun, the scars humming and my wings flaring as if linked to me, rising behind me, reaching almost to the ceiling of the dome. My captor held his hands up. Alia was behind him, arm around his throat, dagger pointed to his neck. Reece and Gellie stood ready with their mops.

"You fanatic!" I screamed at him. My wings beat, blasting the piercing power of my voice, the room resonating with crazed energy. All four of them took a step back, the hair on their arms standing up.

"Melasquez is the fanatic, Saya!" Favian held his voice steady, dried blood on his eyebrow.

"I can't believe you!" Alia shouted back at me. "Traitor!"

I could hardly see her through my singular fury. A crackling sound filled the air, like lightning whipping through the dome, and the dark roots around us began to seethe.

"I was trying to stop it! Do you think the Entangling was an accident?" he begged. "The giant wants to bind you! It is the loop that started it all!"

"When did you know?" I asked him, my wings hissing with sibilant lightning that burst and popped in blinding cobalt.

"The Sifter saw it in the pools. One of the throne room guards must have dreamed of it!" he cried out. "Please, Saya! I was trying to protect you!"

Reece hit him with her mop. I could not believe that he would risk everything for me. He had exploited me from the moment he'd dropped those jingling coins into my mother's hand.

"Shut up!" Alia shouted, her voice panicked, unable to bear being sidelined. "Where is the Traveler?"

Favian pointed at me with a crooked finger.

The realization came over Alia without mercy. *It was I who was your supposed savior this entire time. And it was not me who betrayed the resistance but you who could not trust. You, Alia, who sent your companions to their deaths. You, my former jailor, sister, friend.*

Favian took his moment, his intellect slicing through the confusion. "Saya, darling, I didn't know, I swear it. But now I have what we have always needed to escape Melasquez forever!"

"Swear it on your father's grave!" I cried, gathering myself.

Alia's face was ashen. Reece understood it then too. Neither could believe what she was hearing. But it was true. Favian had crooned to me many a dark night that together we would find the weak point in the armor of this parasitic city. That together we would find the Traveler and bring the giant to his knees. But now that we had done it, he would never give up a power like that. He would use me forever. The scars on my back tingled, begging for vengeance.

"Am I the prophecy?" I asked him.

Alia was stricken, and Favian sensed it. He suddenly ducked and slithered out of her grasp. Reece chased him with the mop and he backed away, stumbling over a smoking opium pot, as Gellie cowered away from the rearing wings.

"Please, Alia! Please!" Favian dodged Reece's next swipes. Did I hear genuine regret? He seemed to care what Alia thought of him.

"Shut up!" Alia roared, unable to bear it. Their shadows danced in darker relief as the hissing energy of my wings grew. Favian caught the mop and twisted Reece off balance.

Gellie recovered himself and was about to jump him too, but Favian held his hands up in peace. Alia waved Gellie off, needing to hear what Favian had to say.

"It's her. It's always been her," he started to explain. But before he could continue, lightning crackled from my wings, blasting my handler from his feet. The force threw him into the wall, limbs splayed like a rag doll, seething veins of energy crawling over his chest as the others dived for cover.

"Little bird, what are you going to do?" Alia cried from her knees, using her pet name for me.

I stared down at her. She looked at me as if she'd never seen me before as the changeling ignited in me, a thousand colors of the universe running through my body.

"I am going to break the world."

·18·

ANDREAS

New Time

I SAT TOGETHER WITH ROSANA IN the vast groove of the branch under the deep blue leaves. The wind tickled our hair in the dappled sunshine, and a few honey-winged butterflies danced between curtains of gold light. The day was still bright, the horizon endless—puffy clouds, the faraway edges of the floating landmass, the snowcapped mountains, a few bird calls. Aside from the gentle sounds of the wind, the brush of butterfly wings, and the starlings' calls, the world was silent.

Far below us, a ring-shaped cloud boiled and crackled, coiling like a black halo. On the ground, specks were scattering, tiny as ants. And there in the eye of the storm, a shining figure flew around in circles, her leash running from her neck all the way past us, between branches, up into the canopy, and then down into the secret hollow of the Tree's stump, suspended by a power all its own. The branch upon which we sat reached outward like the fingers of the Fates, reaching, splitting, and reaching again into the skyline.

"You already know, don't you?" said Rosana, turning her cheek so I could see the hood of her veil.

"Why should I . . ." I felt it then, a tingling fear, an excitement, a terror even, bubbling below the surface.

"Her name is Saya," Rosana said, a note of sympathy in her voice.

It couldn't be. I had seen her, in that final moment, her inescapable violet eyes shining with devastation. It was impossible. I stood up, squinting at the glowing winged figure as she pirouetted around the eye of the maelstrom, light crackling around her. An awful thumping rose in my heart, as if it were punching me for something I'd known all along. The scars on her back!

"There are two Sayas in this new circle of time, Andreas," Rosana said, "as in the old stories, where the Travelers go into the past to meet themselves. This is how time is broken, at the touch of two who should be one."

The apocalyptic stories I'd heard in the temples. Surely they had only been myths. And yet the story of the First Traveler was so close to mine.

"Saya of the present is here, the young, naive girl you were Entangled with. But also the Saya you gave the giant in the old time—she is here also, living on through all these years."

"That is impossible! There cannot be two of a single person!"

"That is why your dream girl is breaking apart. And why you cannot try to save her. Or all of this will happen again and again for all eternity."

"No!" I got up, pulling my hand away from Rosana. I turned on her, desperate, looking for a way out. Rosana was implacable, a white ghostess, her delicate veined feet poking out the bottom of her robes, her cyan and green eyes older than I'd ever known them.

Before us, the storm was dissipating, wisps of boiling purple-gray clouds spinning in a vortex of air as the figure twirled up through the sky. It beat its wings weakly and then began to plummet down toward the earth. My heart was in my throat, but then she elegantly looped back up toward us, scything *backward* through the air and into the canopy. How was that possible? Her wings weren't moving, I realized—the root was dragging her in! The shining figure's wings beat again, as if tasting the air one last time, before she was dragged in by her leash and swallowed by the cavernous trunk. Was it just my imagination, or did she see me as she dipped into the gaping mouth?

"I don't believe in any of this! I don't believe in the Fates!"

The pellet of fur and blood was in my belly again, the guilt ugly and revolting. All of this was my doing. And I had done it to the one girl I had loved most in this world.

"It doesn't matter what you believe," said Rosana, her multicolored eyes and lilac lips so different from how I remembered them.

"What about the other Saya, the girl I was Entangled with?" I demanded, wanting to smash something, anything.

"You may see her again." Rosana's voice was as brittle as her skin, suctioned of all emotion, gray with the dust of time. "But only as the dream she was. Your lost memories from the Dreaming are in the pool," she said, opening her arms.

"Why would you do this?" I roared at her, pacing up and down like a caged animal, my father's rope tightening around my waist. "What is this? Revenge?"

"Oh, dear Andreas," my former fiancée said, "you and I could never have been happy. When will you heal the bleeding hole in your heart?"

"You are the one who betrayed all of us!" I lashed out, my fingers clawed. "You were working with Melasquez!"

"Who is to blame in a world without choices? Am I? Are you? Are the Fates?" Rosana's implacable resolve seemed to crack, her voice weakening. "Perhaps we are all blameless in the end. It doesn't matter." She struggled to her feet, and despite myself, I went to help her. I felt how frail she was, saw the spots on her papery skin.

As she stood, she unfurled the cape. The black wool fabric cascaded to the ground, revealing the white dragon Aiyan flying in a circle, consuming his own tail, striking and compact as a lightning bolt. It was meticulously stitched, the work of decades. Again I had the awful premonition that I had seen it before. I towered over her.

From the pockets of her abaya, Rosana drew a pair of scissors. Carefully, she pincered a thread of the black wool and snipped it. "Andreas, this was the only thing your mother left you." She swept it around my broad shoulders. I could not speak.

I had left my mother to perish alone wrapped in her shroud. And the obsession she'd nursed for my father's return was the only thing she had left me. Her accusation rang once more in my heart, as it had every time he had left her. "Where is your papa?" she would ask me, as if I was the one who had driven him away. The dark wool of my inheritance fit perfectly, wrapping around me like the pain I'd always heard yet been unable to answer to.

I wanted to tear it off, but Rosana stopped me. "Wear this on your way back through the Rift," she said, tying the strings around my throat. She ran her hands down over my chest, over the rope looped around my hips, the emotion finally cracking through. "This will lead you to the first cause," she said.

I had the sudden feeling that we were saying goodbye to each other.

"I don't know the way back," I said helplessly.

"Saya knows," Rosana replied. "For it has already happened." An image of that falling angel, leashed by the throat and tumbling into the Tree, came to me.

"But—"

"Please, Andreas, do not try to find love. It is in seeking that you are lost. To save her and yourself . . . let her go."

❖

I plunged down through the vines with a momentum beyond my control, not bothering to hold on any longer. The black cape flapped loudly through the air, pulling at my neck, pulling with the sins of my father.

"It is in seeking that you are lost."

No! I have dreamed of and found love. Unlike that bastard, who left us when we needed him most. It is in seeking that I have found. I felt the vines preemptively loosen, ready to drop me at terrifying speeds into the luminous memories, memories of Saya. Would I have to say goodbye? Would I see the life we had lived together? Would it break me again, as it broke me back then? Was there any escape from the loops we lost ourselves in?

Saya!

I waited for the final moment, the sound of the bird wings scattering, the glow of the pool beginning to glimmer beneath me. The vines let go and I held my arms tightly to my sides like a piston, pointing my feet.

The liquid memory sucked me in without wetness or impact, warm and enveloping, the pool suctioning down. No turning back. I felt a quiver, a humming in my ears, rising in intensity. My entire body was absorbed, and I heard the sound of foreign voices speaking alien languages, words awash with strange meanings. Symbols distorted as if deep underwater, until it all blurred into vibrations. In resonance with it, my physical form rotated, spiraling, swirling, and disappearing.

Space and time lost all proportion—the time between heartbeats was eternity. Plantlike forms floated through my vision, exquisite colors, mutating. A living crowd of beings, thousands and thousands of innumerable lives. And then, in the quivering and exultant, in the sweet and the pure, in the poignant and the incomprehensible, in the lives of every one of us, I was Andreas no longer.

The Dreaming

OUR NOSES PRESSED TOGETHER. WITHIN her eyes, a riot of orchid and lavender petals radiated from a warm gray flame that encircled her pupils, a violent explosion of color. I drew back and ran my thumb gently over her lips, her small, freckled nose. Down her dusky cheeks cascaded her tangled silver-white hair, and I drank in the smell of her, like warm summer rain.

My dream girl.

She was young, in her late teens, and already excruciatingly lovely. I could not believe this moment could exist, the two of us so close to each other under the covers in our beach tent, the surf brushing the shore outside.

"What if I told you you're not real?" I wondered out loud, my thumb running over her lips. "That I just made you up so I don't feel so lonely all the time?"

Saya smiled. "I would like that," she said, nipping at my thumb. "It would mean something inside you poured itself into making me. Just so I could love you." Her fingers played with my long mane, possessive and exciting. "So, in a way, I am a love letter to you. From your deepest self." She propped herself up above me, her body pressing against mine.

"Wouldn't you want to be something so beautiful?" she asked, holding my face up to hers.

✦

Together we watched the ocean at the end of time, the shifting waves black and luminous, sheathed in a silvery miasma of moonlight. The stars overhead were like dewdrops in the cosmos. Above us, the golden tree's limbs reached out into the surf, gently swaying with pink and brown leaves. Its warm glow reached into the sky, shimmering like the stars themselves. I dragged the boat up the beach, white sand like powder under my toes. The phosphorescent waters twinkled and lit up with tiny creatures as the waves rippled up and down the shore.

Saya was on a low-hanging branch over the waves, legs dangling, tucking a strand of hair behind her braid as she stared out at the moon. It was setting slowly below the ocean, taking up half the horizon.

She stuck out her bottom lip. She was infinitely cute when she was sad. Soon, it would be daylight, and although time was not time as I had known it, she would wake with the third dawn and disappear for a while from me, evaporating like the morning mist.

"When are you coming down from there?" I asked, tying up the boat.

"Go away." She ignored me, kicking her feet. The fireflies were twinkling around her.

I came and stood under the branch. "What's up?"

"You don't know?"

"No," I shot back. I'd been rowing her in the small boat around the shallow surf. She'd been staring into the distance, perched on the end like a mermaid. The moment had been intimate. The beat of oars in the steady current, the beat of the purple-and-blue universe above us. She'd been telling me about the searing hope she felt since we met, how boundless the future was, high and endless like the sky.

"Useless," she grunted.

I pursed my lips, trying my best to recall what I'd done or said. I'd encouraged her, excited by the tremulous hope I saw beneath her carefully hidden sadness. She'd been happy at first, whimsical, contemplating the push and tug of the waves. But then a shadow had crossed her face.

"Sometimes when my feelings are too big, I want to sing them," she groaned, "to no one in particular." She was so dramatic. I climbed up into the tree and sat down next to her.

"Why won't you talk to me?" I tried to turn her to face me but she wouldn't.

"Don't wipe away my tears. I want to feel them on my face." She sniffed. Melodramatic. Was it because she was going to disappear in the morning from this dream world, as she did every morning?

Or was it because even if she felt hope here, it wasn't real?

She had not told me anything about her true home. Neither had I told her about mine. We wanted to keep this, us, our secret, as if any mention of the real world would destroy us. But I knew also that our denial was keeping us from really knowing each other.

"Stop sulking and pretending that if I loved you, I would know why you're upset. I can't read your mind." I held her arm. "Just because we have a connection, it's not wordless. You have to talk to me, Saya. I'm not attacking you."

She pouted, burrowing her head into my shoulder.

"I'll just take a nap. That's how you solve that," she grumbled. I stroked her face, tugging her lovely little earlobes.

"You need to teach me," I said, keeping my voice firm while I hugged her. "Not out of pain or anger. And I will not always get it . . . that's okay. But Saya, I want to learn. I want to learn everything about you." I lifted her chin with my finger and looked deep into her violet eyes, with all of their breathtaking radiance accentuated by her tawny skin and silver hair. She was impossibly gorgeous. "Will you teach me?"

✦

I was leaning back into the groove in the branches, glaring at the resin I'd used to bind the planks of the tree house. I'd just touched it five minutes ago. It was still sticky. I wanted to test the planks so badly, but I couldn't. It would pull apart. I touched it again. Sticky.

"How is it still sticky?" I roared.

"Are you hungry?" Saya called up. She put down her baskets happily and turned on her heel. She'd been picking apples and berries in the forest.

"How am I supposed to know if I am hungry or bored? They feel the same!"

"Are you mad? I'm hugging you with my mind."

"I don't care, and I'm not caring anymore today. Argh!" I touched the resin again and clambered up with my rock and wooden peg. I placed the peg into the gap that ran between two planks and hammered it in, the wood squeaking and squealing. I let go and leaned back. Finally! I took a careful step onto the floor of our tree house and with a sickening lurch, the entire platform swung out and collapsed onto the sand.

I jumped down from the World Tree into the remains of my tree house, then proceeded to smash at them with my rock hammer, kicking over uprooted plants, cursing the Fates, the skies, the apples, the fish, the octopus, and the turtles.

"You're making a mess." Saya had come to observe.

"This whole dreamscape is a mess! What are we even doing here? What is this?" I kicked the broken supports and they crunched inward with a satisfying crack. Behind, I saw the yellow eyes of the creature watching me from an inland thicket. "You don't even know your own name!" I shouted at it.

"Calm down!" Saya marched up to me, clasping my face in her hands. "Angry Boy, listen to me. You do not have to rise above your rage. But you also do not have to let it own you. You are what you are. You will get angry sometimes. You cannot change that. But you can accept it, honor it, feel it, understand it, and let it go."

I was looking over her shoulder at the beast, but as she spoke, she pulled me back.

"I didn't mean to," I growled, trying to make light of it.

"Just don't stay here. Don't hang on to it, because then it gets dangerous. Acknowledge it, and let it go or let it be. It will get better, and if it doesn't, we'll make it. You are still loved and you are still safe, and I am not going anywhere, okay?"

I flicked a look at the beast's yellow eyes. It was patient, hungry.

"Let's walk together. You can throw rocks, smash waves, whatever you need to do to make you feel better, okay? Now kiss me and let's go." She pressed her lips against mine, and finally the anger disappeared. It was just us. I sighed and clutched her to my chest. Together we set off down the beach.

The beast padded after us.

✦

We were walking together on the beach beyond time toward the glowing World Tree, coming home together. The coming dawn was painted in rose, cream, and buttermilk across the surface of the ocean. Although the pillows of the tree house were comfortable, neither of us wanted to arrive yet. I couldn't bear it when she disappeared from my arms in the bed I'd made every morning. She clung to me, a warm wind brushing her hair against me.

"I'm scared," Saya said.

"What are you scared of?" I said softly.

"That one day I'll never find my way back . . ." She leaned into me. I felt protective, fierce, sad all at once.

"You won't. Your dream will come true. You believed that."

"I dreamed that you were . . . real. That you came back for me." She stopped, looking up at me. It tugged my heart to see her afraid.

"How?" I asked.

In answer, she kissed me, her warm tongue seeking mine. I could feel a wild, lost hunger in her. "I want you, forever," she whispered in my ear.

She took my hand and led me into the surf, the phosphorescence glossing our ankles. Glancing over her shoulder, she slipped out of her pale dress. The lights of the ocean danced over her legs, the arch of her buttocks, as the dress fell into the water. She stepped into the waves, her hands rippling the luminous memories.

"Angry Boy?"

I pulled my shirt off. My heart pounded as I undid the strings of my pants, hurrying after her, the ocean yielding around my calves, thighs, and then mercifully hiding me as I stroked in after her.

She was crouched, watching, the moonlight reflected in her hair. She paddled toward me, the glowing tree behind her, the stars twinkling as fireflies danced over the surface of the water. Her eyes were vulnerable, her lips slightly open. She bit them as she stood, nearing me, the ocean only to her waist. The liquid dripped off her, running down her belly, over her breasts with their dark nipples. I let the water hold me, half kneeling before her. She ran her hands over the muscles of my shoulders and up my neck, raising me to her.

"Don't say anything," she whispered. She ran her other hand down my chest as if sculpting me, over my ribs, the groove of my hip. The fireflies congregated around us, twinkling. Our movements made the water dance with sparkling green. She put both her hands around my neck and pulled herself onto me. Instinctively I supported her, hands squeezing her buttocks, her legs wrapping around my hips. She felt light, the liquid buoying us, the currents rocking us in rhythm as we responded to each other's heat.

"Have you ever done this before?"

I shook my head, dumbstruck by the magnitude of the gift she was implying. She smiled in a lonely kind of way. This too was her first and only.

I placed my hand on her breast and squeezed, watching her nipples respond. A thundering began between my legs. Her calves hooked behind mine as she leaned in, devouring, and we moaned into each other's mouths. I bit her lip, and she arched her back. I brought her back, kissing her neck, holding her against me as she lifted her hips, pushing, adjusting until . . . I was right there at her opening in the slippery water, staring into her eyes. As I entered, she winced, her mouth open, her eyes pleading.

"Am I hurting you?" I gasped.

"You could never hurt me," she replied, clutching me. In wonder, we began to rock against each other.

Her moans grew faster, her fingers digging into my back. I felt her groin quivering.

"Promise me," her mouth panted on top of mine, "we'll find each other again."

"I promise!" I cried, shuddering. Her eyes were so close, our bodies crushing one another. As one, we cried out to the sky.

And coming from her back, emerging out of her in light, impossible wings bloomed, shaking with her, arching into the wind.

I clutched her to me desperately, in awe, as the dawn light broke upon us, catching the wings in its first rays. In barely a second, Saya evaporated like the mist, as if she'd never been there at all.

New Time

As I RETURNED FROM THE living memories into my body, I felt my lungs were about to burst. An instinctive surge of energy kicked me upward. I broke the surface, spurting the liquid from my mouth like a dolphin.

I remember. I remember it all. Saya!

Gasping and kicking to stay afloat, head above the memories,

I gulped in breaths, spinning wildly. I was in an enormous pool at the base of the stump, the collected lake of memory that powered the entire city.

Did she know it was me? Did she know the whole time? Why didn't she say anything?

In the center, roots had coalesced into an enormous spire, an island with a single bridge at the peak that led across the water toward a gleaming opening of sunlight. The throne. I had found her again! Around me, the walls echoed with the breathing of the Black Tree, and I saw blue flowers by the thousands all around me on their vines, beautiful and deadly, Leah's dream of children.

Why had I not remembered? How could I be such a coward?

My senses tingled with the smell of earth and secrets, a presence in the air. Forms in my periphery pulsed and quivered, but when I looked, there was nothing there—only the ambience from the glowing liquid. The thin stream of sunlight from the bridge's exit was the only light.

How could I lose Saya again?

I swam toward the island as quietly as I could. Around me, black roots moved like giant worms through the memories, arching and dipping. I felt them crawl past me, unsettling as a deep-sea creature. I had a premonition that they would clutch me by the ankles and drown me in the depths.

A root three times my size arched before me and I dived underneath it. In the liquid, I saw thousands of them, like fingers sifting through the memories. And flashing before me were the final moments of the drained—chained to chairs, pinned to walls and beds, held down, the root tunneling into their chests—men, women, and children.

I burst upward, powering forward, unable to forget, refusing to. *What darkness have you unleashed, Melasquez?* The throne root grew like a monstrous helix hundreds of feet above, and she was chained to it. The Saya who flew through the storm. The Saya who knew the future. I would not follow this destiny, Fates be damned!

I clambered up onto the spiral of root, the liquid slipping right off my cloak without wetting it. The black coils were warm to the touch, knotted with hollows and handholds. A suicidal climb without safety equipment or route. The slightest error would plunge me to death and perhaps beyond. I glanced down at my waist. But this time, my father was with me.

I remembered those night climbs up the cliff face in the Passage of Ravines, the beast below me, hoping to feast when I fell. Was that truly fear? Or encouragement? I unspooled the rope and began my ascent, wincing in pain. Blood caked my bandaged hand, but nothing would stop me from finding her again. Distantly, I could hear explosions, the cries of battle, the clash of steel on steel.

Hand over hand, I gripped, pulled, lunged, digging my fingers into hairpin cracks in the coiled root, hanging by a single arm, swinging my body weight to catch another hold. My fingers ached as I clung by thumb and forefinger. There was no wind, only the suctioning breath of the Tree, heady with oxygen. Bees, frogs, and birds jumped from invisible cracks, scaring me.

I looked up. The gnarled spire seemed massive, never-ending. I gritted my teeth and pressed onward, digging into an obsidian groove, pulling myself from one shallow divot to the next, clawing like an animal. Then, a narrow cranny, and I leaned into the edge and pushed my feet against an adjacent root mass, squirming up as if it were a chimney, my thighs aching and shaking, the fall sickening below me.

At the crest of it, I rested in a hollow fang, planning my next move. There was a vertical opening about two hands wide on the left. I wedged half my body in and wriggled my way upward, inch by inch. I'd secured the rope to a lone root that looped out of the throne below, but I had no way of knowing if it would hold my weight. I gripped and pulled myself out, swinging my right leg into a foothold barely a pencil width wide.

Too small. Too slippery. I teased it again. My toe slipped off again and again, my hamstring burning. I tried farther to the left. It was worse. Then the other way. Worse still, not a single crack. My heart racing, I felt panic. Lost, hundreds of feet above the gaping mouth of the Tree.

I would have to stand up on my right foot and rise or die.

I dreamed that you were real. That you . . . came back for me.

I pushed off.

I careened into weightlessness, gasping in terror. Then my waist constricted, my father's climbing rope biting into my flesh as it caught hard and gravity swung me into the throne, driving the air from my lungs. My eyes flashed and I heard the rope groaning as I swayed, listless, hundreds of feet above the turquoise pools of memory.

Move.

I reached out, gasping, flailing at the smooth roots. But I floated away before I could grab on to anything, the rope biting into my abs, crushing my breathing. I swung back, the rope twisting and groaning.

Please.

My hands caught. My legs moved automatically, toes scrabbling for holds, finding them. The moment I felt my weight in my hands, I clung to the side of the throne in relief, my adrenaline kicking wildly. I breathed, eyes closed. The amber slits of the beast rose in my vision, and I was shocked at their ferocity.

Move.

Shaking, I kicked into a little dimple aggressively so I could reach out with my opposing hand. I hooked both hands into a more stable grip, then swung into a deeper hold where I could finally stabilize myself on firm footing. I loosened the harness enough to gulp air, took some huge breaths, then paused to take stock of the final ascent. There was an alternate route to the one I'd taken. I picked my way up it, gratefully unspooling my father's rope that had saved me.

Thank you, Papa.

I could see the summit now, closer and closer every time I reached for it. *Saya, where are you?* I coiled my legs under me, a loaded spring. To reach the top, I would have to jump backward and grip the ledge of the throne that hung above. This was it; this was everything. A single-handed jump. No time to think.

Just go.

I leaped, and my hand scuttled onto the edge of it, my shoulder ripping in pain. I roared, swinging, my fingers biting, skidding. I flung out my other hand, the wound pumping blood down my arm. *Saya!*

Promise me.

Shaking, I pulled and dragged my head up, then my elbows, and at last my chest flopped over the edge. The balance was precarious, my legs kicking air, and for a split second, I thought I wasn't going to make it. And then, with a gut wrench of pain, I was over, rolling on my back, dust coughing up around me. Just my ragged breathing and the pain of victory.

Saya.

I hunkered down on my knees, holding my bleeding palm. I was behind the throne, built now into a massive chair twice the height of a man on horseback. Beyond it, the bridge spanned three hundred feet to the great doorway of light. It was quiet, eerily quiet.

An impossibly large knee moved into view, legs standing. A black form twisted off the throne. Its girth was incredible, the size of ten men at least.

Melasquez, grown even bigger these decades into the future, arms hanging almost to his knees, each as wide as my chest. His layers of fat and muscle were immense and overwhelming. He hunched over as he lumbered toward me, dragging his knuckles in futility along the ground, the whites of his eyes showing under his hooded brows.

"Oh my hmmm, here you are. The one person I could not save." His apelike lips smirked. "The sacrifice."

And before I could react, he swatted me off the edge, as casually as if I were a fly.

+ ✦ +

Tumbling into the dark, floating. A flash of blue under my back. A gust like a torrent of flapping wind.

Arms, I was holding on to them, flipping through the air. I glimpsed a rush of feathers, a cavern, crackling energy—mesmerizing in deep blue—and then someone laid me onto pillows. A shining figure stepped back, her raven-black wings folding in behind her. She kneeled, caressing my cheek.

It was Saya, but not Saya. Her hair was pale and to her knees, glacial blue at its roots. Her eyes, almost transparent, showed only the barest hint of purple. Her skin was bleached and wrinkled, like a creature that had lived its whole life in the darkest caves. Old, older than time. Delirious, happy tears poured from her face.

We were inside a cavern built from the throne's roots. Threadbare pillows and blankets nested in a circle around a single melted candle. There were chalk drawings all over the roof and walls, cave paintings of the stars, of creatures and worlds I had never imagined, all arranged around a World Tree painted upside down. This was the Saya whose dreams had been taken from her. All of her yearnings, all of her soul, all of her broken love.

"Saya, Saya, what happened to you?"

Her mouth opened, but only a moan came from it. Her eyes were shining with wretched bliss, a final joyful ending. Had she waited all these years to see me one last time?

"Saya, my pet!" the giant shrieked from above us. "Where are you?"

The leash around her neck pulled taut, and she clasped it with her hands. The whites of her eyes darkened with the blue poison of the tears as it choked her.

"What happened to us?" I cried at her, my voice low. The root whiplashed out of the nest, flipping her outward, upward to the throne. I swore violently, rushing after her, grasping at empty air.

Cautiously, I poked my head out. Shadows bustled past the doorway of light at the end of the bridge. I heard shouting, hooting, steel clanking. Then a low, manic chuckle that amplified, echoing off the walls. Melasquez's laughter. That bastard!

I winced, glancing left and right for a hold and levering myself carefully up the side with my good arm, staying pressed against the root wall. My entire left side was numb from the giant's blow. The figures were closer now, soldiers marching down the bridge, *kai talan* and bleeding prisoners in chains.

And at the center of the procession, Heron, being wheeled in on his wooden throne. How had they gotten to him? The light seemed to be shifting, and the speed of the oncoming soldiers seemed to slow, their steps murkier as if walking through a swamp. I saw a bee floating next to my head. It blinked five inches to the right, and then back again in an instant.

I dragged myself up to the ledge, daring a look. Melasquez stood with his back to me, his fist wrapped around the leash. Saya lay crumpled on her knees at his feet, draped in her wings, her pale hair falling in a waterfall across the darkly gleaming roots.

The victorious soldiers of the Tree were shouting and catcalling their prizes. At the front was Favian, the bastard unmasked and unrepentant, and behind him Alia, haggard, her cover seemingly still intact. The snake was holding his ribs, wearing a grim expression of rictus pain that would not be denied.

The Tree around us felt sibilant, alive, the heady wind of its breath making my head swim as the giant's mad laughter echoed in the chamber. The soldiers stopped a little way back, still afraid of the giant after the tears had poured from the sky.

Favian pushed Heron's chair forward. I could hear the wheels squeaking. My ancient friend's swan robe was torn and bloodied, his long hair and mustache disheveled, but his bearing was fierce, unbowed. The giant beckoned them forward with both hands. Pushing the chair from behind, Favian bared his teeth with the effort.

"You shut your doomsayer mouth," mocked the giant, "or I'll be back to shut it for you." The same threat Heron and his friends had spat at the starving inventor on the nights before his rise. Melasquez did an absurd little jiggle, his laughter pinging off the walls.

"You won't be back, Melasquez," replied Heron bravely. "I swear it in the name of Leah's blue flowers."

The giant stopped his dance, put off by the old leader's confidence.

Favian had wheeled Heron right up to the mad Regent, and then, with a bored expression, he had sidled past the distracted giant, drifting toward Saya, who lifted her head like a dreamer awakened in the night. That snake!

Favian kneeled before the fallen Saya, and her raven wings wrapped around them, her arm coming up to caress his face. That's when I spotted it—the bastard had the ribbon of our Entangling around his wrist. I couldn't take it anymore; I pulled myself up over the edge.

A blinding light erupted, blasting over the entire cavern, shaking my bones and convulsing the ground beneath our feet. I shielded my eyes and pushed forward despite a massive gravitational pull, forcing my way through time itself, squinting and seeing. It wasn't Favian any longer; it had never been Favian.

It was Saya, my Saya, with the ancient's translucent hand grazing her cheek. And where they touched, the light emitted was unbearable. Saya and her second self, my dream girl and her nightmare, the past and the present, colliding. She had the loveliest expression on her face, as if she was . . . finally sure of herself.

"Saya!" I screamed, running toward her.

She didn't seem to hear. The giant too was roaring, but it was as if we were moving underwater. I saw her nuzzle her head into her old self and whisper something in her ear as they embraced, the light cutting through both of them as if bursting from within. The ancient disintegrated into particles of dust that dissipated into the shaking air. The entire Tree cracked open overhead, letting in streaks of sun and starlight split by the comet. The canopy had broken open!

Light consumed Saya, her whole body a being of pure, impenetrable burning, widening into a raw reality, the ribbon of the Entangling gleaming on her wrist. I'd only ever seen something like this once before—in the reaching man of the portal.

"Saya!" I pushed through the blinding light, my forearms burning, feeling as if I too were disintegrating, my flesh dissolving in particles. I saw the giant too, his hooded eyes wide in panic, pushing through the otherworldly haze. Heron was laughing, his hands clasped together in prayer while he looked around at the blue flowers. They were wilting and falling all around us, plopping like raindrops into the memories beneath, as the entire earth began to fall away beneath our feet, the soldiers and Alia running back along the bridge.

Melasquez and I kept pushing through the light, which grew brighter and brighter, growing, elongating, enveloping it all.

Promise me.

·19·

SAYA

The Dreaming

"**YOU ARE FREE NOW**," I whispered to my ancient self. I hugged her to me, the unbearable lightness of her, parting with this moment particle by particle. Within us was a boundless ocean of infinite light, cracking open the world. In its vastness, I was free, like a fragrance lifting into space. In that first moment, the stars scattered, and the singing and contemplating within me were whole and infinite as love.

Then with a shattering rush, I came into being again.

I was meditating in a forest, wearing a new white dress, the ribbon of the Entangling around my wrist the only thing that had survived the journey.

The moon had risen.

I uncrossed my legs, stood, and padded toward it, the grass lush on the soles of my feet. The dark trees parted before me, opening the way into a clearing. There I saw a young girl coming down from the moon, stepping through the sky as if on puddles of water, wearing the same gossamer dress I was. The first snow drifted down through the leaves, the flakes illuminated by the pale moonlight.

Her toes touched the grass, daintily, unsure, expectant. Flakes alighted on her dove-white hair. Oh, Saya, just a little girl, dreaming of finding someone to show her who she was. Her first time here, she looked around her like a deer, lost, brave, vulnerable, her teenage anxieties so raw and aching for love it made my heart ache for her.

But the clearing of her dreams was empty. This time, he wasn't here. A wave of grief overwhelmed me. Andreas truly had been forgotten.

The young girl stood there in the dark forest, alone.

I couldn't tell her everything was going to be okay. It wasn't. I had seen our future already. A wilted husk, imprisoned until the end of her days.

"This world is a prison," I said, stepping out into the clearing.

"Is there no key?" she asked.

I was about to reply when a howl echoed distantly through the trees. It was heartrending, lonely. A beast, forgotten at the end of time. The girl heard it and instead of being afraid, she looked at me.

"Why does it howl?" she asked. Could I tell her he was howling for her? Perhaps it was for nothing at all. Perhaps it was for all he had forgotten. Perhaps it was only a figment of this beautiful girl's imagination.

The look on her face told me he was howling in hopes that we would hear him. He was hoping we would follow the sound across time and come back for him.

As always, Andreas, you bring hope to my heart. But I will not follow that folly again.

I saw again the face of my imprisoned self, her shrunken body splayed on the floor of the throne room, Melasquez's fist holding the chain around her neck. And as she disappeared, perhaps worst of all was the gratitude in her eyes as I set her free from herself, forever.

"It howls to the moon, to the Fates that scattered the stars in the sky," I said.

She looked up, the snowflakes settling in her hair, on her eyelashes. "I would like to meet mine. My Fate."

"Shall we go together?" I said, holding out my hand.

The cloth from the Entangling glowed faintly on my palm.

+ ✦ +

We stood on the shoreline.

The phosphorescent ocean washed up, then retreated. The rush, break, and recession comforted me like a lullaby. It was the sound of the only home I had ever known. Shells crunched beneath our feet as we walked, hand in hand, our fingers wrapped around the ribbon of the Entangling.

The way was different, and it had taken longer to leave the forest than I remembered. It was so long ago that I had dreamed it with Andreas, I wasn't completely sure. The night had deepened as the trees had parted for us, the light from the ribbon wrapped around our hands guiding the way. But now that I saw our tree, I knew I had come to the right place.

It glowed golden at the edge of the break line, its pink and brown leaves rustling in the night wind coming in off the waves. I looked for our tree house, but of course, he hadn't built it yet. He never would.

We walked toward it, past the spot where Andreas and I had made love, where I had found my wings. The water was darker, bluer than I remembered. No boat landing, no rope. *Of course it isn't the same, Saya. He isn't here.* The Entangling ribbon around my wrist was burning now, as if in warning, and I rubbed my arm.

"Are you okay?" my younger self asked me.

"Yes," I lied. "I'm just . . . missing someone."

"I know what you mean," she sighed. "I'm missing someone I've never met."

I smiled, tears pricking my eyes. She squeezed my hand, her smile brave.

We reached the tree and stood underneath it. Our World Tree's branches reached up into the sky. Where were the fireflies? I missed them, too. Suddenly I had no idea what to do. Should I pray? How does one talk to a god? To Fate? I didn't know.

I had never known.

"Do you know any songs?" the girl asked me. "I think singing could cheer you up." She sat down on the warm sand and patted the white powder next to her. I watched her tuck a strand of hair behind her ear as the ocean wind tickled it. She was so innocent, unbroken.

It reminded me of a secret song I had never sung before but whose melody I could hear in my heart—lyrics and a beat that had been bouncing around my mind for years since I had read Angry Boy's poem.

I should sing it to say farewell, I thought, sitting down next to her. We watched the waves together, each one glistening with green phosphorescence, none the same as any other but all from the same waters, building, crashing, and receding. I opened my lips and sang his song for the first time.

What is love?
To offer a hand
In a secret forest
To crack the shell
Of your own understanding
To let go of fate,
To leap without feet,
In the keen light of the moon
In the presence of all things
To always know
I want you, forever.

The tree stirred. I heard a voice in my mind: *I am the becoming, seeing myself divided. I am my metamorphosis; I am my return. For here, all selves become one.*

"Give us something to hope for!" I shouted.

As if in answer, I heard a small crack. And from the top of the tree, a fruit dropped into my lap: heart-shaped, decorated with tiny aquamarine seeds, shiny and succulent. I blinked up into the tree in surprise.

"Can you hear it?" the young girl beside me asked, her cheeks flushed with wonder.

I could see no others, only the branches reaching and merging with the sky, the stars twinkling in the deep blue-purple of the heavens.

Of what do you dream?

It was not speaking our language, and yet I could understand it. Where first it had been primordial and frightening, now the voice was familiar. I might even have said it was my own.

I dream of him, but he's not here.
Eat freely of what is given.

I stood up and looked down into that girl's eyes. I saw all of her pain. I saw how lost she was. I looked at the fruit in my hand. I imagined tasting it, freeing her from the pain that had imprisoned her, allowing her to escape herself, at last. The Entangling ribbon around my wrist had looped down my forearm. It tangled in the light winds, still burning in warning.

That howl, distant as a memory, ached in my heartbeat. There was another lost boy out there somewhere, running from himself, fighting himself. "I want you, forever," I had whispered in his ear. I missed him in my bones, as if he had remade me from the inside, filled me with an invincible longing to be his again.

The boy who had made my wings bloom from the depths of me, with all the colors of my hope. Was it his love that set them free? Or my own?

"You need to be your true self. No matter the cost." Andreas's words, in that room a thousand years ago, on a morning when I wanted him more than anything.

I dropped the fruit, kneeling before my younger self.

"Nothing can help you, Saya. Not the Fates. Not this fruit. Not falling in love." I stroked her cheek, the pity swelling inside me. She was so young. Was it fair that she should have to hear this? "Only you can make yourself hope again. I am going to let you choose, but know that I will love you, no matter what you decide."

I hugged her and felt her arms wrap around me. I felt her inside of me. Radiant, complete. And from my back, with the joy of acceptance, came my wings, bursting forth into the world.

I breathed in the sweet air, the sweet pain, and knew that I would fly again. And from the firmament came the fireflies, dancing down around me, bathing us in golden light as if they were the stars themselves.

"You are a miracle mmmhmmm, just as my little brother was." From behind the tree, an apelike figure emerged. Melasquez was even bigger here than he was at the keep, where I had seen him laughing in madness, relishing the end of his enemies, with my ancient self broken at his feet. The waves picked up, pounding the shore next to me and rushing over my calves.

"The girl with a dream so powerful it came true," he said, stomping into the water and towering over me, looking my wings up and down. "Just as my brother's did hmm." He reached down into the water and picked up the fruit that bobbed like a tiny ship in a storm. "The Entangling ribbon draws you to Andreas. If you accept the fruit, your past self will find him again. At least she will find love again."

The brown and pink leaves of the tree were falling in the wind, swept away into the ocean. A bigger wave crashed onto the shore, and I jumped above it, my wings lifting me. The tree was darkening, its leaves wilting, its branches growing blacker and blacker.

"Eat what is given," he said, holding the fruit out to me. "Give yourself the hope you always needed."

I remembered Melasquez's surgeons standing above me, sawing off the wings that now drove me higher and higher, above his waist and now to his eye level. Behind him, the tree was barren now and black as the Fate of the city I had escaped.

The fruit was a trap. This was the loop. This was the end and the beginning.

He snatched at me with his monstrous fingers, grabbing, reaching. With a whoosh of my wings, I lifted myself above his grip, darting beneath his other arm as it clutched the air. Up and up, wings pounding, I lifted myself into the stars, but he grew with me, huger and huger, his godlike arms stretching up behind me, trying to snatch me from the sky. Far below us, the Fate turned to black—it had never been our World Tree.

I won't give up hope, my love.

I'll find you, in this world or any other.

Higher and higher, I flew up to the moon.

·20·

ANDREAS

☾

The Dreaming

THE DISSIPATING LIGHT NARROWED TO pinpricks, and once more I was tunneling into vast and unknowable space. The pinpricks glistened like stars, punctures in the fabric of the universe. I saw the galaxies of purple and green, the branches of light growing around me. I was spinning like a corkscrew, gaining momentum, the cloak my mother had left me wrapped around my body. I passed through space beyond time at unfathomable speed.

It grew dark and suddenly cold, and I knew I'd reached a point older than time. I saw a circle of light. I drew closer. The design on my cloak of the white dragon eating its own tail began to burn. I could feel every stitch of it searing. The circle of light before me was spinning, and I heard a song, just a melody. The song of Aiyan, the Eternally Blooming, the dragon who tasted his tail.

As I neared through the vastness, I saw the circle of light was a dragon itself. A blinding white dragon devoured its own tail, a great circle of beginning and ending. I came closer and closer, so close I could see the stars in his scales and his fangs that bit into his own flesh, greater than mountains. He opened his jaws to bite ever deeper, and for a second, I paused before the strand of time, a puny human consciousness, my black cloak with its insignia whipping around me.

Then, as I once entered the Rift between time so long ago, I entered between the dragon's teeth and into the light.

Old Time

I OPENED MY EYES. I was curled in a ball, tendrils of smoke hissing off me and up into the foliage. I was under a bush, in the muddy dawn, tiny icicles dripping around me. A dandelion, its silver tufts broken, floated in front of my nose. There was wild grass tamed into a pathway, a small wooden house, a river trickling by. I recognized the thatched roof, the green window frames, daffodils cultivated into bursts of canary yellow, white wildflowers, and lavender. It was my garden, dotted with the squishy red balls Papa had brought me from a faraway land, laden with melting sleet from last night's storm.

I shivered and shook my head to clear away the bizarre image of the godlike beast in the everlasting starscapes, cobwebs of memories from the Dreaming. Rosana had told me to find the first cause. Was this where the great loop had led me? But why here?

Our front door opened, creaking in the gentle morning. My father stomped out, a backpack slung over his shoulder. He wore a green cloak and the same indestructible hiking boots I had seen on the soldiers when the Dreaming had first begun.

He rubbed his grizzled beard and smacked his lips in satisfaction, his eyes alive with the challenge of the unknown. I recognized his outfit; I recognized everything. This very day had haunted me all of these years since, the day before the Marauda arrived, the day before the Dreaming. The last day I saw my father. The day he'd promised to come back. And never had.

I struggled to speak; my voice wasn't working. I could hardly move.

He marched past me, strong as a mountain, stopping to close the gate behind him so it didn't squawk and wake us. He stopped and looked back fondly at the grass we had played on so many times, at the last of the frost winking after the storm's passing. I tried with everything I could to move, to shout out to him, but my body wasn't responding.

Then, with a curt grin, he was gone.

I finally regained movement and forced myself upright. With ungodly effort, I got to my feet and staggered toward the gate, past my own window where an angry young man slept, hoping in his deepest heart his father had not lied to him.

Up the lane, I saw flashes of his olive cloak disappearing around a corner. I followed unsteadily, wrapping my darker hood around myself for warmth. He was striding at an incredible pace. The man had walked innumerable tundras, always restless. What made a man leave his family and stride into the unknown?

I could hardly keep up with him. I staggered around a corner and caught a glimpse of him at the top of a hill next to the tavern. As he strode past, a cloaked figure tottered out, hunched over itself. The stooped figure paused and swayed, almost falling into a thawing puddle, looking at my father. And then it began zigzagging after him.

Was this the man who murdered him?

Ignoring the nausea and the weakness in my legs, I pushed myself to the crest of the hill. There, at the bottom of the hill, the drunk was still wobbling after him. My father took the winding path toward the old well, the dirt road that would take him past Melasquez's shack.

My rage powered my recovery, and I forced my legs into a jog. The village was pristinely quiet in the early dawn, just the smell of baking bread drifting through the warm air. The sun was rising and I'd lost both of them. But this was not the first quarry I had tracked, and I saw the uneven footprints of the drunk in the dirt and slush, winding out of town.

I tracked them as I would a wounded animal, my body recovering with every step, moving faster and more urgently. I was running now at full pace, leaping over puddles and ducking under thatched roofs, past the multicolored flags of my people, my heart in my throat. An early riser yawned and frowned at me from a round window.

I sprinted along the dirt track out of town, desperate not to slip on black ice with each pounding step. Around me in the trees, life was awakening. Birds sang and gave rustling calls, and dewdrops lit up spiderwebs built in the sunrise.

As I neared, I saw the door to Melasquez's shack standing wide open. His many stray animals, goats, and scrawny dogs blinked up at me blearily. He was known to be an ugly drunk, full of resentment and malice. He'd been thrown out of every watering hole in the village. He'd not come home this night.

No!

A hundred feet away, my father was watching the sunrise, crouched on a glistening boulder, munching on a straw of mountain weed. Before him was a magnificent view of the Passage of

Ravines, trees shaking off the storm's passing, waterfalls, eagles' nests, and the rising sun his vista. Directly beneath him was the sheer rock face of the valley.

The drunk was creeping up behind him, bent over as if in pain. The drunk called to him by name, and my father turned in surprise.

"Revanan!"

As he spun and stood, my father's boot heels slid off the slick boulder. His hands flung outward, grasping at thin air as he went careening over backward in awful slow motion.

The drunk sprinted forward and leaped, his hands outstretched. He caught Papa's flailing hand and was dragged along with him, but he managed to hook his free arm around the boulder and braced his legs on another. My father's body swung terrifyingly down into open space. His head cannoned sickeningly into the rock face, and he fell limp.

Is this where you drop him, you bastard?

"No!" I roared, sprinting toward them, but it was as though I was running through thick liquid. I saw a swallow suspended in mid-flight, a dog frozen as it leaped away. I looked around desperately. The clearing was silent, vibrating. And then the drunk somehow found purchase in the mud to drag my father's prone body back up and away from the glinting rock. I saw the light flashing from within them, suctioning, blasting.

My father's limp form became brighter and brighter as a warped hole opened, emitting an unearthly light, revolving into a thousand patterns, growing to consume his entire form. And on the ground behind the shack lay the drunkard, having staggered backward holding himself. I saw his cloak curl in the wind, disintegrating into particles.

History repeating itself. The Rift opened.

I sprinted toward the fallen figure as the particles of him were being suctioned into the portal. I skidded to a halt on my knees. I had to know! Melasquez? I tore off the muslin hood.

"My Little Explorer?" The bandaged face was my father, but not my father. A rugged jaw, purple rings under his eyes, a vicious scar on his forehead where he had smashed into the cliff face. He'd shaved his neck beard, and his expressive lips were dry and cracked, his nose even more broken, if it were possible. He looked like a crumbling statue with a vision of a thousand cataclysmic futures in its dusty eyes.

He was thinner than I remembered, drunk with shame and confusion. The tears in his eyes at the sight of me rose up into the morning light, disappearing into nothingness.

"My Little Explorer," he said to himself, his voice listing with relief. His calloused hands, the ones I had played with as a child, held on to me in desperation. I dragged him away from the light with all my might.

"Papa!"

"I tried to save myself . . . from this . . . forever . . ."

"Don't say that!" His feet were disappearing like strands of smoke. I pulled his arm over my shoulder and heaved.

"I didn't know . . ." His moan of regret was like a wound on my heart.

My father had lost himself trying to save himself. He would have died slipping off that boulder if his old self hadn't saved him and cracked open the Rift into the Dreaming. Without remembering his rescuer, he would return to do the same again and again. Like the old stories of the First Traveler, a paradox, an infinite loop through time.

He had not left us as I had always believed. He had not left me.

He had trapped himself, just as I had. I heard a keen, unearthly tearing. I glanced over my shoulder. The portal was in the shape of my father's outline, a shining hole in the world shaped like a man hanging off a cliff by a single hand. From that hand, I saw black veins creeping up through his fingers, crawling upward and outward into space, coming out of the eternal distance. A malignant root, clawing its first steps into our world, reaching onto the bare mud in a ball of five roots. A black hand on the earth.

This was the beginning! This was how the Black Fate had entered into our circle of time.

I dragged my father away from the black root as time shuddered around us. The stray animals had scattered. I was terrified by how much lighter he was.

"My Little Explorer . . ." he said, his gaze fixated on the swallow frozen in mid-flight. "I was lost in a time of dreams . . . so many worlds, all the possibilities of this earth . . . but could not return. Don't you see? I became the greatest explorer. I became . . ."

"Papa!" He was a husk of himself, his chest transparent and empty. The greatest explorer? It had cost him everything. His family. His son. And now, his life. How had he not remembered his own hand in his fall? I glared at the jagged scar on his forehead. Did he think he had fallen into another time on this very cliff?

Rain began to patter around us, right through the bright morning sunlight. I risked a glance above us. Through a rainbow that arched across the heavens, I saw the flash of the Black Tree greater than all the sky, haloed with black-ringed clouds.

"This time is dying . . ." my father said, the rainbow reflected in his eyes.

"Did you eat the fruit?" I half snarled.

"Do not touch it!" He recoiled as if bitten, struggling to breathe.

"You will never escape the . . . !" He saw my face again, how pain had aged it. I was so far from the fresh-faced youth he had left back at home. He reached a shaking hand up to my cheek, tracing the lines of my jaw.

"The future decides the past," I said, repeating the words Melasquez had spoken to me in this very place. My father understood then that even now my child self was just awakening for breakfast in the village. I too was a Traveler. A son following in his father's footsteps. The forbidden way, inherited.

He averted his face in shame.

"Papa!" I cried. "Am I to lose you again, forever, and again?"

"I'm so sorry . . ." His voice was breaking. He loved me; that was the truth of it. It was emanating from him, as if it was stripping him of his essence.

"How do we break the loop?" I begged him.

My father closed his eyes. Particles were breaking apart from his cheeks, rising up like rain. He pointed a shaking finger behind me and I turned. There was the beast, its yellow eyes fixated on us, its fangs glinting between its scarlet tongue as it flicked the air.

"He knows."

"Get away from us!" I screamed at the fiend. It stared at me sadly, grinned like a Cheshire cat, then turned and padded away into the trees. My papa must have been hallucinating to say such a thing, the Dreaming already leaking through the Rift.

I lifted him into my arms—he felt light as the clothes he wore—and ran back to the village. I followed the same trail I had chased him along, sprinting down that same path as if I could rewrite history.

"Papa! Mother, she . . . wanted me to tell you . . . she never gave up loving you."

My father began to cry gently, his tears disappearing right through my chest as I ran, ducked under branches, and leaped over logs.

"Take us home." His eyes were clouding; he couldn't see. There was so much pain in his voice. Is that why he'd been drinking?

"We're almost there, Papa!" He felt like nothing now. I ran faster than I had ever run, but it felt as if time had slowed, as if I was running through thick air. I couldn't even feel him anymore; it was like carrying a ghost.

"Are we there yet?" he whispered. He was staring up at the sky, his eyes white.

Down the winding path, I could see the thatched roofs of the village, the first smoke of morning fires rising from the chimneys. "Yes," I lied, sliding to a halt, falling to my knees. "We're standing just beyond the window. We can see into the house. I'm having breakfast with Mother. I am so angry with you, but also full of hope. This is the last time you will leave us. She's comforting me because she loves you so much."

"Andreas, was I a good father?" he whispered, his voice like the last whispers of wind in the spinning dust.

"No," I said, crying. "But you were *mine* . . ." My hands were empty as I knelt watching the smoke rising from the village chimneys, the morning rays sweeping through the clouds. I put my forehead to the ground, to the land from which he had come and to which he had returned. "Papa, you're home now."

I meandered back toward Melasquez's shack, wandering on instinct as the sun burned away the morning dew. I too felt myself becoming transparent. I wondered if I should find my boyhood self and hug him, do myself a kindness and send me into the everlasting.

No one should have to lose their father twice, again and again, forever. It was too much. I could see now why you could be saved by forgetting. Perhaps Melasquez was right. Perhaps this world and all its pain should disappear into the grateful silence of the void.

I remembered this day with such clarity, and I could already see the lavender clouds sailing like a fleet of ships across the pale green sky. It was the day before the first Marauda invasion, before the Dreaming, before it all began. The day my father left us, in the mighty stillness of the morning.

I collapsed outside the shack, chewing on a strand of mountain weed I'd mindlessly pulled out of my pocket. I chomped on the soggy, nutty strands as if it could bring him back, looking over the cliff face where my father had destroyed himself. I cried for a while like a child. Then my mind began to clear.

I had entered through the mouth of that great dragon in the Dreaming and it had brought me to the beginning of the loop. This was what Rosana had spoken of.

The first cause. My father, the First Traveler.

From this moment, the Dreaming would begin to leak into the village from the Rift my father had created. The Black Tree would grow into Melasquez's shack and around the wrist of his little brother, feeding on his dream of the giant. The Marauda would come in a few weeks, and Melasquez the giant would save us. The village would be plunged into the Dreaming. I would become the beast. And Saya would tiptoe down from the moon and save me.

Was this all written in the dreams of the Fates?

Was there any way to change our paths?

I stood up warily, glancing around. Melasquez's stray animals were returning, scruffy dogs and spindly kittens and cats peeking blearily at me from the long grass, a skinny monkey glaring out from the trees. The door to the shack was open. Inside were dusty books, rusted metals, and chemicals that wrinkled the nose.

The light slanted through a small window at the back. The cot where the little boy with the bright, fevered eyes had lain was empty. Melasquez was using him as a prop in his begging act again or had taken him foraging for materials for his automatons.

Would destroying the root save the boy from his elder brother's crimes?

I stepped around the shack to the edge of the cliff. There, just beneath the shack edge, lay the root. It was an ugly black claw, the size of a human hand, and behind it, the outline of a man like afterburn in the fabric of the world. The shape of my father, reaching up as if falling, clutching to an unseen arm.

Would destroying the Black Tree fix anything? The Rift had already opened, the Dreaming would still happen, I would still meet Saya, and the Marauda would still be repelled the first time. But without the Tree, would Melasquez be able to save the village when they returned in two years' time? Would all my people be slaughtered by the Marauda, including his little brother?

It was impossible to untangle the strands of time, woven as they were in circles.

There was only one thing I was sure of.

The Dreaming would happen regardless. But if I never came to know Saya, I would never love her and she would never be jailed. She would never be broken. She would never be hurt. The only way to save her was to prevent her from ever knowing me. And in this choice, I would remake the future.

My life was in my hands, in the sinews of my will, just as it had always been climbing those rocky cliffs. Before me, the Rift burst into light.

I will break our loop, Saya. For you. For both of us. The rest of the world be damned.

I fastened the black cloak around my neck and stepped into the light.

The Dreaming

THE MOON WAS RISING ON the night I had found Saya, the night I had followed the Marauda soldiers and my friends into the forest, thinking I would save them. I found myself running, my senses sharpened by fear, the dragon that ate its own tail billowing out behind me. In my hands was the knife I'd used to fight Favian, the hunter's weapon I used to put down the wounded animals in my traps in the forest.

Parallel to me, the fires of the Marauda soldiers flickered in the trees, licking up into the night. I saw the chains on Heron, on the others from the village. Whether they were real or illusions of my own making, I could not tell. I only knew what was hunting them lay behind, hungry to feast on its own destruction.

"He knows," my father had said of the beast.

The clearing was around this hill. It would not be long now. I raced diagonally toward it, the trees seeming to part to make way. I could feel its sickening rage, its thirst for the feast, stalking through the undergrowth.

"It's me you want!" I hissed, leaping into the path, my heart pounding in my throat.

I sensed it stop, tasting the air with its bladed tongue, swallowing my scent. It was dark, only the gray light of the moon on the trail.

The hairs on my arms stood up, goose pimples prickling my skin. It prowled onto the trail and stretched its neck and jaw like a lion. Its muscular clawed legs dragged over the dirt. Crazed yellow eyes swayed with its shaggy head. Blood dripped from a wound open and gaping on its chest. It had no nose or ears, just a mouth, razor-shaped eyes, and black-and-gray striped fur that absorbed light like tar. Its five-pointed claws were like hands, flexing for the carnage ahead.

"You cannot have them."

It grinned, its maw bristling with fangs. Chunks of meat, soldiers' flesh, were lodged between its teeth.

My blood pumped in terror, my senses alight with the keenest movement. I unsheathed the knife, holding it backhand like an ice pick, and crouched, the climbing rope wrapped around my left arm as before. "You don't have to fight anymore." I used Saya's words.

The beast grunted, opening its mouth so wide it seemed to dislocate its jaw, and roared at me, a terrible lonely howl that started deep and ended in a high-pitched scream.

"But if you need to"—I steeled myself—"it will be the honor of my life to put you down."

It slouched toward me, swaying and leaving a trail of blood from its chest, the moon looming over its hunched back. It was only a few feet away and staring directly at me with its amber eyes, blank and pitiless as the sun.

Closer. I could smell its fetid breath, taste the blood in its mouth. It shrieked again in my face, an almost human sound, flashing fangs like a hundred knives, tongue covered in tiny pink hooks for stripping flesh with a lick. *For Saya, you can die here a happy man*, I told myself. "I will take your soul," I roared back at it, refusing to budge, my hands shaking, ready to defend with the meager rope. But I did not strike.

With an inconsolable howl of rage and pain, the beast turned tail and ran and ran and ran. And I howled too, my voice joining its cries, the sound echoing up into the moon as I raced after it. The creature was fast, incredibly nimble through the forest. But as if by magic, the trees bowed and the path opened up before me. Overhead, the moon dropped and the sun rose and the sun set and the moon rose, revolving over and over in a matter of seconds, accelerating days and nights without end.

As I ran, the terrain morphed through a thousand landscapes, from rocky mountains to snow-covered valleys, across tundra and arid plains and fields of endless grass, to black swamps, eerie marshlands, and lakes of alabaster flowers.

I ran and ran for I didn't know how long. My body was burning itself out, my mind with it, begging for respite from the pain, for rest, just a moment of relief. But I could not stop. I would not stop. I would hunt this beast, outwork it, and find its limits. There was no escape from it, and it had no escape from me. And always ahead was the trail of blood it left that only I could see.

+ ✦ +

Time had lost its meaning.

I had been hunting the beast for weeks through the Dreaming, years, perhaps forever.

Deep in the deserts of the Great Thirst, I kicked up the red dust. I had tracked it into the dunes and a ruined temple, tracing the droplets of its bleeding wound deep in the sands.

The sky was a rose color punctuated with the cries of indignant desert birds. Bamboo canoes were abandoned in the sacred mud near the only river in these wastes. The temple had been abandoned for decades, except by the diseased and the devotees of the old gods of the Beginnings.

I tracked the droplets of its blood across the sands toward the structure. They led me between broken pillars, through the ashes scattered at the entrance. The lepers who sought solace had fled before I'd arrived. A single fly buzzed over their sleeping mats. I crept through the dust of the stone entrance. I was crouched, alert, my knife ready. It was cold in here. I had heard of such places in the Strange Tales. Here it was whispered gray men crawled from the sluggish rivers to worship forgotten deities, dreaming themselves back into flesh to reanimate themselves. My boots crunched over broken pottery decorated with strange, repeating patterns, splattered with the dark trails of the creature.

I heard a voice bouncing off the walls, its timbre disturbed by madness. I ducked into a niche in the wall. Carefully, I crept farther down the corridor toward the inner sanctum, past concentric circles carved into the walls. Scorpions scuttled over my boots, their sharp legs making a ticking sound. The voice came again, high and unhinged.

"Mhmmm are you awake, little brother?" Those odd speech patterns could only belong to one person. The doorway to the sanctum was between two leaning pillars, forming a triangle. I peeked my head in.

Inside, a man was weeping before a shrine of candles and roots. Melasquez as he had once been—not a giant, but the scrawny beggar we had known from the village. Cracks of light from the ceiling were enough to see the pale body of a small child entombed in the trunk of a tree. I flipped my blade into reverse, the light gleaming along its point. Melasquez was manic, clawing at his patchy red hair.

"Hmmmmm!"

My gaze traveled past his hunched shoulders to the boy entombed in the black trunk. Roots traveled outward from his body, as if they had grown from a seed in his chest. Was this the moment the giant had sacrificed his own brother in the Dreaming? The boy's eyes were only showing the whites, but he was the same child who had been in the cot in Melasquez's workshop, bright, fevered eyes once gazing up at his brother in adoration, deep in an incurable delirium.

"You will be a giant!" the little boy had whispered to his brother.

Guilt soared through me. I could not believe I had left the child to this, for I could no longer tell if this had already happened or whether it lay now in the future.

"Please!" Melasquez cried plaintively. The beggar began to scream at the altar. The wasted body of the child had so fused into the roots I had an awful premonition that the boy would begin replying with the voice of the Tree. The trunk rose into the cracked dome, the branches consuming and obliterating the depictions of the old gods, leaves glistening blue with stolen dreams.

Melasquez was kneeling, listening to a voice only he could hear. He bowed his head, hands outstretched before him, supplicant before the Black Fate. The man who had wanted the power to save his people but instead had delivered their dreams to this parasitic tree. A doomsayer who had imprisoned the love of my life in a time loop in which we would lose each other again and again, for all eternity.

My grip tightened around the blade, and with it, my intent. I felt something slithering around my leg: a black root the size of a python. A thundering darkness pounded into me, knocking me from my feet. I gasped and scrambled, running as hundreds of roots burst from the ceiling and the walls of the narrow rooms, streaming after me.

I sprinted back through the broken stone and the dust of ages, past shattered vases and down the temple steps, the ash powdering under my boots. I could hear the roots crawling after me over the ceilings, but as I burst through the temple gates and dived onto the red sands, they coiled around the pillars, as if unable to seek farther. I dashed out into the dunes, over the first and the second before turning around to check behind me.

There was no pursuit. The Black Fate seemed only to have power over the broken temple, where the priests had reincarnated themselves for generations. I took a breath and wondered what had hit me, saving me from the grasp of that black thing that had wrapped around my ankle. Blood dripped from a deep cut over my right eyebrow, pouring red into my vision.

On the dune opposite, I saw a silhouette, shaggy and slouching against the sun. The beast.

"Are you my enemy or my friend?" I cried out. It watched me for a few seconds, then turned and disappeared into the desert.

I glanced back at the living roots, which had already grown into an impenetrable mass that coiled and writhed around the towers of the temple. The little boy was gone, I knew. Devoured by the darkness that lay within.

I set my jaw, tucking my blade away, and followed my creature into the dunes.

+ ✦ +

I didn't find the beast, that year or the next.

But I never stopped tracking it. And it never stopped bleeding. Its yellow eyes followed me in my dreams as they had that night of fitful sleep in the tree, the sound of a horse's bell tinkling in my ears.

I followed it east beyond the seas of ice, always east, deeper into the lands of the Marauda with each season. Stories grew of the creature—terrorizing battlements, besieging camps, ambushing supply trains, slipping behind cordons to tear apart captains in their tents. The bounty for its head doubled and doubled again, along with its legend and the bloodied pride of the Empire.

Perhaps none of this was true; perhaps all of it was true. Maybe some of it really happened; maybe none of it did. In the Dreaming, it didn't matter if an event was true or not. Only that it meant something.

The Marauda wouldn't let a son of the cursed Village of the Second Sun near the creature. How could they let the heretics save them? It was only when they understood I was the only one who could track its bloody trail that they managed to even get close to it. Three times. Three tragedies. No matter how many soldiers they brought or how badly they wounded it, it just wouldn't die. The beast, spiked with broken arrows and crossbow bolts or alight with burning oil, just grinned, showing its fangs dripping with blood and vengeance. It wanted more.

They didn't believe me when I told them. Every time they hurt it, it got stronger.

Now it had made its way into the Karaka, the Burning Keep itself, the general's stronghold. I stood waiting under his banners, the crimson *V* on Marauda yellow, as the evil northeasterly drove frost into the cracks and castle's fortifications. My shadow was slanting the wrong way, stretching before me into the firelight instead of away.

The guards' shadows were behind them as they stood with fearful sneers on their lips and torches in their hands. Once, it was said, this keep was lit by fires that never extinguished. The Marauda believed the flames were holy, and their priests built a fortress over the great fires that gushed without end from the earth. But then one day, the flames stopped.

Perhaps the gas that fueled those flames from within the earth had run out. But that was not a story that could be disseminated. The empty holes where the holy flames once burned had to mean something more. Their living gods had abandoned them. The apocalypse was coming. Someone had to be blamed.

"How are you not cold?" The soldier next to me peered at me, his mouth twisted. His chin was shaved, like all Marauda. I'd adopted the style for camouflage but left my hair long, bound in a ponytail. "Heretic?" He wrapped his red cloak around himself, his teeth chattering inside his helmet. I wore only my black dragon cape, a threadbare gray shirt, and short pants, my feet, arms, and legs bare.

"You're wishing it was warmer, aren't you? Hoping we will go inside." I gestured to the warm firelight coming from the anteroom. "I'm wishing it was colder and we could stay out here a little longer. That's the difference between you and me." I smiled at him. He hawked and spat at my feet.

Perhaps there was some meaning too in Melasquez's crusade against poisonous dreams.

A whistle came from within, and I was led into the firelit banner room. The guards at the door bristled with each step I took. Leaning on a strategy table was a severe man with close-cropped hair, stern features, and grave eyes, wearing a high-collared jacket similar to the one I'd worn as the ambassador but plainer, only the red *V* on his breast. Around him stood six shaggy wolfhounds.

His armor was on a stand to his right, his helmet with its visor placed on top. Empty. It reminded me of Melasquez's automatons. Unconsciously I rubbed the jagged scar on my right eyebrow where the fiend had torn the flesh, saving me at the temple.

"Sir, the tracker." My guard announced me as if he'd eaten something bad. The Marauda general appraised me critically. The dragon that ate its own tail was no longer white, but the design was still unmistakable. I'd lost muscle on my travels, but I'd grown leaner, harder.

"I am told the man-eater is starting its . . . taste for us . . . in your village." He looked at me from under his eyebrows, speaking in the present tense, as did all Marauda, forbidden to mention the past or future.

"The cursed village," the guard behind me added quietly.

The general's lips twitched with distaste, but he did not reprimand the man. I noticed on the walls behind him banners emblazoned with the crimson *V* and beneath it the words *We vow to live now and now alone.*

"The beast takes a prince," he said.

"Decapitated," I added. His eyebrows twitched. I shouldn't have known. But I trusted what I saw in my dreams, such that I had in this time. They were visions.

"I'm told you can find it. How?"

I shrugged. "It's me that it wants, not you." The guards behind me rankled, a feeling I was quite used to. "The fiend is mine," I told him. "It's my responsibility."

"Is that so?" said the general. "Where is it then?"

"In the walls. Behind the banners."

A low growl came from the dogs as they bared their teeth. And from behind the red *V*, the beast slunk out, its electric eyes flashing. It grinned a mouthful of fangs at the terrified guards. The dogs exploded into a frenzy, and the general dived for his sword.

"I came to talk," I said to the creature.

It bared its fangs, flexing its claws, blood dripping from its chest. A brown wolfhound lunged at the beast, but it swatted the dog into a shaggy pulp that slid down the wall. The others backed off, mewling.

The general was dragged away by trembling guards as the beast continued advancing out of the wall as if it lived in it, walking on two legs, towering over us and blacking out the fires.

"Hold!" I cried at the soldiers who were pouring in from the keep. They stood with shaking weapons. The Marauda general nodded, holding his hand over his mouth.

I felt something tighten around my chest. My father's rope ran like a leash around my waist into the gaping wound in the center of the beast's bleeding heart. I tugged it and the monster roared.

"You're still bleeding," I said. The beast snarled, an ugly guttural sound. "You still blame, still hate, want to die, to hurt. I know. It's the memories. The reason Papa kept leaving? You were only a little boy. He loved you."

I grasped the rope leash with both hands and pulled the beast toward me. It bared its bristling teeth, tearing down the banners of the Vow as it swiped its claws in rage.

"It wasn't your fault," I continued. "And the girl you forgot in the dream?" The beast hissed at me, its hooked pink tongue lolling from its mouth. "You couldn't tell her you loved her. You couldn't love anyone. They'd leave you, just like Papa." I pulled at the rope again. It shrieked at me, that high-pitched, almost human scream, but grimly, I drew it onward. "But she forgave you. You felt her forgive you.

"And the Rift? You wanted to be a hero. It's okay not to be a hero." I dug in my heels, my arms straining against the leash. "It's okay to be angry, sad, and broken. Remember what she said?"

It shrieked again, its cry becoming high pitched at the end, almost like a boy's. It tried to run, scrambling away, bleeding on the floor. But I wouldn't let it escape.

"You can't stay here forever!" I wrenched it toward me, and it fell onto its back, growling. I drove my hand into its mouth. It clamped down on my arm, its teeth biting into my skin. I was reaching for something, pushing my arm deeper down its throat, the pain excruciating as its fangs tore into my flesh. "Let go!"

Finally my hand clamped on to a tough leathery object. And as I clutched it, the flesh began to strip off the beast, curling into tendrils of smoke that rose through the anteroom. Only its eyes remained locked on mine, the rest of it peeling away, leaving a skeleton of claw and bone. I could see now my arm holding a pair of boots. They were tied together with the climbing rope, the leash that ran from the beast's chest through its ribcage to around my waist.

"It's okay, Andreas." I felt the fangs sinking into my arms, but through the pain I stroked its skull. "Please. You can let go now . . ."

It opened its jaws and released my arm. Suddenly the pain was gone, the wounds disappeared. The relief staggered me, and I fell to my knees. I heard the guards gasp in awe.

In my hands were my father's boots.

The skeleton of the beast rose on its four bone legs above me. With its bare skull, it nuzzled my hair, flowing into me, merging into my bones. I suddenly knew what I had to do, what he would have wanted for me. His Little Explorer.

I untied the rope around the hiking boots and one by one slid my feet in. *Please, just be proud of yourself. Forgive yourself for all your many mistakes. You have a choice to be happy, if you want it. You have a choice to make. Will you make it?*

Then I turned to the Marauda soldiers and the general.

"Heretic," the guard whispered.

"We believe in the Beginnings," I replied, nodding my farewells to them.

✦

"She's not coming tonight, buddy," I said to the beast.

He was crouched on his haunches in the clearing, looking up at the moon obscured by clouds. I sighed. I'd found him here every full moon for months. The light wind brushed his spiky hairs.

"Let's light the candles. Come on." I opened the lantern that hung from a nearby branch, held the candle to my torch, then replaced it with a small click.

The beast whined.

"Don't howl again tonight, okay?"

The creature huffed and I smiled, pursing my lips. It was a cold, misty autumn evening, and I wrapped my cloak closer around me.

We hiked up the path toward my cabin, lighting candles in the lanterns every hundred feet along the way. They glowed behind us like faerie lights in the forest. The beast padded parallel to me as I climbed the steps to my home and turned around. He was sitting on his haunches again, looking mournful.

"No howling." I wagged my finger at him. He cocked his head.

I closed the door and went to the fireplace, placing the torch in it. On the walls were sketches of plant life and people from the Village of the Second Sun. Heron, as a boy and a grown man. Leah and their sons. Drawn from memory to keep me company.

The flames licked hungrily at the log in the fireplace, the embers glowing, igniting. I sat down on the pillows and adjusted my blankets, listening to the fire crackling. The flames danced, filling the cabin with the smell of wood smoke, the warm light hot on my cheeks. I tossed another log in and watched the sparks fly.

No howling. That was strange. He was always upset, every full moon. I chewed on the inside of my lip. Better check on him.

I stood up and went to the door, stretching the shoulder where he'd bitten me. It still hurt, after all these years. What was that sound? I pressed my ear to the wood. Chuffing, yelping . . . purring?

I opened the door. He was lying on his back like a puppy. And there she was in a flowing white dress split at her thigh, tickling him and giggling, her hair braided over her shoulder. His tongue was lolling out of his mouth in joy.

Saya looked up at me and smiled. "He's not so scary, is he?"

"Saya!" My heart burst.

I ran to her.

She opened her arms, and I lifted her up and held her, spinning her and laughing. The beast leaped up and pranced around us, yipping playfully.

"Saya!"

"Angry Boy," she whispered.

"Yes, yes! Saya, I remember everything. I remember."

"I love you," she said, kissing me. The world went away. "I love you so much . . ."

"You came back." I crushed her to me, her hair soft against my cheeks. She had grown into herself, her lean angles curving and filled out, the touch of her lush and confident.

"We promised each other, didn't we?" She was choked up.

"That I may follow you, in this world or the next." I repeated the vows of our Entangling as I gently set her down. She was so beautiful when she was crying, shining, so unbearably alive it strained my heart to see her. I saw around her wrist she'd wrapped the binding, still glowing faintly around the spot where our blood had mingled and joined. "Is this how you found me?"

"In this world or the next." She nodded, smiling through her tears. "I want to show you something. You have to promise you won't be a scaredy cat, okay? I know how you get." She laughed and sniffled and laughed again.

"What do you mean?" I said. I would do anything for her. She nestled herself to my chest and I put my arms around her. She was so warm.

From her back, wings bloomed into the night, spanning triple the size I remembered, silvery, iridescent in the moonlight. I looked upon her in awe. She was a living miracle. They arched and folded protectively around us.

"See you later." She blew a kiss at the beast.

With an immense gust, she powered us upward. My arms clamped around her shoulders, panic surging through my chest. We soared up and up, above the forest, into the clouds. I closed my eyes, listening to the beat, holding on for dear life.

"Where are we go—" The rush of air silenced me.

Through the sky, higher and higher. I dared to peek. We were above the clouds, above the earth itself. The curve of blue went all the way into forever, and above us were only stars and the universe.

"Home," she said.

· 21 ·

SAYA

☾

The Dreaming

WE WERE GLIDING BACKWARD ABOVE the clouds, weightless, my wings like silver brushstrokes around us. Clutching Andreas to my breast, I stroked his hair gently, nuzzling into the scent of him, woody, smoky, like the forest. I gazed up into the starry constellations and the purple-and-green aurora, twinkling their blessing of our passage through the universe.

My silvery wings banked and arched us down from above the clouds. They had grown brighter and broader than I'd ever dreamed they could be, effortlessly carrying us toward the glistening oceans and a shore that stretched beyond the horizon. I loved the feel of him against me, hard and lithe, our legs tangled in each other as we descended from the sky.

In that rushing silence, in the touch of him, I was grateful. I wanted it to go on forever. But I glanced over my shoulder at a pink light beckoning me on the beach, our tree, the beacon that had guided me from the giant's reaching fingers, and I let it go. I'd escaped the giant because I'd stopped grasping for what I thought I wanted. He forever would be.

As we neared the sands, I corkscrewed gently and then came upright, alighting us onto the powdery sands. When our feet touched the warm ground, Andreas's whole body relaxed. My wings folded back into my shoulder blades, the quicksilver feathers coalescing into me, my flowing white dress finally at rest from the ripples.

I rubbed myself into his neck, searching for and savoring the smell of him, which drove prickles down my back. "Mmmmmm . . . You can open your eyes now," I whispered in his ear, my cheeks aching.

He let out a breath and laughed down at me, half at himself and his fear of flying. My joy was mirrored in his impish grin and heart-thumping look of wonder, as if he didn't quite believe I was possible.

It was beautiful to see him again, and I ran my fingers gently over the weathered lines of his jaw, his harsh cheekbones cut of all their boyish shine, the wrinkles around his eyes, the jagged scar clawed in his right eyebrow, skin burned almost darker than mine after so many years away from home. I could see he'd suffered without me, no matter how well he hid his grief, and my heart went to him.

He broke our locked gaze as if it had become too much. When he saw the tree house he had built for us, he let me go, whooping so loudly it made me giggle. His hands lifted me up and swung me around, and he was laughing, a pure contagious laugh, one I wanted to remember all my life. He turned me in circles, laughing as stars streaked across the sky. He set me down and pulled me toward the tree house.

The spiral staircase he'd built wound around the trunk and led to our little room, open to the ocean breeze. I couldn't wait for him to see inside, where our bed overflowed with fur blankets and pillows I'd sewn for us, a tiny kitchen with a fireplace to one side. It was shaded by the rouge-pink and brown canopy of the World Tree, hung with lanterns like the ones that had led me to him.

"You found it," he said, the world-weariness melting from him as we looked around, drinking it in. The branches of the World Tree seemed to glow with light, reaching up to merge with the stars, their pink and russet-brown leaves rustling in the sea wind.

"Yes. It's ours."

"The boat!" He spotted the skiff tethered to the base and ran toward it as if he were a boy again. "It's our house!" he cried as he jumped into the boat. Then he leaped out and toward the stairs, testing the struts he'd worked so hard on. "The resin is holding!" he shouted joyously.

He hopped down and ran back to me, grabbing my hands and twirling me. Then he kissed me, breathlessly, warm and hungry, and I kissed him back. I couldn't stop laughing into his lips; I was so happy. I spun with his hand and leaped like a ballerina. Then I grabbed his shirt and jumped on him, bowling him over. He caught me, and we tumbled down into the sand.

"I want you, forever," he repeated my words, cupping my face in his hands.

I was bursting with colors, my whole being alive with the heat of him. "I that is tethered to thee," I replied, unwrapping the binding of the Entangling from my wrist and looping it around his neck.

He rested his forehead against mine. We lay there for a while, lost in each other's certain warmth, just feeling each other again.

Around us, the rose and cinnamon leaves of the tree fell, drifting and swaying through the autumn night.

"Andreas, when you traveled, did you meet something?" I said after a while.

"Yes."

"Me too." I lifted myself to my knees, straddling him. "I saw it first as boundless light, and I was a part of it. But as I spent more time flying, free from all the world, I began to sense it everywhere." I hesitated, anxious about his natural skepticism, and then went on.

"In the shape of things, clouds, the rush of leaves, the winds down the beach, the bugs on their way to who knows where—the smallest touches of life." It was bubbling up now, and I wanted to tell him all the secrets of my life, everything we'd missed together. I got up, overflowing with feeling, my voice brimming, and he followed me. "And I began to listen, really listen! Because I felt it spoke in my own voice."

"What did you hear?" Andreas's intensity scared me as he came close to me once more.

I bit my lip, running my fingers down his arms, feeling the hard contours of him. I looked up into his demanding eyes, hoping. "I felt . . . that the source of things lies beyond time. That this tree is only how we see it. In our shared dream." I heard a hint of a plea in me, that he would understand.

A frown troubled his forehead. He gently shook his head. I broke away and grabbed his hand, leading him to the steps of the tree house. We stopped and looked up together into the leaves.

"This . . . Fate is ours?" he asked.

"Yes. These World Trees are made from stories of people's lives, their memories and their dreams." The wind rustled and in the leaves I saw them, our old friends, the fireflies, dancing down through the branches as though the stars had come to share this moment with us. "Stories are how we make sense of the world. Stories are magic." I felt the truth of it in my bones.

"What do you think it wants from us?" he hedged.

"Each one of these trees is the living universe, seeking to understand itself. They dream of us so that we make meaning for them." I squeezed his hand.

He took the Entangled binding from his shoulders and wrapped it around mine like a ribbon. Then he tugged me up the steps, up the spiral staircase. My pulse quickened. "The only Fate I ever wanted," he said, "was you."

With one arm, he pushed open the hatch and pulled me up into our home. Around us were pillows and blankets and buckets of berries and along the branches the fireflies blinked and dived. I heard the rushing of the waves.

Andreas pulled me to his chest and I came to him willingly. "Let us show it then," he said, cupping my chin with his strong fingers, "that the meaning of life is love." His lips curled with the regret of so many years in the wilderness.

I lost myself in the green starbursts of his eyes, so alive with his fierce, beautiful, primal essence. I felt how big he was around me, how far he had wandered without me. I wanted him inside me more than anything in the world.

"Yes," I whispered.

He tore my long dress from my back in an instant, hunting for my lips before it was even off. I ripped blindly at his buttons, at the strings of his pants, our bodies hungry for each other. I couldn't see anything, only felt him hard against my belly as he tilted me off balance and pulled me toward the bed. I collapsed into the cushions with his muscular heat on top of me, his lips devouring my neck as I bit into his shoulder. I squeezed his taut buttocks, guiding him into me, guiding him home.

The beating waves of the sea drowned us in eternity, the dark heat opening, the pressure swirling like a whirlpool between my thighs. I gave myself to it, to all of it and all of me, pleaded for it, each pulse swelling inward again, funneling waves from the depths of me into my belly.

The gravity drove the beats of us over and over and over, the waves crashing through my body. I clutched his back to me, moaning his name, feeling him twitch and drive inside me. "Wait!" I cried out. "Andreas, not yet!"

I held on to his neck, my eyes pleading with him as my orgasm quivered through my body. I was shuddering beneath him, his hand still grasping on to my breast. I could feel him straining inside me, and he somehow withstood it. His chest heaved, his hips not moving, eyes glazed as he fought not to follow.

"Saya?" he said tenderly.

"I want more, all of you," I said as the final spasm rippled through me. He leaned back and I ran my nails down his glistening chest, over the contours of his abs. The hunger came deep between my thighs again, wild as before. I grabbed his neck and turned him over. He held my legs and slid into me effortlessly.

I arched my back and leaned into the pleasure, the pressure running, swelling as our fingers joined together. I moaned, unable to take it, throwing myself further into that mysterious pull, riding him, giving myself to him, feeling his hands holding my breasts. Within his dark waves curling deeper inside me, I felt the light between us growing and revolving. No more Saya or Andreas, no more names, only that which called to us, answered in the light of our love for each other.

We came then, together, as we had the first time, crying out wordlessly in the other's name. I felt a glimmer of him, bright and liquid in my belly, as we collapsed into ourselves once more, sweating and exhausted, wrapped in each other's arms. We breathed together until we disappeared in each other's embrace, separate yet bound forever in that moment.

Then we fell asleep, awash in a dreamless sea.

✦

I felt Andreas's arms shifting around me in the sweet, fuzzy heaviness of sleep. I listened to him breathing, relishing his warmth, how perfectly we fit together.

"Thank you for existing," he whispered, not aware I was awake. I dozed in the bliss of him, a smile rising within me as I dipped back into sleep.

I woke up slowly, unhurried, to the sounds of waves. Saliva filled my mouth as the smell of frying eggs tickled my nose. I wrapped myself in a blanket and came down the steps of the tree house. It was dawn, and for the first time, I had not disappeared from him with the sun.

Andreas was on the beach, making breakfast among the fallen leaves next to the swing. They had been falling all night, blanketing the beach, and more teased the air this morning. I stepped over the dewy leaves and sat down next to him in the sand. Wordlessly he stroked my hair and kissed my forehead. I leaned into him, the sunny yolks of the eggs in the pan sizzling and tingling my saliva as I breathed in the clean ocean air through my nose.

"Do you think we broke it, our loop?" he said after a while. His eyes kept flicking to the swing.

"We both had old wounds that were driving our decisions. Forcing us to repeat the same old patterns, the same pain again and again," I mused. Beyond us, the waves rippled in the sunlight, sparkling blue and turquoise. "But we both chose differently." *And I'm so grateful you did, my love,* I thought as I studied the stubble on his jaw, the scars I could see accumulated inside him.

"Does that set us free to love each other?" he said to the tides, an edge to his voice.

"Yes," I replied, turning to the sun. "But freedom is nothing without doing something with it."

"We are doing something. We are being happy." He levered the four eggs off the hot stone and placed them onto two plates. We ate together, watching the water as the coral-pink and russet leaves fell around us.

"It's dying, isn't it? This strand of time?" he said, watching the waves lapping up and down the beach, taking the leaves away. The ebb and flow of the world.

"Yes," I replied. "The travel destabilized our thread of time, both new and old. It was never meant to happen."

"I want to stay here forever with you." He bit off his words, anger as ever quick to rise.

"We escaped the Black Fate once. We can do it again, for everyone this time." I put my arm around him, finding his shoulders tense and hard.

"There's something I should have said. A long time ago." He moved away slightly so he could look at me directly. Suddenly, I was scared, yearning, thrilled all at once. We'd both aged in our time apart, grown into ourselves.

His gaze traveled to the swing. I'd waited for him, swinging my girlish feet out into the empty waves, the night he'd never come back. But now I saw before me a fuller Andreas, older but sure, frank and unflinching, with a single white hair in his beard.

"I love you," he said simply.

"I love you too," I said instantly. "Honestly, completely, with everything that I am."

He closed his eyes, grinding his jaw with all of the guilt and recrimination he had buried for so long.

"I hope you always know that," I said, "and that somewhere inside you, you always knew it."

He sighed, reverberating within himself. I waited for him to recover himself with grace.

"Were we made from the same star, do you think?" he said, looking up into the unblemished blue sky. He wasn't serious.

"From the beginning of beginnings." I smiled. "Yearning to be whole."

"And we have found each other, across time and starlight. Is it any wonder, then, we want to run away together?"

We heard the sound of something falling into the sand next to us.

It was a fruit, pale and heart-shaped with turquoise seeds. It lay in the white powder next to us, like a message. And without speaking, we both understood what our Fate was telling us.

New Time

WE CAME BACK INTO THE world smoking, holding each other. The crescents of our fetal bodies had pressed half-moons into a field of bright blue flowers.

Andreas was also awake and unable to speak, his hand gripping mine, sunburnt brown on my honey. His fierce eyes were open, calm and counseling patience. He'd coached me on what to expect, and I waited it out in the field of stalks, watching the smoke rise into the steely daylight. The sky was sapphire and cloudless, seeming farther away than I'd ever seen it.

Nothing disturbed the silence, no bird, insect, or person. I didn't expect to be wearing a lily-white dress with a soft V neckline, my thighs slipping through the slit in front. My forearms were wrapped in ribbons of fine lace and I was wearing calf-high sandals. Andreas's dragon cloak and ancient hiking footwear seemed to translate through time. My pale hair hung loose and wild among the stalks.

When we were ready, we nodded slightly to one another and helped each other up. I swallowed back the aftereffects of the nausea and dizziness, letting myself reinhabit reality. But nothing could have prepared us for what we then saw.

The Black Fate was before us, split down the center as if cleft in two by the Marauda living god's bolt of lightning. The immense trunk had cracked open and fallen, smashing the city beneath. Ugly cracks like dragon's claws ran through the earth around its base, with gargantuan spines of bedrock spiking up through the village, now fallen from the sky. There were scorched patches, stone darkened by flame and smoke.

We were lying in the old village square, and while it had been crushed to rubble by impacts from above and below, the ruin had been reclaimed by a carpet of flowers. We stood in a field of thousands of them, their petals bright baby blue, as far as we could see. Shaped like poppies, the blooms were smaller versions of the ones we'd seen under the city, the cups of color bursting from cracks in the broken walls. They played in the splintered roads, popped over twisted gates, and tickled out from between wood and stone to cloak the entire ruin in a strange ethereal beauty. Tendrils of mist circled around our knees.

"So, Heron got what he wanted," Andreas said grimly. A fallen world.

"Where is everyone?" I felt as if we were standing in the remnants of a cataclysm, a world-breaking event. And it was my doing.

"Where these are not," Andreas said. His heavy hiking boots stomped down the poppy petals. As he crushed the flowers into the ground, the black tears leaked onto the earth. I looked around us for any other sign of life, but in this silent world, only the flowers swayed, thousands and thousands across every surface.

The museum of the Last Men was many miles to the west of here, near the Outer Rim. It might have survived, but anything on the edges was likely most affected by the fall. Before us, the palace, the keeps, and all of the concentric circles of the city were shattered. The Tree had been ripped open like a fruit. The only way anyone could have survived . . . perhaps the automatons Heron had planned to escape on. But could they have swooped in in time to save them?

It seemed unlikely enough to be impossible.

"Do you think . . ." I couldn't bear to say it.

"Saya!" Andreas turned, preempting me. "Listen to me. You cannot hope for a different past."

I tried to control myself but he didn't like what he was seeing.

The sun caught his eyes and made them flash, starbursts of green and hazel. "This is what they wanted. The Black Fate would have devoured everyone."

I nodded, trying to believe him. "There is someone who . . . might have made it," I thought aloud. "Someone I locked away a long time ago."

The compassion in Andreas was enough to encourage me. I took a deep breath.

"Inside the Temple of Beginnings there is a *sai maran*, a sanctuary of dreaming. For the First Mothers to pray again for the beginning of the world."

"There is another, older interpretation of that word." He looked at me significantly. "The *sai maran* can also be translated as . . . an *arkh* of dreaming."

✦

We meandered through the ruins of the city together, down the roads lined in baby-blue petals. Andreas held my hand but kept his other on the knife at his hip. But we didn't see or hear another soul. The flowers gave off a strange euphoric perfume, vanilla, jasmine, cinnamon, a hint of spice that tickled the throat. I couldn't decide if it was pleasant or cloying.

His faded dragon cloak dragged through the flowers and I scanned the rubble, the creepers that wrapped around every boulder, and the cerulean sky above. No sign of the black tears. Just streets of broken and fallen homes. Between were fearsome cracks that spread out like root systems. The city was riven and cut by sheer chasms, so deep they disappeared into darkness, as if the earth had been shattered and roughly reassembled.

And always, before us, were the monstrous hollow logs of the fallen Fate, gaping like the mouth of a living creature, teeth of black wood splitting the sky.

We came to the prayer ground and Andreas stopped, swaying slightly in the breeze.

"What is it?" I whispered.

"They came here," he said, looking across the horizon. "I can see the memories of them, coming down from above in jagged time as the Fate shattered and cracked behind them."

A tingle of hope danced in my chest. He'd told me of how he could see memories of the past overlaid in the present. Perhaps, only perhaps, the break in time had gifted them a way out, forestalling the cataclysm long enough for them to escape.

"The survivors." He pointed to the half-cracked dome of the Temple of Beginnings. "Not just Last Men, but city folk too."

The broken dome was the only place for miles around not covered in flowers, aside from the sundered Fate itself. I squeezed his hand. Carefully, we picked our way deeper into the rubble.

I wondered how many stars he saw in the sky. I should ask him if he could see their memories too.

The entrance of the temple had collapsed, so we climbed up the dome itself, with Andreas leading the way. I could sense we were both grateful to be free of the sea of blue petals and that disconcerting scent, knowing what we had seen together under the earth. He swung down onto a boulder and helped me down into the dome. The pews had crumbled, the dust thick and undisturbed. Our footprints made it feel as if we were the first to enter in years. Light came through the cracked roof in jagged beams.

As I watched him pad through the aisles, lithe as a big cat, I remembered myself as the First Mother, dragging him covered in mud before the children. Their delighted giggles, the housewife Elena's unashamed admiration as she and Tabitha took him for a bath, how infuriated I'd been. How simple things had been back then.

I wondered if he could see those memories too, and if so, whether he would share them with me. We should honor the moments we had of happiness—they were so fragile. But Andreas was too engrossed with the task at hand.

Cautiously he booted open a circular doorway and ducked past the dry wood into the courtyard. The cliff had crumbled completely onto the shower where I had first feasted my eyes on his sculpted body in the firelight.

"Confession," I whispered, indicating where it had happened with my eyes, "I did peek."

He glanced over his shoulder at me, baring his teeth in a cheerful grin. The Mother's residence, miraculously, had survived the fall and the smashing boulders. We climbed over the boulders in silence, avoiding the flowers that crept between the cracks.

Inside it was dusty, deserted—the fireplace destroyed, the wicker chair crumpled, the remnants of a teacup in the corner. I pushed Andreas aside and went to the back wall, my fingers searching for the familiar grooves. I pressed and turned, cogs and wheels groaning, the mechanism miraculously still working. The stone slab slid aside. We both let out a sigh of relief.

Within the *arkh* of dreaming, beams of light refracted through the shards of shattered crystals into the living and sleeping spaces carved from the rock. Inside the beds in the walls were dreamers. The shrines of the Beginnings were lit with life, and around us, the sacred plants growing and sprouting in the water fed them. As one, we ran to the sleeping bodies entombed in the walls, searching frantically among them for familiar faces.

Last Men fighters, some of them I may have recognized. Soldiers, villagers, children, men, and women, even a ragged girl with a gemstone on her forehead marking her as Marauda—all peacefully resting and unresponsive to our urgent whispers for them to wake. And as we went deeper, we both were astonished at the size of the cavern, the hundreds and hundreds of bedchambers built up into the walls with pathways leading up the rock and plants growing around them. It just kept going into the cliffside like a honeycomb.

"Found her!" Andreas called. "Alia!"

I ran to him, up on the third level. She was sleeping hand in hand with Favian on a stone slab, the plants of life growing around them. Had they finally found their way to each other after the world fell? Had she finally found a way to forgive? I looked beyond them and there in a nearby chamber were Salerio and Lady Flower Pot, and my heart swelled with relief.

Favian's right hand was held over his heart, grasping his pocket. Andreas reached to pull it aside, and I made a small noise of protest. But from my former handler's breast pocket, Andreas withdrew a faded scroll.

"It's our poem." He swallowed and seemed to choke up for a moment. "I should read it to you." He looked at me, a magnetic anguish in his eyes, and I found it suddenly harder to breathe. He seemed to struggle too, but as he spoke, the scroll began to glow, exactly as Favian had intended on the train.

What is love?
To offer a hand
In a secret forest
To crack the shell
Of your own understanding
To let go of fate,
To leap without feet,
In the keen light of the moon
In the presence of all things
To always know
I want you, forever.

"Was there really no hope left in you when you first heard it?" I replied, my voice thick.

"When I forgot you, I don't think I wanted to keep going anymore."

I rushed to hug him, and we held each other in that cavern of sleeping dreamers. "Never forget me again," I whispered. Slowly, we pulled away. We both took a deep breath and smiled at each other.

"Why do they not wake?" Andreas said, running his hand through his mane, the muscles of his forearms gleaming in the crystal light. Their greenish tinge and peaceful expressions made Alia, Favian, the children, all of them seem far away, like figures in a grand painting from another time.

"They are dreaming," came a quiet, iron voice. "Of a new world." Standing on the path down below us was a staunch figure in a gray habit tied with a knotted rope. Close-cropped white hair and dusky skin, a bronze circlet shining from her forehead, she looked just as I had left her.

The Mother was holding a cloth and two pots under her habit, one a steaming broth made from the plants and waters of life. We came down together from Alia and Favian's chamber. I ran to her.

"First Mother!" I knelt before her, offering my hand in the old ways, as Andreas had offered his to me. "I am so sorry . . . It was I who—!"

"Child." She put the tray aside and took my hand in hers. Purple fingernails, I noticed with a sting of regret. "As are all things, you are born and forgiven."

Andreas came to stand behind me, dropped to his knees, and offered his hand likewise. She took it.

"I dreamed that you would come back," she said, with a sigh of reverence. How long had she been down here, feeding the dreamers from the waters and plants of the *arkh*?

"First Mother, is the Fates' dream of this world dying?" I asked.

"Our world has finite possibilities," the First Mother replied. "Finite meanings."

"Is that why the Black Fate came?" I pressed.

She released our hands and picked up her pots. We followed her to a dreamer, a fair-haired woman with a long braid next to two children, a boy and a girl, their blond hair similarly intricate, their ragged shirts and skirts scarred with old soot and grime. City folk. Gently, she held up the woman's head and blew lightly on her mouth. It opened, and she poured the soup in as her charge swallowed obediently.

"The Fates forget so that they may dream a new dream, an infinite rebirth of possibility. The Black Fate? It is the ending that enables the beginning."

I knew her pragmatism—she did not come to this conclusion lightly. This woman had dedicated her life to saving orphans, the forgotten boys and girls of this world, and through them had nurtured a resistance that brought the city to its knees. Was this her pyrrhic victory?

But I could feel Andreas's anger even without seeing it, and I held his arm to still him. He didn't swear, but his tone was brutal. "So everything we've done, all our stories, memories, dreams, they're just forgotten?" His anger was controlled but still frightening. "What is the point of any of this?" He threw his arm out at the honeycombed cavern of dreamers.

The First Mother dipped the cloth into her other pot of crystal water and dabbed the boy's forehead, then cleaned away some spilled soup on his bottom lip. She regarded Andreas with equanimity. "The memory of us may be lost, my child, but what we mean to each other won't be." She moved to the boy's hands and the soles of his feet. "The essence of us is never really forgotten."

"That does not console me!" Andreas snorted.

"Please, First Mother. How do we make the Fates dream again?" I implored her, ignoring him. "We are its instruments, are we not?"

"The scriptures do not mention it." I saw her immaculate control dip for a second and saw the resignation beneath. "They only ask us that we . . . believe in the Beginnings." She moved on to the girl next, feeding her just as she had her brother. Perhaps it was the light from the crystals, but she seemed slightly unreal, as if in an instant she could fade into a tapestry.

Andreas prowled the room, unsatisfied. Every dreamer he looked at seemed to agitate him. Whatever he had found in his Dreaming, it certainly wasn't peace. "The Beginnings. Our beginnings?"

The First Mother simply moved on to the blond woman, continuing to minister to her flock.

I looked down at the two children and their mother and the tough old lady who refused to show us her guilt. No one had all the answers. There were no answers. That was why the trees dreamed of us. "As are all things, you are born and forgiven," I repeated the Mother's words.

"Where were you *born*, Saya?" Andreas swiveled.

"I don't know," I replied, taken aback. "I was . . . found. In a riverbed, on the northern shore. In the Uncharted Lands."

"Mine is closer. My parents' house is nearby. But . . . I need to bring them with us."

He stalked back toward the entrance of the *arkh*, climbing up through the honeycomb of chambers. Moving among the dreamers, he squeezed the water of life from the plants onto his blade.

Then he knelt before each sleeper, pricked their finger with the tip of his knife, and touched the finger to his. Each time he inhaled sharply, swaying with the impact of the memories.

The Mother turned to me, finished with the family. "All of you were in the vision I received, locked away in the *sai maran*."

"All of us?" I replied sharply.

She regarded me steadily. It was the same penetrating warmth I'd felt when I'd first met her as Ciana, pretending to adopt one of her orphans. "Saya, you have a seed within you."

◆

As we left the temple together, I sensed in the set of Andreas's shoulders the burden he had taken upon himself. The memories of the survivors in the *arkh* sang through his veins, and he felt a responsibility to them. For a while, he'd wanted to be alone in the *arkh*, closing his eyes and meditating before a pool of crystalline water.

I'd left him to help the Mother minister to the dreamers. I felt so proud of him, of the man he had become. He didn't come back with me to prove that he was a hero; he did it to save others. It made me proud to walk alongside him as his woman. No matter where this thread of time would take us, we would go together. He'd emerged eventually from beside the pool, a glare of purpose in his eye.

"What did you see in their memories?" I had asked him. He'd taken some time to answer, his sea-deep green eyes turning inward, searching within. Eventually, when his voice came, it was raw with emotion.

"There are so many it's hard to . . . remember them all. But there was one memory I was gifted about a jar of dirt," he began slowly.

"It was from a Marauda woman whose marriage was falling apart. She'd just had a brutal talk with her husband, in a remote cottage near a lake. It was their last chance. They cried and laughed and argued and kissed. Somewhere on the seventh day, they found each other again. Now she loves him more than she ever felt possible. The one thing she remembers is the jar of dirt she brought back from the lake." He looked at me in sweet anguish. "Then there is another, and another like this. All of them gave me stories of the beginnings of love. That's all they want to remember."

"I love you, Andreas." I hugged him, at a loss for words. "It's going to be okay." It didn't matter that I wasn't sure of that. And now, as we scouted the landscape of blue petals and chasms, his focus had returned, honed and sharper even than before.

"My family home." He pointed to the remains of a cottage. A cavernous crack had ripped open the earth between us and the broken building. In order to reach it, we would have to cross hundreds of jagged holes that made for treacherous footing, some of them undoubtedly hidden by beds of blue flowers.

Running diagonally alongside it was the rotting trunk of the Black Fate, massive and decomposing. The wood was spotted with holes, entire pieces rotted away, allowing entrance. Suddenly, I was afraid. But Andreas strode forward, his ancient hiking boots seemingly invincible, as if they could walk across the whole earth. The mist in the blue petals was curling into ominous rings.

We came to the dark entrance, sniffing the fetid mush of decomposing wood. His posture told me he'd recovered from the impact of the blood stories. I was about to tell him what the Mother had said, but he interrupted me.

"A better date than a cave," said Andreas, "although even there, I still delivered."

I smiled. "How long had you been planning to kiss me?"

"Since the moment I first saw you." He winked. "Grannies are kind of my thing. Actually, that old bird back there . . ."

"You're disgusting!" I laughed, feeling lighter. He always made me feel better, even when I couldn't stand him. I suddenly wanted to jump on his back and make him piggyback me, but it wasn't the time. I opened my mouth to say something, but he had already ducked into the stump.

The piece of trunk had fallen at an angle so that it lay like a half-moon. The footing was uneven, filled with potential pitfalls, and any misstep onto a blue flower would crush its petals and release the black tears. There'd be no coming back this time if the tears took us. We stepped down into the diseased heartwood, entering the shrunken tunnel that led into the trunk.

It was silent down here, save for the squishing sounds of our footfalls. In the walls, there were soft wounds of gray-pink wood tissue, exposed without the bark, slowly ingesting itself. It got darker too the deeper we went, the cracks above us letting in occasional sunlight.

I followed Andreas as he led our way through the tomb-like tunnels, the floor littered with dry and crumbly detritus. The same fog we had seen outside now curled around our calves. It was as humid as a crypt, and I felt a bead of sweat slip down my spine.

"Look for the nearest exit," Andreas said. "We're past the crevice now."

We saw a hole in the tunnel ahead, and he leaped up, pulling himself up and over. After glancing around him, he reached a hand down to help me.

Around us hung a curtain of vines sprinkled with the blue petals; some of them reached all the way to the ground, dimming the sun. And within, something was moving. Andreas held a finger to his lips, then pointed two fingers to his eyes and then to the floor. Watch for pitfalls. I winced and nodded. Suddenly I was afraid I would cough in the dust.

Brushing vines aside, careful not to touch the deadly poppies, we advanced toward a moaning noise. Through the hanging curtain, we spied a clearing and instinctively crouched down.

A hulking figure waddled away from us, overweight, his torn orange robe filthy with scratch marks and soot.

"Dreams are not ours to keep mmhhmm . . ." Swaying, Melasquez carried a load of spiked black logs to a pile and dumped them. He tested the wood with his sandaled feet, his fat legs shaking with the effort of lifting his swollen body. With the help of a handful of thick vines, the mammoth figure pulled himself up with his hairy, apelike arms. The wood pile held.

Satisfied, he stepped down, groped for a pale blue bottle that lay next to the dump, and gripped it like a toy ship in two fingers. He drained the liquor with a savage shake, the last drops catching in the muted sunshine. *He's going blind*, I thought, watching his pudgy eyes blink sightlessly, his drooping jowls sucking up the drops. Bloated by grief and waste.

"They are not ours!" he cried out pathetically as soon as he was done, his voice rising like a preacher's. "We must give them to the Fates . . ." The monstrous man-baby reached up to a bundle of vines and pulled himself once more onto the pile, almost falling this time. He turned around to face the clearing, gray cataracts spreading under his pronounced brow. We pressed ourselves flat on the ground, hidden by the vines.

"For with our dreams, we only cause pain and horror . . ." he whimpered to a nonexistent audience. We saw him wrapping the vines around his neck and beginning to tie it fast behind his bald skull. "For us to be saved, I must forget . . . I must forget . . ."

From the mist rose shadows, transparent and flickering where the sun touched them. Dogs, cats, goats, and monkeys arranged themselves on their haunches before his blind eyes. And as he moaned and ranted, I almost gasped as the shadow of a little boy across from us parted the vines like the veil between worlds.

He must have been very young when he had been forgotten, no more than seven or eight. The little boy watched as what remained of the Regent fastened another knot around his neck. Melasquez blubbered now, his nipples hairy through his torn robe.

Andreas glanced back at me and indicated with a jerk of his head we should leave. He leopard-crawled backward, my heart jumping into my throat as I saw a hanging flower brush the black hood of his cape.

Before us, Melasquez made a guttural noise and kicked off the broken logs he was standing on. I stiffened at the snap of the noose tightening, the patter of his sandals falling, his shaking feet half a foot above the dust. The shadow of the little boy sat down among the animals, calmly joining his audience.

Andreas gestured urgently again with his head, trying to break the spell I was under.

What the monster had done to me flashed into my mind. He'd sawed off my first wings, imprisoned and enslaved my future self. I wanted him to die. He deserved to die. Alone in misery, forgotten, a coward's justice.

And yet something inside me wondered whether in his futility, he might not . . . give us an answer. An answer we needed more than vengeance, more than pain, more than justice. "Should we . . . save him?" I whispered. Andreas looked at me incredulously.

We heard a taut snap like the string of a boat and an ugly tumble as his body collapsed into the spiked woodpile, scattering the logs and puffing dust into the sunlight. A horrid mewling came from his swollen lips.

"That is no accident," Andreas hissed. "The Black Fate is still alive!" With a low creaking noise, the surface we lay on sank inward.

"Who's there hmmm? I am your savior!" the giant cried, groping blindly toward the shadows. "Leave me be!"

"Even now, you won't stop lying. Even to yourself." Andreas stood, drawing his knife, the same one he used to put down animals. He stepped forward, pushing aside the vines. "So—"

"Tell us how we bring everyone back!" I finished for him, holding Andreas back.

The giant's blind eyes searched for us as he strained to recognize our voices. "Eeeeee!" he screamed. "To be saved, we must be forgotten!"

The animals got up and circled around him, leaving a path for his brother. But this also cleared the way for Andreas, who left my hand to drop at my side. He loomed up behind the little figure, flipping his dagger into the ice-pick grip.

"Melasquez, we have the seed!" I cried.

Andreas halted in shock as Melasquez squealed like a pig.

"The sins of this world cannot be remembered!"

"Put your own sins aside!" roared Andreas. "For once in your forsaken life!"

"Forget me! Forget me!" the giant squealed blindly, unable to stand, his pudgy fingers shaking. The little boy knelt before his brother, staying Andreas's strike. My love crouched, glancing left and right at the other shadows, who remained unmoved.

The little boy hugged his tiny arms around the giant's swollen skull. Veins of black ink raced over Melasquez's sweaty dome, tunneling voraciously into his brain.

"I am sorryyyyy, little one!" He screamed and spasmed as the veins split through his flesh like rivulets of oil. The shadow of his brother hugged his cheek. The giant's shriek stiffened, softened, and faded. His eyes closed, and all the tension went out of him as his last breath gushed from his lungs. And then I watched my enemy say farewell to the world, with all the dreadful peace of forgetting he ever existed. Freed at last from hearing, sight, touch, dawn, forgiveness, time, debt, stories, strays, and hope.

From above us came the boom of distant thunder.

Andreas backed away slowly, but from all around us I saw shadows walking through the vines, the petals gleaming faintly around them. The flower's spicy perfume was strong now, intoxicating. I spun around. There were thousands of shadows rising up from the hollow corpse of the Fate, surrounding us. The coming storm filled the air with jumpy static.

"Andreas!"

From the bones of Andreas's back emerged the beast. It bounded toward the shadows, snapping and snarling. They hesitated before the pure ferocity of its life force. But from behind us and all around, there were thousands more waking up in the deadwood.

And from before Andreas, Melasquez rose again, a hulking shadow looming over us, faceless with the forgotten shade of eternity. I backed toward Andreas as the beast circled us, roaring and biting. The creature slashed with its claws, snapping at the hordes pressing in. Andreas raised his knife in his right again, shifting his feet into a fighting stance, the swirling winds picking up his cloak.

The giant's hands rested lightly on the shoulders of the little boy, who had turned to face us.

"Andreas!" I shouted at him, backing almost into him, searching for an exit. There were thousands of shadows pushing closer. The space around us was shrinking, the light fading impossibly fast, the swaying vines casting shadows like bars of a prison cell. I glanced behind me at Andreas and spotted a streak of sunlight like a beacon on an outcrop of onyx close by.

The beast bounded in front of the giant and shrieked a high-pitched, almost human roar. Andreas pointed at the giant's heart, the storm wind rippling the dragon on his cloak. I bumped into him, the mass of shadow people mere feet away. I knew what he wanted, what he'd always wanted. To be a hero, to save the day, to put down the monster. Even if it cost him his life.

"Angry Boy!" I screamed.

For a heartbeat, I saw his finger pointing at the giant, the beast's coiled shoulders, the lust for blood and vengeance. More than his own life, he wanted to let the beast follow his finger and destroy the enemy of his heart. But when he heard me, the fear in my voice won in him. He snarled and ducked away, and the beast bounded toward the hill in the last of the light.

Roaring, the beast slashed a shrinking path through the curtain of flowered vines before us, and I sprinted after. As we scrambled up the dry wooden outcrop, I slipped. But Andreas caught my wrist and pulled me up past him. We were clear. Sunlight burst down in a beam of gold onto the spike of black deadwood. But in the sky there were rings of dark clouds like chainmail.

I heard the shimmer of rain.

Beneath us, the beast roared and hissed. Thousands and thousands of shadows had surrounded us, closing in like an army from the rotting Fate. More dotted the tips of the crescent-shaped log for miles, eyeing us from every spike and outcrop.

"Hold on to me," I cried, my wings opening in a brushstroke of incandescent light. He glanced to the sky and back at me, and for the first time I saw fear shining in his face. "There's nowhere else to go!" I bellowed, raising my wings above us like the roof of a house, ready to leap.

He clutched on to my back, gripping tightly. The beast turned from the enclosing horde of figures and pounced onto his spine.

"I love you, Saya," Andreas said.

I lifted us upward, wings pounding, buffeted by swirling winds. The shimmer of rain fell like an echo as we powered higher and higher, twisting through the circling storms. Down below us, thousands of shadows stood on the deadwood hill, staring after us. The giant, a gargantuan shadow, still with his hands on the shoulders of the child, looked up at us too. The storm was breaking, the clouds closing over the gap of light. We weren't going to make it.

I flew toward the sun.

· 22 ·

ANDREAS

New Time

I SAW THE WARMTH SPREADING BEHIND my eyelids, and I opened them.

We were drifting above a fluffy white paradise, soft ravines and spires of cloud, the sun streaming before us. Saya's pearly locks danced against my cheeks in the wind. Below us, thunder boomed and crashed, illuminating the unnatural rings of the crackling nightmare we'd erupted from.

I tried to keep my eyes open, to beat my fear, but being stranded so high up without the next handhold was too bewildering. I clung to her and let us glide. Every now and again, I peeked to see the same view—clouds, blooming with the ringed tempest below. We flew for a while like that, in that dreamy silence punctuated by ominous thunder. The rush of wind was too loud to speak over. It was strangely peaceful.

The world was ending.

Her wings dipped and banked, and we began our descent. I squinted, spotting the tear she'd seen in the cloud wall. The thunder seemed to have receded. We were both getting tired; my arms ached from holding on to her. I kissed the back of her head and closed my eyes, adjusting my grip around her torso. We swooped in and I listened to the beat of her vast wings, reassuring and powerful.

She still hadn't said anything.

We broke through the clouds and I opened my eyes as we got nearer. I saw a windswept landscape of mesas and mineral colorations, greens and pinks dotted with fields of blue petals. A single river sparkled, thatched huts around it, and she curved us down. As before, she swooped until the last moment and then righted herself, her wings stirring up whirlwinds of dust as they pumped, and landed us gently on our feet in the mudbanks.

I let go and sank my head into her shoulder. There was no one around, but the river steamed, the last beams of sun coming in from the hole in the clouds above us. All around, storm clouds hung heavy but had not yet coalesced into rings.

My nose tingled with the scent of rusting iron. A desolate wind blew against us, and when I pulled away from her, a pale dust coated my arms and hers. I glanced around at the blue poppies that grew over the papyrus and spiked acacia trees, as my boots sank into the hot red-and-brown mud.

I remembered this place, a feeling of a world before it was lived. It was where I had come to say goodbye to her. Where I had sent the poem into the mists, praying that if time was indeed a circle, we would find each other again.

Her legs gave out.

"Saya!" I caught her. Her wings did not fold neatly into her as they had before, and she was impossibly heavy, the shimmering feathers dragging in the squidgy mud as I sank in up to my calves.

"Saya, talk to me!" I tried to keep the panic from my voice. I tried to pull her from the mud, but her wings were stuck and blotted as if fossilized. And then I saw it. The scattering of black droplets on her left wing and skirt, darkness creeping over the shimmering white.

"It's okay, Angry Boy . . ." She smiled weakly. I cradled her head. Her lovely honey skin had lost all of its color. She was completely pale, her lips and eyes translucent as paper.

"No! I can't lose you again, not again!" I grasped her hand. It felt light, too light.

"This is . . . where I was found." The river, her birthplace. Her beginning?

"Saya, no, stay with me! I want to grow old with you!" Panic overwhelmed me. Her eyes fluttered, their violet so pale it was almost gone. "Please, no, I want our bodies to fall apart together, become the same as each other, please!"

Her pupils filled up with ink. I could see right through her wings as the red-brown mud overtook her color. I was growing more and more manic. "I love you so much. I don't need to tell you more of my heart, but I want to! You know how much I want to."

"Promise me . . . you'll find me . . ." She trailed off. The wind blew in a thin mist, rustled through the blue petals. I couldn't speak, I heard myself whining yes, nodding, hoping she could still see me, hot tears streaming over my cheeks. She put her hand on her belly. "We made it together." What was she saying?

There was a flash of light and, a split second later, a terrible rumble from the heavens. I glanced up. The rings were forming, the tear we'd come in from now barely a crack between gray clouds, a tiny blue crevice in which I could see the ghostly outline of the moon. Did she mean making it here?

"You have to let go now, Andreas." A black rivulet trickled down her cheek. I clasped her hand in both of mine. Her grip was weakening.

"Never!" I glanced around, whimpering. From the mist that rose among the poppy petals, I saw a shadow staring at me from the opposite bank. As I watched, hundreds more rose beyond him. Not just people, but animals and plants too. I swiveled and saw more on our side, coming through the spiked trees. Too many to count, blotting out the road I'd once wandered down.

"Until we meet again . . . on this journey . . ." Saya whispered, streaks of inky tears running down her face.

"No!" I screamed as the peace of forgetting overcame her.

I howled my lungs out as the roots of the forgetting grew through her chest. I couldn't let go. I wanted them to take me too; I wanted to follow her into nothingness. From my back the beast raged to life, leaping to defend me from the oncoming shadows. There were hundreds of thousands of them, too many to count, emerging from both banks.

Above us, the opening in the sky had closed. The rings of black chainmail clouds coiled and rumbled. It was the end. The end of everything. The beast slashed and hissed at the shadows and joined its voice to mine, its desperate howl disappearing into the sky. But this time there were too many, and I saw his fangs outlined against the flashing storm before he was consumed by shadow. The figures closed in, lining the banks of the river.

Promise me.

I released her hand as it darkened into shadow and collapsed into the mud. Her whole body had faded with the veins of the root now, even her wings disintegrating like streaks of translucent smoke. The wind went right through her. I couldn't take it. I screamed my rage at the shadows all around me, refusing to back away.

I felt my blood singing with memories. A jar of lake dirt. Rocks tapping on a window. An umbrella in the rain. Love's first moments. They tore me apart.

And from her belly, I saw a light rising in the shadow, like a lost star. The shadows stopped and waited, watching the star as one. It floated upward and then came toward me. I held out two hands and it alighted in them. Instinctively I clutched it to my chest like a child. The last of her!

I waded into the steaming water backward, clutching the star to my breast, the thunder booming and flashing. The shadows let me pass. There were so many, as though every creature in the world had lined up at the last river.

"Saya! I love you!" I cried out to all of them. I couldn't. I had to.

I let the star go. It alighted on the water's surface, its rays sending prismatic rainbows through the mist and into the flowing liquid beneath. It floated downriver in the current. Every single shadow watched it go. And then all of us looked up as the star rose into the sky, its light bursting over us all.

Saya, I can hear the rain.

EPILOGUE

A LITTLE BOY TODDLED OVER A pebbled beach. The stones were white in the sun and he reached down to inspect a few of them. He wobbled onward and kept looking. Finally he found one to his satisfaction and held it up to the sun. As he brought it down, he blinked.

There was a girl in the turquoise waves with her back to him. She had nice shiny hair. He stomped over the rocks and into the water.

"Excuse me, do you like my rock?" He held it out to her.

"No," she said, dipping her hands into the rush of foam.

He was offended. She turned, mischief in her eyes.

"Are you from my village?" the boy asked her. "Have I seen you before?"

She smiled.

ACKNOWLEDGMENTS

For those who served me innumerable coffees and teas, to the castles and oceans that invited me to their shores. For my many mentors, for my father, who fed me books for as long as I can remember, for my mom, who taught me kindness to the world. For those who added their voices to this story—Dorian, Anne, Teniya, Kirstin—and for the passion of my wife, Meghana, who helped me believe it into being. I am forever grateful.

Photo by Sikandar Heman of Drama Galleries

ABOUT THE AUTHOR

ALESSANDRO CANDOTTI has long been a spellbound reader of fantasy and spent years crafting his own magical worlds in both fiction and poetry. Born and raised in South Africa, he holds a degree in English and psychology from Rhodes University and is an award-winning creative. When not writing, Alessandro trains in Muay Thai, cheers for the Springboks, and battles his cat for his wife's attention. He hopes his words help to inspire compassion for the flaws in all our hearts.